ENDURING
CHAOS

A novel of Elderra

Other tales from Elderra

Ruins of Change
by J. R. Dwornik

Also by the author

Aurius
Halcyon

ENDURING CHAOS

BOOK ONE OF THE *SISTERS OF CHAOS* TRILOGY

CATHERINE FITZSIMMONS

Brain Lag

Ontario, Canada
http://www.brain-lag.com/

Brain Lag Publishing
Ontario, Canada
http://www.brain-lag.com/

Cover artwork by Catherine Fitzsimmons

Library and Archives Canada Cataloguing in Publication

Fitzsimmons, Catherine, 1981-, author
      Enduring chaos / Catherine Fitzsimmons.

ISBN 978-0-9866493-8-7 (pbk.)

      I. Title.

PS8611.I8973E52 2013   C813'.6   C2013-906718-3

In memory of
Charles Fitzsimmons

as well as
Grandma Betty
Grandpa Al
Grandma Val

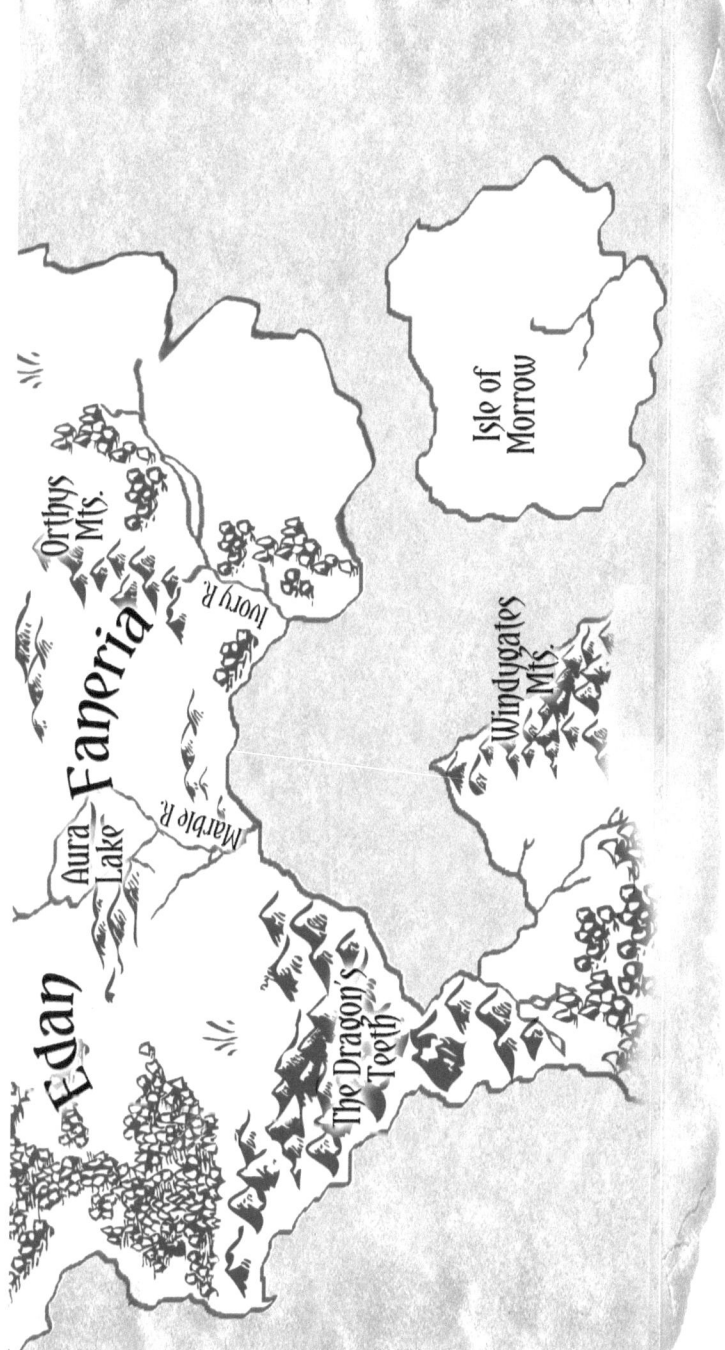

PROLOGUE

The world has changed. Everything has changed. Father keeps telling me it is for the best, but I don't know what to believe anymore.

When did it all begin? I feel we may never know. It is clear now that events were set into motion years, generations, centuries ago.

Of one thing I am certain: the catalyst for everything was the Century Storm. Nothing like it was ever recorded throughout history and everyone agrees it was unnatural. Thunder and lightning, howling wind and torrential rain swept across almost all of Elderra in a matter of minutes. Homes were destroyed, fields set ablaze, and many lives were lost. I might not have been there but it remains a living memory. I have heard enough people speak of it that I can picture it as vividly as if I had seen it with my own eyes.

The Century Storm. That was the moment that it all began again.

CHAPTER 1
A YEAR OF CHANGE

DAMIAN SIRES STOOD at the bow of the ship, her veil and gown rippling softly in the breeze. The river water lapped at the hull close below, the deck of the flat-bottomed barge floating barely out of arm's reach above the surface. To her right, rolling pasture broken up with groves of trees and the occasional rocky bluff stretched to the horizon, flocks of sheep or cattle grazing in the distance. To her left, forest encroached straight to the bank, trees reaching over the river and even growing out of the water, roots submerged beneath banks flooded from the spring melt. The single sail, used to carry the barge against the current, remained furled, the river's flow pulling the ship downstream.

One other person stood at the prow, staring out where the river disappeared in the distance. He let out a breath.

"Well, here we go again."

Butterflies fluttered in Damian's stomach with the thought.

Her father, Claude, turned to her with a smile. She wondered if she reminded him of his late wife, the mother Damian never knew. Damian's movements and manners replicated her father more than her appearance. His hair, now half gone to grey, had given her some of its darkness and its straight texture, though his square and moustached face, darker than Damian's fair complexion, showed only a passing resemblance to his daughter. Both, however, dressed well.

More slender than shapely, Damian's jade green gown drew more looks for its style than for the small curves it enhanced. She had pulled her long auburn hair into a plait with ribbons and pewter clasps for travelling. As for her oval-shaped face with its high forehead and delicate features, that remained covered by a charcoal-coloured veil, patterned with flowers about the brow and the hem that rippled across her shoulders.

Her father was one of very few people who smiled even when he saw Damian without the veil, when he looked upon the feature she kept hidden from everyone else. The eyes with irises of yellow, as vivid as polished gold.

"Are you ready for another market season?" he asked.

Their home village, Aether, lay three leagues behind them. Bolts of the town's fine wool and linen filled the hold beneath their feet, the cargo that would accompany Damian and her father across the kingdom of Faneria from one market to the next. Summer would be only a memory by the time they returned.

Damian smiled, trying to look as steady and convincing as she could. "Yes."

Even as she stood there, she felt energy roiling through her and sparking around her fingertips. She curled her hands into fists, barely managing to keep the sensations contained. Yesterday she left blackened hand prints on a barrel in Aether, embers glowing as she hurried out of the alley where the barrel sat. A week before, the wind had been drawn to her, following her around the town and through the windows into her and her father's home.

Nearly a year now this has been getting worse, she thought. She had been young when she first made fire and it hadn't taken long for her to realize she could do more. Lightning, a mist of light, voices on the air, even changing wood to stone with a touch. She never did it around anyone else but it became her private escape.

Those enthralled nights spent practising her strange ability alone in her room now were a distant memory. The first time Damian lost control was on the journey last year. Fortunately, she was alone, and it had not happened again until she returned to Aether. Since then her power surged out of her control more and more. Usually the effects were mild, but occasionally it manifested in a greater way such as with the wind last week. It was bad enough at home where rumours about her circled the town even though she hadn't been caught causing some strange effect on the world around her. With busy markets filling her days ahead, she desperately hoped nothing would happen that would expose her in the weeks to come. Terrible visions had appeared in her mind and troubled her sleep.

Her father's brow furrowed. "Are you alright?"

Damian averted her gaze, allowing her smile to fade but forcing the fear out of her eyes and voice. "I just feel a little ill." It wasn't entirely a lie. A queasy feeling tickled beneath her jaw and behind her temples. Standing at the prow and staring at the horizon seemed to help though she feared it would get worse before long.

Her father's expression fell. "Oh, no. Seasick again?"

She nodded.

"I'm sorry, Damian. I forgot you got sick last year. You always took the ship fine growing up."

She smiled wanly. "Yes, I did. I'm sure I'll be fine tomorrow. And anyway, I'm more worried about your back. You've been running around the ship all day. You should lie down."

"The pain's gone more than a week."

"I just don't want it to act up again, especially with you being on your feet all day once we reach Trent."

"I would feel much worse if I was lying back while you were sick. I'll go see if the captain has any ginger."

Damian opened her mouth to protest as he walked away but as her innards burbled, she stopped herself. Much as she wanted her father to rest while he could, he was as stubborn as her, and she would be glad for some ginger. She felt bad about asking anything of the captain. After running their barge for many years, he treated Damian fairly, and she knew he'd had a bad year. A harsh winter kept him grounded longer than usual, causing him to miss a regular shipment. She vowed to repay him for anything he offered. She hoped she could keep the energy bubbling through her body from damaging his barge.

Closing her eyes, Damian prayed to the Gods of Light for help to control her ability. Perhaps the God of Justice might reward her for piousness, or the God of Strength would give her his own to control it, or the Goddess of Love would bestow her care on Damian. Maybe this time they would listen.

Opening her eyes, Damian tried to ease her thoughts as she looked toward the horizon. The scenery drifted slowly past as the barge floated silently south. They had passed no other ships in their hours on the water, though she knew that they would meet many once they reached Trent, where the eastern fork of the Ivory River connected with the southbound current that the barge floated down.

Despite the worry over her ability gnawing at her, the thought that they would arrive at the first stop along their market journey in a few days cheered her. No matter how long Damian and her father spent preparing for the journey each year, their departure always seemed to arrive suddenly. After a few hours on the river, Damian could hardly believe that she had woken up in her own bed in Aether that morning. The new year was nearly upon them.

Damian's thoughts drifted to the days and weeks ahead. After Trent, the barge would carry them downriver until they reached the coast. From there, the travel continued by caravan across the countryside, stopping in cities here and there to sell Aether's cloth for a few days before moving on. Making their way across central Faneria with only the wagon crew accompanying them, days and nights would pass under the stars or inside inns and taverns she had not seen in a year. There she would visit people who weren't tainted by the rumours that had circulated around Aether for as long as she could remember. Damian would do her best to draw in those customers passing through the market who looked like local officials, prosperous merchants, or servants of minor lords and knights, and she could speak with them of the cloth as though she had nothing to hide. Nobody would judge her, all questions would be left behind as she and her father moved on, and the only comments about her veil would be in good humour. Much as she would miss her home and the people who knew her better, if not well, the thought of the journey livened her. She was particularly excited about their first stop in Trent.

Nothing compared to Relhan, the new year festival, in Trent. Crowds thronged Plaza Medalia, where the two prongs of the Ivory River intersected and where the annual market was set up. People from all walks of life and from lands near and far constantly passed back and forth in front of the stall. Exotic sights, sounds, and aromas filled the air and goods Damian saw nowhere else filled the stalls that crowded the market. Bands of minstrels, tumblers, and performers from all corners of Elderra wove down the rows of stalls and once the market shut down for the night the city came alive with lights, dances, feasting, and games.

As the river current carried the barge inexorably toward Trent and caused Damian's stomach to churn, she couldn't help anticipating the journey. The year was almost over. It was a time for rebirth and renewal. Relhan was six days long this year. A lucky year or a year of great change, depending who and where she asked. The market director in Trent used to give her and other children of merchants bright blue envelopes at Relhan, embossed with gold patterns and filled with candy and coins with special surprises on lucky years. Now that she was a grown woman, she knew she couldn't expect such gifts. A wistful look crossed her face.

The sound of footsteps tore Damian from her reverie. Turning, she found her father approaching and clutching something. He smiled apologetically as he held out his hand.

"It's old and this is all he had left, but he said you're welcome to it."

In his palm she found a small, wrinkled knot of ginger root. Damian's stomach roiled, the nauseated feeling in her head stronger than it had been earlier. She raised her hand to take the ginger but hesitated.

"Are you certain?"

Her father grinned. "You need it more than he ever will."

She took the root. "Thank you."

"I asked one of the sailors to bring some water to our cabin and I stoked the coals in the brazier. Would you like me to brew you some tea with that so you can stay here?"

"I will get it. I want to repay the captain for this."

An amused smile crossed her father's face. "Alright. Let me know if you need anything."

Damian nodded. "Thank you, Papa." Reaching up, she kissed him on the cheek, then turned and made her way down the starboard side of the barge.

When she passed by the hatch leading into the hold, she glanced within, barely able to see the bolts of cloth filling the dark hold. Over the years as Damian accompanied her father on his journey, she had seen their stock and their acclaim grow. Often they would return with only scraps, enough for Damian to sew a bodice, a tunic for her father, or occasionally a full gown. The weavers had outdone themselves this year, producing some cloth that almost looked fit for dukes and earls.

Damian hurried, anxious to reach her and her father's cabin and boil the ginger. As she passed by the captain's cabin a strong breeze tugged at her veil. She grabbed at the lacy edge before it lifted right off her face.

Eyes on the deck in front of her feet while she straightened the veil, Damian had nearly run into someone before she noticed him. She lurched back with a start. "Oh, I'm sorry." She hesitated as she raised her eyes to the man before her. Standing almost a head taller than her, his broad shoulders were swathed in a black cloak that covered his entire body. Light brown hair brushed back from his forehead and hanging down to his shoulder blades rippled in the river breeze as he stared impassively at her.

He said nothing.

A chill rippled through her. Nodding awkwardly, she moved around him and continued down the deck, hurrying around the corner of the captain's cabin. There she paused and peered around the corner at the strange man, now looking silently over the river.

A hand laid on her shoulder. She started and turned to find Morrie Deacon, the oldest sailor among the handful that ran the barge. Morrie nodded toward the black-cloaked man. "Best keep your distance from that one, Miss Sires."

Damian glanced at the man she had nearly run into, still unmoving where he stood when she came upon him. "Who is he?"

"Cap'n hired him on for security on the voyage, what with all the bandits skulking around the woods these days. Don't even know if he can talk. None of us have heard him say a word. We don't even know his name."

She regarded the sailor curiously. "How did you know he was a mercenary if he didn't say anything?"

Morrie shrugged. "Ask the captain. Strange bloke just showed up on board one day after we'd been at port."

With that, Morrie walked off. Damian sent a last look to the silent mercenary, uttering a prayer to the God of Wisdom that the black-cloaked man was as trustworthy as the captain believed.

Yanuk strode leisurely across the courtyard, looking at the activity within. Once an old border fort, it had been abandoned as Faneria expanded into lands that formerly belonged to the neighbouring kingdom of Edan. The fort's rotting palisade, weathered exterior, and distant location beyond the reach of major roads kept them well hidden in the heart of Hesperia, that most loyal of provinces known for providing the most—and the most elite—knights in the kingdom.

Stocky, shorter than average, with thinning pale hair cropped to his ears and greying blue eyes, Yanuk hardly cut an impressive figure, but here he walked with his head held high. His knees ached as they did most mornings, though the warm sunlight loosened his joints quicker than usual, reminding him that spring was nearly half over and the new year would begin at the end of the week. He never placed much value in Relhan celebrations, nor did many of his fellows, but he knew the apprentices appreciated the ceremony. Whether or not Yanuk believed in adopting an attitude of renewal based solely on man's measure of time, it would be nice to enjoy an early season feast.

Yanuk brushed his hair out of his eyes, his fingers passing over a scar on his forehead. Eighteen years had healed neither the wound nor the deeper hurt it represented. The mark of an outcast. Touching the permanently marred skin brought the memory of that day into his mind. Standing on a balcony looking over the courtyard at the entrance to the castle and the crowd gathered below, hollering and jeering as they glared at him and spewed hateful names. The sharp pain near his temple when a stone smashed his skull. He never saw who threw it. Then it was cheers and darkness as he was led out of the castle in chains, surrounded by guards and shoved into the back of an enclosed wagon meant for transporting criminals to the stocks.

A scowl crossed Yanuk's face, but it faded as he glimpsed another man his age entering the courtyard down the hall. Patrus's arms ended in wooden cups with slender hooks instead of hands. Yanuk had gotten off lucky.

Shaking off the memories, Yanuk looked over the courtyard. The eastern half was covered by the garden, neat rows of vegetables and herbs germinating under the long hours of sunlight, with a few larger than sprouts. The days had grown warm enough that often Yanuk only needed a light cloak over a short-sleeved tunic and the plants revelled in the change. Inside the garden, one young underling cut back some squash that encroached on the plots for other vegetables. Yanuk frowned.

"It seems a shame to trim perfectly good squash. Perhaps we should consider planting outside the walls. Surely there is some way we could conceal it from outside interest."

Fedris, the young man inside the garden, looked up at Yanuk's mumbled words. The curious look on Fedris's face faded into a slightly forced smile when he saw that Yanuk walked alone. The youth smiled and nodded, holding up a hand. "Good morning, master Alganov."

Yanuk smiled in return. "Good day, Fedris." Yanuk walked on as Fedris returned to his task. At the northwest corner of the courtyard, a woman Yanuk's age led their community's small flock of sheep and goats out of the large side room they used as a barn. Lambs and kids bleated and scampered beneath the adults' hooves as they marched through the main entrance to graze in the open fields.

"I see no reason why we must continue to maintain this derelict facade so assiduously," Yanuk grumbled, continuing his line of thought. "We have resided here in peace for fifteen years. I grow weary of hiding."

His attention diverted as he passed an open doorway leading into a small room off the courtyard. Inside, a humpbacked old woman with short white curls and a hard look on her face stood behind a table. Atop its surface sat a brass scale, small jars, and stone weights and she faced two youths behind desks similarly laden.

"We are the last vestiges of magic in this world and we are nearly gone," she said to the young man and woman. "No matter how skilled you are or how much promise you show, you will never have enough power to cast magic on your own. What we have is the power to release energy from those items that do have it." She waved a hand over the jars, inside which lay an assortment of roots, stones, animal parts, and other objects. "Unless you prepare your ingredients precisely and speak the incantation properly, your spell will fail and perhaps with catastrophic consequences."

The young man and woman exchanged an uncomfortable glance.

The old woman's scowl darkened. "You will learn nothing from each other, you cretins. You may have learned to read, but do not think yourselves knowledgeable. Until you can cast magic successfully you are nothing but labourers here."

Her students jumped at the sharpness in her voice and fixed their eyes on the old woman with muttered apologies. Yanuk chuckled as he walked on. They would grow used to, if perhaps not comfortable with, Miria's sharp voice and short temper. They all did.

"That is the bond that ties us together," Yanuk mused as he strode down one of the open-air corridors lining the courtyard. Here in this old border fort hidden from the outside world, Yanuk and his fellows could practise the gift for which they were condemned and teach it to the next generation. Never again would he and his comrades have to face the judgement of ignorant peasants, nor did they have to bend the knee to any lord who ordered them to use their magic for sinister or mundane purposes. Here they could practise and expand their knowledge at their leisure. This home Yanuk had helped build was not just study, but sanctuary.

Suddenly, a pulse thrummed through Yanuk's chest. He inhaled sharply, pressing a hand against his heart, then smiled. He slipped into another small room off the central courtyard used as a storage area. Reaching beneath his tunic he pulled out a leather cord hanging around his neck. A crystal the size of his small thumb joint hung off it, cheap and cloudy and rough-hewn but for one smooth, flat side. Covering the crystal with his hand, he uttered an ancient phrase under his breath. A different voice droned out of the crystal in response, distorted.

"Yanuk? Can you hear me?"

Yanuk smiled. "Yes, Rhyslen. I am here. How goes your journey?"

"Fairly well, master. I have located her, but she has just left town.

I fear it may be several days yet before I can speak with her alone."

Yanuk could hear the unease in Rhyslen's voice. One of the first apprentices Yanuk recruited into the little community of mages, Rhyslen had learned much and become a senior among the younger generation, despite that he was still less than half Yanuk's age. However, the youth was terrified about venturing halfway across the kingdom and discussing magic, a topic so feared and loathed by the common man. Yanuk feared Rhyslen being discovered as well, but he had faith in his apprentice and the girl Rhyslen sought could be a boon to them or a grave threat.

"Be patient and continue following her. Concentrate first on learning how she was able to find you." Yanuk heard commotion in the courtyard as what sounded like another mage returned from a trip acquiring supplies.

"Of course, master. I will contact you before the week has ended."

Yanuk nodded, though he knew the gesture would not carry. "I shall eagerly await your report, Rhyslen. Good luck."

"Thank you, Yanuk. Good day to you."

"And to you." With that, Yanuk rubbed the crystal, severing the link between it and its twin hanging around Rhyslen's neck so far away.

"Yanuk!"

Yanuk glanced up at the urgency of the cry. Standing, he strode to the doorway. Patrus, the amputee, searched the courtyard from where he stood beside a mule-drawn wagon full of sacks of grain, candles, leather, and other dry goods. Fedris, having emerged from the garden, loitered around the wagon along with the middle-aged man and young woman who had just retrieved the goods. A mixture of uneasy and suspicious looks crossed their faces. Finding Yanuk, Patrus strode quickly over, a small white square clutched to his chest with one hook.

"Yanuk, a message came for you."

Yanuk's brow creased. "A message? From whom? Where was it?"

Patrus shook his head. "We do not know who left it. There is no sender listed on the outside, but it is addressed to you. Apparently it was slipped into the wagon here."

Yanuk tensed and turned a wide-eyed look to Edrand, the man who led the wagon. A few years Yanuk's senior, Edrand's face was badly scarred from escaping villagers who tried to burn him at the stake many years ago. "You were seen?"

The young woman flinched. "No, master, I swear it!"

Edrand shook his head, the salt-and-pepper hair on the side of his face that still grew swaying with the motion. "No one saw us." He gave Yanuk a flat stare. "Aside from those with whom we traded that tin, of course."

Yanuk frowned. Edrand had always opposed the idea of taking things they did not need when they stole the supplies they required to continue surviving in their isolated home, preferring to never have contact with the outside world. Yanuk firmly believed that some of their necessities could only be obtained through trade. If they could no longer trust their contact, however, then they could all be in danger.

"Neither of us had any indication that we were seen," Edrand went on. "I do not know how it got there and only discovered it just now."

Yanuk snatched the envelope out of Patrus's hook. Yanuk's name was written in shaky, but clearly practised script on the front. No seal marked the back of the page, only a misshapen glob of wax held it shut. Yanuk's dark look deepened as he broke the seal and unfolded the letter. Patrus leaned forward and Edrand watched intently as Yanuk's eyes scanned the short page. Upon reaching the end, Yanuk's lips pursed into a tight line.

"What is it, Yanuk?" Patrus asked.

Yanuk folded the letter and slid it into a sleeve, gauging the reactions of the senior and younger mages. "Someone knows about us. And wishes to meet with me 'to our mutual benefit.'"

CHAPTER 2
AN ENDING, A BEGINNING

FLICKERING LIGHT FILLED the tiny cabin as the barge drifted downstream. Damian sat alone at the small table, its surface covered with the remains of her supper and the lamp lighting the room. She absently sewed a new shirt for her father, listening to the muffled conversation and laughter from the next cabin. The captain's voice and her father's drifted through the wall. Damian bowed her head with a sigh, wishing sleep would take her as she had for the last hour or more since she exiled herself to the cabin. Her surroundings were clear for a change, as her veil hung on a peg behind her. Another round of boisterous laughter rang out from the room that held almost the entire crew but for the man at the helm and her.

The first night is always the hardest, she told herself. Damian's stomach churned though she dared not leave her cabin for fresh air. She and her father claimed she wore the veil because her eyes were too sensitive to light. At night the excuse fell flat, though there remained the chance that one of the sailors would see her eyes if she went without. Instead she confined herself to her cabin, shut away from the world while the rest of the crew and her father carried on jovially. It wasn't that she wanted to spend more time with the sailors. She simply longed for company while she heard them having such a good time. Her thoughts drifted to the people in Aether that she spent time with as a child and people she had met across Faneria with the cloth trade. All of them were very far away.

Maybe I should go onto the deck anyway, she thought. *Almost everyone is in that room and as long as I stay to the aft the helmsman shouldn't see me.* She paused in her work, glancing around the small, empty cabin as the thought gripped her mind.

Damian had lowered the shirt to the other chair when she remembered the mercenary she met that afternoon. Her hands paused in midair. Then, with a sigh, she sat down and resumed her work, wishing her cabin at least had a window to admit the moonlight or a view of the river.

After another round of laughter rang out she rose and retreated to the small bunk bolted to the wall. The ship rocked gently and her stomach swelled with it and it took all her willpower to keep from rising and escaping to the open deck. She curled in on herself, too ill to even move her bag or cloak, both lying on the edge of the bed where she dropped them that afternoon.

Please grant me sleep, she prayed to the God of Strength.

When she finally drifted to sleep some time later, haunting dreams troubled her slumber. Had she been awake the bizarre images would have bothered her little, but with the clarity and presence of dreams her fear and anxiety rose. Images flashed through her mind of Aether as it only existed in her dream, strangers and familiar faces rejecting her or ignoring her as she cried for help, shadows and frightening beasts and being exposed, reaching and grasping but unable to pull the veil over her head. Her body twitched in her sleep, desperately trying to escape as terror overwhelmed her unconscious mind, and she grew warm. Very warm.

She awoke with a start to find her cabin engulfed with flames.

Damian yelped. Heat and smoke beat down on her, her eyes and nose stinging from the assault. The firelight hurt her eyes. Every wall, floor and ceiling, and the edges of her bunk were ablaze. Through the walls she could hear the screams and crackles that told her the entire ship burned.

She scrambled out of her bunk, kicking her bag off the mattress in her haste. As her foot dropped onto the floor, the weakened wood splintered and broke under her weight. With a shriek, she plummeted below deck. Quicker than she anticipated, she landed, hitting the pile of cloth filling the hold. Shards of burning wood bounced around her as she rolled down the stack of cloth to slam into the floor of the cargo hold. Coughing, she turned onto her back and sat up. The entire ship roared and the light of the fire burning through the hold nearly blinded her. The bolts of cloth to either side of her burned. The heat pressed against her and smoke filled her nose and throat, making her nearly choke. No one else was below deck with her.

As Damian raised her hands to push herself up, she found both

covered with flames. She yelped and the flames sparked, heat
flooding her hands. Yet they did not hurt. Trying to stem her fear,
she closed her eyes and curled her hands into fists. The crackling of
the fire and pounding of feet above deck rang in her ears. After a
long moment struggling to breathe and control her fear, she opened
her eyes. No flames covered her and her hands were unscathed.

Glancing around, she found her cloak and bag had fallen through
the floor with her. Part of the bag burned and she hastily smothered
the flames with her cloak. She grabbed both and rose, stumbling
toward the ladder leading above deck as boards from the deck
rained into the hold. Halfway to the ladder near the bow, she heard
the splashes of sailors jumping overboard. The hull cracked in
several places and water hissed inside.

Finally, Damian passed the mounds of cargo and provisions and
hurried toward the ladder. A few feet away, a large, shadowy form
suddenly dropped through the hatch. Damian lurched back with a
gasp. The figure rose, revealing the mercenary she saw earlier that
day. He turned, his eyes settling on her after quickly scanning the
burning hold.

A loud groan and a series of cracks rang over the snaps of the fire
almost directly above Damian. She glanced up as the floor above
shattered and the mast dropped straight down into the hold.

The mercenary moved quicker than she did. Lunging, he grabbed
her around the waist and pulled her aside and down to the floor as
the mast slammed into the floor of the hold. The hull held beneath it
and the deck tore apart as the severed mast tipped over. It crashed
through the deck at the bow of the ship and water poured in through
the gap it cut in the hull. Through the opening in the hull, Damian
just made out the flicker of moonlight on the river. She thought she
saw a shape splashing in the water.

The mercenary rose, grabbing her wrist and pulling her to her feet
as he hurried toward the break in the hull. Damian struggled to keep
up with him, torn lines and broken boards from shattered barrels
scattered over the floor. By the time they reached the remains of the
hatch, the ladder splintered and crushed under the burning mast,
water splashed around her ankles. The torrent of river water pouring
in tugged at her skirt and cloak, slowing her. Only the mercenary's
strong grip kept her moving forward.

He slowed as they reached where the mast had broken through
the hull, the cascade of frigid water beating down on them. Damian
clung to his arm, the only thing keeping her from being swept deep
into the hold. She struggled to breathe as the biting cold water

flowed over her, barely able to open her eyes to see. The mercenary managed to step onto the mast and pushed toward the broken hull. Damian hung on his arm like seaweed, unable to get any footing. The cold water forced her underneath and her lungs ached, desperate for air.

She could no longer tell what was happening when his other arm wrapped around her waist and dragged her through the rushing water. A moment later, the pull of the water eased. She fought toward the river surface, the night sky a brilliant orange above the water.

Damian broke the surface and gasped in a deep lungful of air, fighting to stay afloat and swim away from the current rushing in to the ship. Panting, she glanced over her shoulder. The barge was a silhouette against the fire licking up its entire face, the bow sinking as the river rushed in where the mast had broken through. Voices cried out in every direction around her, though she couldn't make out the words through the water in her ears.

The river began pulling her under again. Her bag weighed her down and her skirt and cloak tangled about her legs. The frigid water made her limbs numb and no matter how she fought, she started sinking. She took in one last desperate gulp of air as the water rose over her head and everything went dark.

The city engulfed him before he had even passed within its walls.

Garrick frowned as he rode through the field of tents being erected outside the city. Trent was large on its own, but with the added crowds flocking to the city, the press of people would engulf the streets.

Finding his quarry here was going to be difficult.

Glancing around, the knight realized that most of the tents were being set up. More than twice as much ground had been cleared in anticipation for further arrivals and no doubt the areas north and east of the city were also being prepared to accept more travellers. By the time he reached the outlying tanneries and chandleries and passed through the southern gate into the city, he had ridden through half a mile of what would be a temporary town outside Trent's borders.

Not only did Garrick have to continue his search during the biggest festival of the year, but it had to happen in the city with one of the largest celebrations in Faneria.

The townspeople paid him little mind as he rode leisurely through the cobbled streets. Heads down, hurrying through their tasks, even the most influential and well-known locals would be hard-pressed to recognize any particular new face with so many flocking in.

Garrick was considering his strategy when a voice called out from the side of the road, "Well, good day, good Sir!"

Garrick turned his head to find a stout merchant behind a hand cart crowded with small bottles and jars.

"What brings such a fine gentleman out here?"

Reining in his horse, Garrick leaned his arms against his knee and grinned, tempering his western accent. "Why, Relhan, my good man. I hear Trent has the finest new year celebrations in all of Faneria."

The merchant laughed. "Right you are, Sir. You'll see things here you won't see anywhere else and that's a fact. Folk come from all over to take part in Trent's Relhan festivities. We even get dancers from the wild lands for the closing ceremonies."

Garrick raised an eyebrow in genuine interest. "Is that right?" Coming from the western side of the kingdom, Garrick had never had any interactions with the tribes from the eastern territories of Zahn. He knew that this part of Faneria had some trade with the natives largely isolated across the mountains along the border, though he hadn't expected enough familiarity to find Zahni performing here.

"Nothing like it in the world, I'll tell you straight, Sir. And the music festival's one of a kind. You couldn't see everything there is to see if you never slept throughout Relhan."

"Well, I hope I can still find a room with all these people coming into town."

The merchant waved a hand. "Not to worry, most folk don't usually start coming in 'til later in the week."

The knight tilted his head aside. "So soon before the festival?"

"Oh, these merchants and entertainers can set up lickety-split, just you wait, Sir."

Garrick grinned wryly. "I wonder if you don't also get some people leaving early on account of the noise."

The merchant barked out a laugh. "Us locals're all quite tired come the new year, but anyone comes here for Relhan knows it'll be loud."

Garrick sat up, smiling wider. "I suppose so. Well, I appreciate your welcome, good man."

The merchant gestured to his cart. "Can I interest you in some mink oil for your leathers, Sir?"

"I think I am in dire need of some after my journey." Reaching into a pouch on his belt, Garrick flipped a coin to the merchant. Taking the proffered bottle, Garrick dropped it into a saddlebag next to another bottle of mink oil. He dipped his head to the merchant. "You've been most helpful, good man. I hope we see each other again before the new year begins."

The merchant perked up. "I look forward to it, Sir, and if you have any other questions, feel free to come find me. You have yourself a nice day."

"You as well." With that, Garrick tossed the reins and continued through the streets.

So Trent was used to all sorts of foreign people visiting during new year celebrations, though someone might have taken note of his quarry arriving so early. And Garrick's target might have raised interest if, perhaps, his journey continued past Trent before Relhan began. Still, the knight had seen that the spread of Trent was large and more people arrived every day. Letting on to the oil-seller that he was looking for someone from his own region of Hesperia could have helped him find his quarry quicker, but he couldn't risk his prey knowing that Garrick was looking for him. Trying to find Garrick's prey in the city, let alone what he might have done while here, was going to be very difficult when trying to keep his own pursuit secret. Garrick glanced at the crowds around him.

Where are you, Yanuk?

CHAPTER 3
THE GAMBLE

DAMIAN AWOKE TO stillness. Opening her eyes, she found a roof of bare branches crisscrossing the sky overhead. She sat up with a start, but the movement caused her head to spin and she dropped back to the ground. After a long moment, she opened her eyes again and looked around without rising. Forest surrounded her in every direction, silent and barren. Her cloak lay over her like a blanket. She could see nothing through the trees, not even the river.

Crackling to the side drew her attention. Twisting her head around, she found a fire burning some paces away. The black-cloaked mercenary crouched before it. Her eyes widened as he looked at her. His broad face was smooth, his features not prominent, and he looked five to ten years her senior. His skin was tanned, though most of his body was covered by brown clothes, gloves, boots, and a leather breastplate. A sword in scabbard, an unstrung bow, a quiver with a row of arrows laid out, and a satchel lay on the forest floor beside him. Damian looked around. They were alone.

The memory of the barge sinking, wrapped with flames, came to her. It seemed like a nightmare, something that couldn't possibly have been real. Yet there the mercenary kneeled, silent as he had been when she met him on board and when he helped her out of the burning cargo hold. Dread settled with a heavy weight in her stomach as she sat up.

"The barge?"

He turned his eyes to the fire, his reticence saying more than any words could.

A chill stole over Damian. She didn't want to know the answer yet she had to ask. "My father?"

The mercenary made no reaction.

Damian's hands trembled and she leaned forward. *He's gone. My father is dead.* Choking back a sob, she pulled her knees to her chest and wrapped her arms around them. *Oh, divine Light, what have I done?* The feeling of the fire surging over her hands and the terror that accompanied her nightmares washed over her anew. *What have I done?* She knew she caused the fire on the ship. The captain and entire crew of the ship were dead and it was her fault.

She had killed her father.

Damian clasped her hands over her head. She was alone. She had lost the only important person in her life, the only one who truly knew her, accepted her, and loved her. She knew she had been losing control over her condition of late, but never before had it caused such destruction. There was no undoing the horror she had wrought. Six good men were dead and Aether would be devastated from the loss of the cargo the town had taken almost a year to make.

As her breath rushed in and out of her, misery overwhelming her, the earth rumbled around her. The mercenary looked up and Damian gasped as the tremors grew stronger.

No, no, no! She grasped her head tighter but the realization consumed her that she was losing control once again. The trembling grew so strong that she could hardly maintain her balance sitting upright.

Then, a tree nearby cracked. Turning, she saw a sharp spine of pale inner wood shoot out from the trunk as fast as a loosed arrow. Tears ran down her face as more sprouted from the other trees and the ground around her. *No matter how hard I try, I can't control it.*

"Why is this happening to me?" she cried out, curling up as tight as she could get. "I'm sorry! I'm sorry! Just stop!" Her agitation fuelled the tremors and more spires of wood ripped out of the trees and earth, some inches away from where she sat. The crackling of wood and rumbling of ground filled the forest. She trembled almost as hard as the earth, wracked with sobs as she realized there was nothing she could do.

Then, a voice spoke over the noise.

"This will not help him."

She struggled to look up through her tears. The mercenary stepped forward and crouched before her, taking her shoulders with a firm grasp. She gasped as he caught her gaze, his crystal blue eyes boring into hers. She had never seen such a clear and vibrant colour.

"Do not let your despair control you."

His deep, earthy voice washed over her and sent a chill up her spine. There was a firmness in his eyes that was full of meaning, more emotion than Damian had yet seen from him. She stared at him for a long moment, measuring that look and his words, as the rumbling around them diminished.

Closing her eyes, she focused her attention inward. She pushed away thoughts of her father, of the guilt, shame, and horror of what had happened and set them at the back of her mind, gradually calming down.

Finally, the forest fell still and steady. She sighed. The emotions that had overwhelmed her were not gone, but they were distant, something she could look on from afar.

She opened her eyes. The mercenary still kneeled before her, holding her shoulders, though he looked as impassive as ever. Over his shoulders she could see the spears of wood sticking out of the trees like the scales of a pine cone. The depth in the look he gave stayed with her. She was struck by how powerful it had been and the brilliance of those blue eyes amazed her.

It took a long moment before she realized why his eyes looked so stunningly bright. She was not seeing them through her veil.

She gasped, but he didn't seem to notice her alarm. His eyes passed over her body, glancing briefly at the barbs of wood sticking up around her, before he returned her look. He didn't flinch at the sight of her eyes. She could only stare back at him.

Releasing her shoulders, he stood, his face twitching slightly as he rose. Damian's head lowered and she sucked in a breath. A spine of wood jutted out of the ground a pace before her, the tip stained with blood, and she saw an open gash on the mercenary's lower leg. Horror threatened to steal over her but as she faced him he calmly shook his head. Inhaling deeply, she forced the feelings back.

"I'm sorry."

He merely nodded and turned to walk back to the fire. His weapons had shifted and the fire was scattered from the trembling earth but his satchel remained unscathed. Kneeling, he dug inside and pulled out a water skin. Without a word, he poured water on the wound on his leg.

Damian shifted, pulling off her cloak. Her throat grew thick as she looked at the clasp on the garment, a tiger iron brooch carved into an owl with tiny gilt dots for eyes. Her father had given it to her years ago. Swallowing hard, she swung the cloak around her shoulders.

As she looked at the ground around her, she cringed. Her bag hung off a spear of wood nearby, the canvas torn where the sharp tip stabbed into it. Another side of the bag was blackened from the fire on the barge. Damian paused as she noticed all her belongings spread on the forest floor. A brush and clips for her hair, some supplies for sewing, a little money. The new gown she had made for the new year hung over a branch nearby. Nothing of any particular value but even all the coins in their singed pouch were accounted for. She then discovered the ashes of several small fires circling the spot where she awoke. Reaching down, she touched the hem of her dress. It was still damp and cool. The rest of her body felt warm and dry, her cloak most of all. Damian hesitated with a sidelong glance at the mercenary, stoking the fire that burned a few paces away.

All of their possessions would have been soaked by the time they escaped the river. Nothing could have been dry enough to warm them up. He must have built fires all around her as close as he dared to dry her off after carrying her dripping wet body this far into the forest. Her cheeks flushed with the thought.

Damian swallowed. "Thank you."

He looked at her.

"For saving me." She glanced at the spikes jutting out of the forest around her. "Both on the ship and just now."

He nodded once and turned back to the fire.

She frowned a little at his silence.

Do not let your despair control you.

She considered asking the mercenary about himself, but his large, dark stature and the words of Morrie Deacon on the ship kept her silent. Instead, she turned her thoughts to her next steps.

She couldn't go back to Aether. She knew she couldn't face the townspeople or her father's weavers who had spent three seasons making that cloth as the only survivor of the ship. She couldn't explain what had happened to the barge. She would return sometime, but not now.

What can I do? Anxiety ate at her as she felt lost. Even if she wanted to, she couldn't just run. She wouldn't know where to go and would never make it on her own. Also, she knew she couldn't simply ignore the markets across the kingdom that would be expecting her and her father and their stock. Perhaps something could be done for some of the cloth.

That one fact quelled her uncertainty. Damian knew where she had to go. The first stop on the market circuit, the city she and her father had been sailing to, the place their long journey began every year. Carefully, she stood, moving gingerly around the spines of wood sticking out of the ground.

"I have to go to Trent."

She met the mercenary's eyes, that brilliant blue that met her own yellow without hesitation. She fought not to squirm under his emotionless stare. He said nothing.

Clearing her throat, she glanced around. She could see no sign of the river nor any other landmarks. "Which way is east?"

He paused, staring at her for a moment. Then, he nodded to his other side. Damian waited for any other response but he gave none, his eyes fixed on the fire. Crouching, she gathered her belongings and packed them in the damaged bag. Unfortunately, she had not brought an extra veil, since she had been short on space and decided she could buy a new one in town if she needed. She closed the bag and rose, swinging it over her shoulders. She struggled to think of something to say to the mercenary, then gave up and walked in the direction he indicated, carefully striding around the far side of the fire from him.

She had moved a few paces deeper into the forest before his voice rang out.

"The road is rife with highwaymen."

She stopped in her tracks, her eyes widening at his sudden statement. After a moment, she averted her eyes with a frown.

She knew he was right. Bandits plagued the roads in this part of Faneria where many of the province's soldiers had to hold vigil along the eastern border with the territory of Zahn. Last year the caravan had been attacked twice and a stray arrow nearly ruined one bolt of cloth. With spring crops coming in and many people carting their wares to the first market of the year, pickings were ripe for thieves.

And for a young woman travelling alone on the road? She shuddered at the thought of what a group of bandits would do to her.

Swallowing hard, Damian glanced to her right. The forest rose and fell, creeks winding under carpets of fallen leaves, the undergrowth too thick to pass in places, and no path to be seen. She could try to make her way to the river bank and follow it south but she knew the trees clustered too tightly together to remain on the bank. It would be too easy to become lost or turned around.

Slowly, she looked behind her. The mercenary sat before the fire, staring at it as though he never spoke. Her eyes were drawn to the sheathed sword lying near him. What had he used that blade on? She began to move farther away from him but stopped herself.

He was hired on for protection. The captain trusted him enough for that. She let out a sigh as she looked eastward. *What choice do I have?*

"Do you know the way to Trent through the forest?"

The only response she received was a rustle. Turning, she found the mercenary standing and gathering his belongings. She watched, her throat tightening as he replaced the arrows in the quiver, tied it and the bow to his satchel, clipped the sword to his belt, and removed his cloak to hang the bag over his shoulder. As he did, she caught a glimpse of a pendant hanging on a chain around his neck that glinted silver. Before she made out the design of the pendant, he swung the cloak over his shoulders, leaving it parted beneath his right shoulder and obscuring the pendant from view.

Damian shifted as he stamped out the fire. "I cannot pay you what you were promised."

He said nothing nor did he stop. Once the fire was out, he straightened and looked at her. She hesitated, forcing herself not to turn away.

Is he waiting for me to say something?

She gave him an awkward nod.

Dipping his head slightly, he turned and strode south. Damian watched for a few paces, then hurried to catch up, falling in step behind him. They were climbing the next hill before she worked up the courage to say, "Thank you."

He said nothing.

She bit her tongue, hoping she had not made a mistake in trusting him.

"My name is Damian Sires."

She said it on a whim and did not expect a response. Part of her hoped that by giving him her name it would make her seem more human in his eyes and that he might feel guilty if he tried to betray her. Her throat tightened with the thought that such a sentiment likely meant little to one so hardened and so aloof. Yet he had taken great care of her and her belongings when he could simply have left her drenched and shivering. She didn't know what to make of that. Her thoughts faded as she struggled to find footing across the wild forest. She picked her way over the uneven ground, stepping on half-buried logs and jutting bedrock to gain purchase as she made her way up the incline after the mercenary.

"Domino."

Damian's eyes widened. She stared at him but he didn't turn. She saw only cloak, hair, and boots ahead of her. Pursing her lips, she fell silent as she followed him over the rise and toward what looked like a deer trail.

Gods of Light, please shine on me.

*   *   *

The tavern rocked with life, almost every table filled in the light of tallow candles. In one corner, a group of heavy labourers belted out drinking songs while other, more sedate patrons struggled to make themselves heard over the din. Bar maids sashayed through the crowd while two tenders behind the bar furiously pumped ale to keep up with the demand.

Garrick took another pull on his drink as the middle-aged man sitting across the table from him ranted.

"What am I supposed to tell my customers, you know? I have quotas to keep, too, and it ain't my fault a rough winter hurt their pepper plants. What happens when the local lords come looking to restock their larders? They'll look elsewhere, that's what! It's right inconsiderate of them, keeping just as much of their stock as last year when there ain't as much to go around. And those bloody heathens ain't trading with anyone anymore."

Garrick smiled and glanced at the tavern's inhabitants. Locals, almost exclusively, yet they nearly filled the common room. His information gathering had brought him deeper into Trent and he had singled out the spicer as a likely source of talk. The problem was the spicer liked to talk a little too much.

I could have saved the coin on drinks for this one, Garrick thought, looking at the spicer's miraculously near-empty second mug. How the spicer could have downed as much drink as Garrick, talking as much as he did, the knight couldn't imagine.

"Not that the lords are much better. Just because they can have whatever herbs and spices they want year round they think it's always available. Their servants are coming in every other day asking if I got more of this or that. It's all imported! They know I won't have any 'til the suppliers come for Relhan. No matter how many times I tell them, they don't listen."

No sooner had Garrick peered into his own empty mug, wondering if he was going to get any useful information out of the spicer, than a bar maid appeared at his side, rosy-cheeked and grinning.

"Would you like another drink, Sir?"

The knight gave her his most charming smile as he slid the mug toward her. "That would be lovely."

Less buxom than the other tavern girls with her straight brown hair pinned up at the back, her eyes shone with anticipation as she took up the leather mug. "Another brown ale?"

Garrick leaned against the table, inching closer to her. "Why don't you surprise me?" He winked.

She shivered, cheeks reddening further as she bit her lower lip playfully.

With a nod toward the spicer, he added, "You'd better get my friend a refill as well. I think he's going to need some more to keep going."

Tittering, the bar maid picked up the other mug, though Garrick's companion failed to notice as he bemoaned the struggles of his trade.

Garrick tuned out the spicer's complaints as the tavern girl scurried off. He thought about the mission that had brought him so far from home.

"We began seeing Yanuk in town two years ago," Captain Warwick had said when Garrick stood in his office in Misengrad, seat of the Duke of Hesperia. "Though it turns out he had been visiting occasionally for some time before that. We only took notice when he was accompanied by another, also known to be an outcast mage."

That news surprised Garrick, though he carefully responded, "Surely it is not a crime for him to associate with someone with whom he has that in common."

"No, but he was soon sighted with two others."

Garrick's eyes widened at that.

"Coupled with some of the purchases he made in town, we fear he may be gathering mages together for some specific purpose."

"What did he buy?"

"Powders. Roots. Animal parts. Known spell ingredients. Along with ink and enough paper to fill two books." Sir Warwick shook his head. "An outcast mage with no known whereabouts or trade purchasing that quantity of goods certainly caught our attention. Yet somehow he has eluded our spies every time we try to follow him and so have all his companions. They seem to have a way of masking their passage so that they cannot be followed."

"What are my orders, Sir?"

The captain had leaned forward against the desk. "We still have no leads on Yanuk, but one of his accomplices was spotted riding eastward two days ago. He is not trying to cover his tracks and he clearly is not a man of the wilds, so you should be able to follow him based on the towns he passes through. Clearly, his mission is urgent, and if it is important to him, it is important to Yanuk."

"I understand. I will find him."

"Remember," Sir Warwick stressed, "do not let your pursuit be known to him. We must assume that this man is a mage. If captured, he will probably have a way of notifying Yanuk. We want him to lead you back to wherever Yanuk is hiding."

"How soon do you want me to set out, Sir?"

"As soon as you can get some supplies packed."

"I will be ready to ride within the hour."

"Light shine on your journey." Sir Warwick gazed meaningfully at Garrick and the younger knight didn't need his experience with reading people to see the lifetime of thoughts behind the elder's eyes. The guilt, the uncertainty, the worry that his belief was misplaced, and the hope that it wasn't all melded together, Warwick's desire for Garrick to succeed almost as great as Garrick's own. The captain's parting words sent a chill through Garrick then and now. "I have faith in you, Garrick. Good luck."

True to his word, Garrick left shortly after the meeting with Sir Warwick and had not looked back. The thought of two mages together was hard to fathom, but four or more gathering had not happened since the Time of Gods and Magic, before the Gods of Light won out over the old Gods of Time centuries ago. A force of that power could pose an enormous threat to the kingdom and it was vital that they discover Yanuk's purpose.

It was the first time Garrick had been entrusted with a mission alone, never mind the first involving magic, and he was determined to prove himself at last. Only vague directions spurred by chance encounters with townspeople had drawn him across all of southern Faneria to end up in Trent. With the new year festival approaching in a city known for its diversions, this had been the most difficult stop to search for his quarry. If anyone recognized Garrick for his unique knightly order they would know he was from Hesperia and any knowledge of his search for someone from his home province would raise immediate interest. Thus he could no longer ask directly whether people had seen Yanuk's companion and Garrick had to mask his accent and leave his distinctive armour at his inn every day.

It seemed a glorious opportunity in the beginning, one particularly suited to his expertise. Yet sitting here trying to coax information out of a drunken spicemonger when he knew that Yanuk was back in Hesperia, Garrick couldn't help feeling frustrated.

He half listened to the spicer complain about a customer as the bar maid returned with their drinks. Visibly anxious, she set a mug in front of Garrick. He smiled as he took a sip. A darker concoction, its woody texture held a tang of blackcurrant. The result was a little fruitier than he liked, but it had a pleasantly heady flavor with a mild aftertaste. Garrick held up the mug with a grin.

"Very nice."

She tittered. "I thought you might like it, Sir. It's a house speciality." A call from another table drew her away. She waggled her fingers at him as she turned. Garrick watched her in amusement while the spicer continued his tirade.

"I told the stupid bloke that fennel wasn't in season yet, but he wouldn't let me hear the end of it, like his life was on the line for finding some."

Garrick snapped his attention to the spicer and was immediately relieved that the merchant hadn't noticed his sudden interest. Could the spicer be speaking about Yanuk's accomplice? Garrick wasn't certain if fennel was used as a spell ingredient but anyone looking for it for flavour or medicinal purposes could suffice with a replacement.

He chuckled, trying to press the spicer further. "Foreigners."

"I know! Told him we might get some when my suppliers come in for Relhan, but he said he wasn't planning to stay that long."

"Leaving before Relhan? What business could he possibly have that would take him away from Trent right at the end of the year?"

The spicer threw up his hands. "Got me. I just told him the truth, that I ain't got any fennel, and he stormed out. These westerners." He scoffed and took a pull of his drink.

Garrick returned his attention to his own ale, knowing that he would get nothing further of use from the spicer. Garrick seemed to be on the right track and further enquiry in the area might yield a direction of travel.

After another polite interlude, when his drink was finished, Garrick bid the spicer well and headed toward the exit. Spying the tavern maid who had brought him his drinks, Garrick veered through the crowd. She spotted him a few paces away and straightened with a quick breath. He leaned closer, bringing his mouth right up to her ear, and uttered, "Come to the Crossroads Inn once you're done here." He winked, her cheeks flushing red, before he casually turned and strolled out of the tavern.

A grin spread on Garrick's face as he entered the dark street. The tavern girl might not have the robust curls or curvaceous figure of her companions, but that made her more endearing. Between her and the progress he made in his search, this would be a good night.

CHAPTER 4
TRENT

THE MERCENARY STOPPED in his tracks, lifting a hand over his shoulder.

Damian froze, wondering what he saw. Standing a few paces behind him, she could see little around his large form with his cloak spread out. Without making a sound, he shifted, his right arm apparently digging in his satchel. Hanging back, Damian watched, hoping it wasn't trouble ahead. They had not encountered any in their travels over the past days but she felt uneasy all the same.

It wasn't until he shifted to his right that she could see what caught his attention. Forty paces away, a herd of deer made its way through the forest. Turning her attention back to Domino, she found he had pulled out and strung his bow and held an arrow nocked to the string.

Crouching, he gathered the tail of his cloak and wrapped it around his shoulders, keeping it from dragging the ground. Then, he began moving to the right. Damian's eyes widened. Each footstep dropped so slowly and so carefully that he stepped out of the path without making a sound, his eyes fixed on the deer as though he had some instinctive knowledge of the forest floor. When she had tried to soften her footfalls and watch where she stepped, twigs snapped and leaves crunched under her boots with each pace. His silence captivated her as he made his way deeper into the undergrowth.

She heard no change in his movements, but suddenly the deer all raised their heads and stared at Damian and Domino. The mercenary froze, standing still as a statue.

One of the bucks snorted, stamping a hoof as it stared in their direction. A fawn with a heavily spotted coat scampered behind its mother. The rest of the deer waited unmoving.

The movement was so slow it took Damian a moment to realize the mercenary gradually swung his bow into position. Damian held her breath, not daring to move anything but her eyes as her attention returned to the deer.

Something fell to the forest floor on the other side of the deer. A few jumped or snorted and most turned toward the noise. In that moment the mercenary drew the arrow and released. Damian could barely track the flight of the arrow before it impaled the hindquarters of a buck. The injured hart leaped and bleated while the rest of the herd snorted and fled, their hooves drumming across the forest floor. Before the stag could flee, Domino loosed another arrow. The second caught the buck in the shoulder. The mercenary dropped his bow and raced through the forest as the hart staggered and fell to the ground. Damian's heart hammered in her chest as she watched Domino dart effortlessly across the forest floor. The stag, panicking and stumbling, screamed and tried to flee after the rest of the herd now gone.

As the mercenary ran, he drew his sword. The scuffed brass hilt glimmered like pure gold, set with red stones and forged into flowing curves, topped a black blade, wide as a broadsword but curving and single-edged.

The mercenary slipped between the trees as the hart fled over a rise and Damian could see nothing more. She stood still for a moment while she listened to the chase, transfixed by the mercenary's silence and swiftness. He seemed more like an animal, a creature of the forest, than a man. Strangely, she found that thought comforting.

A thump sounded in the distance. Damian held her breath for five heartbeats, then lifted the tail of her skirt and ran down the path. Halfway to the rise, she paused, glancing through the undergrowth to where the mercenary had loosed his arrows. Picking her way through the bushes and ferns, she retrieved the fallen bow, then continued up the incline. At the top of the rise, she stopped and looked down the far side.

The mercenary stood forty paces ahead, clutching the legs of the unmoving stag draped over his shoulders. He turned to look at her, saying nothing. Without a word, Damian strode down the incline. He didn't speak as she approached, nodding when she handed him his bow. Attaching it to his satchel, he turned and walked on, carrying the hart. Damian's stomach grumbled merely to look at the beast. It was the first meat they had acquired in half a week of travel.

They continued in silence, picking their way over the rough, uneven forest floor while the wind stirred the trees. Damian's feet ached, a now familiar soreness that she still preferred to standing in the same place all day like when she sold Aether's cloth behind her father's stand. The horror with the memory of the barge sinking and the knowledge of what she had done clawed at the dark recesses of her consciousness, but she pushed those thoughts back and pressed on. She couldn't face the guilt or the worry over what would happen next.

Some time later, the mercenary merely held a hand up and nodded ahead to stop for rest and food. He didn't speak when he offered her a handful of berries they had gathered, nor did he say anything while they ate. When it was time to move on he simply stood, gathered the stag, and continued walking. Damian fell into step behind him just as taciturn. In truth, they had exchanged fewer words in the days since they began travelling than they had that first time she awoke after he rescued her from the sinking barge.

Every night, she fell asleep anxiously and reluctantly on the forest floor with the mercenary looming nearby. With exhaustion brought on by the days of walking, sleep took her quickly despite her unease. By the time she awoke in the morning Domino was usually already up. A few nights she had seen him nodding off but otherwise he had remained as emotionless and unchanging as ever.

A creature of the forest, she often thought.

Damian lost count of the days that passed since she awoke in the forest with Domino but she knew the year had ended. In quiet moments when she was desperate to keep her thoughts away from the horror that lingered so close, she immersed her thoughts in memories of Relhan in Trent. Paper lanterns swung through the cobbled streets with dancers swirling torches of brightly coloured flame. People drank and sang together and exchanged gifts and anyone who revelled in the beginning of a new year was welcomed in the celebrations. The festivity made the city come alive with colour, light, and noise.

All the while she trudged through the wild forest toward a market that had already begun, if not ended, without her.

Hours dragged into days as they made their way south. The time felt interminable, as though she had never lived before she entered this forest nor would there ever be any end to it. The mercenary silently pointed out trees, bushes, or undergrowth that hid edible plants and soon she noticed them without his assistance. As out of place as she felt next to this man of the wilds, she was glad to be of use. Much of her time was spent searching for sources of food as Domino's stores depleted so they would not subsist entirely on the stag's meat. Enough plants had begun sprouting by this time that she had little worry for quantity, if not selection of food.

The sun dipped toward the horizon, hanging at eye level through the branches of the trees as Damian followed Domino up a tall hill. She panted as she climbed, the backs of her legs trembling from the effort. She felt dirty and tired and sore and looked forward to sleeping on the ground. At least it meant rest at the end of that long spring day.

When she reached the crest of the hill where the mercenary waited and looked ahead, she straightened. The forest ended abruptly at the base of the hill and across an open field a city rose.

Trent.

Damian stared at the city for a long moment, taking in the sight. She had always approached the city by boat and coming around the last hill out of the forest to find Trent filling the horizon had been impressive. From above she could truly appreciate the immensity of the city, the outer wall spread out almost farther than she could see. Within, the buildings clustered thick and even as trees in an orchard, a net of cobbled streets twining among them with city squares and the occasional arbour. The southbound and westbound forks of the Ivory River, glinting in the sunlight, flowed steadily underneath the outer wall. In the distance she could just see where they met inside the city. The late afternoon sun painted the scene in gold.

Patches of darkness and light spotted the ground outside the city wall. Most of the tents that recently occupied that land had been taken down, leaving heavily trodden earth behind, though a few squares of light or brightly coloured canvas still stood. Tiny figures swarmed the area and a group of people lined up outside the northern gate trying to enter the city before the sun set.

Damian drew in a breath as she took in the sight. As she held it inside her, her throat grew thick. Travelling through the forest and focusing on keeping her footing and her bearings, it had been easy to set aside the tragedy that lay behind her and the struggles she faced ahead. Looking upon the first stop on the journey with her father every year, the memory of the burning ship sprang into her mind along with the thought of everything that had been destroyed. She pushed the emotions back before guilt overwhelmed her.

I must look ahead, she told herself. *Not behind. Even if nothing waits for me in Trent. If I look back, I will be lost.*

She turned her head. Domino stood beside her, impassively

surveying the city. His size, lack of emotion, and that sword in its scabbard still intimidated her but he had guided her here as she asked without any hope of reward.

He turned at her glance, giving her the same expressionless look he gave everything. Yet, looking at him she couldn't help but remember the meaningful glint in his eyes after she awoke a week or more ago.

Do not let your despair control you.

She didn't know what those words meant to him but they had helped keep her sane these past days.

"Thank you." She cleared her throat, her voice rough from misuse. "Thank you for guiding me here… for all your help."

Nodding in response, he turned to continue down the hill.

"Wait."

He stopped a few paces ahead and looked back.

"I want to repay you." She opened her singed coin pouch, but frowned at its meagre contents. It would not last her long in Trent and she would need every coin she had. She considered whether she had anything else of value to offer him. Her hand was drawn to the clasp of her cloak.

No, she thought immediately, but soon relented. *He saved my life.* Closing her eyes, she resigned herself to it.

"I know I cannot pay you what you were promised to help guard the barge, but I owe you this much at least." Reaching up, she removed the tiger iron owl pinned over her cloak clasp and held it out. The thought of giving up the brooch made her heart wrench, but she kept her hand held out toward Domino.

He simply shook his head and turned to continue toward the city.

She watched him for a few paces, torn between accepting his refusal and insisting. Finally, she said louder, "I do not like to owe people."

He stopped. He turned to face her as she climbed down the hill. Standing within arm's reach of him, she held out the brooch once more.

"I know it is not worth much, but it is all I have. My father gave it to me the first year I helped him with his stall." She shifted as he watched her. "That is, the first time I actually worked it with him. I have been accompanying him since I could barely walk, but it wasn't until I was eight years old that I began truly helping him."

Domino's eyes fell to the brooch. Lifting his hand slowly, his gloved fingertips brushed across her palm with a feather-light touch. He held the stone bird as though it was alive. To Damian's surprise, she found a hint of the meaningful look she had seen in his eyes when she awoke in the forest with him.

"I am sorry I have nothing more to give you."

He didn't move his gaze from the brooch. "It will do."

Her eyes enlarged. Without another word, he opened his satchel and carefully lowered the brooch inside. Raising his eyes, he nodded, then turned to continue toward the city. She fell into step beside him as they walked in silence.

The sun gradually sank closer to the horizon as they made their way down the hill and across the field. Damian increased her pace, anxious to pass the gates before the guards closed them for the night.

Eventually, they reached what remained of the temporary merchant village set up outside the city. Damian stepped carefully, deep muddy ruts worn into the ground from the wagons that had passed and droppings from horses and oxen dotting the earth. Large empty spots gaped where tents had stood with only half or fewer of the structures left. The people that remained busily packed their belongings or prepared their stock for one last night around Trent before departing. Damian felt a pang of remorse at the sight, realizing that Relhan must have ended that afternoon and she had missed the new year celebrations by a matter of hours.

Around her, people herded sparse flocks of sheep and goats into pens now far too large for them. Other people carefully wrapped glass bottles, clay figures, cuttings of exotic plants, or stranger objects. Several turned to look at Damian as she and Domino made their way toward the gates. She tried to avoid their eyes, though her cheeks heated up with the feeling of being watched.

The northern gate in the wall was already shadowed and the portcullis half lowered as the line of people waiting to enter Trent shrank. Damian's pace quickened, desperate to retreat into the city proper before she was locked out with these merchants for the night.

The sun had sunk halfway beneath the horizon by the time Damian finally reached the gate. The guards prepared to drop the portcullis and close the gates, most of the mail-clad guardsmen inside the walls. Only two remained to admit the remaining people, both looking tired and bored and eager to be done with their duties for the evening. Damian and Domino stepped into the line behind a man pushing an empty wheelbarrow.

Murmurs rumbled around them from outside and inside the wall, seeming to grow louder as they approached the gate. Damian fidgeted and swallowed uncomfortably as she felt eyes boring into her.

Finally, the man ahead of her was waved inside and the guards at the gate gestured for her and Domino to approach. The nearer guard frowned as he stared at Domino. "Names?"

Damian opened her mouth to respond, but she never got the words out. As the guard turned to face her, he yelped and started, jumping back with wide eyes as he looked at her.

A chill stole over her and her throat tightened. After all the time spent wandering through the forest with only Domino for company, she had forgotten that she no longer had a veil to keep her eyes hidden.

"What darkness-plagued sorcery is this?" the guard snapped, crouched to flee or attack. Damian trembled and shrank away as both guards slid swords out of their scabbards. People all around turned to look at the guard's cry and Damian felt naked, helpless against their anger.

Then, Domino stepped in front of her.

Damian caught her breath as the guards turned their attention and their swords on him. The first one's eyes narrowed. "And just who are you?"

The second guard's expression darkened. "Wait a minute. I know who he is. That's the Crow!"

For half a breath, Damian forgot her fear. *The Crow?* The name tickled something in her memory but she couldn't place it. Before she could give it more thought, two more city guards rushed out from inside the gate. One tried to move around Domino closer to her, but the mercenary shifted, keeping Damian behind him. Four bare swords rose menacingly at him.

Damian's heart pounded. "Wait! I-I'm here to speak to Caleb Nazeerad!" She hoped the name of the market director in Trent would mollify the guards. The words poured out in her terror and desperation. "My father runs a cloth trade out of Aether. We were supposed to sell during Relhan, but the… there was an accident. The ship sank in the river." Her throat constricted and she shoved away the dark thoughts that rose up in her like bile. "Please, I need to speak to Caleb Nazeerad."

The voice that responded dripped scorn. "And what's your story, Hawk-killer?"

Damian chanced a look around Domino's cloak, her memory touched by the new alias. All of the swords pointed at him. The guards scarcely spared a glance for her.

The mercenary said nothing.

One of the guards took a step closer, raising his sword. "Talk!"

"Please," Damian attempted. "He was hired on for protection on our journey. The captain of the barge hired him."

A guard turned to her, a look in his eyes like a cat that has sighted prey. "Protection? So he's a mercenary?" The expression was mirrored by the others and two of them grinned.

Cautiously, she answered, "Yes."

The nearest guard pointed at Domino's cloak, where she could see the tip of his sword pushing the cloth outward. "Aha! It's true!"

The guard that had first addressed them straightened, a smug grin on his face. "Commoners aren't allowed to carry swords in Trent."

One of the other guards drew nearer. "You're under arrest. Cuff his hands and I'll have that sword."

A cold feeling spread through Damian. Frozen, she could only watch as the guards advanced, one producing a pair of heavy handcuffs as they approached Domino. Cheers rang up from either side of the gate, from the crowd Damian realized had formed a ring around them. Domino didn't move while the guards cuffed his wrists and removed his sword belt.

Only when the guards led him through the gates could Damian tear herself from her daze. "Wait! He wasn't even in the city!" She tried to hurry after them as they escorted Domino down the street but one of the remaining guards at the gate stepped in front of her, pushing her back before she passed under the portcullis.

"Hey, we're not done with you yet, demon-eyes."

She flinched. Moving back a pace, she leaned over to look around the guard at the group escorting the mercenary. "Domino!" Domino glanced over his shoulder at her. His face betrayed nothing. No anger, no resentment, no guilt. Just acceptance. The same acceptance he had shown her. Before she could say anything more, the guards surrounding him pushed him on, two bare swords held out. Her stomach tightened as she watched the group disappear into the crowd. Several people lingered on either side of the wall to stare at her in the waning dusk.

"Alright, missy. You'd better start over at the beginning."

Closing her eyes, she let out a sigh as she answered the guard's questions, now completely alone.

Fewer people sat inside the tavern now that Relhan had ended but the conversations filling the common room remained excited and lively. Garrick nearly shouted to make himself heard at the table he occupied and those sitting at the far end of the group had half his words relayed to them. Over a dozen townspeople listened raptly to him.

Merchants loved stories about shoplifters being caught. And this one, which happened a few weeks ago on his journey to Trent, had become an instant favourite.

"So I go out into the street and there he is, running straight towards me. He doesn't even slow down when I tell him he's under arrest. I'm thinking this buffoon must be looking to be caught, and then the butcher comes out of the shop behind him. The man casts a shadow down the street. I swear, I've seen oxen smaller than this butcher. He's chasing after the thief with a cleaver the size of my leg and suddenly it's all I can do to keep him from killing the poor bastard!"

Raucous laughter rang out among the assembled townspeople and one pointed at him. "You should've let him!"

Garrick gestured with his mug with a grin. "Ah, but then I wouldn't be a very good knight. I had to stand between that butcher and the thief for half an hour before he calmed down, and you can bet that thief went meekly in irons to the reeve." More laughter rang out and Garrick felt a lurch in his stomach. He glanced into his nearly empty mug, wondering about the quality of this tavern's ale. He had barely softened up the crowd but the sensation wouldn't fade.

"And on that note, my friends, I had best be going."

Groans rang out and one of the townspeople waved.

"You only just got here."

"Come on, have another drink!"

The others echoed the sentiments as Garrick stood, smiling and wishing his stomach would settle.

"My apologies, but I still have business to attend to tonight." Garrick wished it was true but feared his only business would be in a nearby latrine. As he exchanged farewells with the townspeople he noticed them chatting with each other. He knew some of them had not met others until now. Garrick grinned as he passed. He hadn't learned anything during Relhan and the celebrations had kept him busy but getting the merchants to talk to each other would help pass word along. He hoped that the mage's trail was not too cold.

One of the townspeople, the spicer Garrick met a few days ago, accompanied him out the door. No sooner had Garrick stepped into the cool night air than the sensation hit him again. He realized it had nothing to do with sickness. Stumbling, he leaned against a wooden pillar outside the tavern, eyes widening.

"You alright, Sir?" the spicer asked, grabbing Garrick's arm though he swayed in place.

The knight nodded, donning a smile. "I guess I had more to drink than I realized. I'll be fine." The spicer bid him goodnight and staggered down the street. Garrick looked in the opposite direction.

I've never felt anything like this.

Inside the tavern, the sensation had felt similar to the light-headedness of too much drink, but in the open he could sense something far different.

Magic.

The thrum of energy resonated down the road, far more powerful than anything he had ever sensed. The pulse was so strong Garrick was surprised it didn't affect anyone else out in the darkened streets. Could it be his mage? If so, then his quarry was far more powerful than he or Sir Warwick anticipated.

Garrick walked into the street, following the incredible surge of energy. Few people remained outside in the dark roads and no one paid him any mind as he crossed through alleys in search of the source of the magic. His heart beat faster and he flexed his fingers, loosening them up. He could never imagine feeling something so intense that wasn't a spell in active progress but no one who could use magic would dare use it anywhere near Trent.

When he neared the source of the aura, he pressed himself against the wall of an alley and crept close to the corner. No plate armour, no voulge. He only had his mail tunic and his dagger to protect him. *Great. I'm finally actually facing magic, in the one place where I can't be known for doing so.*

He sensed the aura moving. Steeling his nerves, he peered around the corner.

The street was almost empty. Few lights still burned after dark on these long spring days, most of the townspeople retiring as soon as the sun set. One person occupied the street. Likely a woman based on the size. He could make out little else of her form in the darkness and with the cloak draped about her, the hood drawn up over her head. He watched her for a moment, studying her movements and trying to determine what type of spell she cast.

As she made her way down the street, his expression grew more curious. She did nothing with her hands nor did she seem to be saying anything. She walked haltingly, casting furtive glances about, and as the sound of his passage fell silent he could hear sniffles as she breathed. Garrick looked around, trying to see if the aura he detected came from anywhere else. While he waited, she moved on, and so did the aura.

Garrick watched her for another half block, trying to decide what to do. Then, backtracking through the alley, he jogged toward the next street corner. His heart pounded in anticipation and he clenched his fingers, honing his senses to better absorb the aura.

By the time he neared the next corner he could sense the woman one block over. For a moment he weighed his options. Power of that magnitude could threaten the entire city but she clearly wasn't in the process of casting a spell. She herself was the source of the magic, which made no sense at all. And she seemed upset.

Perhaps she's cursed. He frowned at that thought. No curse he knew of was that powerful, nor could he imagine that she carried some enchanted object that would emit such strong magic.

Was some creature of old walking among people once more? *Yeah, right,* he thought. *Sir Warwick would probably laugh at me if I said that.*

While Garrick waited, he sensed the woman turning down the street in his direction.

It's all up to me.

Relaxing his posture he strode around the corner, moving directly in her path. She stepped back with a gasp at his sudden appearance.

He held up his hands, raising his eyebrows in a look of surprise. "Oh, excuse me, miss."

She nodded awkwardly. Then, without a word, she began moving around him.

Leaning down, he tried to look in her eyes while she passed. "Miss? Are you alright?"

She started, reluctantly meeting his eyes for a brief moment. "Yes. Thank you. Forgive me."

Flashing his most charming smile, he stepped closer. She moved back a pace as he approached but remained close enough that he could make out her face beneath the hood, oval-shaped and delicate. Nothing about her seemed anything other than human nor even that remarkable. Fashionable gown, sturdy boots, a bag over her shoulder, the smell of the forest about her. He found himself intrigued.

Smiling wider, he bowed. "My name is Sir Garrick Magni."

Her eyes enlarged at the title and she curtseyed a little stiffly. "Damian Sires, Sir."

What an interesting name. "It's a pleasure to make your acquaintance, Miss Sires."

She avoided his eyes.

"Are you lost?" he asked in a voice smooth as cream.

An uncomfortable look crossed her face and she glanced around. He couldn't tell if she sought familiar landmarks or escape from him.

After a moment, she sighed. "Yes."

He held out an arm. "Well, then, Damian, would you permit me to escort you to your destination?"

She blinked. "Ah, of course, Sir. I am trying to find the Black Duck Inn."

"I'm afraid I don't know that one."

"It is near Plaza Medalia."

"Plaza Medalia? That's halfway across the city from here." He nodded down the street. "I know an inn a few blocks away that has a number of rooms available now. Shall I show you the way?" She frowned, then nodded and stepped aside as he led the way down the street.

Garrick glanced at her, wishing he could see her better in the starlight. Her aura tickled the side of his body, a constant companion. Nothing else about her seemed very unusual. She seemed content to walk in silence, so he tried to draw information out of her. "So where are you from?"

She glanced away. "Aether, Sir."

"Aether, eh? That's north of here?"

She only nodded.

"What brings you to Trent?"

Her head bowed and she opened her mouth a few times before answering simply, "Business."

He tilted his head aside. "What business?"

His interest was lost on her. She shifted uncomfortably. "Trade. In cloth."

Giving up, he nodded. "A good trade." He kept his face straight as they continued toward the inn. He doubted she was lying but nothing added up. She looked younger than him. How she could carry such incredible, unsuppressed power, he couldn't imagine, but this was something he couldn't ignore.

"Here we are." Garrick gestured up to the sign of the Boar Pit hanging over the door. "Not a flattering name, I know, but the rooms are deceptively comfortable." She pulled her hood higher over her head as he opened the door. He followed her inside, the common room nearly as busy as the one he had left recently.

"Sir Magni!" came a bellow from the bar. Garrick grinned as the bearded innkeeper spread his arms wide. "An ale for you tonight?"

Garrick made his way to the bar. "That would be wonderful, but first this lovely young woman needs a room for the night." Damian slipped her bag off her shoulder and opened it. Garrick reached into a pouch on his belt before she could and laid a coin on the counter.

"No, I will…" she began, inhaling sharply as she glimpsed the silver coin. It was worth more than double the asking price for a room, even during Relhan. She turned to Garrick as he turned to wink at her. As he looked her in the eye he leaned back in surprise, his smile fading.

Yellow eyes?

She hastily looked away. The innkeeper, clearly missing what the knight had seen, rummaged underneath the bar. Garrick's attention remained on the girl beside him. She stared toward the wall, keeping her eyes hidden.

Before Garrick had time to react, the innkeeper straightened and set a key on the bar.

"There you are, miss. Let me know if you need anything else."

Snatching up the key, Damian gave Garrick and the innkeeper both a curt nod and hurried to the stairs.

"Wait!" Garrick called after her, but she climbed the stairs without looking back. He stared toward the second floor, lost in thought. Only when another patron of the inn called for Garrick could he snap out of his reverie. Even as he approached and chatted with the townsperson, Garrick couldn't get his mind off the girl who had retreated upstairs.

What is she?

CHAPTER 5
UNVEILED

THE TAVERN'S COMMON room was busy despite the town's small size and its proximity to Misengrad and many conversations filled the air. They were field workers and shepherds mostly, from the look of them and the smell. Yanuk wrinkled his nose as he glanced over the crowd, uncomfortable with being close to so many commoners when all could see him plain as their own hands. Yanuk absently brushed his hair over the scar on his forehead. He tried to tell himself that no one here would likely know him on sight but the fear remained. A few people near the door looked up as he stepped inside. He gave them his best attempt at a casual smile and nod.

"Why did I have to come here?" Yanuk muttered under his breath, the words drowned out by the conversations filling the room. The smell of strong ale and brandy tickled the air, enticing behind the smoky tang of the large hearth centred in the common room. His mouth watered with the aroma of the drinks, so much heavier and richer than the plain ale he and his comrades subsisted on. Yanuk would not partake of the finer drinks, no matter how he thirsted for them. Not when the others went without.

Yanuk sighed as he looked about the room while standing just inside the door and drawing stares and curious glances from bar maids and patrons. A figure at the back of the common room caught his eye. In an isolated corner, a man waved to Yanuk. Yanuk made his way to the distant table, weaving between other patrons with quick, muttered apologies when his fleshy stomach bumped someone's chair.

Whatever Yanuk had been expecting from the message left for him, this man wasn't it. The man was old. Not completely frail but his grayish skin was deeply lined and no trace of colour remained in his thinning hair. A cane rested against the table beside his chair. Well-groomed, the clothes covering his ample paunch were very fine but worn, the style out of fashion for some years.

The man spread his arms with a wrinkled smile as Yanuk approached. The lines at the corners of his mouth looked more accustomed to frowning. "Yanuk Alganov. I have been waiting quite some time to speak with you. Sit down. Do you want a drink?"

Yanuk reluctantly lowered onto the chair across from the well-dressed man. "How do you know me?" The elderly man didn't look like any noble Yanuk met before he was cast out.

The man smiled enigmatically as he swirled the drink in his goblet. The wine had a potent aroma. It had been so long since Yanuk encountered wine that he wasn't certain if it indicated a cheaper vintage.

"Yours is a name of some renown in this region. You used to hold some power here, did you not?"

Yanuk pursed his lips, wondering how much to reveal. The elderly man knew enough to be damaging. "I was once advisor to the Duke of Hesperia himself." Advisor was perhaps a generous title but Yanuk hoped his former status would command some respect. His companion nodded, not seemingly impressed. "Who are you?"

"Alas, my name is not so well known any longer, though I once held far greater power." He waited for a response but Yanuk gave none. The man set his goblet down, focusing on Yanuk. "My name is Parn Gawthrain, and I was duke over a much greater territory than your Hesperia."

Yanuk regarded him, taking in the lord's far western inflection and searching his own memory of politics, dated though it was. "You are from Edan?"

Gawthrain looked pleased. "You have heard of me?"

Yanuk shrugged. "I recall hearing something many years ago about a mad duke losing his hold over southern Edan before the new royal line took the throne. I paid little attention to the information, as I was being ostracized at the time."

Gawthrain's expression darkened. "The usurper. He was no less a warlord than I, with no royal lineage."

"What do you want with me?"

The lord sobered. "Do you want a drink?"

"No. How do you know about me?"

"The right money in the right hands. You are cunning, Yanuk Alganov, but you are not infallible. Others might also be looking for you. You should be more cautious."

"Is that what you brought me here to tell me?"

The disingenuous smile returned to Gawthrain's face. "No, that information I give out freely. I brought you here to make you an offer."

Yanuk stared cautiously at him. "For what?"

The lord leaned against the table, drawing closer. "The opportunity to gain power you and your fellow mages never had, right now."

Yanuk gave him a skeptical look. Reaching into his doublet, Gawthrain pulled out an amulet and tossed it across the table. Yanuk dropped his eyes to it before facing the former lord again. Gawthrain gestured impatiently toward the amulet. Frowning, Yanuk picked it up, realizing that it was a locket. Opening it, he found a deeply yellowed sheet of parchment folded up inside. His expression shifted from curiosity to wonderment to confusion as he unfolded the page. It was covered in ancient writing, the script so old he had rarely encountered it even in the castle library in Misengrad.

Yanuk raised his eyes to the former duke. "What is this?"

"That is all that remains in my possession of a spell book, one of enormous power. With that spell, we would be unstoppable."

Yanuk narrowed his eyes at the lord's casual inclusion in the mages' group. "To do what?"

Smiling, Gawthrain laced his fingers together and leaned over the table. "To storm Albrith, of course."

Yanuk straightened, then shook his head. "I have no desire to attack the king of Faneria. My comrades and I live a life of peace."

Gawthrain snorted. "Peace? You live apart from civilization, hiding in desperation from ants. That is not peace. That is subjugation. Humiliation." He waved a hand, the gesture encompassing the rest of the tavern's occupants. "You are like gods among these filthy peasants. Is it fair or just for you to cower in your hidden home, you who are so much better than this rabble?"

Yanuk pursed his lips. He thought of Patrus, Edrand, and the other old mages he had gathered, maimed and marred for life though they had committed no crime, for the crime of being themselves. The aroma of sizzling mutton and bitter ale wafted across the room to Yanuk, making his stomach grumble.

Gawthrain leaned over the table. "You and I know what your mages are capable of, Yanuk. Let us work together so that we can reclaim the respect and status you deserve."

Yanuk raised his eyes to the former duke. "What do you get out of this?"

Gawthrain spread his hands. "An equal share. Is that not fair for the one who gives you such power? I need a mage to use that spell, and you need extra strength to achieve your goals." He held a hand forward. "A mutually beneficial partnership."

Yanuk hesitated. He looked at the page in his hand. The bottom edge was torn. "You said this page came from a spell book."

"Yes, and it will need to be recovered."

"Where is it?"

"Not beyond our reach, I assure you. If you wish to proceed I would be glad to give you the location of the book and you could be casting that spell within a week." Gawthrain held the hand forward more blatantly. "Do we have a partnership?"

Yanuk stared at the lord's outstretched hand. Years of hard work had brought Yanuk and his fellow mages a life of contentment. Yet they had to hide from the rest of the world, sneaking into towns and stealing what supplies they needed merely to survive. Their hands, which in ages past had wrought miracles and expanded all knowledge, now suffered the scars and callouses of ordinary peasants. He and his brethren still suffered nearly twenty years later because the common man thought they created the Century Storm.

Slowly, Yanuk refolded the page and replaced it in the locket. "I must discuss this with my fellows."

Gawthrain nodded. "Of course. But you will permit me to come speak with them as well, yes?"

Yanuk shot him a suspicious look.

"Come now, Yanuk, do not look so troubled. I would not have shown you this were my offer not genuine." Gawthrain held up the amulet before pocketing it inside his doublet.

Yanuk frowned. He had never seen a spell so old, seemingly written in old Styrian, the words that crafted the incantations to cast any spell. And Gawthrain offered an entire book of spells like this? Yanuk should be the last among his fellows to bring a stranger to their home, but there was no denying what Gawthrain offered and Yanuk knew he would not be the only one curious about this opportunity. Some of Yanuk's comrades were content with the life they had created, free from persecution. Most of those who remained after their exile held resentment for how they were treated when they were cast out, as Yanuk did.

And if Yanuk refused this lord? Gawthrain knew enough to expose them. Yanuk didn't know what the former duke would get out of doing so but Gawthrain didn't seem the forgiving type. Yanuk also took note of the fact that Gawthrain had not refuted the 'mad duke' title. Such an alias would not come about lightly. Yanuk didn't want to let Gawthrain out of his sight until he could be convinced of the lord's intentions.

Yanuk let a smile crawl onto his face, trying to hide his trepidations and suspicions. "Very well." He held out his hand. "We have an agreement."

Gawthrain shook his hand. The former lord held up his goblet with his other hand. "Well, then, let us toast this new partnership." Yanuk nodded and at last called a bar maid over for a drink. Gawthrain smiled at Yanuk, yet about the eyes it looked more like the frown he was clearly accustomed to.

"To glory restored."

A scent of lavender tickled Damian's nose as she awoke. She nestled deeper into the plush mattress and pillow for several minutes, relishing the softness of the bed, the warmth of the blankets, and the silence of the enclosed room after spending so many nights sleeping on the ground in the forest. For a moment, she simply lay there, enjoying the comfort and ignoring everything else.

The sleep had been so restful, so deep, so dreamless, that she awoke with her mind cleared and unable to focus on anything. As the day outside the yellow window brightened, thoughts crept back, scattered and disjointed.

Alone. The word weighed on her as much as the thoughts about the barge that circled at the back of her mind, ever searching for a moment of weakness. Damian thought she had always been alone, but now she truly was in a way she never had been. Her father was gone, the captain and crew of the barge were gone, even Domino was gone.

Until last night, Domino was her world. He was all she had and all she needed. He was her reason, her purpose, and her strength. Then she got him arrested. Her throat constricted with the thought. It was her fault. She told the guards he was a mercenary. She had never dealt with the occasional trouble other merchants or her father faced. Only once, years ago, had she been told that no one but city guards, knights, and nobility could carry swords within Trent. Last night she had forgotten about it entirely. Now Domino was in prison for his weapon.

Who was Damian without him, without the cloth trade? Alone. So many winters in Aether staying at home and avoiding others as much as she could had shown her that. It wasn't a bad thing. She felt comfortable by herself the way she couldn't with almost anyone else.

Yet she missed selling the cloth. She had been looking forward to it. It was a mask, the facade of someone who was perfectly at ease speaking with others, but in ways it felt more real than her preferred solitude. She felt rejuvenated afterwards.

That person was her and it was not her. Damian slipped into that persona so easily that she had joked with customers and fellow merchants about the person she was when not selling the cloth. Usually they didn't believe her. As a merchant she was confident, determined, light-hearted, and at ease with herself. She wanted to be that woman.

Could I?

Some of that other Damian slipped out the last night when she explained her connections with the cloth trade to the guard at the gate after Domino was taken away. The guard seemed to relent. That hint of fear and scorn in his eyes as he looked into hers never faded but for a brief moment it didn't matter to her.

What would the merchant Damian do?

She wouldn't simply lie in bed when there were things to do. Pulling back the covers, Damian swung her legs off the bed and stood. Opening her bag, she drew out a brush and worked out the tangles in her auburn hair before clipping it back in a simple style.

She packed the brush but paused as she glimpsed the gown folded within. She pulled it out and held it up, letting the garment drape to the floor. Thankfully, after Domino hung it up to dry after its trip through the river it had not suffered any noticeable damage. Deep crimson with black and gold accents, she had designed it after a handful of gowns she had seen at the end of the trade journey last year in Windermere in central Faneria. The style was just coming into fashion there at the time. It was the dress Damian had made for the new year now already begun.

Looking at the garment made dark thoughts reach up from the back of her mind. A lump formed in her throat as images of the burning barge flashed through her memories, along with the darker thoughts of having lost her father. Pushing them back, she changed out of the dirty gown she had worn since she boarded the barge and pulled on the new dress for the first time. She had rarely owned a red garment for the cost, nor had she worn a gown before that was cut so low. The style suited both and she found herself standing a little straighter as she wore it.

She hesitated as she glanced at the door. The reaction of the guards at the gate the last night weighed on her. Once they had taken Domino into custody, the remaining guard allowed her to pass without much trouble, though the unease never left his eyes as he spoke with her. She had avoided letting anyone else see her eyes in the crowded common room the last night but the knight's reaction emphasized the disdain and fear she knew she would face if she stepped outside without a veil. Wearing her cloak with the hood up would not hide her eyes so well but she had nothing else with which to cover them.

She caught a glimpse of her reflection in a mirror across the room. Cut close in the bodice with its low neckline, the new gown enhanced her features, making her look more a woman than anything she had worn before. She raised her gaze to her own eyes, the same yellow that had always stared back at her. She thought of how Domino had looked into them without concern.

I don't want to have to hide.

She hesitated. The mere thought of looking at strangers without the shield of a veil made her skin crawl.

I just have to see Caleb first. Then I can look for another veil.

Before she could allow herself to doubt the decision, she turned and swiftly strode out of the room, locking the door behind her.

She descended the stairs to a nearly empty common room. The quietness did not surprise her though she had never awoken in Trent at the beginning of the year. She and her father always spent the last night of Relhan reloading the cloth onto the barge, sleeping on the ship and departing at first light. Most merchants, performers, and visitors made haste to depart at the end of the new year festival, if not before, leaving Trent to return to normal business in very short order and leaving its inns barren. One other person occupied the common room, an older man who watched her climb down the stairs and walk up to the bar.

"Hello?" she called toward the kitchen.

Soon, the innkeeper emerged, smiling as he strode behind the bar from the kitchen. "Good morning, miss. How was your…"

He cut himself off with a gasp, backing away with wide eyes when he came close enough to see hers. Her throat grew thick and she looked down at the bar.

"May I have something to eat, please?"

The innkeeper's eyes darted over her, weighing his options. After a moment he escaped into the kitchen without a word. Damian let out a sigh, wondering if he intended to return. Turning, she found the other occupant of the room watching her, though he hastily returned his attention to his drink. He wondered what so startled the innkeeper, no doubt, and likely he would be looking for the oddity in her.

It's going to be a long day.

Through the door into the kitchen, she heard something sizzle loudly. She smiled faintly but realized the knight's generous payment the previous evening probably influenced the innkeeper's decision more than her politeness.

Inhaling deeply, she focused on how she had made customers out of browsers while she stood behind her father's stall. A lump formed in her throat.

I can do this.

After a few minutes the innkeeper emerged, holding a tray with steaming eggs, bacon, and biscuits in his hands.

Damian smiled as pleasantly as she could, failing to keep her chin raised as she reached out to take the food. "Thank you."

The innkeeper gave her a stiff smile and nod. He stepped back a pace as she relieved him of his burden and watched her while she retreated to a table to eat. She tried to ignore him as she sat down. The common room remained silent while she ate and stared toward the windows that glowed from the light of the morning sun.

Finally, Damian finished and stood, taking a moment to steel her nerves before she crossed the room and stepped outside. She winced and shaded her eyes against the glaring sunlight. Compared to the dense crowds that thronged the streets when she was normally here, with two dozen or so people in view in either direction the city seemed barren. It was nothing like Relhan, when she could barely walk down the sidewalk without bumping into others the entire way.

When her eyes adjusted to the light, the first thing that struck her was the details and colours. For a long moment, she stood still and stared around in amazement. She noted the minute differences in the colours of the bricks making up a shop, the grain of wood in the carts that rolled through the streets, the subtle plaid pattern in a townswoman's skirt, the many different colours of hairs that made up the coat of a bay mare. The world looked so much more vibrant and alive without the screen of a veil, and much brighter.

People moved around Damian on the sidewalk, none stopping long enough to look her in the eyes. A few walking down the road nodded when she caught their glances but they passed too far away to make out the colour beneath her hand. Damian's skin crawled as she glanced out, her eyes bared to all, but she felt slightly emboldened by the lack of reaction. Inhaling deeply, she turned and headed south.

The first gasp and start came before she had walked one block down. Damian forced herself to keep her shoulders back as a woman going the opposite direction glanced at her, only to recoil when she saw Damian's eyes, giving her a wide berth and almost running into a donkey as she passed. More reactions sprang up as Damian made her way through the town, mutters, jests, jeers, and gestures for the Gods of Light coming all around. Damian suppressed a cringe but stopped noticing them as thoughts of her purpose filled her mind. As she passed into familiar streets, her stomach grew tight at the idea of what she was about to face.

Finally, she reached a narrow building a block away from Plaza Medalia where the north and east forks of the Ivory River intersected. Damian's insides twisted and her breath sped. For a long moment she stood in front of the building, bracing herself to address what she had avoided since that first night on the river. Then, steadying her breath, she stepped forward and knocked on the door. Hurried footsteps approached the door from within.

A fair-haired man opened the door. "Can I help—" He cut off with a gasp and start as he looked at her.

Damian forced her expression to remain neutral. "Hello, Horace. Can I speak to Mr. Nazeerad?"

The man swallowed uncomfortably, leaning back while holding the door ajar. "M-Mr. Nazeerad is not to be—"

"Please," she cut across him. "Just tell him Damian Sires is here."

"I—"

"Damian Sires?" exclaimed a deep, booming voice from within. Horace looked over his shoulder, opening the door wider, and Damian managed a faint smile at the figure sitting behind a desk inside. "It is you!" The chair scraped across the floor as Caleb Nazeerad, market director for Trent, pushed to his feet and hurried around the desk toward the door. "I am so relieved that you are here! And you are not wearing your veil! But your eyes…"

As he drew close enough to see her he stopped in his place, his eyes enlarging. "Oh."

She gave him a wry smile, stringing a lock of hair behind her ear. "It wasn't my vision that had a problem."

A bewildered look remained on Caleb's face. "I see, yes."

Her smile faded and she glanced away. "I'm sorry we lied to you all these years."

Caleb cleared his throat. "Well, you have hidden that from

everyone, yes? People always speak of you as the veiled girl. I think it is nice to see your lovely face free from that veil." Before she could respond, Caleb stepped aside and gestured toward the room. "But come inside! I have been wondering about you. And where is your father?"

Damian stepped into Caleb's office, Horace closing the door behind her and moving a few paces back. Her throat thickened. "That is why I've come."

She glanced around Caleb's office. Little floor space remained clear as crates and neat piles of books and papers stacked along every wall, blocking off the shelves against the wall that held more ledgers, along with strange and exotic figurines, bottles, boxes, and bowls from all over Elderra. Papers, seals, horns of wax and ink and a set of brass scales buried under more sheaves of parchment covered Caleb's desk, decidedly messier than the rest of the office.

Damian turned her attention back to the occupants of the office. Horace stared uncomfortably at her. He had been Caleb's assistant as long as she could remember, younger than she was now when he started working for Caleb. The market director himself seemed not to have changed in all the years Damian had accompanied her father to Trent. Though Caleb had lived in Faneria longer than she'd been alive, he looked like he had just come from the far northern desert yesterday. Little of his red-brown skin could be seen under his white clothes, gold tunic, and matching turban, and a thick black beard covered half his face before falling down to a point on his chest. Barrel chested, large as an ox, with arms like hocks of ham and a girth Damian could hardly reach halfway around, his size and deep, loud, rolling voice intimidated her as a child, but the sight of him was welcome now.

She tried to keep her voice steady. "There was an accident on the barge. It sank the first night out of Aether."

Caleb put a hand over his heart, a horrified look crossing his face. "Oh no! I feared the worst when you did not arrive for Relhan, nor was any word sent. I sent a messenger to Aether, but only two days ago. Then your father…?"

She looked away, biting her lip.

"Oh, this is dreadful news! My heart breaks for you, Damian."

She nodded, her voice taking on a tremor. "Thank you." Speaking of what she had avoided for a week and a half allowed dark thoughts to claw their way through her mind.

I'm all alone. I've lost the only person who could take care of me.

Caleb opened his arms and stepped forward as she trembled. Drawing in a shaky breath, she let him come close and wrap his huge arms around her. The vicious thoughts, like evil spirits, tore at her.

It's my fault. I killed him.

I'm a monster.

Her body shook with silent sobs and she felt energy boiling inside her, threatening to break loose. Horror rose with the thought that she would lose control here in Caleb's office.

Do not let your despair control you.

The words returned suddenly to her mind and she recalled the feeling of the mercenary's gloved hands on her shoulders, his eyes gazing deeply into hers. With a deep, shaky breath, Damian pushed down the dark thoughts and the energy.

Don't look back, she told herself. *Don't look back. There is only now.*

She breathed in quick gasps, slowly steadying her thoughts and her hands. Wiping her eyes, she leaned back, Caleb's arms releasing her as she moved.

"Thank you," she uttered. "I think I will be alright." As she looked at Caleb, smiling sadly at her, she caught a glimpse of Horace behind him, eyes averted and discomfort of a different kind marking his face.

"Ah, this is so sad." Caleb sighed. "Claude was one of my best merchants. I will never forget the first day I met him, when he approached me for a stall at the market during Relhan." He chuckled. "I was having such a bad day and dismissed him without even listening to him. But he persisted. He caught me when I went out for dinner and bought my meal for me. He offered to pay double the fees I was asking! I could not rob him like that, but I gave him a chance, and never has a day passed that I regretted it."

She smiled softly. "He was always so patient. Especially the first year that I stood behind the stall with him. I complained of boredom so much and I'm certain I was more a hindrance than help."

"He was glad to have you there." Caleb laid a large hand on her shoulder. "Horace! What about you?"

The assistant jumped at the thunder of Caleb's voice. "Master?"

"Claude Sires, man! What is your best memory of him?"

Horace frowned with a furtive glance at Damian. "The year that he helped organize that scavenger hunt in the market." Horace shifted. "My own father had passed away the winter before. My little brother didn't take it so well and that made him so happy."

Damian looked up in surprise, not remembering that. Of course, that year she had been six.

Caleb nodded slowly. "Claude was very kind. He will be missed."

She frowned. "I hope our absence did not make things too difficult for you."

Caleb waved a hand. "Fah, you've nothing to apologize for. You are still here, and for that I am glad." He spread his hands. "But what can I do for you?"

She breathed slowly, trying to focus on what she had come to do. "I need to contact the guild's insurers." She shifted. "And I was wondering if I could arrange for a team to try to recover what cloth might not be damaged beyond repair."

"Of course, of course!" Caleb approached his desk. "I hope you will forgive me if it takes a few days to arrange everything."

"Of course."

The market director threw up his hands. "I am still trying to resolve all the issues from Relhan. Complaints from customers about the noise, complaints from merchants about placement or displays hanging into their stalls, complaints from the city about refuse, complaints from sailors about warehousing, never mind all the merchants who still have not paid their taxes or fees. Fah! It makes me want to quit and return to Enseros."

Damian couldn't help smiling at the familiar rant, something she had heard almost every year, never mind Caleb's fevered opinions of the politics in his homeland. It felt nice to take her mind off her own troubles.

"But I will do everything I can for you, Damian." He shuffled through the papers on his desk. "Is there anything else you need? You have a place to stay? Someone to take care of you?"

Her first thoughts went to Domino and a pang of guilt struck her at his imprisonment. She shook her head. "We put a deposit down last year for the inn where we usually stay. I was going there next." She didn't want to address the larger issue yet.

"You are certain there is nothing else you need?" Caleb straightened. "Let me pay your expenses until those insurers get back to you."

She shook her head. "That's alright, thank you."

"No, no, no, I insist! It is the least I can do for you, in Claude's memory."

"I couldn't, but thank you for the offer."

He put his fists on his hips, gazing sternly down at her but for the smile on his face. "Just like your father. Very well, then. Consider it a loan."

Damian smiled. "I am fine for now. But I will let you know if I need a loan."

Chuckling, Caleb shook his head and continued looking through the mess of his desk, papers falling to the floor as he searched. Horace hurried over to gather up the fallen pages.

"So prideful," Caleb said. "Well, do not let your pride stop you if you need some coin to tide you over. I know how those insurers work. Fah!" Leaning over, he opened a drawer under his desk. "Ah, here it is!" Standing straight, he held up a blue envelope patterned with gold. Metal jingled and something rattled as it moved. "I meant to give this to you for the new year. I do not know if you are too old for the candy now."

Surprise, delight, nostalgia, and guilt swept through Damian at once as she took the envelope. Opening it, she saw a handful of candies and shiny, newly minted coins inside. She smiled. "I don't know if I will ever be too old for this candy. Thank you." She frowned. "I should have a gift for you as well. I'm sorry."

He waved a hand. "Think nothing of it. With all you have been through, that should be the least of your worries. Is there anything else I can do for you?"

"You have done more than enough." Only after she said that did she remember that she still had no veil. She hesitated very briefly, but decided that she didn't want to ask that of him. The coins in the envelope would pay for one. "Thank you so much, Mr. Nazeerad."

He waved a hand in dismissal. "Fah, we have known each other too long for such formality. Please call me Caleb. Anyway, I hope that you will return with new stock next year. You would run a fine stall on your own."

The mere thought made her stomach tighten but she smiled and nodded.

"Feel free to come visit anytime you like, Damian."

"I will. Thank you again, Caleb. Have a nice day."

"You as well, my dear. Now, Horace, what in blazes was I working on again?"

Damian smirked as she strode outside, Caleb's assistant scrambling to his desk while she left. "We were trying to settle the accounts for the Manhausers..." She closed the door to the sound of Caleb groaning in exasperation.

She clutched the envelope tightly in her hands, the sight of it making her feel like a child again. Protected. Guided. The gold patterns on the envelope shone reflectively and she caught a glimpse of her eyes inside the patterns, the same colour as the paint on the paper. Part of the weight lifted off her shoulders as she stood outside Caleb's office having been treated the same way he had always treated her, if a little less jovial under the circumstances. Though he seemed to stare a little harder at her eyes than usual he had said nothing about them after she walked into the room.

It's the best I can hope for.

Even those few who had seen and accepted her for the colour of her eyes did so in spite of them, not truly seeing them as anything but strange.

Except for Domino.

That thought and the realization that her mind had turned to the mercenary twice in such a short period made her cheeks grow warm. Shaking her head, she turned toward the inn she had tried to find the last night.

Now that the more difficult task had been completed, Damian noticed the reactions to her eyes more as she walked through the streets. They didn't catch the interest of anyone not already looking toward her eyes, one in ten passers-by at best. However, no one who did see their colour failed to show anything less than surprise at the sight. Damian's chest tightened with the reactions but she bit her tongue and kept her chin up as she walked. Much as she wanted to hide, it was nice not to have to wear a veil and she found herself putting off searching for another when she passed by shops where she might find material for one inside. She might be facing fear and disdain but at least it was genuine, a reaction to who she really was. She prayed to the Gods of Light that she would not face anything worse.

Her meeting with the keeper of the Black Duck Inn was briefer and less amiable than with Caleb but she earned a few extra nights' lodging out of her negotiations. With thoughts of her father fresh on her mind she set out for another destination.

The garden stood in the middle of a square, a haven of green in the midst of the city. Several people passed within the bordering pillars of the garden as they made their way through the late morning streets but the lawn remained full and verdant. Neat arrangements of daffodils, mums, snapdragons, orchids, geraniums, and blue hydrangea lined the outer border of the garden, broken by the dirt paths onto the lawn that quickly faded into plush grass. Songbirds chirruped as they perched in the trees planted evenly between the decorative pillars that supported nothing above them. Cherry trees in full bloom grew at each cardinal direction, raining soft pink petals onto the lawn with each breeze, while tall green ash trees, silver birch, and two maple trees with dark red foliage stood between them. She heard squirrels chittering in the trees, though the garden was too small for them to venture down from the high branches.

At the centre of the garden lay a pool, rimmed in stone and smooth as glass. Walking through one of the paths, Damian approached the pool. She looked up at the statue at its centre. The Goddess of Life rose majestically from the water, white marble robe draped about her as she gazed into the distance, one hand holding a growing oak branch and a wreath of laurel circling her brow.

Damian looked at the pool, the water dark and unmoving. She could not see deeper into the water than she could reach with her arm. No one knew how deep the pool ran. Holding up her skirt, she kneeled at the water's edge. Other people spoke softly nearby and Damian could tell one person watched her, though she paid none of them any mind. Reaching out, Damian gently set the tulip she had bought—bulb, roots and all—into the pool, careful not to touch the water with her fingers. A tiny ripple spread out from the flower as it dropped into the water, fading before it touched the stone edges of the pool. Damian sat back, her throat feeling thick.

"Please guide my father to your side, so that he may walk your golden halls." Tears welled in her eyes and her voice quavered. "And let him find my mother there." She squeezed her eyes shut, holding back a sob as the tears streamed down her face. She forced back the thoughts that reached up from the depths of her mind, focusing only on the simple idea that she had lost someone she loved.

She had no doubt that her father would find his way to the goddess's sanctuary as he had never lived but to the principles of Light. Strength, Justice, Wisdom, Love, and Life. Opening her eyes, Damian watched the water slowly absorb the tulip until it sank into the depths of the pool, soon disappearing from sight. The motion seemed to finalize it, and in that moment Damian knew that her father was truly gone. She shrank in on herself, sitting alone at the edge of the pool for a long moment in silence while she battled with her thoughts.

Finally, she wiped her eyes and rose. Turning, she found the knight she had met the last night leaning against one of the bordering pillars of the garden, framed by cherry blossoms and painted in dappled sunlight as it streamed through the branches. It was a beautiful sight and only under the light of day did she notice how handsome he looked. His brown hair, glinting red in the light, was tied back in a loose tail. With a rectangular face, large green eyes, a straight nose, and an easy smile, his entire visage seemed a perfect compromise between masculine and boyish, and he must have been only a few years older than her. Dressed in a grey shirt and brown pants and clad in a plain mail tunic over his lean and sharply muscled body, armed with nothing more than a dagger, it had been easy to mistake him for a city guard the previous night. She could imagine him looking threatening, yet his relaxed posture and gentle expression gave him a companionable air.

Damian wasn't surprised to see him, as she thought she heard someone join her when she came to the pool. A solemn expression marked his face.

"I'm sorry."

She studied him for a long moment, wondering what he was doing here. The condolences seemed sincere but she found it strange that he would act so casual and open. She had seen his true nature when he recoiled at the sight of her eyes the last night. She didn't want to deal with someone being dishonest with her. Even if the sight of her eyes didn't bother him anymore, which she found unlikely, he was either curious about them or wanted something from her.

He gestured over his shoulder. "Would you like to get some lunch?"

A chill crept up her spine. His accent had sounded off for a local, but now she knew the truth. This was a knight from far to the west. Could he be a dragon knight? Stories of the Agaesi, the ancient, mysterious, and secluded order of knights, rippled through Damian's mind. Rumours told of them displaying uncanny power and being tasked with clandestine, even arcane assignments. Damian's father always warned her not to believe the tales though even he spoke of them with a softer voice.

Hesperia prided itself on its army and all the stories said that scarcely a few dozen dragon knights remained. It had to be coincidence. Still, she couldn't help feeling uncomfortable with this knight's presence.

She tried to keep her feelings hidden and her voice uninterested. "No, thank you, Sir."

He nodded, his expression not changing. Trying to cast aside her unease, she strode toward him and dug in her coin pouch. He didn't falter as he looked into her eyes with a smile.

She held out a coin. "Thank you for your assistance last night,

Sir. This is repayment for the room." It wasn't nearly what he had paid the innkeeper, but the coin covered what the room was worth, for it being the end of Relhan.

The knight shook his head with a smile. "Don't worry about it, Damian. You don't have to repay me."

The casual use of her name felt like a rope tied around her throat. "Take it, Sir, please. I do not like to be beholden to anyone. I can pay for my own room."

Tilting his head aside, he regarded her a moment. She remained firm and steady under his scrutiny. Finally, his face broke in a grin. "Alright." Taking the coin, he dropped it into a pouch on his belt. "May I walk with you, at least?"

Her discomfort heightened at the thought and all she wanted to do was hide in her room at the Black Duck Inn. A different thought crossed her mind. *What would the merchant Damian do?* She wouldn't be afraid of this knight.

She nodded. "Of course, Sir." Turning, she strode out of the garden and into the late morning streets. The knight's mail jingled as he walked alongside her.

"I suppose if you come here on business, then you probably know all the best places to eat."

She increased her pace a little, acutely aware of the fact that she didn't know where she was going next and that it was dinnertime. "I have not had the time to try much of Trent's fare, Sir. My father and I usually ate at the same places each year."

"Well, there must be something special about them if they kept you coming back."

She shrugged. "We knew them. The only place I would truly recommend is Talmot's Bakery."

"Oh? I've been dying to find some good cinnamon flip-pockets. I think my tastes are too spoiled for a traveller's life."

Damian's mouth twitched almost into a smile. "They do make nice pastries, but my favourite is their butter cream cakes. My father and I would always share one during the closing ceremony parade." Her eyes widened, surprised that she had told Sir Magni so much.

He smiled wider. "That sounds delightful. You'll have to show me that bakery."

She gave him an uncomfortable look and fell silent. She turned at the next corner, hoping she could get away from the knight.

As they continued through the streets, the occasional townsperson greeted Sir Magni by name with a wide smile and the knight usually asked about their specific trade or family. To

Damian's surprise, the reactions toward her diminished around him. She frowned, disappointed that she would only be more accepted in Sir Magni's presence. Glancing away as he greeted a local cooper, she continued across the street. He soon caught up and continued speaking as though nothing had happened.

"You grew up in Aether?"

She let out a sigh, resigning herself to his company. "Mostly. The cloth trade took me across much of Faneria for nearly two seasons every year."

"That must have been hard, being away from home so much."

Was he goading her? No, it was clear from the affected accent that he was trying to make others believe that he was from Trent or near to it. Seeing a chance, she took it. "I like to travel, Sir. Besides, Hesperia is much farther away from here than Aether."

He glanced at her in surprise. "What makes you think I'm from Hesperia?"

She gave him a cautious look. "No one this side of the Marble River uses the word 'lunch.' "

He blinked a few times, apparently caught off guard by her statement. After a pause, he chuckled and his gaze deepened. "You are a very clever woman, Damian."

She frowned, uncertain what he meant by that, and continued in silence.

Soon, Sir Magni stopped and held up a hand. "Ah, here we are." Blinking, Damian glanced at the building in front of them, a tavern called the Hawk and Hare. Only then did she realize he had subtly guided her here, drawing close to her on one side to make her retreat in a different direction. She took a step back, staring suspiciously at him, but he smiled warmly at her.

"The food here is exquisite. I hear the chef once served a high lord of Edan."

As the door opened to admit another townsperson, an aroma of herbed meat and freshly baked bread drifted onto the street, making her mouth water and stomach grumble.

"Would you like to eat?"

Damian stared at him, incensed and terrified at the ease with which he had tricked her into coming here. Yet she was hungry and the scent of the food within surpassed anything she could remember eating. She straightened, giving the knight a cautious look.

"Very well."

He opened the door for her and she stepped inside. The common room in the tavern looked much the same as any other in Trent, about half the tables occupied for the dinner rush. She quietly followed Sir Magni to a table. Before she could take a seat, he pulled a chair out for her. The action gave her pause. No one had ever done that for her. Reluctantly, she lowered onto the chair and he tucked it under the table before he took a seat.

A bar maid sashayed up to them. "Good day, Sir, miss. What can I get you?" She started and gasped as Damian turned and the maid met her eyes. Damian sighed as the bar maid scrambled back a few paces, leaning against the next table over. Several patrons looked over at the commotion and one couple at a table nearby whispered animatedly to each other.

"We'll have whatever the cook is making that smells so delightful," Sir Magni said quickly and calmly, "and I'll have a brown ale." He turned his eyes to Damian as the bar maid faced him and straightened a little.

"Mead, please," Damian said tiredly, "with ginger and cinnamon." The bar maid muttered something and scampered off.

Sir Magni watched the bar maid disappear, his smile fading. "I take it you get that a lot."

"No. Usually I wear a veil."

His eyes returned to hers with a smile. "So what made you change your mind about it?"

Her gaze on him was firm. "Losing it when my ship burned down in the river."

His smile disappeared and he stared at her in surprise. "I'm sorry. It must be hard."

"Being judged on something over which I have no control? Yes, Sir, it is."

He hesitated and a strange thoughtful look crossed his eyes. After a moment, he opened his mouth to continue. Before he could say another word the bar maid returned, setting their meals and two leather mugs on the table before darting away. The sizzling duck filled Damian's senses and as she began to eat she forgot all else. The juicy, spiced bird was more flavourful than perhaps anything she had ever eaten and the hunk of warm crusty bread and roasted new potatoes complemented it divinely. Even the mead, sweet and dry with its delicate flavors, ranked among the best she had drunk.

As the delicious food filled her stomach, so it soothed her spirit. Her discomfort with the knight faded, her misery over her father's death diminished, and her anxiety over dealing with taking over the cloth trade eased. For a moment while she enjoyed her meal, everything seemed alright.

"I'm sorry."

She looked up at the knight's sudden words. A solemn expression marked his face.

"I'm sorry for the way I reacted to your eyes last night. That's what I was going to say earlier."

She sighed and returned her attention to her dinner. Her irritation with him seemed petty now. She could hardly blame him for his reaction. Even Caleb Nazeerad had been surprised, despite knowing her all her life.

"It is fine, Sir."

Snickers rose from a table nearby, from the couple Damian noticed earlier. Their speech slurred a little and a few words of their conversation drifted to her.

"Little yellow-eyed birdie nesting with a Crow."

Guilt weighed in Damian's stomach like a lead ball and she lowered her knife to the table without a word.

Sir Magni turned to stare pointedly at them. "Do you have something you would like to say to us?"

The man held up his hands, eyes widening. "N-not you, Sir. We were talkin' about the Crow."

A skeptical look crossed the knight's face. "He hasn't been seen in this part of Faneria in years."

Damian watched him, noting the guarded look in his eyes as he referred to the mercenary.

"He's here in town, Sir," the woman insisted. "I saw him with my own eyes, getting hauled off by the city guard just last night for carrying a sword into town."

Sir Magni sat up straighter. "What?"

"Yeah!" The man pointed. "And I heard it straight from one of the guards who arrested him. He came into town with that girl!"

Sir Magni shot a wide-eyed look to Damian. "*What?*"

She squirmed under his scrutiny. "He guided me here through the forest."

With that, the knight leaned against the table while the couple snickered. "Don't you know who he is?"

Anxiety gave way to anger at the disgusted look in his eyes. "I know he saved my life, Sir." Her reaction came instinctively. It was true, she knew nothing about Domino. He could be the worst kind of person and she had no way to refute it. Yet what did Sir Magni and the couple at the next table know about him? They had not travelled through the wilderness with Domino. Damian couldn't help seething at their accusations.

"He's a criminal. He murdered his—"

"Enough," she snapped, her eyes narrowing. "He is already in prison. Is it so honourable to attack someone who cannot defend himself?"

Sir Magni blinked, entirely nonplussed. "Are you kidding? What in the world did he say to you?"

"Nothing." She shoved her chair back and stood. "But he was far kinder to me than you have been." Reaching into the pouch on her belt, she threw a pair of copper coins onto the table, turning away as the knight shielded his face from the coins bouncing against him. Without a backward glance, Damian stormed out of the tavern.

She had passed two other shops before the knight's voice called out.

"Damian!"

Ignoring him, she stalked on, townspeople edging out of the way as she passed. To her irritation, she heard the knight hurrying through the crowd to catch up to her.

"Damian..."

She whirled on him, swinging an arm through the air. "Just leave me alone!" Fire roared through her veins and smoldered in the look she shot him. A small, dark part of her wanted him to push harder, wanted the excuse to lash out in a way she never had before. Instead of reaching for her again, he leaned back and stared uncertainly at her. In his moment of indecision, she turned and continued, leaving him behind.

CHAPTER 6
LOSING CONTROL

LYLE AWOKE BEFORE dawn. He looked around his bedroom, trying to pick out shapes in the darkness, before glancing over his shoulder. Evelyn slept softly beside him. Quietly, he rose, dressed, and slipped out of the room.

To his surprise, as he descended the stairs the common room was well lit. Reaching the main floor, he found the hearth fire and a number of candles burning. Marise, dressed down to her boots, stood in the kitchen busily slicing bread. He watched her for a moment. She barely reached up to his chest but looked nearly a woman in the flickering firelight. At least, she might have looked like a woman if she hadn't kept her brown hair close-cropped and dressed in a men's shirt and close-fitting trousers. He frowned at that as he did every morning.

Lyle turned to the hearth as he heard the water in the kettle shifting, picking it off the hook as it whistled. Marise turned at the noise and straightened.

"Father. Good morning."

"Morning." He brought the kettle into the kitchen. "Where is your brother?"

She kept her voice even, but he could hear the scowl in her words. "He is still asleep." Spreading some preserves on a slice of bread, she offered it to him.

He took it with a nod. "Make certain he gets to his training on time."

"I will."

Finishing the bread, Lyle crossed the room to the stand holding his scuffed and aged armour. He shrugged on the mail tunic, then began strapping on the pieces of plate.

"Here, let me help you with that, Father."

He glanced at Marise as she took the straps of his armour from his hands and buckled the breastplate and backplate together. She worked quickly, securing the chest armour before moving on to an arm.

"You seem quite able at this."

She didn't look at him, though he could see a glint of pride in her eyes. "I have watched you don your armour almost every day of my life." Attaching the last piece, she stepped back and stood straight, facing him.

He glanced at the armour, fastened well though he would need to adjust it. Daven should have been the one to assist him. Lyle nodded at her. "Thank you."

Marise stood taller, her chest puffing out. "Have a good day, Father."

He nodded. "Work hard at your training today." Buckling on his sword belt and slipping on his helmet, he turned and walked into the rosy dawn.

Though the streets of Misengrad remained quiet, Lyle heard the murmurings of industry starting behind closed doors. He strode purposefully down the road, his tall frame and broad shoulders larger than most people he passed. Clad in his armour with his sword at his hip, those that he saw bowed and ducked out of his way. The lines in his face and grey in his dark hair and beard remained hidden beneath his helmet. The visage he showed to the world commanded respect.

A few blocks away, he came across another man similarly armed. The second waited at a corner, smiling as Lyle approached.

"Captain Hitchcliffe."

Lyle nodded. "Gravier." Gravier fell into step as Lyle continued without pause. "How is your family?"

"Good. Lilana says the morning sickness has nearly passed. How are Evelyn and the children?"

"Fine."

Gravier raised an eyebrow at the curtness of his reply.

Catching the look, Lyle frowned. "Daven got into trouble at practice again. He will not stay focused on his training."

"Give him time." Gravier grinned. "I'm certain when you were a boy you did not always do as you were told."

Lyle gave him a hard look. "I knew the importance of my training and my duties, even when very young."

"Look, I know you…" Gravier paused and his eyes swept Lyle's body. "Is your armour on straight?"

Lyle glanced briefly at the armour. It didn't look off to him, but it was too loose around the waist and weighed too heavily on his shoulders. "Marise helped me put it on. I will fix it when we get to my office."

Gravier paused and his expression sobered. "I hear her swordsmanship is coming along quite well."

"Mm."

"Kearney tells me she is his most promising student, and the hardest-working."

"Mm."

"Apparently, she is as much as two years ahead of some of her fellow recruits."

Lyle raised an eyebrow at his second in surprise.

Gravier nodded.

Lyle stared ahead with a frown. It had never sat well with him that Marise trained to be a soldier, even though she had fought hard for the right. Why couldn't Daven show the same promise and initiative?

"You know, if you would like my help with Daven, I could—"

"I will deal with him later," Lyle cut in and fell silent.

Gravier didn't press the point.

Soon, they neared Lyle's office nestled along the outer wall surrounding Misengrad. The city guards standing at either side of the door straightened and saluted as he and Gravier approached.

"Good morning, Captain!"

Lyle merely nodded, lost in thought as he retrieved a key ring from his belt. Only when he slid the key in to the lock did he pause.

"Captain?" Gravier asked, seeing the cautious look on his face. "What is it?"

Lyle examined the door. "The lock is off." He turned on the guards standing beside the door. "Was anyone here last night?"

The guard he faced paled. "N-no, Captain. At least, the night shift didn't say so."

Lyle turned to the door, his eyes narrowing. Something had been tampered with. He did not like that at all. As he turned the key, he slid his sword out of his scabbard. Gravier followed suit, both of them crouching as Lyle opened the door.

Inside, everything looked in order. Lyle's eyes scanned the room, sword held out. None of the furniture seemed to be disturbed, the coats-of-arms on the wall hung as they always did, and the papers scattered over his desk had not been moved.

"Everything looks alright," Gravier remarked. "Of course, I doubt anyone would be very interested in your bookkeeping."

Lyle grunted. He lowered his sword tip but kept the blade out as he crossed the room to another door. He couldn't tell whether this one had been disturbed. Tensing, he unlocked and opened the door, climbing down the stairs within. Gravier followed with a candle from the office.

The storeroom looked in order. The rows of swords, pikes, bows and arrows, stands holding mail, barrels of sand and provisions, and shelves of records did not seem to have been disturbed. Lyle moved slowly into the room, glancing around and counting the arms and dry goods. Someone had been in here the last night leaving almost no trace of their passing yet had taken nothing of value.

As Lyle came to the back wall and looked to his left, he stiffened. The false stone in the wall in the corner had been left slightly askew. Not enough for those who didn't know it was there to see it, but to Lyle's eye the change was plain as day. His armour rattled as he strode quickly to the corner, followed by Gravier with the flickering candle. Using a narrow board as a pry bar, Lyle edged the false stone out enough so he could hoist it clear of the wall. Gravier held the candle over Lyle's shoulder to illuminate the opening in the wall. Lyle let out a hiss.

The cubbyhole was empty. The book was gone.

Damian visited Caleb Nazeerad a few times over the following days as they arranged the recovery of the cloth from the river. Thoughts of the barge and of word reaching Aether about what happened threatened to bring guilt and horror to the surface of her mind but the logistical discussions with the market director gave her enough distance from the event to keep those thoughts at bay.

While Caleb contacted the insurers and gathered the men and resources for the expedition, Damian's days passed in tedium. She largely stayed at the inn, working on her sewing and watching the street outside her room, occasionally visiting local tailors and weavers to barter for leftover scraps of material they had no use for. Dealing with the remaining pieces of Aether's cloth after the end of the market circuit had given Damian plenty of experience working with such small quantities and her initially reluctant suppliers became eager to sell her handiwork and split the costs with her. The extra coin helped to tide her over those days spent in Trent and it gave her something to do.

Alone and with Relhan over, interest in seeing more of Trent waned. She rarely left to explore the city, not often interacting with others and avoiding letting people see her eyes. Much as she didn't want to hide any longer, it was taxing to get those she spoke with to accept her in spite of her eyes.

Given time to reflect on those few interactions she had in her time in Trent, she realized that she overreacted to Sir Magni's opinions of Domino. Worse, she knew her anger at him almost made her lose control in the middle of the city. The memory still shamed her and she thanked all the Gods of Light that she had managed not to cause anything unexpected to happen.

She had since learned the truth about Domino, as much truth as stories conveyed.

After getting over the initial shock of seeing her eyes unveiled, Filias, the keeper of the Black Duck Inn, had been cordial enough. As one of few patrons and the only one not usually scrambling about her own business, she had taken to chatting with him. After a day at his inn she broached the subject.

"Do you know the Crow?"

Filias looked up from where he wiped out a leather mug with a cloth. His bushy, pale eyebrows lowered, the lines at the corners of his mouth deepening. "Y'mean the criminal who took down the Red Hawks?"

That name Damian knew. She had grown up hearing stories of the band of warriors belonging to no man, who wandered the countryside righting wrongs and battling evil wherever it reared its head. They had been told to uncover corrupt lords, rescue kidnapped princesses, and steal from greedy magistrates to give to suffering peasants. She realized then that she had heard little spoken of them in the past few years.

"The vigilante group?"

Filias snorted. "Mercenaries, more like. I guess all those old stories about 'em were… embellished somewhat. Heard say they slit throats and lined their own pockets much the same as any sellsword, only they kept all their bad deeds hush-hush, made themselves sound like heroes."

Damian frowned, disappointed that one of the noblest names in the stories of her childhood turned out to be just as cruel and selfish as the ones the Red Hawks were reported to have vanquished.

"O'course, no one knew that 'til the Crow killed most of 'em."

Her breath fell short. "What?"

Filias gave her a baffled look, his thick eyebrows quirking.

"Y'haven't heard this? Happened a few years ago."

She shifted. "I do not tend to get out much at home."

The innkeeper frowned and nodded slightly, his eyes fixed on hers. "I suppose you've reason not to. He murdered 'em in the night, then shortly after, the truth started comin' out."

Damian's chest tightened as she looked away. The first time she saw Domino on the barge, he had looked dangerous. That never changed.

But he guided me here, she thought. *And asked nothing in return.* As uneasy as she had felt with his silent company during the long trek through the forest, he had helped her, had never done anything untoward with her, nor had he complained at having to accompany her for so long. And the way he had looked into her eyes that first day after the barge sank sent a shiver up her spine.

Could he be a murderer? He had treated her with all the chivalry of a knight.

Frowning, she traced circles on the bar, not meeting Filias's eyes. "If the Red Hawks were doing bad things, though, he probably only wanted justice."

"Yeah," the innkeeper replied flatly. "'Cept he was one of 'em."

She froze. Slowly, she looked up at him.

Filias nodded solemnly. "They were his partners an' he killed 'em while they slept. People don't have much love for the Hawks anymore but you won't find any for a traitor." The innkeeper shook his head and rubbed harder at a stain inside the mug. "Can you believe I've heard he's here in Trent?"

Swallowing roughly, she faced away. Emotion dropped out of her voice. "Well, you need not worry about that. He is in prison."

He let out a breath. "Good. I'll sleep better tonight knowing that."

She nodded, though she didn't face him. "Thank you for the information."

"Anytime, Mis'Sires."

With that, she hopped off the stool and returned to her room, spending the rest of the day lost in her thoughts. The stories varied among those she asked over the following days but the core facts remained the same. Domino had murdered his own partners, a lot of them, and only a lack of conclusive evidence identifying him and his avoidance of towns had kept him free.

Damian couldn't help feeling defensive of him when she thought of the long journey they had taken through the forest. She wished she had been kinder to him. He had protected her, guided her, and shared his food with her, and though he rarely spoke or showed her any emotion she had felt unnecessarily suspicious of him. It seemed wrong now.

Even if he was a cold-blooded killer.

As the days dragged on and she longed for company, missing her father more and more and struggling to keep her emotions under control, she found her thoughts returning to Domino. She missed his reticence, that unassuming silence he held around her. And it was her fault he suffered in prison now.

A week after Damian entered Trent, the confusion and guilt reached a peak. She left the inn, seeking the first city guard she could find to direct her to the prison. She remained steady as he turned a baffled look to her only to start and back away when he saw her eyes. Keeping her gaze firm, she gleaned directions from him and made her way through the city.

As usual, stares accompanied her travel, though fewer people showed as much surprise since word had spread through Trent of the yellow-eyed girl residing near Plaza Medalia. Instead, many shied away from her or murmured to others as she passed. Not facing their reactions, Damian continued with her shoulders back and gait steady.

The evenly paved roads gave way to muddy, poorly tended tracks, the houses and buildings looking dismal and worn. This sector of the city, once another town entirely, had been absorbed by Trent long ago and remained the oldest part of the city. Built on marshy soil upstream of the joining of the currents along the East Ivory River, it gradually fell into disrepair and disuse. Some buildings Damian passed looked as though they had remained unchanged for generations, if not centuries.

Half the afternoon passed by the time she reached the prison. The stone building set in a patchy lawn looked imposing, though it was smaller than many of the other buildings around it. Steeling herself, she opened the door and stepped inside.

The door opened into a small anteroom lit by torches and small barred windows on the side walls. Through an open doorway in the stone wall a few paces away, a short hall stretched to the other end of the building, lined with rows of iron bars. In the entrance, two armoured guards sat at a table no larger than a bar stool, its top covered with a game board with an arrangement of tiles scattered across it. Another soldier with a thick, dark beard, a pot belly and a mail coat underneath his leather leaned back in a chair next to the doorway.

All three looked up with baffled expressions as she stepped in.

The two playing the game fell silent and the only noise murmured from the hallway. The man wearing the mail lowered the front legs of his chair to the floor with a bang and stood, tugging his belt up over his round belly. It slid down to where it rested before.

"You've got the wrong building, missy." He stepped forward to usher her out, but she moved forward a pace, standing straight. He started as he caught a glimpse of her eyes.

"I want to see the Crow."

He gave her a suspicious look. "Who are you? What do you want with him?"

Reaching into her pouch, she pulled out a coin and held it out. "I want to speak with him."

He frowned at her and her outstretched hand. Silence lay heavily over the room for a long moment. The guards at the table exchanged a glance, though the one wearing the mail kept his attention fixed on Damian. She didn't move.

With a shrug, he grabbed the coin and turned toward the hall. "Whatever you say, missy. I won't be responsible for whatever happens in here."

A frown crossed her face. *Your prisoners are all locked up behind bars,* she thought. She said nothing as she followed after him.

In the torch-lit hallway, Damian saw that the building held six cells, four of them occupied. The guard guided her to the back of the prison. From the corner of her eye she made out reactions from those imprisoned in the other cells, though she didn't face them. The guard stopped before the last cell on the left and folded his arms.

Damian turned to look into the cell. In the darkness, she could just make out a form sitting cross-legged on a straw pallet. He turned his head to look at her. Making no reaction, he stood and strode to the bars.

The mercenary had been stripped of most of his equipment. He stood beyond the barred gate wearing only shirt and trousers. His weapons, his cloak, his satchel, even the pendant she had never seen clearly was missing. She noted with dismay that the owl brooch she had given him was nowhere to be seen. With the collar of his shirt open to his chest, she saw how well built he was. She remembered how he pushed through the water rushing into the barge's hold, dragging her limp body behind him. Then he had carried her deep into the forest after reaching the river bank with her and her belongings soaking wet. It was a humbling and discomforting thought.

For a long moment she looked at him, her feelings battling with each other. It was difficult to imagine that stoic form murdering his associates, though she did not doubt he was physically capable of it. Her thoughts were drawn to the journey they undertook. She didn't know what to think.

"I'm sorry. It's my fault you are in here."

He shook his head. "The mistake is mine, not yours."

She stared at him curiously. "You could have just left before we reached the gates."

"I could have."

She waited a moment for him to continue, but he said nothing more. *Why didn't you?* she thought. For some reason she felt she didn't need to know the answer.

She shifted. "I know who you are now."

Whether his expression changed, she couldn't tell in the darkness. He remained silent.

She cleared her throat, the sound echoing through the passage. "Is it true? What you did to the Red Hawks?"

This time she knew the look on his face didn't change. He simply nodded.

Her chest tightened and she realized how foolish it was of her to ask that here in the prison under the eyes of the guard. She didn't want to believe she had travelled so far with such a criminal. She tried to turn her thoughts elsewhere but the stories she had heard over the past week ate at her.

"Why did you do it?"

Still he showed no reaction. "It does not matter."

Her eyes widened and she hesitated as she absorbed his words. Slowly, she shook her head. "Of course it does."

He remained unmoving within arm's reach on the other side of the bars from her. "No, it does not."

She could only stare back, stunned at his reaction.

The guard reacted before she did and let out a snort. "You see? Admits he's guilty and he'd no reason to do it."

"I did not pay to speak with you," Damian snapped, glancing at the guard from the corner of her eye.

The guard straightened, glaring at her. "Listen, you…"

She turned to face him fully. "Do not make me repeat myself. I expected that coin to buy me some privacy."

The guard clenched his teeth, looking like he wanted to say something else. Instead, he folded his arms, planted his feet on the floor, and fell silent.

She turned back to Domino. In the darkness, she could barely make out his eyes. "Well, what you did in the past does not change what you did for me." She shifted. "And you still don't deserve to be in here. I'm sorry."

Domino shook his head, saying nothing.

She frowned, trying to think of something to say. She realized that for all the time she spent trying to find the prison she didn't know what she wanted to say to him. It merely seemed important that she see him. All she had learned was that he was guilty of murder and offered no explanation or apologies for it.

She let out a sigh. "Is there anything I can do for you?"

He shook his head.

She shifted. "I'll pray for Justice for you."

"Truth. Pray for Truth."

She stared at him in surprise and she could see the guard's attention dart over to Domino. The God of Justice was one of the principal deities of Light, the five beings worshipped throughout Faneria, Edan, and Enseros. The deeper Truth belonged to the ancient, dead Gods of Time, the malicious beings who reigned over much of Elderra before the Gods of Light appeared. The true gods' victory over the old gods in an ancient war sealed their place among their followers and allowed Light to spread across all lands. No one still worshipped the old gods, or so Damian thought. Nor could she imagine why anyone would want to, given their uncontrolled ways. Justice favoured the pious.

Staring back at Domino, watching her impassively, she wanted to reassure him but couldn't bring herself to tell him she would pray to the old gods. Before she could think of anything else to say, the guard stepped closer.

"Alright, come on, time's up."

Damian's eyes remained on the mercenary as she moved through the prison before the guard could nudge her on. Her mouth opened as Domino disappeared from view but she remained at a loss for words and left without saying anything else.

"Some talk," the guard grumbled. "He can't be trusted, that one."

Without another word as they left the rows of cells behind them, Damian crossed the entrance and walked out. She squinted and shaded her eyes against the late afternoon sun. The scattered downtrodden souls trapped in this weary part of the city hurried through the street outside the prison, not seeming to notice the squat stone structure as they walked past. Once Damian's eyes adjusted, she walked through the streets once more.

She could feel the change in the air as people wound down their business for the day. Errands seemed more hurried as men and women tried to finish their tasks before sundown. Children darted between the adults' feet, often emerging from behind some other figure with a pouch in hand where none had been before. Clutching her own coin pouch, Damian strode swiftly through the streets, eager to leave this part of the city behind.

Her thoughts remained on Domino as she walked. She felt no less conflicted than she had before she saw him. The Red Hawks were vile, all the stories agreed upon that, yet Domino didn't claim that was the reason he murdered his former partners.

He admitted his guilt and he doesn't try to excuse it. That means he accepts that he did something wrong, right?

Or did that make him unrepentant?

But if he was truly uncaring, then why did he help me here with no hope of reward? He even let himself suffer imprisonment to accompany me all the way to the gates when he could have just left me before we reached the wall.

She tried to remember the look in Domino's eyes when the city guards led him away. It had been too dark to make out his expression clearly and she couldn't recall if he looked the same as he had through the whole journey.

All Damian had heard of him both from others and from his own mouth was that he couldn't be trusted. The journey they had undertaken together told her otherwise.

Does it even matter? He's in prison now. She wrapped her arms around herself, guilt making her chest constrict.

The stares and murmurs and a few starts and curses resumed as she crossed the decrepit city streets. Her shoulders sagged as she strode down the sidewalks, her expression falling with each suspicious look cast her way. She couldn't help but remember how Domino had looked into her eyes as though he saw nothing unusual there. Her throat tightened. Her own father, as she had been told, took nearly a year after her birth to truly warm to the sight of her eyes.

The only person who has ever accepted me without hesitation is a backstabber.

Tears welled in Damian's eyes as the reactions continued. After another couple blocks of the same, when she saw a Temple of Light rising to her left, she hurriedly crossed the lawn and escaped inside.

Through the cracked and faded portico and into the main chamber, Damian leaned her head back and let out a shaky breath. When she opened her eyes and looked around the empty building, a bemused expression crossed her face. The statues rising in a semicircle along the back wall looked all wrong, one was missing from its pedestal, and she didn't recognize any of the scenes carved in crumbling relief along the walls. She couldn't even identify a number of the strange creatures depicted in those scenes, huge and bizarre beasts like no animal she had ever seen. And where were the Seers and acolytes? Why was the mortar crumbled and stone so weathered, as though no one had maintained this temple in centuries?

The answer struck her far too late and she gasped. This was not a Temple of Light. She had wandered into an ancient temple to the Gods of Time.

Her first reaction was to turn and flee, but the gods depicted here were long gone. No one stood in here to judge her. As sacrilegious as she knew it was to be in this temple to the old gods, she supposed she could spend a few minutes enjoying the silence and settling down before returning to the Black Duck.

Slowly, Damian strode toward the statues, her footfalls ringing through the deserted temple. Cracks marred the stone floor, some tiles pitching wildly from their breaks, and she stepped carefully around the upturned floor. The scenes carved along the wall had lost much of their definition, leaving simple shapes. The figures portrayed by the statues appeared along the wall, visages Damian had seen in tapestries and carvings celebrating the true gods' victory over these older deities. Without the Gods of Light reigning over the old gods' defeat, the ancient temple looked foreign. Instead these figures dominated, basking in the attention lavished upon them by other figures as great as kings.

Damian's head leaned back as she drew near to the statues, three times the size of a man. Five gods, just like the Gods of Light, but these were very different. Instead of three gods and two goddesses, there were two gods and one goddess with the statue in the middle nothing more than an abstract swirl of stone. Damian couldn't tell what the missing fifth statue once portrayed. As she examined the statues, there seemed to be parts missing. Weathered, but elegantly carved robes, hair, and skin sported bizarre indentations.

Then she noticed a pattern in the indentations. A wrist here, the waist of a robe there, a crease around one's brow. She recalled the teachings that the old gods coveted grand offerings while they reigned. Once, fine baubles must have adorned these statues, polished brass or perhaps silver and gold beset with jewels which had clearly been looted after these gods' downfall. Damian's eyes were drawn to the pile of rubble. She wondered what riches ornamented that statue that the entire thing had been taken, leaving fragments of stone she could carry in her hands.

Coming upon the first statue to the right, she looked at the plaque carved into the pedestal. The letters were strangely shaped and the words had archaic spellings, but she managed to interpret the inscription.

Nemir, the God of Fortune.

Damian frowned as her eyes travelled up the old god's visage. That was what bothered her and so many others about the Gods of Time. Their governing virtues could be used for evil as much as for good. Beings of such power without the constraints of honour unnerved her, as did their names. Though the name was unlike anything she would hear in common usage, it made them seem too human. Too fallible. The statue itself seemed to enforce that in the cunning, inscrutable eyes carved into his weathered face.

Damian's eyes dropped as she moved to the missing statue. For a long moment she examined the inscription, but the spelling was so unusual that she could not make out the goddess's commanding aspect. All Damian could read was that her name was Destine. Damian stared at the pile of rubble, able to make out pieces of fingers and perhaps what had once been a nose. Eventually, Damian moved to the statue in the middle.

The abstract swirl of stone had no name, nor even any gender. It was simply Mystery. The idea of worshipping such an unknown being made her uneasy.

The next plaque gave Damian pause. Athios, the God of Truth.

He stood imperiously over her, one arm outstretched with a circular hole through his hand, clutching some kind of rod that was no longer there. Even staring into the distance, high above her, there was something piercing about his gaze, deep and inescapable, as though he could see through anything. She shivered at the sight, feeling as though she was being watched.

This was the god that Domino wanted her to pray to for… what? If he had not lied about the Red Hawks, then Truth would only condemn him. Her expression fell.

What is the truth?

Damian turned to walk out, wanting nothing more to do with the old gods, but paused. Her eyes moved back to the statue. Then, with a frown, she lifted her skirt and kneeled before the statue as she would before a depiction of one of the true gods.

"Athios," she began, a tingle running up her spine with the

thought of addressing a god like a common man. She stumbled over her words. "I know that I am not a follower of the Gods of Time." Her frown deepened. "Nor do I think you are even still around to hear this." Pausing, she considered how to refer to the mercenary. "But my companion Domino asked me to pray to you for him, and out of respect to his beliefs I ask for your help. I… I don't know what you can do to help, but he was imprisoned and…" Her throat grew thick and she swallowed uncomfortably. "And I don't know what to think. He tells me he murdered his own companions, but he saved my life, and he helped me without asking anything in return. He has done nothing to the people of Trent and he was kind to me in a way that no one else has been." The feeling of being watched heightened and her cheeks grew warm. "If there is anything you can do for him… for me, I would greatly appreciate it."

She hastened to her feet and spun to flee from the decrepit temple. Before she faced the entrance, the last statue drew her eyes. This goddess almost looked kind, motherly, though the expression in her stone face was unreadable as she stared forward. Damian lowered her eyes to the inscription.

Veran, the Goddess of Change.

Curiously, Damian drew closer. A second, smaller plaque rested above the one bearing Veran's name. Above it sat a small, flat-topped mound on the pedestal that looked added some time after the statue was erected. A small stone chip lay on the flat top. Damian peered closer, reading the second plaque.

The Eirheart, blessed by Veran.

Damian's eyes widened. Had an item actually blessed by the goddess once resided here? The stone fragment, hardly larger than Damian's thumbnail, was rounded on one side but with an uneven flat surface on the other. The piece must have chipped off the original artifact. What had happened to the rest of the Eirheart, she could only wonder.

Something tickled at the edge of Damian's awareness as her fingers ran over the cool stone mound. It grew stronger, but still unidentifiable, as her hand drew nearer to the stone chip. She started, only just realizing she had been reaching for it. Shaking her head, she pulled her hand back and the sensation faded.

Damian looked up at the statue. It gave her no indication of what the chipped piece of the amulet was or what the goddess's blessing had imparted on it.

Slowly, Damian's eyes fell to the stone fragment. Something drew her to it. She reached forward, the sensation returning the closer her fingers came to the stone chip. A voice whispered in her mind a heartbeat before she touched it, too brief for her to react.

The stone felt warm. No, hot. Its heat seared Damian's fingertips before she yanked her hand back. The heat consumed her, rushing through her body. A blinding light filled her vision. She cried out and staggered back as the temple rumbled around her, dust and fragments of the stone walls and ceiling raining through the air.

When she could see again, she gasped. Flares of brilliant light flashed out from her body, swirling through the air and leaving black scores on the floor. Stumbling against the trembling earth, she grabbed the altar to Nemir to steady herself, but the stone crumbled to ash beneath her hand and she nearly fell with a yelp. The streams of light slashed into the statue of the God of Fortune, rending deep, scorching gashes in the stone and soon breaking it in half. Her breath raced as she looked around at the quaking temple.

"What… what's happening?" Damian felt immense power radiating through her and consuming her like the strange energy that bubbled through her when her emotions grew too strong. The horror at losing control rose like a forgotten dream after she had kept her power contained since the barge sank.

A tongue of light dug into the wall and the carvings there, a shower of stone fragments spilling through the air. The statue of Veran tipped over. Damian barely flung herself clear as it crashed into the floor, the neck cracking and a chunk of the shoulder breaking off and tumbling away.

Closing her eyes, Damian tried to draw the power back, to settle her emotions as she had the day she awoke in the forest with Domino.

Nothing happened.

Fear overwhelmed her and she darted her eyes around, seeing the blocks of stone shift in place. A column supporting the ceiling broke in two and crashed to the floor, cracks spreading over the ceiling above it.

"No, no!" she cried out, grasping the sides of her head.

"Damian!"

Spinning around, she found Sir Magni standing in the doorway of the temple.

Her mouth went dry at the sight. The knight showed neither horror nor surprise. He only looked around at the damage before his eyes returned to her.

"I can't stop it." She stumbled back, grabbing the altar to Mystery to steady herself. The stone broke under her touch and she fell to the floor. Hurriedly, she rose to her feet, sending the knight a desperate look. "I can't stop it! I don't know what to do!"

Sir Magni jogged toward her, shading his eyes. "Damian, you have to control this. Focus!"

The composed look in his face soothed her fear and she shut her eyes. Clenching her teeth, she tried with all her concentration to draw the power back into her as she had always done before.

It had no effect. The rumbling continued stronger, the walls bowing and ceiling sagging.

"I can't." Her muscles tensed, trying desperately to still the waves of energy rippling through her, but it was like trying to stop the tide coming in to the shore. She gazed desperately at Sir Magni. "It's not working!"

He took a step back, twisting aside as a tendril of light streaked toward him. Then, his eyes narrowed faintly, resigned yet focused.

"Then I'm sorry about this."

He moved so quickly it seemed he crossed the distance to her in one bound. She never felt the blow land.

CHAPTER 7
TAKING CONTROL

COMMOTION IN THE courtyard drifted through the air.

Yanuk looked up from the table where he sat, its surface littered with small stones. "Have they returned?" he asked to the empty room. His heart pounded in excitement. Pushing up from his chair, he rushed out of the room, though a stitch gnawed at his side and his knees ached from the effort.

Throwing open the door, he stared into the courtyard. The entire community of mages gathered at the entrance to the fort, all their daily chores abandoned. Tools lay forgotten in the garden, doors stood ajar, and a few sheep milled outside their indoor pen.

As the mages shifted, Yanuk caught a glimpse of White, the tall youth who had left them two days earlier. A thrill rushed through Yanuk's heart. He hurried over, the last to arrive among them, and several people on the edge of the crowd turned to watch him approach.

"Let me through, let me see it." Yanuk laid his hands on the shoulders of two others, who stepped to either side with his light nudge, and made his way to the front of the crowd. His breath caught in his throat. Broad-shouldered White and matronly Helena, who had gone to Misengrad, stood in the middle of the semi-circle of people. White held an empty canvas sack.

Another of the mages held the book. Yanuk's eyes widened as he glimpsed it. With a nod, the other handed it over. Yanuk gingerly took the heavy tome and stared at it in wonder. The leather cover was dry and cracked, the imprinting almost entirely rubbed away, and only traces remained of the gilt that once decorated its now greying surface.

A book of spells unlike any Yanuk had ever seen, written in the original language of magic. The thought of the extraordinary potential within his hands sent a chill through him, as though the power of the book crackled with an electric charge. Stolen from the city guard of Misengrad itself. The thought exhilarated him. Anything was within their grasp.

The conversations of the others fell silent as Yanuk opened the creaking cover to look at the pages within. The parchment was yellow and the edges of the pages dark and fraying, but the ink was dark and crisp. He only recognized a handful of the characters filling the pages. His eyes were drawn to the illuminations that had lost nearly all of their colour.

Even Edrand's voice was subdued. "I have never seen a book so old."

"It is as Gawthrain said it would be," added Patrus, the amputee.

Old Miria scoffed. "If it says what he thinks it says."

Yanuk gently turned the pages at her words. Near the end, he found a page torn all the way to the spine, the top half of the sheet missing. It was ripped along an even gap in the text and appeared to be the same size as the page in Gawthrain's locket. Raising his eyes, Yanuk carefully shut the book. "Then it is time we found out." He turned to willowy Laryn, one of their apprentices who had taken on the job of cataloguing their small library. "Do we have any books on translating old Styrian?"

She shifted. "Perhaps, master. I am not entirely certain."

He nodded. "I shall have a look. I must begin translating this book at once." The mages straightened with the focus in Yanuk's voice. He turned to Helena and White. "You had no trouble obtaining this?"

Helena smiled proudly. "None at all. Finding the book and taking it were easy. We paid a young maid to help distract the night guards to be certain, but the unseeing spell kept us hidden."

Yanuk smiled. Years ago, he and Patrus devised the spell that the entire community used and no one outside of it knew about, a spell that allowed them to move anywhere they liked without being seen by others. It was how they acquired most of their supplies and it had availed them once more with their most daring theft yet.

"Excellent work, my friends. You have done splendidly." Dropping his eyes, Yanuk gently stroked his thumb over the ancient leather cover. "I hope you will forgive me if I neglect my regular duties for the near future while I attempt to discern the value in this book."

"What of Gawthrain?" asked another of their young mages.

Yanuk hesitated. The former duke left shortly after returning to the fort with Yanuk and helping to convince the rest of the community to seek out the book, claiming he had things to address and sundries to acquire. His departure had been a blessing, for many of the mages distrusted him and most had balked at his plans to storm Albrith. Only with careful persuasion had Yanuk convinced them to look into the book and Gawthrain to be satisfied with that. Tensions in their home eased once the former duke left though a few of those gathered looked uncomfortable with the mention of the old lord.

"Gawthrain has thus far upheld his end of the bargain, and I think we can all agree that this book may indeed hold incredible power."

A few of the mages grumbled assent. Others looked excited by the prospect of the book.

"He has earned a measure of confidence. Not enough, of course, to allow him to remain free with the knowledge of our home."

The others nodded in agreement.

Yanuk laid a hand on the shoulder of the apprentice nearest to him with a smile. "Thank you again for all your hard work, my friends. Whether or not Gawthrain is right or his intentions just, our lives will be enriched by this book." He turned to their librarian. "Laryn, please show me the books you think will allow us to translate this." Nodding, she turned and led him toward the library in one corner of the fort and the others dispersed to resume their daily chores.

The following days passed in a blur. Yanuk spent the hours sequestered in a room he claimed as a study, learning how to translate the language he had seen in other books. However, no other books he encountered were written entirely in old Styrian. Often the work so engrossed him that he forgot to stop and eat and the other mages brought in meals for him. Usually the food was cold by the time Yanuk got around to it. He never minded, begrudging more the time spent away from his books than the flavour of old food and drink. He stayed up well after dark on those longest days of the year, ancient characters swirling through his mind before he fell fast asleep and hurried up the next morning to resume his work. His progress was slow as he struggled to learn the foreign language with no assistance other than equally old books. The task so engrossed him that he didn't care. It consumed him, body and mind, and rejuvenated him in a way he had not felt in years. The rest of his companions took on his usual chores and organized the rest of the mages in their work. All his attention focused on the ancient book.

Half a week passed before something interrupted him.

"*Seras. Na. Al'gen. Muharthas…* no, *muharthen.*"

Books and papers covered Yanuk's desk. Directly before him, the most prized. The ancient spell book lay open, surrounded by the other books and handwritten pages. Yanuk worked ceaselessly, his mind blank and ignoring the growing noise from the central courtyard. He revelled in the tedious task, a feat of scholarly study like he had not experienced since he was cast out.

As the chatter in the courtyard heightened and cut into his concentration, he snapped his head up, eyes narrowing. Gruff, yet amused voices rang through the courtyard, apparently just inside the entrance of their fort.

"What in blazes is going on out there?" Yanuk emptied his quill into the horn of ink, replaced it in its stand on his desk, and strode to the door.

He opened the door and froze, unable to move for a moment. Twenty rough-looking men, well armed and dusty from the road, milled in the courtyard. Some of them glanced around the fort in interest, some looked impatient or bored, and all seemed to have a greedy, deceptive, or callous gleam in their eyes. The mages in the courtyard murmured to each other and stared or glowered at the intruders, their chores abandoned.

One of the men near the front of the group shifted and Yanuk spotted Gawthrain's finely-dressed form between them, leaning on his cane while he spoke with one at the front of the group. Yanuk hurried to the former duke, his expression darkening as he gave the men a wide berth.

"Ah, Yanuk. There you are." Gawthrain glanced sidelong at the group with poorly concealed distaste. "I would like you to meet Vitro Norgssen." Gawthrain gestured to the tall, rugged man standing beside him, who held out a hand to Yanuk with a smirk. Vitro's short blonde hair was ruffled from the wind and his long, sun-darkened face was marred by scars over his eyebrow, chin, and cheekbone.

Yanuk cast an uncertain look at the outstretched hand before returning his attention to Gawthrain. "Who are these people?"

"Vitro here is the leader of this band of mercenaries. I have hired them to accompany us to Albrith."

Leaning back, Yanuk's eyes widened. "We have not even agreed to undertake this absurd idea of yours, let alone to prepare to leave already."

The former duke gave him a flat stare. "You have the book, do you not?"

"Under no obligation to use it."

"And what will you do with it instead?" Gawthrain waved a hand, gesturing at their home. "Keep it here in your dilapidated fort while you continue stealing the supplies you need to survive from peons? We can be ready to march—"

"You are not lord over us!" Yanuk snapped over him. "And we do not follow your orders. You have no authority to make such decisions over us."

The mercenaries exchanged interested looks, a few elbowing others and whispering remarks as they watched the exchange. The mages listening at a few paces' greater distance straightened with his words, shouting support for Yanuk.

Gawthrain glanced at the mages and mercenaries. "May we speak in private?"

Yanuk set his shoulders back. "No. Anything you have to say can be said to us all. We are all equals here."

The old duke spread his free hand with the same sneering smile he shared at their first meeting. "This is precisely what I mean, Yanuk."

Yanuk's eyes narrowed.

"There is no such thing as equality. People are leaders or they are followers. If none of you lead, then you are all followers."

Yanuk's blood boiled. "If you dare to refer to us like the servants and peasants you no longer have—"

Gawthrain stamped his cane against the ground. "I did not make a partnership with eighteen of you. If you wish for me to respect your authority, then you need to show that you have some." Gawthrain turned to face the mages present, almost all of them gathered in the courtyard. "And would you not follow him? He, who has provided you safety and companionship since your exile? He, who can guide you and ensure your protection, as all good lords do?"

"As though you know anything of that," piped in one of the old mages, eliciting snickers throughout the entire crowd and a few guffaws from the mercenaries.

Yanuk blinked, barely hearing the barb or seeing Gawthrain's eyes narrow as he considered the former duke's words. Several mages glared at Gawthrain or turned uncomfortably away as the old lord's eyes passed across them. Others turned questioning looks to Yanuk. Faithful looks. Trusting.

Slowly, Yanuk shook his head. "I will not be a lord over my

brothers and sisters."

Gawthrain scoffed. "No one will ever mistake you for a lord, Yanuk Alganov."

Some of the mercenaries laughed.

The former duke waved a hand dismissively. "Think of yourself as a village elder if it soothes your conscience. But I can only treat with one who represents your entire horde."

That thought amused Yanuk. A few of the exiles were older than him, some by a wide margin. Yet Yanuk had been the one to draw them together and they often looked to him for guidance. He had never imagined, nor desired, commanding them.

Did they desire a leader? Most of his fellow exiled mages had told him that they preferred their society the way it was. However, occasionally they bickered over some detail of their lives such as stealing things they did not need to trade for things they did. Those arguments would often be difficult to resolve to everyone's satisfaction. The way the apprentices looked to him made it clear they longed for guidance.

None of the mages who returned his look spoke up. No one else challenged Gawthrain's suggestion that Yanuk should lead.

Yanuk held up his chin. "Very well. I shall lead my comrades." He fixed his gaze on the former duke. "But that means you will share all your information with me."

The self-satisfied grin crossed Gawthrain's face. "Then you have agreed to my plans?" Yanuk's expression darkened and Gawthrain held out his free hand, though he failed to look innocent. "I shall reveal all when you agree to cast that spell and march on Albrith."

Yanuk sneered back. He pointed at Vitro. "We still do not need mercenaries and I do not want them in our home."

Gawthrain sniffed. "They have their own horses and supplies. They can camp outside."

Yanuk caught a glimpse of Vitro shooting Gawthrain a dirty look before the mercenary leader rallied his men and filed outside. Yanuk pursed his lips as he watched them leave. Their presence outside the walls would jeopardize the abandoned look of the fort that helped keep them hidden from the rest of society.

A thrum of energy resonated through Yanuk's heart. He straightened in response, then turned to Gawthrain. "You are lucky we do not lynch you right now. You overstepped your boundaries and endangered us all by hiring mercenaries for a venture we have not even agreed upon."

The old duke growled. "Well, you are the leader now. What are you waiting for?"

Yanuk's eyes narrowed. "All the information we require to make an informed decision. When I have completed my study of the book, then I will notify you as to our plans. In the meanwhile, you are to remain in your chambers unless summoned otherwise and will make no more arrangements before consulting me. White, see him to his room." Turning, Yanuk marched swiftly across the courtyard, the mages dispersing and returning to their tasks as large White approached Gawthrain.

Back inside his study, Yanuk shut the door and let out a quick breath. The looks on his comrades' faces as they accepted him as their leader remained etched into his mind. Some of the mages, particularly the older ones who had lived through exile and suffered the whims of lords or officials in their past lives, seemed suspicious or reluctant. Many others looked content, if not glad of his decision. They wanted him to lead.

But to what purpose? They needed no leader if they refused Gawthrain's offer and stayed here. They would have said as much if they wanted nothing to do with Gawthrain's plans.

Yanuk strode slowly to his desk. Leaning against it, he looked down at the books and pages scattered across its surface. Even if they did not march on Albrith, it seemed a travesty that such an ancient and powerful relic remained hidden here where it could do no good to anyone. He recalled what one of the mages said when the old duke tried to convince them to join in his plans.

"Is this the legacy we are to leave behind?" Yanuk muttered aloud, repeating his comrade's words. "We have the power to shape the world and all we have to show for it are a few outcast apprentices who are trapped in a dilapidated home and will never have the opportunity to use magic as it was intended."

Yanuk's back ached from leaning over the table. He straightened with a frown. One of their number who had survived exile and lived among them all these years had died of a fever over the winter. While Miria, nearly old enough to be Yanuk's grandmother, was proof enough that he may have many years yet, Yanuk knew that was unlikely. One day not very far from now they would all be gone, leaving only the young ones they had taught.

Another ripple of energy spread from his chest. Reaching beneath his tunic, Yanuk retrieved the crystal he used to speak with young Rhyslen. Yanuk uttered the incantation to unlock the spell.

"Rhyslen. It has been awhile since we last spoke. How fares your journey?"

The young mage's voice ebbed out of the crystal until it sounded as though Rhyslen spoke on the other side of glass, rather than the other side of Faneria. "I apologize for not contacting you sooner, master. I have only just returned to Trent. I am afraid I have lost her trail."

In all the excitement of the book, Yanuk had forgotten about Rhyslen's mission. The girl he sought, whom the apprentice encountered last year on an expedition to acquire supplies, was the only person any of the mages had ever met who could see through their spell to move unseen. It hardly seemed important any longer.

"That is fine," Yanuk answered distractedly. He hesitated, still lost in thought over the conversation in the courtyard.

"Yanuk?" Rhyslen asked after a pause.

"Rhyslen… what would you say if we had an opportunity to regain power and respect?"

Silence followed. When the youth replied, he spoke slowly and carefully. "I am certain you would act in the best interests of us all."

Yanuk straightened. What was in their community's best interests? Disposing of Gawthrain and returning to their struggling existence, thereby sending the mercenaries away unpaid with the location of their home? Cruelly and unnecessarily slaying them all along with the old duke, which would certainly be noticed? Or pursuing a reckless plan that could get them all killed but might win them back their standing in society after nearly twenty years in exile?

Yanuk's eyes fell upon the book. The answers lay there.

He held the crystal up to his mouth. "Thank you, Rhyslen. I think we might have need of your skills here."

Garrick leaned against the window frame, staring at the street outside. While not the throngs of Relhan, the roads swarmed with crowds. The first market days of the new year had arrived and more farmers and craftsmen arrived each week with new crops and goods.

Out of the corner of his eye, Garrick saw Damian sitting on his bed, hands folded on her lap and staring at the floor in front of her.

This really complicates things.

His quarry was the first solid lead that the captain had in two years of trying to track down Yanuk. Garrick had been entrusted with this mission, the first he had ever been assigned alone. Undoubtedly the other knights of his order were still trying to find Yanuk back in Misengrad, but if Garrick could find this mage it could be the break the Agaesi had been looking for.

Damian was another issue entirely.

In an instant she had gone from something he could not ignore to something that demanded his complete and immediate attention. He had kept his distance from her after that first morning in Trent though he had watched her since. It was hard not to. If he stood within two blocks of her, he didn't need to expand his senses to discern precisely where she was. If he did he could find her from nearly half the city away. He knew nothing about what her power was or how she acquired it, though he grew increasingly convinced that she was human and not something else. What she could do and more importantly what had happened to her the last night was beyond any knowledge he had. She didn't seem malicious but she was clearly unstable. With the power she commanded, that posed an enormous threat. He was the only one available to deal with it.

"Was anyone hurt?" Her voice sounded thick, though it lacked emotion.

His eyes shut. Left without any other options inside the temple, he had dealt her a swift blow to knock her out. The power radiating out from her with destructive force in the temple had stopped, though the damage had been done. Plunging into the mass of energy she exuded, then gathering her in his arms and rushing out of the collapsing temple had been the most excitement and danger he had seen in his life. Fortunately it had happened in a building that almost never saw visitors in a neglected sector of the city. Undoubtedly a few people had seen the glow of magic surging out of the temple. He imagined he would be hearing rumours the moment he stepped outside the inn.

"No one was anywhere around."

Her next words were more hesitant. "What's going to happen to me?"

Garrick sighed as he pushed away from the window and turned. Her eyes looked clear and aside from the headache she mentioned when she awakened she seemed little the worse for wear for his attack. He had told her he aimed for a specific pressure point to minimize injury. He hadn't told her that was the first time he had performed that manoeuvre on an unwilling and unprepared target. He was relieved it had worked as he intended.

The parts of his body that normally revelled in the idea of such a lovely, intelligent, independent, and unusual young woman sitting on his bed remained dormant. There was also the fact that she could expose him, cause connections to be made that might trickle back to his prey. With one word she had been able to determine that he came from Hesperia, the same region as the man Garrick had so carefully coaxed information about. If the mage found out about Garrick's pursuit, his mission was over. How could he have been so careful to disguise his speech to sound more local and have missed something as simple as the word 'lunch'?

Shaking off the thought, Garrick strode to the chair beside the bed where he had spent the night watching her as she slept, senses tuned to her aura. Thankfully, the ether he administered after bringing her to his room kept her asleep and her energy calm.

"First, why don't you tell me about yourself. The truth this time."

Her eyes narrowed. "Everything I've told you has been truth."

He watched her carefully as she spoke, but he could see no discrepancy in the indignant look she shot him. If she was lying, she was as skilled as any schemer at court and he found that unlikely. She even failed to use his title in her unease. Her expression darkened as he continued watching her.

He nodded. "Alright. Then how about you tell me where your power comes from."

A distrustful look remained on her face though her anger softened. "I don't know. I've had it as long as I can remember."

"And how long has it been doing this?"

She glanced away. "It's been almost a year since I first lost control. Since then it's been happening more frequently. Last night was the first time since the barge sank, though. It... tends to happen when I am upset."

He waited for her to continue, but she said nothing more.

"You don't know anything else about it?"

Through the hardness in her eyes, he could see a touch of desperation, of misery. "Who would I speak to of it?" A twitch in her expression followed, though it wasn't a lie. He supposed it came from some memory involving her ability, perhaps of someone she did once speak of it.

"So you don't even know what your magic is."

She started, shooting him a wide-eyed stare. "Magic?"

A wry smile crossed his face. "I take it that would be a 'yes.' "

She shook her head. "That is impossible. Magic is gone."

He couldn't help grinning. "Magic is a part of the world. It can't disappear. As long as there is earth and sky and plants and animals, magic is around. There's just no one around who knows how to use it anymore. Or at least anyone who could was exiled after the Century Storm." He eyed her. "I guess that would have been right around the time you were born."

She rubbed her arm. "I was born during the Century Storm." Garrick's eyebrows rose in interest and Damian shifted. "Lightning struck my house right as my mother was giving birth to me. She died from it. I do not know how I survived."

He considered that. He had never truly believed that the deadly storm that appeared suddenly and covered almost the entire continent eighteen years ago was caused by magic as the rest of the kingdom believed. Yet Damian had been born during a lightning strike from the Century Storm and emerged with yellow eyes and unfathomable magic power? There must be a connection there.

A cautious look marked her face. "You think that is related to my... ability."

"I think it's a distinct possibility, yes. You have to understand, Damian, humans don't have power like you do."

"What do you mean?"

He hesitated. If she truly didn't know anything about magic, could he risk telling her? As he gazed at the genuinely confused look on her face, his expression softened.

"Okay, look. When a mage casts a spell, what he's really doing is channelling energy from some other source. Whether it's through items that have magical power, a spirit bond with some creature that does, or a combination, he pulls in power from somewhere else. In past times, there were supposedly certain types of people that could call forth magic from a well inside themselves, like you can. But humans don't have a source of power within them from which they can cast magic."

She swallowed uncomfortably. "If that's true... then what am I?"

He shook his head. "I wish I knew. This is beyond anything I've ever heard about."

She frowned. "How do you know all this?"

He hesitated again. *Well, why not? She already knows some things that I've been trying to hide.* "Have you ever heard of the Agaesi? The dragon knights of Hesperia?"

She stiffened but showed no surprise. So she had guessed. She gave him a guarded look. "Wild stories. Rumours, mostly."

He grinned. "They're probably more true than you would expect, if a bit embellished. Let's just say we're a very specialized unit. We're trained to deal with matters of magic. That means knowing about it."

She straightened, clearly uncertain what to make of him.

He sighed. "This is beyond my expertise, though." He looked at her, weighing the danger she posed against his mission.

Three years after he was knighted he was finally assigned a mission. He knew that if he failed in this endeavour it might be far longer before he was entrusted with another, if ever. The thought left a sour taste in the back of his throat and the personal vow he made not to return until he succeeded rang in his head. Though the trail of his mage had grown cold it was still his duty and his honour to track down Yanuk's underling.

Garrick knew he couldn't leave Damian unguarded as the only Agaesi he was aware of in this part of Faneria. He could send word to the rest of his order and ask for instructions or for reinforcements to be sent to assist with her, but by the time a messenger could cross nearly the entire kingdom and return to Trent it might be too late. What would happen when Damian lost control of her power entirely, he didn't know, nor did he want to find out.

May the captain forgive me for this.

"I need to take you to Misengrad."

Inhaling sharply, she edged away from him on the bed. "What?"

He saw the reluctance and discomfort in her posture and expression and softened his voice. "The Agaesi are the only ones with the knowledge to do anything for you. They're the only people who can help you."

She shook her head, avoiding his eyes. "I can't go to Misengrad."

"Damian…"

"No. I have to return to Aether, and the expedition to recover the cloth from the river—"

"Damian."

His voice was calm, but she halted and slowly faced him.

She swallowed. "What would you do if I said no?"

He could tell she wasn't serious and was merely testing him. He gazed evenly at her, showing no reaction.

"I wouldn't want to find out."

She tensed though she tried to hide it. Reaching out, he laid a hand on her shoulder, drawing it back when she flinched from the touch. "Damian. What would you do about this? You want to be able to control this, right?"

"Of course I do." Her eyes hardened with her voice.

"But you've been trying to for a year and it hasn't worked."

She didn't respond.

He leaned forward in the chair. "I want to help you, Damian. What if last night happened again and I wasn't around? What would the people of Trent do if they caught you like that?"

Tears welled in her eyes. "I don't lose control that way."

"Except you just did."

She looked away and fell silent.

Letting out a sigh, he rose from the chair. "I'm not going to kidnap you or arrest you. I will not take you to Misengrad as my prisoner." He turned toward the door. "But you know that most people look at magic the same way you do. And I don't want to know what would happen to you if you didn't come with me by choice."

He began to walk out but she leaped to her feet behind him, anger lacing her words. "Do you think I don't see what you're doing?"

He turned to face her, surprised at the venom in her voice and face. "Damian…"

"You're manipulating me! You act like you are giving me a choice but you really aren't. How do I know you are not lying to me? I have been more honest than you have."

He stepped closer, reaching out as her aura surged. "I didn't mean to—" She swung at his extended arm and he barely pulled back before she struck him.

"People like you disgust me. You think you can get anything you want, that you deserve anything you want, and you think that everyone else is beneath you and you don't care who you step on to get your way."

He couldn't help flinching. "I…"

"I cannot believe anything you have told me." Whirling around, she strode around him toward the door. "And I will not let you use me."

Garrick didn't move as she passed. Her words hurt more than he cared to admit. It seemed all his methods of trying to endear himself to her failed and he didn't know what else he could say to make her change her mind. He had never read someone so badly before and feared that if he made one more mistake he would push her away permanently.

Fleetingly, he considered letting her go. It would be so much easier to let others deal with Damian Sires and return to his true mission, the assignment that was so important to him. Besides, her power and lack of control was beyond anything he had been trained to handle. Garrick and perhaps Damian would be better off if he focused on the mission that brought him here in the first place.

Yet what would happen if he returned to Misengrad and it became known that he walked away from such a danger? From something that fell precisely within the realm of their abilities? How could that reflect well on him?

What would happen to the people of Trent if she lost control like that again without an Agaesi to handle it?

His gaze hardening, he turned and grabbed her arm with a firm grip before she reached the door.

"Fine, you want to know the truth? You are a threat because of your magic and it is my responsibility to make certain you don't become more than a threat. So if you don't come with me willingly then I have to arrest you or kill you right now."

Her eyes enlarged, her body tensing and leaning away from his grip. She didn't truly fight him. To his relief, her aura settled a little.

His expression softened. "And I don't want to do that." He released her slowly so she maintained her balance and held his hand out to her. "I'd rather take you to Misengrad as a friend."

She stared at him for a moment before looking away. She didn't reach for his hand.

"I cannot trust you enough for that." She sighed. "But I suppose I have no choice."

It was clear that she thought otherwise but he said nothing. He could find her if she tried to escape. He lowered his arm with a nod. Then he turned, walking to the window and looking tiredly outside. "We'll leave first thing in the morning."

Not another word passed between them as she walked out of his room, closing the door behind her. He let out a breath.

What have I gotten myself into?

CHAPTER 8
FACING THE UNKNOWN

DAMIAN AWOKE TO the murmur of crowds outside. The yellow window in her room at the Black Duck Inn glowed, newly risen sunlight gleaming through the room. She stared at the small space in silence for a few minutes.

An empty feeling clung to the pit of her stomach as she tried to will herself to rise. So much had gone wrong in such a short time that it overwhelmed her. She wasn't certain what upset her the most so she lay there in silence, feeling numb.

The first thought that crossed her mind was the memory of losing control of her power in the Temple of Time. A chill crept up her spine as she reflected on it. She had never lost control with such intensity before. Were the true gods punishing her for visiting the temple, even praying to their sworn enemies? She shivered.

What have I done to deserve this?

Damian recalled the first time she knew her power manifested, when she was a third her age. She insisted on helping her father light the hearth fire and when her failure to strike a spark led to frustration, a stream of flames flew forth from her hands and ignited the wood. Stunned at the reaction, she had turned to her father. The look of horror on his face remained etched into her mind.

Tears slipped out of her eyes and she trembled, tugging the covers up tighter. She had lost her father, the ship, and Domino. Now she was losing Trent and her freedom. The tightness in her stomach heightened as she wondered what else she could lose before everything was over. Travelling alone in unfamiliar company all the way across Faneria to Misengrad bothered her enough but the reason for the journey would haunt every step of it.

And what then? What would happen when she was surrounded

by the Agaesi, the mysterious order of knights that was rumoured to have strange powers? The stories Damian had heard about the dragon knights over the years ran through her mind. The kingdom held them in very high esteem but supposedly they lived nowhere, came from nowhere, accepted no outsiders into their ranks, and resided in complete secrecy. Stranger stories than that circulated about them and while she doubted they were true, they continued with such consistency that she couldn't deny something fuelled them. Sir Magni claimed they knew about magic and were the only people left in Faneria who could do anything about her power. What would they do to her? Could they help her or was it too late already?

Would my father still be alive if I had sought help before now?

More tears streamed onto the pillow and energy prickled inside her.

No. I must not look back.

Sniffling, Damian pushed back those thoughts and reflected on the travel itself. It would be nice to start moving again. She had been getting restless these past days in Trent and had been looking forward to accompanying the expedition to recover the cloth from the river.

The cloth. I should have gone to see Caleb yesterday... and Domino.

Upon returning to the Black Duck yesterday morning she disappeared into her room and emerged as little as possible the rest of the day. Now she regretted not taking the time to inform Caleb or the mercenary of her departure. The latter she likely would never see again.

And I never told him how much I now appreciate what he did for me.

Biting her tongue, she finally pulled back the covers and rose. She focused on dressing, packing her belongings, and weaving her hair into a plait for the travel. She prayed to the Gods of Light for forgiveness and that the Agaesi could help her. She hoped they didn't find that idea sacrilegious.

With a last look around the room that had been a home to her for a week, Damian slung her bag over her shoulder and walked out. The inn was quiet. She crossed the upstairs hall and descended the stairs.

As she glanced over the common room and saw Sir Magni sitting at a table, she paused. He wore a full suit of plate armour over his mail unlike any she had ever seen. Only parade and jousting armour looked so exotic. Forged in sweeping curves with strange subtle ribbing in the blued steel, it looked organic and it suited him so well it seemed a part of him. To her relief, he wore no helmet, his face and hair clearly visible above the breastplate and the attached armour around his throat. A forked blue-grey cloak fell to about knee-length behind him. Beneath that a voulge, a glaive-like weapon, hung in a harness over his shoulders, angled sharply as it leaned up against the chair.

Damian hesitated as she watched him. The thought of travelling alone with Sir Magni all the way to Misengrad left a lump in her throat. He might be a knight but she had seen some who thought little of those beneath their station. She couldn't help feeling the same was true of him after his attempts to manipulate her. How much of what he told her was true? If he had no such qualms about using people for his own purposes, what would he do when he had her alone, far away from anyone else?

What would she do if she didn't follow him? She had gone two weeks without losing control after the barge sank but she couldn't deny that she had been unable to do anything to suppress her power in the Temple of Time. What if that happened around other people, innocents like the sailors on the barge and her father? Swallowing hard, she pushed back those thoughts but the unease remained. She felt the energy roiling within her, seeking any slight weakness to escape.

I should have fled last night.

As Sir Magni turned his head and smiled at her, Damian knew that opportunity was lost. She climbed down the stairs and approached his table, one of few occupied that morning. Up close, though his strange armour added little bulk to his frame, she found he looked intimidating, despite the friendly smile on his face.

"Sleep well?"

She nodded in response, not wanting to talk to him. Filias walked over as she took a seat across from Sir Magni and set a dish of eggs, sausage, and fried potatoes in front of her, along with a leather mug of cider.

She gave him a weak smile. "Thank you."

He nodded. "No worries, Mis'Sires. I hear you're leaving Trent."

Damian sent a glance to the knight, wondering what else he had told the innkeeper. "Yes. Thank you so much for all your generosity."

"Well, 'twas the least I could do after all those years of business you and your father gave me."

She frowned, years of memories rushing through her head in a moment. "Would you do me a favour, please?"

Filias straightened with a look of curiosity mixed with apprehension. "What can I do for you?"

"Can you tell Mr. Nazeerad, the market director, that I left? And… tell him I'm sorry for not telling him in person."

Filias seemed to relax at that. "I'll let him know."

"Thank you."

"Safe travels, then."

Damian nodded as he walked away. "Thank you." With that, she turned to her breakfast.

Sir Magni was silent for a moment, glancing over the common room as he sipped his drink. Then he said, "I'm sorry." She eyed him. He faced her with a solemn expression. "I know this must be hard for you, and I regret having to take you away from what's familiar."

She didn't bother to tell him that travelling into unknown territory itself didn't disturb her.

The knight's face broke in a grin. "I'm also sorry I never got to try that bakery you recommended."

Damian hesitated with a bite halfway to her mouth. Staring at him, she wondered what he was trying to get out of her this time.

The chair creaked as he leaned forward, his expression sobering. "Look, Damian, I know we got off on the wrong foot, but I'd really like to make it up to you. I don't want the entire journey to be like this."

She looked away, saying nothing.

Sir Magni leaned closer. "Is there anything I can do to make you feel more comfortable with me?"

Without facing him, she shook her head. She realized her silence came across much like Domino's and thought she understood why the mercenary spoke so little. It felt nice to have at least that amount of control over her life.

Sir Magni sighed as he sat back. For a moment, he opened his mouth, looking like he was going to say something else, but fell quiet and sipped his drink instead. Damian returned to her meal, idly looking around the common room while she ate.

At last, she finished and Sir Magni rose, offering her a hand. "Shall we be off?"

Not taking his outstretched hand, she rose and followed him out the front door of the inn. When she stepped outside, she gasped, stopping in her tracks.

Tied to the hitching post beside the sidewalk stood an enormous stallion. Muscular as a plow horse but not broad-hoofed like one, the saddle sat higher than her eye level. It was a destrier, a warhorse fit for a high lord. With a deep chestnut coat, its curly tail hung to the ground and long feathering draped off its hooves. The bridle and saddle were made of fine leather, recently oiled, the latter stamped with intricate dragons around the edge and the seat marked with the griffin and swords of Hesperia. It was the most magnificent animal Damian had ever seen.

Smiling, Sir Magni patted the horse's neck. "This is my partner, Brenadier. Bren, this is Damian. Say hi." Bending a hoof, the horse leaned back and lowered its head in an imitation of a bow.

Damian smiled at the sight. "He's beautiful. I've seen horses like this before, only…"

"Black," the knight finished for her. "That's why I could afford him. The breeders would have sold him off as a cart horse just because he wasn't their favourite colour." The knight smiled. "They didn't know what they had with him. He's the finest horse I've ever seen." Turning his head, he gestured to Brenadier's other side. "Sorry to say I couldn't spend quite so much coin on yours, but the stable master said she's the best riding horse he had."

Turning, Damian finally noticed a second horse tethered beside the destrier. The other horse looked half a pony beside the huge stallion. The mare had a golden brown coat splashed with white over the face, mane, tail, shoulders, and legs. Damian's smile faded. "That's… my horse?"

Sir Magni grinned. "Unless you want to ride with me."

She stared at him with a mixture of surprise and annoyance.

He sobered. "You're under my protection, Damian. I'm not going to make you walk all the way to Misengrad."

Slowly, Damian turned back to the pinto. The thought had occurred to her and the sight of the mare tacked for her use surprised her. The horse likely cost him a lot. He could have let her walk. Most knights probably would. She swallowed as he mounted his destrier.

"She belongs to you."

Damian reached out a hand to the mare. It nickered and nuzzled her hand, and its warm breath rushed against her skin as it sniffed at her arm and head.

"You might as well give her a name now."

Damian paused, staring at the horse's markings and wondering what to call it. She wasn't certain why the name came to her, but the moment it did, she knew she could call the mare nothing else.

"Hope."

Sir Magni smiled his approval. She glanced at him before mounting the horse and together they rode through the streets.

The roads remained busier than Aether ever was but they felt deserted to Damian. Many people turned to watch them pass as they rode. Damian tensed at the attention though more heads turned toward Sir Magni than her. He sat straight and tall in the saddle, every bit the dashing knight in his elaborate armour and riding his huge warhorse. Despite herself, Damian caught her breath at the sight. She felt ashamed that she had neglected to use his title for so long. The fact that he didn't seem to mind came to her as much a surprise as it was a relief.

Occasionally people recognized him, though the surprise was clear in their voices at seeing him armed and armoured. Sir Magni called out goodbyes to those who noticed him as he and Damian made their way west, offering a smile but no explanations.

The sound of flowing water rose over the buildings as they neared Plaza Medalia, populated only with pigeons and a few statues set at distant intervals. Damian glanced down a side street, looking toward Caleb Nazeerad's office a block away. She wished that she had gone to visit him one last time.

Riding alongside the eastern fork of the Ivory River that bordered Plaza Medalia to the south, they crossed the large bridge spanning the southbound current. She glanced over the bridge at the river. A few small trawlers skimmed the water, dragging their nets behind, and in the distance she saw a barge gradually making its way downstream but the muddy water otherwise flowed open.

Gradually, they made their way through the western side of the city, stopping for a quiet dinner at a local tavern before leaving Trent. Soon, they crossed the western gate out of the city and into open fields. Rolling hills dotted with trees or jutting cliff faces stretched as far as Damian could see and spring brought huge swaths of wildflowers blooming all around. Much of the land along the river was given to pasture and distant flocks of sheep and goats grazed in the open land. Unless they turned north, within half a day's ride they would be surrounded by unmarred wilderness and days could pass between sightings of civilization.

Damian glanced over her shoulder as grass grew over the heavily trodden path beyond the gates, the tracks beaten across the land spreading out in various directions. The outer wall and outlying buildings nearly filled the horizon, but Trent already seemed far away. A lump formed in her throat as she thought of the journey to come.

The sound of the stallion's snorts and an anxious prance to its steps drew her attention to Sir Magni. She eyed the huge destrier, the horse stamping its hooves as it walked and champing at the bit. "What's wrong?"

The knight grinned. "He's just restless and eager to stretch his legs. Been cooped up in a stable too long." The horse snorted, jumping a little at its next step. "Alright, alright." Sir Magni shot a quick grin over his shoulder as Brenadier whinnied. "Take your time, I'll come back for you." With that, the stallion launched into a gallop, racing across the plains.

Before Damian could react, Hope lurched forward after Brenadier, bouncing Damian into a trot before leaning into a canter. Damian let out an uneasy noise as she tried to move with the mare's gait. Occasionally Damian helped the stable master in Aether exercise his horses, though she had little experience riding above a walk and hoped the quicker pace wouldn't jounce her too much. As the mare cantered after Sir Magni and Brenadier, Damian grew used to its motions and she relaxed. She smiled, pleased with the mare's performance. For a moment, Damian enjoyed the feeling of the wind in her hair, the land rushing beneath her as the horse hurried across the fields, and all her worries seemed to be left behind.

She caught up to Sir Magni sooner than she expected. His stallion clearly only galloped for a few minutes before slowing to a walk. Damian pulled Hope into a walk, missing the freedom that faded away as dark thoughts tumbled about the edges of her mind. She was surprised Brenadier galloped so briefly though the horse covered considerable ground in that time.

Sir Magni nodded at Hope as Damian came alongside him. "How's she ride?"

She stroked the mare's mane. "Very well." Raising her eyes, she looked at the knight. "Thank you, Sir."

He smiled. "My pleasure."

With that, their ride fell to silence and hours drifted away as they made their way west. It didn't take long for Damian's seat atop Hope to feel uncomfortable and she was relieved when the knight stopped to lead the horses on foot an hour later. Occasionally, Sir Magni would make some comment about the weather, travel, or the state of Faneria, point out some landmark or lone distant animal, or attempt to draw Damian out in conversation. Away from Trent, his voice took on a western inflection, his affected accent dropping away. It was a curious dialect to Damian, who had never gone farther west than central Faneria, with its clipped vowels and staccato rhythm, but the sincerity of it was refreshing. Damian remained mostly silent and spent her time looking at her surroundings.

She thought of other journeys she had undertaken. In this part of the kingdom, the travel reminded her more of the second half of her father's trade journey when they left the rivers and sea behind and loaded the remaining cloth onto a caravan. With only two horses, one companion, and no wagons, the travel was much quieter, the silence broken only by the occasional breeze, flock of birds soaring overhead, or Sir Magni's voice. The solitude weighed on Damian and she fidgeted as she rode or walked, feeling far less comfortable with the silence here on the open plains than in the encroaching forest. She couldn't work herself up to speaking much when the knight attempted to converse with her.

So the hours drifted away, the long afternoon spent shifting between riding, walking, and pausing for breaks, until finally the late golden sunlight turned orange as the sun dipped toward the horizon ahead. She nearly asked Sir Magni when they would stop for the night when he called a halt. They found shelter at a copse of trees at the base of a long hill and laid blankets on the ground, the clear evening promising a warm and dry night without the need for cover. Damian removed the horses' tack and led them to a creek to drink before tying them up nearby while the knight gathered wood and built a fire. He showed her how to brush the horses' coats and clean their hooves. By the time they finished caring for their mounts, all traces of sunlight had faded from the sky and the land lay dark and quiet.

Finally, Damian sat before the fire. Opening one of Brenadier's saddle bags, the knight handed her a strip of dried mutton, a hunk of crusty bread and hard cheese, and a handful of berries. He winced as he took his first bite of the meat.

"I'm going to miss those inns in Trent. Sorry I've nothing better to offer you than this." He grinned. "Cooking isn't exactly something a knight is trained to do."

Damian tried not to cringe as she bit into the salty but rather flavourless mutton. She glanced at his equipment. "Do you have a pot? A little broth might do this wonders."

He shrugged. "I'm afraid not. Wouldn't know what to do with it if I had one."

"You have nothing you could use to heat water over the fire?"

Setting aside the mutton, he tossed berries into his mouth. "I've heard of some knights who cook noodles in their helmets." He made a face. "Could you imagine the smell, wearing that all day?"

Frowning, she looked over his equipment again. "Do you have a helmet?"

"None of the Agaesi do." He tapped his temple. "It's to keep our minds clear. Of course, some of our rank take that a step further and keep their heads plucked bald." He grinned. "Personally, I feel that I can think well enough with my hair."

Despite her attempts to hide it, she couldn't help smiling.

Sir Magni's smile widened. "Now that's a refreshing sight."

Sobering, she averted her eyes.

He let out a sigh. "How many times do I have to say I'm sorry before you'll forgive me?"

Damian fidgeted, not wanting to have this conversation.

He leaned forward, his armour rustling with the movement. "You know I never meant to hurt you, right?"

Her voice dropped to a whisper. "I know."

"So what's bothering you?"

She let out a breath in frustration. *He's still missing the point.* "It is the way you manipulate people."

He frowned. "Everyone manipulates others. It's how we get what we want."

She levelled a hard look on him. "Not me. It is cruel."

"It's not cruel. People are happier when they feel like they're getting what they want. They're satisfied that way."

Damian bristled. "It is worse than being dishonest. It makes those you use lie to themselves, until they no longer know what is their own belief and what was planted there. It takes away people's freedom."

He leaned to the side, resting a hand on his knee. "Come on, Damian. You're a merchant. Salesmanship is the art of manipulation. Don't tell me you don't make suggestions to your customers to sell your goods."

Straightening, she lifted her chin and gazed firmly at his eyes. "I believe the cloth should speak for itself. It does us no good to sell to people who do not need or want it."

With a sigh, Sir Magni leaned back and shook his head. "You're a rare case then."

She hesitated, watching him. "You seem kind enough. I do not know why you feel you need to manipulate others."

A distant, tired look was in his eyes as he stared across the dark fields. "Yeah, well, we all have our ways of surviving. You chose straightforwardness. I picked a different path."

She blinked, surprised at the depth in his eyes and his words. She opened her mouth to ask him a question, but before she could speak, he rose and strode toward the creek nearby.

"You'd better get some sleep. The nights are short and you'll need the rest for the travel."

She watched him walk away, his mail jingling softly beneath the plate armour. He didn't look back.

Without another word, she settled uneasily onto the blankets, their conversation swimming through her mind.

Everyone manipulates others. Salesmanship is the art of manipulation.

She had often seen such tactics in the markets throughout the kingdom. But she didn't do that. Her sales didn't come because she manipulated others.

"It's not true," she said softly to the quiet night and the crackling fire.

Isn't it?

Lyle drummed his fingers on his desk, his expression hard.

"How is it possible that someone could break into my office and steal something if you two never left your posts?"

Two city guards stood on the other side of his desk. One trembled, his face pale, though the other kept a solemn look on his face. Lyle could see the dread in his eyes.

"I-I don't know, Captain."

Lyle leaned forward against his desk, his mail rustling and the straps of his plate armour creaking. The guards quailed, the first one's hands visibly shaking.

"I swear to all the gods we were here all night, Captain."

His partner nodded so quickly it seemed like a nervous spasm.

Lyle's voice remained even. "Did you fall asleep?"

"No, Captain."

"Did you get distracted by something?"

"Of course not!"

Lyle's eyes narrowed further.

"N-n-not long enough for someone to get in, anyway."

"And yet someone did."

The guards said nothing, the first quaking in fear and the other looking resigned to his fate. Lyle watched them, letting their terror stew. Finally, he said, "You are both suspended without pay."

The first guard paled further. The other asked without meeting Lyle's eyes, "For how long, Captain?"

"Three days. It will be a week if you stay in here any longer." With that, the first guard scrambled out of his office, the other lifting his hand in a quick salute before marching hurriedly after his companion. Lyle turned to the man who had summoned them, also looking uneasy. "Find replacements for them, and make sure they stay focused while on duty."

"Yes, Captain." Bowing stiffly, he departed in haste, leaving Lyle alone in the room with Gravier.

The second's voice was cautious. "You know they were telling the truth, Lyle."

Lyle pinched the bridge of his nose. "I know. They are not incompetent, either. They caught that spy two years ago that fooled the gate guards. But how could someone have broken in here if they did not leave their posts?"

Gravier shrugged. "Perhaps one stepped away to relieve himself and the other got distracted momentarily."

Lyle shot him a look. "And did not hear or see someone come inside the door he was standing right beside? Or back out again?"

"I do not know how it happened but I still do not think they were lying."

Lyle sighed. "Nor do I, and that concerns me a great deal more than if they had left their posts."

Gravier took a half step forward. "Captain, if I may, what was stolen from that compartment?"

Lyle gave him a hard look.

The second held up his hands. "If you want help recovering it, we need to know what was taken."

Lyle stared across the room with a frown. "Something that few people should know about."

Gravier hesitated and Lyle could tell the second was deciding whether to press him for more answers or leave the topic.

Lyle's chair scraped across the floor as he rose, "It was a book."

Gravier blinked. "A book?"

Lyle folded his arms as he stared out the window at the city streets. "A very ancient and dangerous book. That is all you need to know and more than anyone else needs to know."

Gravier nodded. "I understand, Captain. How should we go about finding the thief?"

Lyle watched people walk down the street as his mind whirled.

Who else knew about the book, and more importantly, who else knew that he had it? Was everything that happened almost twenty years ago beginning again? His head sank. Mere chance had brought him into the events that gave him the book and he never had understood everything about it. Without more information, he would never be able to discover who had taken it.

He raised his head. "Talk to everyone who was on duty last night. Either the thief scaled or bypassed the walls or he is still in town. In either case, someone must have seen something even if those two did not."

Gravier saluted. "Yes, Captain. I'll find the names of every soldier on duty last night." He approached Lyle's desk and leafed through the papers there.

"Do that, and start with those posted on the walls." Lyle strode around his desk toward the door.

"Where are you going?"

"Canvassing the neighbourhood." Lyle's voice was dry. "Maybe someone in this area had insomnia and noticed someone skulking about the streets." Without waiting for a response, Lyle stepped outside and closed the door behind him.

He soon discovered that no one had seen anything. Whatever method the thief used to gain access to his office, clearly it kept him from being seen by anyone. Handing off as many of his duties to Gravier as he could, Lyle spent what free moments he had trying to track down the book. The search proved more difficult than Lyle already anticipated. He undoubtedly sounded mad trying to ask about a mysterious object stolen from a hidden cubbyhole by a thief who had not been seen by anyone nor taken or disturbed anything else. Lyle suspected that even Gravier doubted him.

Then Lyle wondered if he knew exactly who had taken it. But if so, then why? That thought consumed him more.

The idea swirled through his mind some nights later as he lay next to Evelyn, staring unseeing into their bedroom. The house lay silent, the room dark and illuminated by the moonlight streaming through the windows.

He felt himself drifting to sleep when Evelyn raised on her elbow beside him. "What is bothering you, Lyle?"

"Nothing."

"You are lying."

He raised an eyebrow at her. In the moonlight reflected off the floorboards, he saw a wry smile cross her face.

"You still hide your feelings well, but I can tell when something is on your mind."

Staring at her, he wondered if he had been rougher with her a few minutes ago than he realized or intended. The release had been welcome and desperately needed though his thoughts remained clouded.

She stared at him, a knowing look on her face. "We have been married fourteen years after all."

He blinked. "Has it been that long?"

"Marise is nearly a woman now."

Grunting, he laid his head back. "One would not think it to look at her."

Evelyn pursed her lips. "She is desperate for your respect. She works hard at her training for you."

"It is unnatural."

She laid a hand on his bare chest. "Children wanting to be like their father is anything but unnatural."

"Girls should not be trying to follow in their father's footsteps."

Evelyn leaned back, her eyes hardening. "Do you want her to be more like Amera? You would pay her even less attention than you do now."

He sat up, his eyes narrowing. "I am not neglecting her."

"No, but you are denying Marise the only thing she desires."

"Daven—"

"Daven is spoiled," she cut across him. "You dote on him too much." He opened his mouth, inhaling deeply for his response, but Evelyn continued in a softer voice, "There is more to the Hitchcliffe line than its name. Marise would show you that." He fell silent and Evelyn went on, "You know I did not want her to learn the sword as well, but she has proven herself very dedicated and very capable. Will you at least go see her at her training?"

The thought of watching his daughter in training reminded him of her swinging a toy wooden sword as a child while wearing his helmet. The helmet had covered her eyes and rested on her shoulders in those days. Lyle couldn't imagine seeing her in training without seeing the same thing.

"I will consider it."

Evelyn gave him a flat look, clearly hearing the reluctance and the lie in his voice. "I suppose that is all I can ask of you. Just think hard about what impact you are having on her before you decide. But you did not answer my question. What is bothering you?"

With a sigh, he rolled over, facing the window. "Entirely too much."

The next day yielded no more results than the previous ones, and much of Lyle's time was spent with his regular duties. Much of the remaining was spent in thoughts of his family and he gave little consideration to the stolen book.

Then, a voice spoke to him unexpectedly on his way home at the end of the day.

"Captain Hitchcliffe?"

Lyle turned around and straightened. A knight in full armour, much finer and newer than his father's old suit of plate, stood a few paces away. It was strangely stylized, serpentine in appearance, yet the knight wore no helmet, his hairless pate bare. The realization struck Lyle.

This was an Agaesi knight.

Lyle bowed. "Sir."

"Our captain would like a word with you. Do you have some free time?"

Lyle didn't show the uncomfortable feeling that rose in his stomach with the question. "Of course, Sir."

The knight turned and led Lyle through the streets toward the castle. Lyle fell silently into step, his thoughts whirling. Those two sentences the knight spoke was the most interaction Lyle ever had with an Agaesi. Lyle had rarely been to the castle and never within the Agaesi's own barracks. From the stories that circulated about them, few people ever had. He didn't believe the stories about the dragon knights but for an order housed within the city they were scarcely seen. No one seemed to know where they came from, lived, or trained.

Strangely, the wild tales Lyle's brother once told him rang through his mind as they came within a few blocks of the castle. Those in particular seemed too far-fetched to have even a grain of truth in them.

Lyle glanced up the wall around the castle grounds, as high as the one surrounding the city. No city guards under his command stood here. Full knights and men-at-arms, under the direct command of the Duke of Hesperia, stood at regular intervals. Lyle and the Agaesi passed under the portcullis and through the gate that admitted a steady stream of people in and out, ranging from peasants come to plead cases to the duke to nobles crossing on finely tacked horses or in carriages. The pair of guards at the gate gave Lyle and his escort a cursory glance before they turned their vigil to the next people.

The castle grounds bustled with activity, servants or local merchants pushing wheelbarrows of food and supplies or clerks scurrying with rolls of parchment wedged under their arms. In a corner of the yard beside a barracks, a sandy training ground writhed with squires and knights sparring with practice weapons.

Soon, the grounds were obscured by a second curtain wall surrounding the castle. The Agaesi knight led Lyle over the drawbridge above the moat of spikes and under the portcullis, and after crossing a brief paved path that ended at the wide stairs of the entrance, they passed into the castle. The knight immediately turned off the cavernous main corridor into a quieter, more secluded passage. Lyle glanced briefly at the main hall with its soaring arches, huge tapestries, and motionless guards in full suits of armour, as well as the throngs of people continuing toward their destinations.

Silence overtook them as the Agaesi led him through empty halls populated only by the occasional guard. There were none of the visitors, servants, clerks, or messengers that filled the main hall. The sound of their footsteps and their armour rattling rang through the corridors. Torches lit the passage, no windows admitting any light along their path.

The emptiness and their long, winding journey pressed on Lyle, making his chest tighten the deeper they went into the castle. He knew he couldn't find his way back out if he tried and the question of what the captain of the Agaesi wanted with him resurfaced and claimed his thoughts.

At last, they made a final turn and approached a set of double doors at the end of the hall. Two Agaesi knights stood guard outside.

Lyle knew he had little to fear from the Agaesi despite this unexpected and secretive meeting. Decades of training kept the thought that he was outnumbered squarely in his mind. Neither of the guards, decked in armour as fine as Lyle's guide, said anything or moved as Lyle's guide led him to the doors and inside. With their heads bare, Lyle could see their eyes watch him enter.

To his surprise, they entered what appeared to be a common room. Two walls were set with windows, dusty light streaming onto old, worn tables scattered about the floor. Nobody sat at any of the age-darkened chairs. The hearth did not burn and nothing adorned the walls but cobwebs. Lyle wondered at the purpose of the Agaesi claiming a common room they clearly did not use. The knight crossed to the right side of the room and passed through a door.

They came into a room lined with shelves stuffed full of leather-bound tomes, ledgers and records by the look of them. Some were so old and brittle they looked like they would crumble to dust from a stiff wind. The mountain of paperwork the Agaesi apparently dealt with felt oddly familiar to Lyle and his tension eased slightly. Two writing desks, one covered with horns of ink, quills, and papers filled out the room, and a young man and woman scrambled between them. A third youth, thin, pale, and gangly, sat in a chair beside a door against the left wall. The knight leading Lyle strode to the boy beside the doors, who scrambled to his feet with a wheezing breath.

"I have brought Captain Hitchcliffe of the city guard. Is the captain available?"

"Yes, Sir." The youth coughed and cleared his throat, his voice growing slightly less frail. "You may see him now."

"Thank you." With a nod to the boy and then to Lyle, the knight continued to the doors and walked inside.

The next room was the same size as the previous. A few shelves holding more books of records lined the walls, along with a pair of tapestries, a coat of arms, and a pair of crossed decorative swords. Windows along two walls let in the late afternoon sunlight. A scribe sat on a stool in the far corner, scribbling notes on a sheaf of parchment supported by a lap desk.

The captain of the Agaesi looked little older than Lyle with medium length dirty blonde hair shot through with grey and a thin, close-trimmed beard beneath steel grey eyes. He wore a plain cream-coloured shirt and leather bracers. His head was bowed toward the large desk he sat behind as he scratched out a letter with a crow quill.

Lyle's guide stopped and straightened as he passed through the doors. The knight held out a hand toward Lyle while facing the captain. "Sir, I have brought Captain Hitchcliffe of the city guard."

The Agaesi commander didn't look up from his letter. His voice sounded distracted. "Mm. Thank you. Please wait outside."

"Sir." The knight bowed and ducked out, shutting the door.

Lyle stood in uncomfortable silence for a moment while the Agaesi captain wrote. The scribe hurriedly jotted a few more words before tearing a blank page out from beneath his current one and placing it on top.

With a flourish, the Agaesi commander finished his letter, emptied the quill into a bottle of ink, and replaced it on a stand on his desk. Then, he finally looked up at Lyle.

"Captain Hitchcliffe." Standing, he gestured toward a chair on the other side of his desk. "Please come in. I am Sir Redge Warwick, Captain of the Agaesi Knights." The scribe scribbled on his page as

Warwick spoke.

Lyle bowed before he approached the desk. "Sir."

Sir Warwick waited for Lyle to sit before he lowered onto his chair. "I would be lying if I said I regret not meeting you sooner, for we wouldn't have much opportunity to meet except under dire circumstances."

"What circumstances would these be then?"

A wry smile crossed Warwick's face. "A matter of curiosity, that's all. But I am glad to meet the man responsible for keeping the rest of Misengrad safe. I understand your family has served the city well for generations."

A lump formed in Lyle's throat as he thought of his lineage, the older and younger Hitchcliffes now gone. The burden of his family line rested on his son, the one whose attention to his training drifted. "Yes, Sir." Despite his years, the idea of being in a private meeting with a knight, let alone commander of the most elite order of knights in the kingdom, left Lyle self-conscious. The scribe scratching at his parchment didn't help matters.

The captain's smile faded as he leaned on his elbows on his desk. "Captain Hitchcliffe, I will get straight to the point. I have heard news that you suffered an unusual theft recently at your office."

Lyle's throat tightened. Why would the Agaesi have any interest in the missing book? Lyle thought his questioning had been discreet and couldn't imagine how such word reached Warwick's ears.

"Am I correct?"

"Yes, Sir."

"And I understand that you have had difficulty tracking down the culprit."

Warning bells rang off in Lyle's head. What else did Warwick know? It seemed entirely too coincidental that the Agaesi would summon him to speak of the theft of a book with an ancient magic spell written inside. The rumours Lyle had always heard about the Agaesi bubbled through his mind.

"Yes, Sir."

Sir Warwick gazed steadily at him. "Can you tell me the circumstances of this theft?"

Lyle shifted, his old armour rattling softly. "I discovered the theft a few days ago just after dawn, when I was arriving for my shift in the morning. The difference was slight but I noticed that the lock had been turned. When I went to the store room below my office I found that an item I thought well hidden had been stolen. The guards on duty claimed never to leave their posts, nor were they distracted long enough for anyone to gain entrance."

"And you are certain they entered through the main door?"

"The lock slides, Sir. A screw is loose, I have not yet tightened it. It was askew that morning."

Slowly, the commander nodded. "I see. So the thief managed to gain entrance, bypassing two guards, without being seen."

There seemed, Lyle thought, a curious emphasis on that last. For a moment, it sounded like the scribe's notation grew more forceful. More intent.

Warwick raised his head. "Forgive me for monitoring you, but I was alerted to this theft by one of my knights, who overheard some of your guards discussing it, and it seemed very curious. Why have you not started a full investigation?"

There was no accusation in Sir Warwick's words, but discomfort crept up Lyle's spine all the same. "It was a… personal item that was taken, Sir. I kept it at my office for safe keeping. I do not have the authority to utilize city coffers to recover it."

Warwick showed no reaction to that. "If I may ask, what was stolen?"

Lyle hesitated, uncertainty swarming over him. The entrance to the castle seemed much too far away. "A book."

Sir Warwick's eyes widened, his surprise not entirely covered up by the look of confusion he then gave Lyle. "A book? What kind of book would interest such a devious thief?"

Lyle glanced at the scribe, who had not looked up since he entered. "I am not certain, Sir. It was written in a language I do not recognize."

That made the Agaesi captain look thoughtful. "How did you come to be in possession of this book?"

"It was entrusted to me."

"I see." Seemingly satisfied by that answer, Sir Warwick stared absently across the room. "Have you anything else to add regarding this theft?"

"No, Sir. I have learned little about it myself."

Warwick nodded. "That will be all, then. Thank you for taking the time to speak with me, Captain. If I find out anything else about your missing book, I will let you know, though I will hold this meeting in strictest confidence. Sir Kedovsky will show you out."

Lyle bowed, then stood and walked out without another word.

Lyle paid little attention to the knight that led him out of the castle, through the outer grounds, and into Misengrad, nor did he spare anyone else he passed much notice as he pondered the meeting he had just left. Even thoughts about his family faded to the back of his mind as thoughts of the book consumed Lyle. The Agaesi knew more about this situation than Sir Warwick let on, of that Lyle was certain. More importantly, the Agaesi captain had shown no surprise or curiosity in response to Lyle's information, aside from the admission of what was stolen. Warwick must have heard of a theft like this before. Lyle never had, and in his position he was privy to a lot of tales told around town.

Were the rumours true? Did the Agaesi deal in matters of magic?

If so, then magic was involved with the theft of his book. And that probably meant another mage was preparing to cast the same spell Lyle helped abort almost two decades ago. Dread settled over him with the thought that it was happening again.

Only this time, he had no idea who was involved or how to stop it.

CHAPTER 9
WARMTH

DAMIAN'S CONVERSATION WITH Sir Magni circled through her mind all the following day. His comments consumed her thoughts and she revisited every memory she had of selling her father's cloth in the market.

Had she manipulated people in her efforts to make sales? Her father always taught her to be honest with customers. But sometimes a customer would hesitate over some aspect of the fabric and Damian would try to turn the inconvenience around in the customer's eyes or gloss over it to highlight some other trait that appealed to the customer better. If she was honest, she had to admit that was a form of manipulation.

Her personal interactions hardly seemed any better. Haggling was a way of getting what she wanted for less than what others desired, even if it was honest about its purpose. Some of the things she had said to Sir Magni or people she knew at home seemed intended to change their thoughts. The way she had spent her life hiding her eyes had the same effect. Was there any time in her life when she had not manipulated others?

The thought made her feel horrible. Misery clung to her throughout the day as they travelled. As she grew accustomed to those dark thoughts, she looked frequently at the knight riding beside her. His confidence, his easygoing manner.

Everyone manipulates others. It's how we get what we want.

To him it wasn't evil, it was simply the way people interacted. Perhaps it was. He did manipulate others but he was kind and compassionate. Damian's eyes were drawn to the mare she rode, a gesture that was not only unnecessary, but one few would offer to a girl of a lower class. She recalled the look on his face the last night, as though a great weight settled over him when he spoke of survival.

It wasn't until they stopped for dinner the day after that she managed to speak about her thoughts. Several minutes passed as she eagerly downed more of Sir Magni's flavourless rations, her stomach growling. He glanced around the countryside while they ate and she watched him.

Finally, she managed to say, "I'm sorry."

He faced her, a curious look on his face. "For what?"

She shifted, not meeting his eyes. "For the way I treated you. I have been thinking a lot about what you said the other night and I understand now what you were trying to tell me. It... it was unfair of me to be so rude to you."

He smiled. "Ah, it's alright. I don't blame you for being upset. And I'm sorry, too. I didn't mean to use you. It's just the way I am." She raised her head, though he gazed into the distance. "I grew up in the Duke of Hesperia's court. That world is far more cutthroat than the market." A wry grin crossed his face. "Or the slums of old Trent, for that matter."

Damian tilted her head aside. "You attend court? But I thought the Agaesi…"

He turned his grin to her as she trailed off. "We can be secretive and mingle with nobility at the same time."

She had heard other knights say otherwise. The Agaesi never appeared at court. They refused to play politics. It seemed stranger that Sir Magni would have attended court as a child, before he had been knighted. Even if he squired for a much greater knight, if Agaesi took squires, he would have little status of his own.

She cleared her throat as he looked at her and could only manage a generic response. "I did not realize."

"Most people don't. It's not a big deal." He held out his hand. "No hard feelings?"

A brief moment of surprise took her at the gesture. Then, with a smile, she shook his hand, his grip firm as though shaking another man's hand.

He tossed the last bite of his strip of meat into his mouth, wincing at the taste. "Well, shall we be off?" Standing, he offered Damian a gauntleted hand. This time, she took it. He pulled her swiftly to her feet, so effortlessly she thought he could have lifted her right off them. With a smile, he fetched Brenadier and Damian approached and mounted Hope.

Clouds scudded across the sky throughout the next day, growing dark as they chased Damian and Sir Magni west throughout the afternoon. As the sun sank toward the horizon, a grey, pillowy blanket covered the sky, casting the land into premature nighttime. The wind tossed Damian's hair and skirt and the first drops fell as the knight called a halt beneath a knot of three scrubby trees.

They dismounted and Sir Magni looked at her while he removed his stallion's saddle bags. "We'll brush them later, just worry about getting them some water."

Damian nodded as she loosened Hope's bridle and removed the bit. "Alright." Much as she enjoyed caring for the horses when they stopped for breaks, she was glad to delay the longer process of brushing Hope's coat and picking out the mare's hooves.

Damian paused in her work. Only then did she realize how the knight had assigned her only the tasks she enjoyed. He allowed her to brush the horses' coats but he took on the more tedious work of combing their manes and tails and picking out their hooves. She glanced over the mare's back as she unstrapped the saddle. Sir Magni smiled as he removed Brenadier's tack.

The scattered drops picked up to a light drizzle by the time Damian secured Hope's rope halter to a tree. Sitting before the fire Sir Magni built, she opened her saddle bag to pull out her cloak.

"Here," he said, opening his own bag and handing her a blanket. "Use this. You should keep your cloak dry so you can warm up quicker once the rain stops."

She hesitated. The blanket he gave her was the one he had been sleeping on. "Are you certain?"

He smiled as he leaned back against a tree, pulling some food out of his satchel. "I've some spare clothes with me. Just keep my bag underneath it, in case I get too wet."

The rain fell heavier. Without another word, Damian wrapped the blanket around herself, pulling the edge of it over her head like a hood. She took the knight's bag and slid it beneath the blanket. The fire leaped, popped, and sizzled under the barrage of rain. Damian's eyes raised and she glanced into the darkness. With clouds covering the sky, she saw little beyond the light of their fire. The sound of the rain washing steadily over the land and tapping against the leaves of the trees soothed her. The sound brought back memories from years past. Closing her eyes, she let out a breath.

Metallic tinks rang out beside her. Turning, she found Sir Magni staring into the dark sky, a serene smile on his face as rain drops glided down his face and hair and tapped against his armour. For a moment she stared at him, captivated by the carefree look in his eyes as he watched the rain.

He turned his smile to her. "What's on your mind?"

His closeness struck her. He had built the fire in the centre of the trees that made an uneven semicircle, yet he sat on the same side of the blaze as her, rather than across it as he had the last night. Although he remained a couple paces away, not too close for her comfort, it was still closer than he had been.

She cleared her throat, turning to the fire. A few days ago she would have dismissed or ignored those small gestures. Now they clung to her like the blanket and only when she focused on the sound of the rain could she recall what crossed her mind moments before.

"I was just remembering last year when we travelled across this part of Faneria. We had a few nights of rain on the road."

"This was for your father's cloth trade?"

She nodded.

"That's unfortunate. Rain always makes for uncomfortable travel."

"The rain itself didn't bother me. I have always found the sound of rain calming."

His smile widened. "I know the feeling. Though getting rained on while you sleep is another matter entirely."

"Actually, in ways those nights were the most comfortable on the road. I got to sleep on the cloth because there was little enough room for everyone to take shelter in the wagons." Her smile faded. "But with the wagon drivers packed in there with us, I had to sleep with my veil on. I slept so fitfully because I was afraid it would fall off and they would see my eyes."

No fear rose from the memory though she remembered it so vividly. Instead, a heavy weight settled over her heart with the thought that there would be no markets for the cloth this year. Never again would the journey be run by her father. Damian trembled and drops of her own slid down her face.

He's gone.

She sniffled, her fingers digging into her arms as she tried to hold back the miserable feelings tearing their way out of the dark part of her mind where she had banished them.

A light weight rested on her shoulder. She flinched from the touch, but Sir Magni's hand remained where it was. She didn't fight it a second time. She pushed back the guilt, the horror, those feelings that persisted in the distance. The journey to Misengrad felt welcome to escape the shame.

I must not look back.

Inhaling deeply, she straightened before turning to the knight. "Thank you."

A solemn expression marked his face. "I'm sorry." He pulled his hand back. "I can imagine how hard it must have been for you growing up this way." He gazed into her eyes steadily as he spoke and she recalled the look on his face the first time he saw them. Surprise, yes, but had there been disgust? She was no longer certain.

"Do they bother you?"

He smiled. "Nah. I admit I was shocked the first night we met, but they're who you are. I wouldn't have you any other way."

She straightened in surprise. Even the other boys and girls her age in Aether, those few who had seen her eyes, said otherwise.

Do you ever wish they were normal? One young man in Aether asked that a few years ago. She had answered, "Sometimes," but never told him the truth. That as much as she wished she didn't have to hide her eyes to be accepted, she couldn't imagine looking in a mirror and seeing blue, green, or brown irises instead.

Damian smiled. "Thank you."

Sir Magni's grin widened. "Nothing to thank me for. It's just the way I feel." He looked toward the dark sky. The sound of the rain softened and the moon glowed behind the clouds. "Looks like the rain's letting up. We should get some sleep."

She nodded and stretched out on the blanket beneath her, draping the knight's slightly damp one over her and the bags.

The night slipped away and they rode out the next morning over dew-kissed grass. Brief showers passed over them as they travelled but gradually the sky cleared and the thirsty earth and warm sun quickly dried off the plains. As they travelled, more wildflowers bloomed around them, the grass bursting with yellow, purple, and red.

Two days later, their travel halted as they came upon a river winding over the plains. They stopped the horses at the bank and examined the water running before them. The river was slow-moving and shallow, a finger's length deep, and stretched some thirty paces across. A smooth, flat stone bed lay beneath the water as though the river had been shaped by man rather than nature. Downstream, the river bed dropped away and reeds choked the dark water. A stone's throw upstream, a short waterfall cascaded down from a hill, the pounding of the water driving out a depression where the water pooled before flowing to where they stood.

Damian dismounted, wincing at the heat and pain on her legs, backside, and palms. Alternating between riding and walking beside the horses, as well as occasionally riding side-saddle, had not prevented soreness from developing, and her hands chafed from the reins. Standing beside the mare, she watched Sir Magni.

The knight kneeled at the bank of the river, removed his gauntlet, and stuck his hand into the water, running his fingers over the river bed.

"It's covered with algae. Very slippery." Shaking the excess water off his hand, he stood, glancing up and downstream. He jogged upstream, climbing a smoother side of the small cliff to stand beside the waterfall. From the top, he stared upstream. Then, he turned and looked downstream.

After a moment, he stepped forward and leaped straight off the cliff. Damian's eyes widened, the drop over twice his height. He landed in a crouch without showing any discomfort. He strode back, shaking his head.

"I don't see any better place to cross unless you want to swim."

A shudder ran through her with the memory of flailing in the Ivory River after the barge sank. The memory remained hazy, more like a nightmare. The knowledge that it had been real frightened her more than the images that remained. Unable to find her voice, she shook her head.

"Didn't think so. I'd hate to get everything wet. Even the horses would have to swim."

She opened her eyes as the sound of his voice dropped. He bent over to unstrap the armour around his lower legs and remove his boots, tying them on top of Brenadier's saddle bags.

"I think we should be okay if we take it really slow. I'll go first with the horses."

She nodded. "Alright."

He patted the horse's necks before taking up their reins. "Okay, Bren, don't let me down. Or take me down. You too, Hope." Damian couldn't help but smile as he spoke to the mare by the name she had given it.

His feet absurdly bare with his trouser legs rolled up beneath the rest of his fully clothed and armoured body, Sir Magni stepped into the water, leading Brenadier and Hope to either side. The horses stepped carefully, their heads bobbing as they felt for purchase.

The horses' back hooves barely entered the water before the knight slid, his arms waving for balance. Damian held her breath but he steadied.

"It's definitely slippery. Be careful."

Damian swallowed, wondering if they should swim. Doing so would make for a very uncomfortable ride for a long time afterward, if not possibly ruining Sir Magni's fine leather saddle and their food, but it would be worse if one of the horses slipped and broke a leg at this ford. As Damian glanced downstream at the deeper water, she realized that the reeds and weeds reaching up to the surface could tangle in the horse's legs, making for a very perilous crossing.

With a sigh, Damian crouched and pulled off her boots, holding them in one hand while she held up the tail of her skirt with the other. Slowly, she stepped into the water.

Her foot slid on the first step. It steadied at a mild depression in the river bed but her heart raced from the brief lack of control. The current was slow, barely pulling at her leg, but the stone river bed was as slippery as melting ice. She placed each foot down slowly, gradually shifting her weight forward as she steadied her feet on the slick river bed. The water that ran over her feet was cold and she was glad it barely reached her ankle. She supposed that was another good reason not to attempt swimming across a deeper part of the river. Undoubtedly the water downstream where it sank farther from the sunlight flowed colder. Here where she could see no town in any direction, getting soaked in this water posed a real risk of freezing.

Damian gradually figured out how to move safely across the slick river bed and managed to catch up to the knight until she walked just behind the horses. Relieved to be close to the horses and Sir Magni, Damian hoped neither of the beasts would decide to kick her. Although her feet frequently slid, she managed to keep her balance.

Then, a sudden, unseen dip in the river bed halfway across made Damian's foot slide quickly out in front of her. Gasping, she flailed her arms, trying to move her other foot back to support her, but she could feel herself toppling over. The knight let go of the reins and shuffled through the water toward her, but he remained a few paces away. Dropping her skirt, she threw her arm back to catch herself.

Something else did before she fell into the shallow river.

Opening her eyes, Damian found Sir Magni's face hovering inches above hers. His arms wrapped around her as he held her up, bent over backward as though he dipped her in a dance. She froze, staring at him while her heart raced. The sun shone behind him, gleaming in a halo around his head and glinting red in his hair. A few strands hung loose and tickled her cheeks. Her eyes were drawn to his and the deep gaze he returned.

The thought of having nothing holding her up except his grip made her tense, desperate for footing. As she hung there supported by him, closer than she had been to almost anyone, she found her heart racing more than it had when she fell. She wanted to pull away from him and lean closer at the same time and draped over his arm unmoving, not knowing what to do. Her cheeks heated up from his closeness.

"Are you alright?"

The smoothness of his voice, resounding so close to her, rippled up and down her spine. "Yes," she uttered, unable to find her voice. "Thank you." He grinned knowingly as he straightened, lifting her up to her feet. He kept one arm circling her as she found her balance at the base of the depression that made her slip. To her surprise, chagrin, and pleasure all at the same time, he kept it there when she was stable and stood close beside her.

He smiled. "If you'd like, you can wait right here and I'll come back and help you once I get the horses across."

"I…" she began, stopping herself before she refused. *No, thank you,* she thought, but her voice only said, "Thank you."

His smile grew warmer. "Sit tight. I'll come back as quick as I can."

She only managed to nod in response as he turned and stepped carefully between the horses. Grabbing their reins, he led them on, leaving her to watch.

They had moved several paces before she finally noticed the ripple of cloth against her ankles. Reaching down, she pulled the tail of her skirt out of the water, the hem now soaked. She had managed to hold onto her boots with her other hand.

Sir Magni slid a couple more times and Brenadier skidded once with a whinny, though the knight spoke softly and calmed the stallion and they made it to the far bank without incident. Damian breathed a sigh of relief as the horses scampered eagerly out of the water.

After patting their necks, Sir Magni turned and strode back into the chill water toward Damian. Unexpectedly, her heart drummed in her chest as he approached. His smile widened as he drew near and held out his hand.

"You ready?"

No, she thought. Switching the tail of her skirt to her other hand, holding it and the boots together, she took his hand. A thrill rushed through her with the touch, his skin surprisingly soft and warm. She hadn't noticed he removed his gauntlets. He gripped her hand tenderly though his arm remained stiff and sturdy to support her.

They continued across the river hand in hand. She tried not to rely on Sir Magni too much but when her feet slipped on the mossy river bed she regained her balance much easier with his steady grip supporting her.

When he slid once, his support barely shifted. He grinned. "Sorry."

At last they made it to the far bank and stepped out of the river. Damian let out a relieved sigh as her feet lifted out of the cold water and onto dry, firm stone. Dropping her skirt, she climbed up the stone bank and onto grass, rubbing her feet as she walked to dry them.

"Well, that wasn't too bad, was it?"

Glancing over her shoulder, she found the knight standing close. He leaned over as he rolled down his trousers, pulled his boots on, and strapped on his armour over them. Her cheeks heated up with the way he smiled at her and she could only shake her head in response. Her dress pulled a little heavier on her due to the wet hem but with her boots on it only added weight, the cold and dampness held at bay. The feeling of being held in his arms clung to her more as they mounted the horses and rode on. Throughout the rest of the day, much as part of her wished otherwise, she told herself that it didn't mean anything. He seemed the type of person who would do that for anyone.

After another full day of travelling they stopped the horses at sundown and set up for the night. Damian's attention shifted to Hope as she brushed out the mare's coat and picked out small stones and other detritus in the horse's hooves. The sky darkened from orange to rose while she worked, the eastern horizon deepening to cobalt as stars glinted to life. Eventually, Damian secured a rope halter around the mare's head and left it to graze. From there, she turned and helped the knight with Brenadier by brushing out the stallion's long, curly mane and tail. Leaving her to the task once he finished cleaning the destrier's hooves, Sir Magni retreated to build a fire. After a few more minutes' work, Damian tied Brenadier some paces away from Hope, a necessary precaution after the stallion tried to mount the mare earlier that day, much to the mare's displeasure.

A fire blazed by the time Damian finished and she took a seat before it, cringing at the soreness from the saddle. Opening one of his saddle bags, Sir Magni approached to hand her food.

"Thank you," she said as she took it. He smiled, then sat down right beside her, his knee almost touching hers. Damian looked away, her heart beating faster, and silently ate. She felt his eyes on her while she ate and scooted away before she could stop herself. Now and then, she glanced toward him from the corner of her eye. He returned a meaningful grin. Each time she saw that smile, her cheeks grew warm and she looked away. The stillness weighed on her, the knight's deliberate silence making her skin crawl. She tried to focus on something else as she finished eating and stared across the starlit fields, but she could feel him beside her as though warmth radiated out of him. Still he did not speak.

Finally, she said, "Um, Sir Magni…"

He cut her off with a rich laugh. Her eyes shot open as she spun toward him, finding him grinning widely at her. "Please, Damian, we have a long journey ahead of us and I respect you too much to make you cow to me. Just call me Garrick."

She hesitated. "Ah… alright, Sir Garrick."

He laughed again. "Come on, the Sir makes me feel old." Reaching forward, he touched her chin with two fingers. "Garrick."

Damian thought her pounding heart would cut off all air to her body, but she uttered, "Garrick."

His smile widened. When had he drawn so close to her? "That's better." He dropped his hand and sat back. "What's on your mind?"

"Ah…" Suddenly, she couldn't remember what she had been about to ask him. She looked ahead, certain the fire couldn't conceal the colour in her cheeks.

"Then how about I tell you what's on my mind?"

Her heart lurched with the husky sound of his voice. Turning, she found him drawing close. Tilting her chin up, he moved his face toward hers.

She flinched. He hesitated, eyes opening. She sat still, conflicting impulses tearing at her as sensation rippled through her body.

After a pause, he closed in until his mouth fell on hers. Her heart rattled in her ribcage, pounding as ferociously as it had the night the barge sank. Her lips tingled and the feeling spread, encompassing her entire being. It was more passionate and riveting than she had dreamed of, his mouth opening and taking in hers over and over. Her whole body swelled in anticipation as he leaned her back against the ground, crouching over her. She laid her hands against his breastplate, part of her glad the cool metal hung between them. Her breathing sped as their kiss lengthened.

Finally, his mouth slid away from hers. Her eyelids fluttered open to find him glancing down with a curious expression. Passion so enraptured her that she hardly noticed.

Then, he cried out, "Damian!"

Blinking, she followed his gaze. Where her hands touched his armour, the metal glowed red-hot. She yanked her hands back with a gasp. He rose on his knees, hurriedly unbuckling the side straps of his breastplate to pull the heated metal away.

Damian covered her mouth, eyes enormous in horror. *No, not again. Not again!* She lunged to her feet and ran away from the fire as fast as her feet would carry her.

"Damian, wait!"

A whinny rang through the cool night air as Damian fled, holding up the tail of her skirt. All the incredible sensations from a moment before had been replaced by panic and she ran as if she was being hunted. Frequently, she stumbled over obstacles she couldn't see in the darkness, but she pressed on, desperate to escape.

"Damian!"

She wasn't certain how far she had gone when the knight caught her arm, pulling her to a stop as she spun to face him.

"I'm sorry, I'm sorry, I didn't mean to—"

"Shh, it's okay." He laid his other hand against her cheek, turning her to face him and the steady look he returned. "Just relax. I'm fine."

Tears gathered in her eyes as she gazed desperately at him. "What's wrong with me?"

Reaching out, he wrapped his arms around her and pulled her close.

She pressed against his chest, trying to break out of his grip. "No…" He held fast, his strong arms keeping her close, and after a moment she stopped fighting. He laid her head against his shoulder. Her cheek pressed up against the mesh of his mail, his breastplate gone.

For a moment, she allowed the feeling of his arms circling her to comfort her as though it felt familiar. She breathed in ragged gasps, overwhelmed by the horror of what she had done.

Finally, her panic faded and discomfort with being so close to him resurged. She pushed away and this time he released her. Wiping her eyes, she looked up at him. His expression was calm in the moonlight.

"Did I…"

He leaned back a little, gesturing at his chest. "I'm fine." Dropping her gaze, she tried to examine his mail, but couldn't discern whether it had suffered damage in the darkness. He laid a hand on her shoulder. "Are you okay?"

She nodded. "I'm sorry."

"I know. No harm done." Turning, he gestured toward the distant fire. "Come on, let's go get some sleep." He fell into step beside her as she made her way back, eyes on the ground. Halfway back, he picked up his armour where he had tossed it aside. She tried to look at the breastplate, but he kept it distant enough that she couldn't see whether she damaged it.

She said nothing more as they returned to the copse of trees where they made camp. The horses nickered at their return. Garrick quietly offered her a blanket. Without another word, she lay down on the grass and tried to sleep. Thoughts of what happened stirred through her mind too much for sleep to take her easily. The feelings of horror remained distant but the thoughts that fuelled them circled through her until she finally drifted off.

The room once meant as a dining hall, now largely used for storage but furnished with several tables, was the only room in the fort that would hold all eighteen mages comfortably. The sight heartened Yanuk as he watched the last two enter, one of the older mages helped along by one of the younger. Yanuk knew Crain's hip had been acting up recently and Yanuk nodded in appreciation as the older man hobbled inside. The apprentice shut the door.

"Finally," Helena remarked with a smirk. "Yanuk has kept us all waiting for you."

Crain grumbled as he slowly lowered onto a chair.

"Friends," Yanuk said to the room of assembled mages. "Thank you all for coming."

One of the apprentices leaned forward in his chair. "So what have you learned, master Yanuk?"

Edrand leaned back in his seat, arms folded across his chest. "Out with it, then. You have been busy enough these last days translating that book. I hope it has been worth the effort and Gawthrain's presence."

"Little would be worth that," old Miria replied, to a few honest or nervous chuckles.

"So what does this spell of his do? Is it really as powerful as he believes?" Edrand asked.

Yanuk rubbed his head, fingering his scar. "There is potential for the spell to prove incredibly powerful, and the language used suggests that it is, but the application of it is curious."

"What in blazes does that mean?" Crain asked.

Yanuk straightened. "The spell Gawthrain wishes us to cast is a control spell. It binds a subject to the will of the caster, forcing the subject to obey the commands of the caster. But I do not know what subject he wishes us to bind."

In the silence that followed, Edrand asked, "What could one bind with that spell?"

Yanuk shrugged. "Animals, humans, beings of magic. Perhaps any living creature."

The mages exchanged looks and some whispered excitedly to each other, voices rising as they discussed the possibilities.

"Now that we know what that spell does," Crain remarked, "we do not need Gawthrain. We could choose our own target."

The mages spoke louder and Yanuk raised his voice to be heard.

"Alas, no." Yanuk frowned as everyone quieted. "Gawthrain still has the ingredients required to cast the control spell in that locket."

Murmurs and groans rang out and Helena sneered. "Darkness take that spell of his, and the torn page. We should throw him out and be done with it. Undoubtedly there is more of practical use within that tome."

Yanuk held up his hand against the agreements and arguments that followed her comments. "I fear being rid of Gawthrain would not be so simple." He waited for the others to fall silent before continuing. "I have been too naive."

"What do you mean, Yanuk?"

"What hinders us from casting him out right now?"

"The mercenaries," Yanuk replied.

"You fear Gawthrain turning them against us?"

"No," Crain answered for Yanuk. "Worse. They could expose us."

Yanuk nodded. "They will not tarry long here, idle as they are, and their knowledge of where our home is presents a grave danger to us all."

The murmuring grew louder, ringing off the walls of the small dining hall.

"What shall we do?"

"Fear not, my friends." Yanuk smiled, silencing them. "Is it not time we moved on regardless? If Gawthrain could track us down here, then surely others could as well. This old fort is falling apart beneath our feet and it is only a matter of time before it becomes uninhabitable. We shall find a new home and perhaps this book can show us a better one than this."

"But all our hard work…"

"The crops are only just beginning to sprout."

"Must we really abandon this place?"

Miria snorted. "It's about time. This place is too cold and I have not slept well in years for the noise of the mice."

"What of Gawthrain?" asked an apprentice. "And the mercenaries?"

Yanuk grinned knowingly. "We shall tell Gawthrain we agree to his plans. We will pack up what we can and prepare to move. He will suspect nothing."

Edrand returned a skeptical look. "Do you really think he will fall for that?"

"Gawthrain is a fool. Clever, but too self-absorbed to see truth if he believes he is getting what he desires. It will be easy to deceive both him and his hired swords."

"What shall we do?"

Yanuk straightened. "I will inform Gawthrain that we have discussed the matter and have agreed to his plans. Begin by making tallies of what we have, what we shall need immediately, and what we can leave behind. We can decide what to do with those things that will be difficult to move, such as the flock, at that point."

The mages murmured and spoke to each other about whatever supplies they presided over and what to do with them.

One apprentice spoke up, "What about the book?"

"I shall continue my work translating it as I can," Yanuk answered. "Wherever I am needed in the preparations, however, I will assist. We have much work to do now. I thank you all again for joining me here today and you have my endless gratitude and appreciation for all the hard work you do to maintain our little home. Do not despair over the loss of this fort. This is the start of a new chapter in our lives, and we shall find much better conditions somewhere new." He smiled wryly. "Perhaps even enough to satisfy Miria."

Edrand smirked with a sidelong glance at the elderly woman. "Not likely."

A few people chuckled as they rose and filed out of the room, though some gave a grumbling Miria a wider berth. Only Patrus lingered as the others left, his hooks resting on the table beside Yanuk. Finally, the room emptied and the last apprentice to leave shut the door.

Yanuk stared at the closed door, listening to the mages cross the courtyard to resume their duties. It had been easier than he thought. He had little opportunity to exercise his newly claimed leadership over the mages, but none of those present questioned his choices today.

"They seemed to take it well," he commented quietly.

The amputee sniffed. "Why should they not? Your reasoning is sound. Unfortunately." Patrus turned to him. "So what have you decided about Gawthrain's spell?"

Yanuk hesitated. Helena was right, of course. Casting the spell was a foolish idea whether or not they followed Gawthrain's plans. The first lesson they passed on to new apprentices was discretion. They should never use magic unless absolutely required. Unless they followed through on Gawthrain's absurd plan to assault Albrith there was no reason to attempt the ancient control spell. Yet the desire to feel the power of that spell swelled in Yanuk like an ache. It felt a crime to let such extraordinary power languish, to bury it in their next decrepit home while they continued living their lives hiding from the rest of the world. The feeling had grown as he studied the book. Much as he tried to convince himself that thinking was irresponsible, he couldn't help being drawn to the spell and wondering what target Gawthrain had in mind.

Yanuk shook his head, trying to cast those thoughts out. "I… we shall decide later. Together. All of us. It is too heavy a decision to make alone."

Reaching out, Patrus laid his forearm on Yanuk's shoulder, keeping his hook carefully clear. "You know I trust you implicitly, Yanuk. I would not have survived those first years after my hands were cut off without your help. The others will come around."

A smile crossed Yanuk's face. "Patrus, my friend, if I could gain but half of your devotion among the rest of our comrades, I should have nothing to worry about."

The amputee smiled. "I shall do what I can to convince them that you know what is best." With that, they stood and left the room.

The following days, the fort became a frenzy of activity as they packed everything that had made their abode a home for more than a dozen years. Yanuk lamented the time spent away from the tantalizing puzzle of the spell book but his help was often needed in preparing things to be taken with them or left behind. Wagons were acquired and filled the courtyard as spare supplies, dry goods, and eventually food items were packed. The mages put away everything they owned faster than Yanuk expected. Within days the familiarity and personalization of home disappeared, leaving only a decrepit old border fort behind. As anxious as Yanuk was with the thought of leaving the only place he had known for so long, another part of him felt young again as they prepared to leave on their journey and set off into the unknown.

The courtyard clattered and chattered with noise, louder than the fort might have been since it was originally in use. Yanuk glanced around as straps were secured, the last supplies were loaded onto wagons, and bags were tied to horses. The mercenaries had thankfully remained outside the walls of their home though Yanuk could hear them preparing to leave over the noise of those inside.

As Yanuk looked at his mages, a smile crossed his face. He crossed from person to person, laying a hand on his comrades' shoulders as they finished their work.

"You have done well, my friends. You should feel proud of yourselves. I know we have a long journey ahead of us, but everything will be alright." He smirked as he watched Miria hauling herself onto the saddle of a pony, slapping off the hand of an apprentice trying to assist her.

"Leave off, I'm not infirm." With a groan, she pulled herself up and settled down on the saddle.

All through the courtyard, the mages mounted horses or climbed to the front of wagons. Yanuk spotted Gawthrain atop a black mare near the exit of the fort, his cane tied to the saddle.

"Is everything secured?" Gawthrain called out. Nods and murmurs of assent rang out and the former duke smiled. "Then let us ride out, everyone, and our journey will begin!"

Yanuk narrowed his eyes at the order but said nothing. Striding forward, Yanuk climbed onto the saddle of his horse, a lanky bay gelding. The remaining mages followed suit.

"Everyone, form a line so that we can have an orderly departure. Wagons, bring up the rear."

Yanuk rode to the former duke as the mages lined up. "So, we are setting out to put your plans into motion. Now will you tell us where we ride?"

Gawthrain gave him a knowing smile. "How do you feel about taking a religious pilgrimage?"

Yanuk blinked. "What?"

"We ride for a temple."

Yanuk was baffled. "That is the great, secret location of the item needed for this spell?"

"That *is* what we need for the spell. The only item we could have used to make the spell work has been out of my hands for years. Without that, the only way we can cast the spell is by going to this temple."

"Why is that worth keeping secret? Anyone can find a temple."

"Not this one. This temple has been forgotten for centuries, buried underground and accessible only by a narrow crevice deep underneath the leaf litter of a forest. It took me years to find its remains."

"And what makes this temple so special?"

Gawthrain gave him a knowing grin. "You shall see."

Yanuk pursed his lips as he watched the former duke. "Still keeping your secrets, are you?" Yanuk mumbled under his breath. "And what will you hold over our heads after I cast that spell to ensure our allegiance?" His horse fell in behind Gawthrain's as they entered the hall leading out of the fort.

Emerging to the field beyond the fort, Yanuk watched Gawthrain order the mercenaries to their tasks with curt, barking commands and waving off any questions or concerns returned.

A grin crawled across Yanuk's face. Ideas swirled in his mind as the mages gathered outside the entrance and one rode up beside him.

"Patrus," Yanuk said, turning a dark smile to the amputee, "I think I know how to handle Gawthrain."

CHAPTER 10
EYE OF THE BEHOLDER

UNDER THE LIGHT of day, Damian thought Garrick's armour looked none the worse for wear.

"See?" He tapped the elegant breastplate. "What did I tell you? No harm done." The thought brought her little comfort. Horror stole over her with the memory of what happened the last night, overriding any joy she took from that moment.

My first kiss, and with a handsome, young knight. I can't believe I ruined it so badly.

Her stomach twisted with shame. She shook her head when he offered her food from his bags.

A weary smile crossed his face. "Eat, please. It won't do either of us any good if you go hungry."

Reluctantly, she took the bread and cheese he offered and choked it down.

His grin widened. "Though I know my food stores leave a bit to be desired."

She said nothing.

"Don't worry so much about last night, Damian. That was nothing like what happened in Trent."

A desperate look crossed her face. "I don't lose control that way. Last night was more like what usually happens."

His eyebrows rose and he let out a breath. "Well, that's a relief." Her expression darkened and he held up his hands. "I'm just saying that day in Trent was the first time I saw you do that. I thought that was what I had to contend with on this journey."

She looked away.

Garrick's voice sobered. "So what did happen in the Temple of Time?"

"I… touched something."

"What?"

She shifted. "There was a stone chip on one of the statues. I felt drawn to it, and when I touched it…"

As she trailed off, a strange look crossed his face. "That's it? You touched a piece of rock and your power surged stronger than it ever had before?"

"Yes." As he continued staring at her in bewilderment, she squirmed and averted her eyes. "There was a plaque on the statue that said it was from something that had been blessed by the Goddess of Change."

Sir Magni straightened, his eyes enlarging. "Wait, you touched something blessed by one of the old gods? And that's what caused you to lose control?"

The shock in his voice made her turn curiously to him. "That was only what the plaque said. It wasn't really…" She hesitated at the unwavering look he returned. "I mean, it couldn't really have been…" Once more, she trailed off as he gazed seriously at her. Her skin crawled. "Th… that's impossible. The old gods are gone."

His expression didn't shift. "So are the new ones."

She frowned. "They still watch over us."

His voice softened. "How do you know the Gods of Time don't as well?"

Damian's breath fell short and her blood chilled. A shudder ran through her and she leaned forward, wrapping her arms around herself. "You mean I…"

The old gods, still alive? And I was in one of their temples. Divine Light, I prayed to them! What if they heard me? What if the true gods did?

"I'm sorry, I'm sorry," she pleaded, raising her hands and face to the morning sunlight and spouting off a prayer to the Gods of Light. Even under the warm spring sunshine, she felt cold.

"Damian…"

She shook her head. "They are punishing me."

Reaching out, the knight laid a hand on her shoulder. "I doubt that. It's probably just coincidence. Although, if you were triggered by touching something blessed by the Gods of Time…"

Sniffling, she turned to him. "But that thing can't possibly still hold any power, can it? It was just a fragment of whatever the Goddess of Change blessed. And it's been centuries since the Gods of Light banished the old gods."

"There's a reason they're gods. Their power is not to be trifled with."

That caused another shiver to run through her body.

He gave her shoulder a squeeze. "Whatever it means, we should keep heading toward Misengrad. Come on." Swallowing uncomfortably, she rose and saddled and bridled Hope while Garrick turned to strap on Brenadier's tack.

Damian felt tense throughout the travel and shied away from Garrick's advances. Her anxiety heightened the following day when he led her into a small village on the edge of a swath of barley fields.

"We're going to need to get more food sometime," he said when she expressed her discomfort with entering the town. "I'd rather do it now than when we actually run out. The horses could use the rest anyway."

Damian frowned but said nothing more as they rode into the village.

Heads turned as soon as they came within sight. The villagers stared far more at Sir Magni than at Damian, giving her cursory glances before their eyes returned to the knight. As soon as their horses' hooves set foot on the dirt path through the hamlet, people swarmed them, welcoming him to the village of Rahgden and pleading to him to buy their wares, offer them blessings, share news from throughout the kingdom, mediate some dispute, or mete out justice to what sounded like a band of raiders that frequently harassed the village. Garrick gave brief blessings but refused the other requests, smiling apologetically as he explained that he was on an important mission already. As they rode through the crowds, he dug in his satchel and tossed out handfuls of small coins to the people around them.

That gave Damian pause. She thought of the expense he must have incurred procuring Hope as well as the expensive coin he had used to obtain a room for her the night she arrived in Trent. If he could spend so much money so carelessly and fling those coins into the street for these villagers, he must carry a fortune on him. Travelling alone with his fine armour and steed, he would be a ripe target for thieves.

That must mean he was able to defend himself from them.

He grinned askance at her and she averted her eyes to the road. Although his armour did not enlarge his stature too greatly, with his forked cloak draped behind him and polearm strapped to his saddle, Sir Garrick looked commanding. Every morning and night Damian saw a glimpse of the man beneath the armour. Though his mail and clothes draped fairly loosely, it was clear they covered well-toned muscle. She recalled when he forcibly held her close after she ran from him. His grip was like iron. A shiver ran through her with the memory.

Thank the Light he wants to take me to Misengrad as a friend rather than a prisoner.

As he gleaned directions to Rahgden's sole tavern, the crowd dispersed and the townspeople returned to their tasks. Damian watched them leave, several people staring as they continued and others whispering excitedly to each other.

"Does this happen everywhere you go?"

Garrick grinned. "Usually in small towns like this. Big cities like Trent are no stranger to knights, but these people might not see someone of even my status but once in their lifetimes." A wistful look crossed his face. "And more the better. Out here in the wilds they're likelier to see knights as a result of conflict than chance."

Damian sent him a curious look but said nothing more.

They made their way to the inn, leaving the horses in the care of stable boys. Garrick paid the innkeeper a handsome sum for rations and for the use of one of the two rooms in the building.

The knight handed her the key. "Go on up, I'm going to take a bath while I have the opportunity."

Nodding, she took the key and retreated upstairs. A bath sounded nice, but perhaps she would have one later.

Leaving the key in the door, Damian dropped her things at the end of one bed. Wincing at the discomfort from the saddle, she sat down and watched the street through the open window. There was little activity in the village and her eyelids drooped as she leaned against the window frame. When her head bowed suddenly forward, she lay down on the bed and was soon asleep.

The creak of the door opening woke her. Turning around, her eyes widened. Garrick stood in the doorway, dressed only in the clothes he wore beneath his armour. His damp hair tumbled loose over his shoulders. Without his mail tunic pressing against his body, his shirt hung open and she could see the chiseled muscles beneath. Her cheeks flushed.

He smiled. "How are you feeling?"

She gave him a jerky nod. "Fine, thank you."

His smile widened. "Glad to hear it. The cook is going to make up some food to take with us, hopefully tastier than what I've had so far." He winked.

She looked away, feeling her cheeks heat up.

He chuckled. "I don't think there's much to do in this village."

She shook her head faintly in agreement. She doubted Rahgden was even half the size of Aether.

"So we have the whole evening to ourselves." Reaching out, he pulled the door closed as he stepped into the room. "What shall we do with it?"

Her heart raced with the sound of his voice.

"Any ideas?"

"I…"

Glancing back, he turned the key until it locked. "We could tell stories to pass the time." He pulled the key out of the lock. "Or see if the innkeeper has a board game or dice we could borrow." Damian's heart hammered in her chest as he twirled the key in his fingers. "I'm told I'm fair with a lyre."

His eyes fixed on her with such intensity that she thought he could see straight through her.

He grinned. "Or maybe we should just entertain ourselves right here." He tossed the key to the side, where it bounced against the floor and slid beneath a chest.

Damian leaped to her feet, eyes growing wide. Rounding the other bed, he approached her.

"Garrick," she uttered shakily. She backed away as he drew near. A few paces back she came up against the wall. Her breath fell short as she pressed up against the wall, pinned between the two beds. "Garrick—"

"I like the way you say that."

He leaned down toward her and her lips parted in anticipation.

Then, she pushed him away and cried, "No!"

He stepped back, blinking in surprise.

She shook her head. "I can't. Not after…"

"Damian," he attempted.

"No." The excitement that swept her up a moment ago vanished and a hollow feeling filled her instead. "If I hurt you again I couldn't take it."

His voice softened. "Damian, you're letting this control you."

She fixed a sharp look on him. "Do you think I haven't tried? I have been trying to control this for three seasons. I have tried everything I can think of. Working myself to exhaustion, meditation, herbs, even changing what I eat. I can't even remember how many times it has happened now."

"That's not what I'm talking about. You're letting it control what you do."

A desperate look crossed her face. "What am I supposed to do? I've spent the last year of my life terrified that someone will find out about this."

To her chagrin, he smiled. "I already do."

She shook her head. "I—"

"Damian," he cut across her, taking a step closer. "This is just a part of you. You shouldn't let it define the rest of your life as well."

Swallowing, she glanced over his body, the firm muscle used to carrying the weight of his armour and swinging his voulge. Willing and eager for her, more so than she could say about almost everyone she had met and more than anyone who had seen her eyes. A thrill trembled over her.

"I... I just don't want to hurt you."

He grinned in a way that made her heart flutter. "I'm a dragon knight. I can handle it."

She looked away as he took a step closer, within arm's reach. A part of her wanted to push him away, but the rest of her body desperately wanted to believe him. He had been able to stop her in the Temple of Time in Trent.

Leaning forward, he rested one hand on the wall beside her head. She took in a sharp breath as he came closer.

"What would you do if you didn't have this power?"

She could only stare into his eyes, unable to speak or think of anything to say in response. Lifting his other hand, he tilted her chin up.

"Focus on that instead."

This time, she allowed him to close in until he kissed her. Her body felt like it melted under his touch, her knees trembling as she struggled to hold herself up. His arms slid around her, pressing her body up against his, and she inhaled sharply at the feel of his desire. Her hands rested on his muscular shoulders and biceps, too nervous to move them anywhere though his hands slid over her. Her body shuddered in anticipation and she forgot all about the reason why she didn't want to do this.

His head moved down but before his mouth separated from hers he slipped an arm behind her legs and swept her into his arms. She let out a soft moan as he stepped aside and laid her on the bed. Her breath sped as he climbed onto the bed and straddled her, kissing her deeply. His hands slid up and down her body, thrills racing over her skin. Tentatively, she moved her hands to his chest, relishing the tautness of his muscles through the fabric of his shirt.

Finally, he slipped his mouth away from hers. Straightening, he pulled his shirt off, exposing the chiseled chest and abdomen beneath. Her heart drummed as he tossed the shirt onto the floor. Leaning down, his mouth traced down her neck to the top of her dress. She clenched her fingers against his shoulders.

A crackle of energy tore through her. She heard a snap where her hands touched him and he groaned, stumbling and rolling off the bed onto the floor.

She gasped. "Garrick!" Launching up to a sitting position, she looked down.

"I'm fine," he said through a cough. Her eyes grew huge, though he smiled as he sat up. He grabbed his shoulder, rolling his arm with a faint wince. "It's alright, I'm fine."

She stared, her breath feeling hollow and terror clenching her heart.

"Damian…"

Scrambling off the bed, she raced around the other bed toward the door.

"Damian!"

She tried to open the door to escape, but it remained locked. She yanked desperately at the knob, the door rattling in its frame.

"Damian, it's okay." Still naked to the waist, Garrick jogged over to her. "Relax. I'm fine." He gently touched her arm and she gave up her struggles, her shoulders sagging.

"I can't. I can't do it."

"That's fine. I won't pressure you."

Turning, she glanced at him. A shiver ran through her as her eyes passed across his bare stomach and chest. Her attention was drawn to his shoulders. She couldn't tell if he suffered any injury.

He opened his arms, eyebrows raising inquisitively. She looked away with a faint shake of her head and leaned against the door, wrapping her arms around herself. Turning, he leaned against the door beside her and folded his arms.

"We'll go at your pace. Whenever you're ready, just let me know."

She let out a shaky breath. "I just wish I knew why this was happening to me."

A pause stretched out. Through her raspy breathing, she heard a faint breeze in the street and the distant footsteps of someone walking through the village. She also heard footsteps nearly directly below. Her cheeks flushed with the thought of what the innkeeper might have heard.

When at last Garrick answered, his voice was uncertain. "There is something I can try."

She looked up at him. "What?"

He looked solemn. "I might be able to find out what your magic is, where it comes from."

Her shoulders sank as she stared at him. "Why didn't you tell me this before? I would do anything to know that!"

He looked uncomfortable. "Well, there are risks."

Her expression fell. "What kind of risks?"

"I've only read about this technique. It's not something the Agaesi teach. But if I did it wrong, it could be very dangerous for both of us."

"Oh." She looked away. *Of course it wouldn't be that easy.*

He ran a hand through his hair, eyeing her. She stared at him with the motion, watching his muscles move. "If it worked, though, it might give us a better idea of how to keep your power in check until we reach Misengrad."

She glanced at him, uncertain what to say.

He smiled. "I'll think about it. I'd certainly like to know what your power is, too. For now, shall we just get some rest?"

She nodded and they turned toward the beds in the room. The covers on the far one were slightly rumpled. Damian's cheeks flushed with the memory of lying on that bed with him.

"I'm sorry."

A grin crossed his face. "No harm done."

She felt his eyes on her as she retreated to the bed. With the afternoon growing late, once she closed the shutters the room deepened into darkness and she soon fell asleep.

They left Rahgden the next morning burdened with many more food stores as well as an iron pot and tripod Garrick bought from the local blacksmith. In his company, Damian met few surprised or uncomfortable looks from the villagers before they left. Her seat atop Hope provided a welcome distance that kept most of the people from seeing her eyes.

Although he often met her looks with a smile, Garrick remained quiet and thoughtful throughout the morning. Occasionally she looked over to find his eyes shut in deep contemplation. Farmland faded into open grasses that surrounded them in three directions. Forest soon grew to the south, stretching closer as they travelled.

They walked some paces beneath the trees when they stopped for dinner and ate quietly beneath the canopy, birds chirping all around. At first Damian watched him while they ate, though he spent most of the time staring absently at their surroundings. What was he thinking? Was he still considering what he said to her last night? That had never left her mind throughout the morning as they put Rahgden behind them. Her skin prickled eagerly with the thought of knowing what was this power that had cursed her for so many years. She forced herself not to press Garrick about it. Despite the distance that remained to Misengrad, for the first time since she left Trent she felt excited to reach the Agaesi, to at last know the truth.

Do I really want to know what the cause of this is? It could be something horrible, something far worse than anything I imagined. Even if I do, would it be worth the risks to both of us? It's hardly fair for me to put him in danger simply because I want to know about my ability.

But I do. I've wanted to know this my entire life. Maybe I will find out when we reach Misengrad, but that's still at least two weeks away. And after what happened on the barge and in the Temple of Time, I'm putting people in danger everywhere I go. If this can help me figure out how to control it better, I have to try.

Damian turned to find Garrick's eyes fixed on her. It was clear he knew exactly what she was thinking.

"You want me to read your energy?"

Her heart raced in anticipation. "Yes. If you are alright with it."

A solemn look remained on his face. "It's up to you. If you're not comfortable trying it, we won't, but if you want to proceed, I'll give it a shot."

She chewed her lip, staring at him and trying to see if he wanted her to refuse. Nothing suggested any course of action in his expression or bearing. Either he kept his emotions very strongly in check, a distinct possibility if he had such experience at court, or he was truly leaving the entire decision in her hands.

She hardly had to consider it. "I do."

He nodded, showing no other reaction. "Then sit here before me."

She scooted over until she sat in front of him, her legs crossed like his. "What are you going to do?"

He removed his gauntlets. "I'm going to connect my energy to yours so I could read it as though it was my own."

She blinked. "I don't understand."

A grin crossed his face. "It's an Agaesi thing." She frowned at that but sobered as he straightened and shut his eyes. Reaching up, he laid his hands on either side of her face. "Just try to relax and please don't fight it. I need you to let me in."

Damian wasn't certain what he meant by that. The sounds of the forest rose as he sat unmoving. She wondered when or if she would know something happened.

It didn't take long. A strange tingling spread through her where his hands touched her though it didn't seem like something she actually felt. The sensation crept slowly into her body, into her muscles and blood and numbing the flesh it passed by. It reverberated through her body as she seemed to gaze into something she knew but couldn't see. It felt like fingers probing her soul, digging deeper and deeper until…

An image appeared before her. She stood at the mouth of a valley filled with writhing figures. Men packed shoulder to shoulder in tight formation, wearing archaic clothes and bearing ancient spears and strange curved swords, their bronze armour glinting in the sunlight. All of them faced her as they shouted a rhythmic chant and banged their swords on their shields in near unison. A dark smile spread on her face as she watched them, the sword hanging from her hand a familiar weight and an electric warmth that resonated through her body. The noise of the army almost drowned out the stomping of the field of men arrayed behind her. She felt their anxious energy, their hunger to charge the men below and win their glory.

A cry rang up and the entire valley roared with the simultaneous shout of the assembled warriors below. Raising their weapons, they surged forward, an unending wall of metal and muscle surging toward her. She thrust her sword point up into the sky and shouted a command of her own. The army behind her yelled its support. Then, she rushed forward.

Arrows flew toward them as they charged, striking down many behind her as the pointed shafts rained down. Any that came close to her she merely slapped out of the air. The battle fuelled her strength and by the time she reached the vanguard she struck so hard she clove two men in half with a single blow. Before their first sword stroke could fall she spun and impaled another man clear through his bronze plate. She dove into the formation, the teeming mass strengthening her strokes and speeding her reactions. She slipped out of time, darting through and between her foes with uncanny speed. She had cut a swath through the enemy formation while her forces still grappled with the vanguard, the men behind them struggling to push through and add their blades to the attack. Man after man fell to her blade, dark light rippling and dancing around her as she moved. Despite the sheer numbers of warriors surrounding her in all directions, nary a blow landed on her. And as the battle progressed, each stroke of her sword grew more powerful. Several men fell with one swing, a dozen the next, and a score after that. She let out a laugh that rang throughout the valley over the crashes of blades and cries of men.

Suddenly, the vision tore away from Damian as though her body ripped apart. Gasping for breath, she fell over backward and collapsed on the forest floor. Over the sound of her laboured breathing, she heard the rattle of Garrick's armour and the sound of him wheezing for air. Aside from an uneasy whinny from one of the horses, the rest of the forest lay eerily quiet around them. The birdsong had silenced in the wake of Damian's vision.

She coughed as she rolled onto her side, her entire body tingling as feeling returned to her. Her head spun and she lay still, waiting for everything to settle down. As she regained control of her body, she realized it wasn't her nerves and muscles that quivered. The energy inside her, that power she struggled to control for most of the last year, roiled like waves breaking on rock and it took all her concentration to keep it from leaching out as she lay there.

Finally, she pushed up to a sitting position and looked at Garrick. He crouched on the forest floor, panting heavily and his body trembling as he held himself up on his knees and elbows.

"Garrick?"

He shook his head, still bowed toward the forest floor. "There's… something there."

She gave him a curious look. "What?"

"Inside you." Groaning, he rose to his hands and knees. The troubled look he sent chilled her straight through.

"What do you mean?"

Shaking his head, he leaned back and sat down. "There's some kind of spirit inside you. That's where your magic comes from."

She blinked. "What? How… how did it even get inside me?"

He rubbed a hand roughly over his face, still breathing heavily. She wondered if there was something else to what he saw that he wasn't telling her.

"I can only guess that it happened to you when you were born. When that lightning struck your house."

"But what is this… spirit?"

He let out a heavy sigh. "That, I couldn't tell you. I didn't get a good enough look at it. All I could tell was that it was very powerful and very ancient." Her stomach clenched as she thought of the image that appeared to her. Was that a memory of this spirit? Was that bloodthirsty, deadly creature what hid inside her? The idea sent a shiver down her spine.

She stared at Garrick, the knight looking like the weight of years rested on his shoulders. Her voice dropped. "Garrick, what did you see?"

Finally, he raised his eyes to hers and she started at the haunted look in them. "That it's almost free. Whatever keeps it inside you, it's tied to your magic. Every time you use your magic, it gets closer to escaping. It almost escaped through me while I was connected to you."

Her eyes widened as she absorbed his words. Suddenly, her body felt too weak to hold her up. She wrapped her arms around her midsection, shrinking in on herself.

I have been carrying this thing inside me my entire life. And every night I spent marvelling at the powers I could conjure, I brought myself closer to releasing something that could effortlessly clear a path through fully armoured warriors.

Am I nothing but a vessel for this spirit? If it is released, will it take over my body and will I be gone? Or was I spared at birth only to be a carrier for this spirit? Is there even anything else to me?

She shut her eyes as memories of her father's cloth trade rushed through her mind, of winter nights spent reminiscing with him at home and visits with the other children her age in Aether, now grown, as well as the journey she had undertaken since she left her home weeks ago.

No, she thought, setting her shoulders back. *My life is my own. I will not let this spirit control it. And I must not let it be released into the world.*

She turned a firm look to Garrick. "Let's go. We have to get to Misengrad."

The knight looked deeply troubled but he seemed mollified by her conviction. Nodding, he rose, offering her a hand. She stood and followed him to where they had tied up the horses.

Whatever happens, I must keep this thing from escaping.

Even as she made the vow she could feel the energy within her churning, struggling to break free, and she hoped she could contain the spirit until they reached Misengrad.

Niabi strode silently through the forest, feeling its life energy flow around her. Ancient as the earth beneath her feet, she felt the struggle and promise of the buds and newly fledged leaves striving to spread and reach the sunlight. Chicks fought to break through the hard eggs in their nests while naked and blind squirrels and rabbits mewled pitifully for their mothers in their dens, their only chance of survival. Life was a struggle, as it was with hers.

Alone as ever, she could sense the presence of humans, distant yet constant. Their energy was different but she did not focus on them. She basked in the life blossoming around her, fresh and decaying, established and rising. The dead leaves of the forest floor shuffled under her bare feet. As she stepped past them, earth, grass, and leaf sprang up unharmed, leaving no trace that she had been there. Even her silken robe brushed across the leaves without disturbing them. The energies of this forest, though the humans encroached on it more each year, glowed soft and steady. All was as it should be.

For centuries untold, she had wandered these lands, doing what she could to encourage the natural cycle of life. Never had she received a sign from her gods, her masters. Despair and desperation had long since peaked. The Gods of Light left this world after claiming it and she knew that few things would cause them to return, and those disastrous. She continued their work here in the world of humans, hoping one day to be reunited with those she served unquestioningly.

Suddenly, a wave of dark energy shuddered through the world. Gasping, she stumbled to her knees and grabbed a tree for balance. The thrum of energy was brief but its icy touch lingered. She paused, panting as the strange force ebbed over her. It felt familiar and yet...

Niabi let out a cry as she raised her head. The wave of energy was similar to the storm that rocked nearly the entire continent years ago, yet this was not the wrath of Light.

It was the will of a different god.

A horrified look on her face, she threw herself to her feet and ran through the forest, paying the briefest of attention to the presence of humans so as to avoid them. Whatever the energy was, it had dissipated for now but she could feel that its threat remained. Something kept it contained and she must ensure that it remain that way.

CHAPTER 11
SHADOWS

GARRICK'S VOICE STIRRED Damian from her reverie.

"Damian."

His voice was steady but at that moment Hope let out a frantic whinny and pranced. Damian blinked, startled, and saw what alarmed them both. The sandy shore beneath the horses churned as much as the waves washing in to the beach a few paces away, though no wind or water touched its dunes. Gasping, Damian shut her eyes, feeling the energy writhing through her. With great effort she grasped at the flaring power, slowly settling it until the mare fell still. When Damian opened her eyes the sand above the tide line did not stir. She let out an uneasy sigh.

Garrick smiled. "Good."

She said nothing in response and stared toward the waves flowing in to the shore. That was the third time in as many days that Damian lost control of her power without any emotional turmoil to ignite it. She kept her power reined in as tightly as she could but all it took was a moment for her mind to wander and it would break free and affect her surroundings once more. Containing it afterward grew more difficult each time.

The sound of surf and the smell of salt had accompanied Damian and Garrick for the past day. As the coastline continued northwest, their path intersected with it and they wove through the patches of forest to ride along the shore, taking the most direct path to Misengrad. Damian spent the day looking at the waves as the horses marched through the sand and watching sea birds float on the water or raptors dive.

She remained silent as the beach disappeared and they climbed a winding path leading up a hill. The waves crashed against a rocky bluff to their left. The forest encroached close on their right though only a few gnarled trees grew across the patch of grass they traversed, hardy specimens whose leaves could weather the strong sea breeze. A grey sky hung low overhead, a threat of rain that had lasted all day. Glimpses of a pale spot in the clouds ahead showed that the afternoon waned.

Damian urged Hope quicker up the hill, nothing but sky visible beyond its crest. Even a small fishing village would be a welcome sight if it meant a roof over her head. The past two nights they had spent sleeping on the forest floor, the wind and night creatures whistling and chittering all around. It made for restless sleep along with the image of Garrick's smile. That clung to her memories every night.

She tried to shake off those thoughts as they reached the summit of the cliff, her pulse hurrying for more reasons than one. As she led the mare forward and saw the land ahead, she drew up short with a gasp. Garrick straightened on Brenadier's saddle beside her with a low whistle.

No villages could be seen, only more forest spread out below. These woods, however, looked nothing like any she had seen. As the hill sloped down to another beach, the occasional red-leafed tree that grew in the forest took over. For a patch of wood that stretched out almost as far as she could see, not a single green tree grew.

"I've heard of the Red Forest of Mierre," Garrick remarked, "but honestly I wasn't expecting the rumours to be true."

Damian could find nothing to say as she stared at the red forest. The foliage wasn't the fiery red-orange of autumn but ranged from a deep burgundy to a purple-red so dark as to be nearly black. There was little colour and less light. It looked ominous.

Garrick shrugged and smiled. "Well, we might as well set up camp in there."

She gave him an uncomfortable look. "You want to sleep in there?"

"We've seen plenty of trees like that in the forest already. I doubt it's dangerous. Besides, I'm sure most people would stay away from it."

Damian frowned. That was likely true and the red forest was so large that they wouldn't be able to reach its other side before nightfall. The hill they stood atop dropped in sharp curves away from the sea so they wouldn't be able to make camp in a normal part of the forest without backtracking. Still, she didn't like the look of that red forest.

"Come on. It'll be fine. I see a creek up ahead, maybe you can make some stew for dinner like you did the other night?" He winked, her heart fluttering in response. Dismounting, he led Brenadier down the hill and Damian reluctantly followed.

If anything, the red forest seemed more foreboding up close. The dark leaves made it very dim inside. With an overcast sky above, it looked like already underneath the canopy. No green foliage could be seen anywhere within. Even the ferns, weeds, and undergrowth grew in the same shades as the leaves of the trees with only an occasional patch of tiny white flowers breaking up the solid curtain of red. Damian shifted uneasily as she followed Garrick into the forest.

She looked around constantly as they removed the horses' tack and set up their camp. The sounds of the forest were the same as any other, the animals that lived here apparently not bothered by their dark home.

The sun hung above the horizon by the time they settled in, golden sky visible through the trees over the water, but deep in the red forest the fire Garrick built provided the only useful illumination. The trees on the edge of the forest rustled from the sea breeze though the wind that stirred the trees farther inland faded with the day.

Night fell while Garrick cared for the horses and Damian simmered the stew she prepared from creek water and their rations. Outside of their bubble of light the forest was the same pitch black as any other at nighttime. The firelight that touched the trees and undergrowth provided a constant reminder of the strangeness of their camp site.

Saddles and bridles under his arm, Garrick strode back to the fire with a smile. "How's it coming?"

Damian shrugged as he set the horses' tack down nearby. "I don't think it will taste as good as it was last time. We used up the rest of the parsley we found last night."

"Well, it'll still be a lot better than anything I could make. Anyway, you go ahead and have your half."

Then, he sat down directly beside her. The impulse to scoot away took Damian before she could chastise herself for it. The knight didn't seem affected by her moving away. He smiled as she picked the small pot off its tripod and ate. The forest lay silent around them, the horses calmly grazing some paces away.

His closeness felt like a furnace, radiating warmth against her. As she had many times since that afternoon in Rahgden, she lamented the loss of his touch and wished she were not alone with him at the same time. A shiver spread over her body with the memory, yet uneasiness clung to the pit of her stomach as she thought of what she had done to him. She saw no signs of burns on his chest from their first kiss nor did she see any wounds from the lightning that passed between them. He had shown no signs of injury. Still, discomfort tempered her desire in equal measure.

She cast a furtive glance to him. He met it with a curious look and she hastily returned her attention to the stew, her cheeks growing warm.

Suddenly, Garrick laughed. She stared at him with wide eyes. He only gave her an amused smile.

"After everything that's happened, you're still thinking about Rahgden?"

Embarrassment flooded her though it was quickly followed up by disappointment so severe it made her chest ache. So there it was. She had ruined her chances with him. Tears stung her eyes and she fought not to let them run free. Without facing him, she pushed the pot of stew, now half empty, toward him. Her voice was thick. "The rest is yours." The weight of the pot lifted from her hands and she snatched her arms back.

"Look, it's not that I'm not interested anymore."

Cautiously, she turned to find a sultry smile cross his face.

"Far from it," he purred.

Her innards spun and her cheeks flushed. Certain her face was as red as the foliage around them, she looked away.

Garrick's voice sobered. "But the message has been made pretty clearly that we have bigger things to worry about at the moment."

Damian hunched her shoulders and wrapped her arms around herself. The energy within her roiled and she struggled to suppress it.

"Tell you what," the knight continued. "Once we get to Misengrad and get this spirit taken care of, then we can take some time alone together. Does that sound good?"

She met his eyes, then nodded very faintly. He laid a hand against her cheek, leaned in, and kissed her deeply. The short hairs flecking his jaw scratched at her chin, but she hardly noticed it. Her heart and her entire body swelled with the sensation.

He pulled away a moment later and looked her in the eye. "Consider that a promise." She leaned back, her heart pounding, as he held the stew pot and began to eat. For a moment, she couldn't help but stare as he slid the spoon she had been using out of his mouth.

Swallowing hard, she rose and walked to the edge of their camp and completely failed to come up with an excuse for departing. "I… will be right back."

He said nothing and gave her an amused smile as she stepped beyond the trees lining their small clearing.

Turning, she took a few steps into the trees but stopped. Beyond the light of their fire the forest was pitch black. Was it darker than a regular forest? Damian couldn't be certain but she felt penned in and exposed at the same time. She could barely make out the outline of her own feet and couldn't see any details in the forest floor.

As she turned to head back to the safety of the fire, a glint of light to the side caught her eye. She turned, but saw nothing.

Then, another flash came closer from her other side. When she turned to its source, a smile crossed her face. A palm-sized orb of light hovered in the air within arm's reach. As she focused on it, another two flickered behind it. Glancing around, she found a dozen of them floating around her. She reached a hand out to the nearest one and it passed over her fingers.

From the corner of her eye, she saw Garrick slowly rise from his place beside the fire. "Sprites."

Damian watched one float in a slow arc around her a handspan from her head. "Is that what they're called?"

"You didn't know?"

She shrugged and stepped closer to the fire, the sprites circling her. "I've never spoken with anyone about them. I always thought they were something else I experienced that no one else did."

"Well, many people see them, though I suppose they would be more interested in you."

She gave him a curious look, a sprite hovering silently beside her ear. "Why?"

"They're attracted to magic. They probably want to have a look at you."

"Oh." She watched another glide over the fire, unconcerned with the sparks that drifted up from the flames. "Have you seen them before?"

"Occasionally, but never this many or this close."

She murmured. "I used to see them on my father's market journey. At first I was afraid of them, but as I grew up I came to enjoy them. The nights we spent camping along the road I would sneak out of the tent to look for them, usually a little bit north of here. I saw them every year. They were always friendly and welcoming and I never had to hide my eyes around them." Grief twisted her stomach as she thought of her father and she struggled to push back the misery. "So… what are they?"

An unreadable look crossed the knight's face. "Memories. They're some of the last fragments of magic left in the world, especially since the Century Storm." Damian peered intently as one passed close to her but as ever, she could make out no shape within the glow. Garrick smiled wryly. "I guess that's why they're drawn to you. When you're so rare, it means that much more to find a kindred soul."

She frowned uncertainly but before she could say anything in response the sprites suddenly scattered, darting up and through the trees in streaks of light. Damian held her breath, watching them leave.

"Did… did I do something to frighten them?"

He grinned. "They're known for being fickle. Sometimes, they'll…"

He cut himself off and he and Damian turned at the same time. Something had caught her attention though she had not heard or seen anything. It was more like a thrum of energy through the forest, something strange and intangible yet discernibly present. Somehow, although Damian could see no difference, the red forest seemed more alive. She heard nothing but the rustle of wind on the leaves.

Shuffling to her left drew her attention. She barely saw Garrick move yet by the time she turned her head to face him he held his voulge in his hands. The wide blade at the end of its long haft hovered above the ground as he scanned the forest. Damian tensed, gazing around at the dark wood.

"Who's there?" Her voice trembled as her eyes darted through the trees.

The only thing that answered her was the wind. It seemed too regular to be a breeze. She looked at Garrick but he remained focused on the forest.

Damian tried to draw more strength into her voice. "Show yourself!"

The sound of footfalls rang out, light as a rabbit. Damian crouched, Garrick brandishing his voulge a few paces away. Following the noises, she caught a glimpse of a pale, silken robe before it disappeared behind a tree. The sound of the leaves shuffling under Damian's shifting feet seemed grating compared to the feathery steps of this approaching being.

As it stepped out from behind the tree, Damian's eyes enlarged and she drew in a breath and Garrick cursed. The robe was a long, elegant garment in shifting shades of pastel colours, rich and delicate as flower petals, shimmering like silk with no seams and cut in a style Damian had never seen before. It covered the impossibly tall body of a woman, standing head and shoulders higher than anyone Damian had ever met, graceful as a willow and thinner than her.

At the top of the robe rose the head of a fox.

Solid golden fur rippling in the breeze, the fox woman turned solid black eyes like a squirrel upon Damian. Damian trembled as she took in the sight before her. "Wh… what is that?"

The long muzzle tilted up slightly and sharp fangs showed as it spoke. "I am Niabi, servant of Ganodu."

Garrick's voice was incredulous. "You're a malakh."

Enthralled at the sight of the animal face speaking, it wasn't until Garrick replied that Damian absorbed the creature's words.

Damian's eyes grew huge. "What?"

The dark eyes shifted, apparently glancing at the knight, though it continued facing Damian. "Yes."

Damian could hardly breathe. In the Time of Gods and Magic, malakhs, mystical servants of the deities, had been common. After the war between the old gods and the new, when the Gods of Light left the world to watch from a distance, most of their servants left with them. Now alive strictly in folklore, malakhs were as ancient, mystical, and revered as the gods themselves.

Damian's words came out haltingly. "What… why have you come here?"

Rounded animal toes with sharp claws peered out from beneath the stunning robe as Niabi stepped forward a pace. "I have come for the being within you."

Damian straightened, though Garrick regarded the malakh cautiously.

"The spirit?"

The fox woman's dark eyes narrowed as she raised a hand, holding it palm down toward Damian. "Spirit is far too kind a word for the being known as Nephrita."

Damian looked curiously at Garrick.

He raised his head, his eyes widening. "Nephrita? Child of the Gods of Time?"

The malakh's next words sent a chill through Damian.

"The Goddess of Chaos. Emissary of destruction. One who

would have destroyed this entire world, as well as the True Gods, to achieve her own ends."

Damian's whole body felt cold and all she could think about was the vision she had when Garrick tried to read her energy. The dozens of warriors she cut down in a matter of seconds, the army of brutal followers at her back. The added strength she seemed to gain from the battle.

A goddess? The Goddess of Chaos? The most infamous, powerful, and dangerous being ever to walk this land? That's what's inside me?

"But how…" Damian gasped as she tried to back away from the advancing malakh but her feet held fast against the forest floor. Looking down, she found dark red vines coiled around her boots, rooting her in place.

"What the…" Garrick tried to draw nearer to Damian but vines snaked over his feet as well. "What are you doing?"

The malakh did not so much as look at him. "The balance must be restored."

Damian shook her head. "I don't understand. How did this goddess even get inside me?"

The fox woman returned an implacable gaze as she approached. "When she was defeated so many centuries ago, she was imprisoned in a void from which there was no escape. Yet some foolish humans who would have resurrected her nearly succeeded in breaking the bonds of her imprisonment eighteen years ago."

Garrick paused in his struggles against the vines binding his legs. "The Century Storm. Are you saying that's what caused it?"

"How…" Damian attempted, trailing off as the fox woman came within a handful of paces. Damian leaned back, nearly falling over as the malakh approached with furred hand held out.

"Damian!" Garrick's eyes flicked between Damian and the fox woman. "What are you going to do to her?"

The malakh simply answered, "What I must."

"Which is what, exactly?"

Damian glanced at Garrick, struggling against the vines holding him in place, before returning her eyes to Niabi. "Can you get her out of me? I don't want to bring the Goddess of Chaos back. Please, tell me you have the power to free me from her influence!"

The malakh stopped, and somehow Damian could see the look in Niabi's eyes grow indifferent. "Your spirits have become too intertwined."

Damian's heart turned to ice. "What?"

Slowly, the fox woman advanced. "There can be no separating her spirit from yours without a chance of her breaking free. I cannot risk that happening."

Damian leaned back though the malakh stood but two paces away.

Garrick looked stricken and angry at once. "Damian is an innocent here. She's done nothing to deserve this."

The malakh did not react. "The balance must be restored."

Damian yanked at her legs, trying to free her feet, but the vines were like oak roots grown over her and wouldn't budge. "Wait! What does that mean?"

"It means," the fox woman stated as she reached her hand toward Damian's chest, "that the threat of Nephrita must be put to an end here and now."

Before Damian could react, the fox woman touched a finger to Damian's heart. A ripple of energy and numbness spread through Damian.

"Damian!" Garrick exclaimed.

Damian heard rustling before feeling returned to her muscles. When she could move, she found vines coiled around her wrists, pulling her arms toward the ground as other strands of ivy wrapped around her shoulders and held her upright. Damian fought to pull her arms or legs free or thrash out of the constricting plants but she was soon trapped, unable to move and helpless as the foliage gripped her. The malakh stood tall before her, dark eyes staring down at her fruitless struggles. More vines and ferns grew and twisted around Damian's body, slowly cocooning her. A hollow feeling spread through her.

Suddenly, Garrick let out an unearthly yell. He slammed the blade of his voulge through the vines coiling around his feet, severing them, then lunged toward the fox woman with inhuman speed.

It all happened so quickly Damian couldn't react. A thick, red-leafed branch beside the malakh snapped aside like a whip, slapping Garrick hard through the air to slam into a tree and crumple to the ground. The fox woman never moved.

"Garrick!" Damian tried to move but her legs up to her knees were encased in ivy and more wrapped around her upper body. Small tendrils poked into her legs, stabbing with increasing pressure as they tried to burrow into her skin.

Then, the roots of the plants at her feet crackled. Damian struggled to look down and found the base of the vines had become stone. As she watched, the stone crept slowly up the strands and leaves toward where the ivy dug into her flesh. Damian's breath raced as she met the uncaring look in the malakh's eyes, the fox face simply watching her.

I'm going to die, Damian thought. *She is going to turn me into stone for this being inside me.* The malakh's words rang in her head, the contempt for Damian's life. *This goddess I have never known.* Damian's hands trembled and curled into fists. *This burden that was placed upon me at birth and then ignored until now.* She stared at the malakh with narrowed eyes.

"This is the gods' solution?" Damian spat. "I have been praying for release from this my entire life!" She fought and strained her muscles yet nothing stopped or slowed the vines creeping over her body and jabbing at her skin or the stone hardening the plants at her feet. Her blood boiled and she cast a withering look at the malakh. "I have done everything the Seers say! Does my devotion mean nothing to them?" Damian pulled and struggled against the ivy, her heart and breath racing, but the malakh did not move, eyes never wavering from Damian's.

"Why would they even give me this trial if they only meant to sacrifice me for it?" Damian's voice rose in pitch and volume in her frustration. The horses tied nearby whinnied and shuffled their hooves. "I never asked for this!" Damian tried to summon magic, but as soon as the energy roiled at her fingertips the vision of the valley flashed through her mind. Curling her hands into fists, she settled her power.

Damian levelled a look at the fox woman as she withheld her magic. "I have done everything I can to try to control this. Are you saying that means nothing to you?"

The malakh did not react.

Tears of frustration streamed down Damian's face as stone encased her feet and vines wrapped around her chest. She looked to Garrick but he could barely move as he lay on the forest floor.

"I cannot believe..." Damian's voice cut off as the ivy pressed in tightly on an exhale and she could no longer breathe. Vines wrapped over her neck and head as she gasped feverishly for air that her chest could no longer hold. Damian sent a last desperate look to the fox woman as leaves shadowed the edges of her vision. Still the malakh made no reaction. Damian felt the strands digging into her legs growing hard and cold.

Crack!

Damian pitched forward as the sound cut through the rustle of spreading leaves. The rock-hard vines tumbled limply as she collapsed, the stone around her feet and ankles crumbling while she dropped. She gasped in a deep lungful of air, panting and coughing as she breathed unobstructed. A tangled web of ivy lay over her like a blanket.

While she tried to push out of the nest of foliage, quiet footfalls drummed over and someone tore the plants away. Damian rose to her knees to find a familiar face before her.

She froze, her eyes enlarging. "Domino?"

The mercenary kneeled before her, his eyes passing over her body.

"Are you injured?"

His deep voice reverberated through her, followed by a shiver. *He came back. He saved my life again.* Fear remained but some of the tension in her shoulders melted away as he helped her up. "No, I'm fine. Thank you." As she raised her head she saw the amulet she had noticed before. Strangely, in the dark night she could see it clearly. A round bloodstone pendant with pewter backing and chain hung around his neck. Pewter bird wings circled the stone and the specks of red within vaguely resembled an eye.

A glint of gold at the corner of her eye caught her attention. Turning, Damian found the fox woman lying unmoving on the forest floor, eyes shut. Domino's sword laid beside the malakh, removed from its belt but still in its scabbard. The leather wrapping was peeling off and a split was visible along the wooden lower edge.

A thousand thoughts rushed through Damian's head. She couldn't focus enough to speak any of them. He nodded toward the horses. She stared at him for a moment. Then, with a shaky nod, she hurried to retrieve the saddles and bridles and stumbled over the uneven forest floor to the grove where Garrick secured the horses.

A third, dark horse waited next to Hope and Brenadier, the starlight casting dappled shadows over its lathered coat. Damian's hands fumbled as she saddled the horses and replaced their rope halters with bridles. She tried to hurry but she could barely see what she did and she could hardly focus on the task after the night's events. Fear, confusion, wonder, and relief swam through her mind at once and caused her heart to race.

By the time she had the horses ready, she found Domino approaching. The mercenary helped Garrick along with one of the knight's arms over his shoulders. Domino carried their equipment and his sheathed sword with his free hand. The fire had been extinguished but by its embers Damian saw that the fox woman's feet and hands had been bound behind her back. The jungle of ivy, some of it petrified, lay beside her.

Domino brought the knight to Brenadier. Before the mercenary could help him onto the horse, Garrick cut in weakly, "Wait. Bren, down." The destrier kneeled on its front legs and Garrick climbed onto the lowered saddle. With a pat to the stallion's neck, the horse rose to its hooves. Domino handed Garrick his voulge and bag, then moved toward the dark horse.

Damian took a step toward the mercenary and hesitantly reached a hand out. "Domino, I…" She trailed off, uncertain what to say.

He stood before her, tall and unfazed and immutable. He simply nodded at her. "Later."

That single word eased so much of her worry that she smiled faintly. She mounted Hope as he climbed onto his horse and without another word the three of them rode away.

Silence hung heavily over the dark night, thick clouds noiselessly creeping closer and blanketing the stars. On the ground the wind had stilled and no creature stirred beneath the restless dark. The crickets that eagerly sang their freedom from their winter slumber seemed subdued. As the clouds tumbled closer it felt like the world held its breath.

The camp site had grown quiet as darkness descended over the land. Tents huddled around the large fire at its centre, helping to shield its light from view. Perched at the top of a ravine and scattered with trees, the camp sat alone and apart from the outside world. As the moon glowed behind the cover of the clouds a few mercenaries wandered. The horses tethered at the edge of camp slept silently. Beneath the canvas cloth of one of the larger tents, however, a beeswax candle burned.

"Is that all of it?"

Yanuk took the wooden box from Patrus's hooks and opened it. It felt heavy. Turning it into the light of the candle, he smiled as he glimpsed the contents.

"Are you certain of this, Yanuk? This is a dangerous gamble. If they should refuse…"

Yanuk gently shut the lid, slipping the box inside his tunic. "Do not worry, Patrus. This should be more than enough to convince them."

"Perhaps I should accompany you."

"No, I need you to find that amulet, as well as the map to this temple if possible. I am certain I can handle this."

Picking up the candle, Yanuk opened the trunk it sat on. Rooting through, he pulled out a small burlap pouch. A grin crept across his face. "Very certain."

Patrus nodded as the first rain drops tapped the roof of the tent. Yanuk's smile widened as he glanced at the dark spots appearing against the canvas. "Helena said the rain would be heavy tonight. This will be perfect." Rising, Yanuk shut the trunk and replaced the candle on it before turning to Patrus and laying a hand on the amputee's shoulder. "Remember, Patrus, discretion is of utmost importance. I have utter faith in you."

Patrus nodded.

Yanuk tied the pouch to his belt and stepped out of the tent, taking up a lantern on his way out.

Outside, Yanuk saw no movement through the steady drizzle, the bonfire popping and sizzling under its assault. He raised his hood, turning the lantern back and forth as he tried to peer through the shadowy trees. He heard nothing. A frown crossed his face. "At least, I certainly hope this will not prove to be a mistake." Carefully, he stepped beyond the light of the central fire and made his way around the camp site to a pond nestled within a grove of trees. There he stopped, glancing around as he waited.

"My man tells me you got somethin' to say to me."

Yanuk gasped, finding Vitro leaning against a tree barely three paces away. Yanuk had not noticed the mercenary though the lantern light illuminated his form clearly. Yanuk breathed slowly, trying to ease his racing heart.

"A question for you, actually."

"Well, out with it. His lordship'll have a fit if he finds out I'm not outside his tent."

"Mm." Yanuk smiled as he glimpsed the measuring expression on the mercenary's face. "You are devoted to him?"

The mercenary gave him a cautious look. "Long as he keeps his word about payin' me."

Yanuk nodded, rain dripping off his hood with the action.

"What's your question?"

"Whether that devotion can be swayed."

Vitro raised an eyebrow. Yanuk reached into his tunic and pulled out the box. Opening the lid, he showed it to the mercenary. Even in the darkness, Yanuk saw Vitro's eyes grow wide as the mercenary glimpsed the gold coins filling the box. Rain clinked against the metal as it dripped through the foliage above. Vitro reached forward and scooped out a handful of coins, listening to them jingle and thud heavily as they fell back in. Yanuk's arms sank under the additional barrage.

"That is, of course, the first half of your payment."

Vitro's eyes snapped up.

Yanuk shut the lid of the box. "The rest will come once we reach our destination. If, that is, you are amenable to this change of plans."

Vitro hesitated though his eyes remained fixed lustily on the box. He glanced in the direction of Gawthrain's tent, eyes narrowing and upper lip curling. Straightening, he faced Yanuk. "I think we can make a deal."

"Excellent." Yanuk gave him the box, leaving his hand outstretched as the mercenary leader took the payment. Vitro shook Yanuk's hand, cradling the box in his free arm.

"So I take it you want us to take care of his lordship, eh?" Vitro reached for a knife on his belt.

Yanuk hesitated. Yes, that would be the sensible solution. Gawthrain would never suspect his own mercenary and the kill would be easy, clean, and perhaps painless, more than the former duke deserved. Yanuk should allow Vitro to rid them of Gawthrain.

Reasonable as Yanuk knew those thoughts were, they failed to change his mind.

"I will handle Gawthrain." Turning, Yanuk continued along the outside of the ring of tents. "But I would recommend you be a little late returning to his tent."

The mercenary grinned as Yanuk stepped away from the pond, the rain falling steadily as he cleared the shelter of the trees. The cold crept through Yanuk's shoulders and his cloak hung heavily as he made his way across the softening ground.

He shivered. "Thank the stars it is nearly summer. Though I could stand warmer nights still."

Picking his way carefully through the trees, Yanuk circled the camp, examining the tents as he passed. After walking past the temporary corral erected for the horses, he found Gawthrain's tent, larger than all the others. Yanuk sneered, remembering the interior with its unnecessarily lavish furnishings, the opulence Gawthrain made Vitro's mercenaries set up every night as though they were his personal servants. Crossing beneath the cover of a large tree east of the tent, Yanuk watched the shelter for a long moment. He saw no light and no movement within.

Suddenly, a burning brand from the fire waved up and down twice in front of Gawthrain's tent. Blinking, Yanuk saw Patrus where no one stood a second earlier, a rolled-up sheet of parchment wedged under the amputee's arm beneath his cloak. Yanuk smiled as Patrus tossed the brand back in the fire and hurried away.

Tugging his wet cloak off his shoulders, Yanuk set the lantern down some paces away and moved to the west side of the tree. He retrieved the burlap pouch off his belt and loosened the strings, careful to hold the opening beneath his cloak and out of the rain. Reaching into his sleeve, he pulled out one of the translated pages he had written from the spell book. He grinned.

"Ah, that your own plans would be your downfall. You think a fortunate birth makes you powerful? I will show you true power."

Carefully holding the page out of the rain, Yanuk chanted the words he had transcribed on it. As he did, he scattered ground-up sea shells from the pouch on the earth around the tree, careful to avoid the roots. Energy thrummed through his fingers as the powder drifted to the earth though he detected no obvious change. Squinting in the hooded lantern light, he spread the ground shells in a semicircle several paces around the western side of the tree.

As he finished his chant and emptied the pouch, he could neither hear nor see any difference in his surroundings. He paused for a moment, every nerve in his body tensed. Then, his feet began sinking into the earth. He hurried backward, his boots squelching through ever softer mud until he cleared the patch of powdered shells.

The feeling of the magic resonating through him made his entire body tremble and each second ticked into eternity. For a long moment Yanuk watched, holding his breath. The grass and flowers around the western side of the tree sank into the mud, leaving an inky pool that splattered with falling rain and glistened in the light of the lantern.

"Come on, come on," he muttered under his breath, staring at the tree.

Then, the tree leaned toward him. Grinning widely, he rushed around the pool of mud and grabbed the lantern while he fled. Outside the circle surrounding the tree, the ground was much firmer. Though the rain continued falling, no water beaded the grass beneath his boots. At a safe distance, he turned and watched.

The western side of the tree sank slowly into the watery mud, the trunk seeping underground as the roots on the eastern side held. As it tipped farther and farther over, the firm earth beneath the eastern roots pulled upward. Yanuk's heart hammered in his chest as he watched, leaning forward and gesturing with his hands as though he cheered on a joust.

Finally, the roots tore up the dry earth on the eastern side and the tree tipped over. To Yanuk's surprise, he heard nothing over the steady wash of rain until the top branches smashed into the ground. Leaves rustled and branches snapped as the tree fell, the thick trunk crashing into and flattening Gawthrain's tent, support beams splintering and the canvas crumpling beneath it. The earth trembled as the tree at last slammed against the ground. Yanuk held his breath while he watched the tree crush the tent, awed and uneasy with the swiftness of the destruction. Yet his blood rushed with the power he had just wielded, the effortlessness with which he had caused such damage.

Tent flaps flew open through the camp, the impact and noise drawing out mage and mercenary alike. Yanuk steeled his features, listening to them chatter anxiously and stare at the smashed tent.

As Yanuk crept around the mound of earth torn from the base of the tree, snarled roots snaking out of the dampening dirt, he saw a dark shape crawl out from the ruined tent through the tangle of tree limbs away from the rest of the camp site. Yanuk paused, frowning, until he saw Vitro slinking around the edges of the tents in pursuit of the figure. Hoisting the lantern, Yanuk hurried around the jagged crater in the earth toward the camp. He turned wide eyes to the smashed tent.

"Gawthrain!"

The mages turned at his call.

"Yanuk?"

Donning a baffled expression, Yanuk faced the mages gathered around Gawthrain's tent. The mercenaries were inconspicuously absent. "What happened?"

Edrand gave him a skeptical look. "Did you not see?"

Yanuk shut the doors on his lantern as he stared at the destroyed tent. "I was answering a call of nature. I heard nothing until the tree fell." He stepped toward the tent, though the snarl of branches made it difficult to draw close. "Gawthrain! Can you hear me?"

"Come now, Yanuk, nobody could have survived that," said one of the other mages.

"I wish," Yanuk mumbled under his breath. He turned toward the crowd. "Is anyone else harmed?" They all murmured assurances and he nodded. "It is an unfortunate accident that has befallen our, ah, ally." He caught a glimpse of Vitro approaching the side of Yanuk's tent, sheathing a sword over his shoulder. "We should perhaps check the stability of the other trees nearby, but for now, let us rest. We shall decide what to do next at daybreak when the weather improves." A couple of the apprentices tried to push through the branches to assess the damage but most of the others nodded assent and made their way back to their tents, drawing hoods up over their heads against the increasing rain.

Yanuk watched for a moment, then strode to his tent where Vitro waited in the shadows.

"Did you hear anythin'?"

Yanuk gave the mercenary a puzzled look.

Vitro scoffed with a grin. "He started to make a ruckus 'til he saw me coming. Got to his horse 'fore I could catch him. You want us to go after him?"

"No need." Yanuk looked to the ravine dropping behind the crushed tent and fallen tree. "He will not get far in his condition. And even if he reaches civilization, what can he do now? Still, keep a close watch tonight to be certain."

Vitro nodded. "Aye, Lord Alganov."

"Lord Alganov," Yanuk murmured as Vitro turned into the darkness surrounding the camp. Yanuk grinned. "I like the sound of that." Turning, he hurried beneath the flap of his tent and peeled off his sodden cloak. Patrus waited inside, the parchment spread out on the trunk of spell ingredients. Yanuk's heart hammered in his chest. "Did you get it?"

Smiling, the amputee reached into his tunic and pulled out the amulet Yanuk had not seen since he met Gawthrain.

Yanuk let out a breath that trembled with anticipation as he took the locket and opened it. The tear along the bottom portion of the sheet inside precisely matched the torn page in the book. He had looked at that page enough times to know the shape of the rip by heart. He had everything he needed to cast one of the most powerful spells in history. The thought sent a thrill of excitement through him.

Patrus gestured at the parchment on the trunk with a hook. "I also got the map, and it is a good one."

Tearing his eyes from the torn page, Yanuk followed the amputee's eyes. To his surprise, he found an excited spark in Patrus's eyes and the amputee could barely restrain himself as he grinned.

"Yanuk… Gawthrain's plans were even more ambitious than we imagined."

Holding his breath, Yanuk leaned forward and studied the map. The entrance to the temple was clearly marked and notes were written as to how to access it. It wasn't until Yanuk lowered his eyes to the legend hand-written at the bottom of the map that he found who the temple paid tribute to and who Gawthrain's target was. Yanuk's eyes widened and an excited smile spread on his face.

"The Goddess of Chaos."

Chapter 12
Nephrita

"How are you feeling?"

Garrick winced as he slowly lay back on the blanket spread out for him. He assessed his symptoms as he glanced around the small hunting shack they had found for refuge. His head ached, though it didn't throb like it had after the malakh hurled him into a tree. No dizziness or vision loss, his memory seemed intact, and he hadn't bitten his tongue from the force of the impact.

I didn't stand a chance against her. Nothing I could do could have stopped her. The thought made him uneasy.

He rubbed his head. "No lasting damage, I don't think. Just sore."

Damian nodded, a halo of orange light surrounding her from the fire on the opposite side of the room. She removed the other blanket from his saddle bag and slid it under his head. He closed his eyes.

And her power comes from a god?

He was way out of his league.

When she spoke, her voice was hesitant. "Who is Ganodu?"

He wasn't surprised she didn't know. The Seers rarely spoke the gods' names, focusing on the purity of their aspects rather than their more human flaws. Even the Agaesi didn't teach their names anymore though Garrick had spent enough time in their library to know.

"The Goddess of Life."

"Oh." An uncomfortable look crossed her face. "And... Nephrita?"

He turned his head to face her. "What do you know of the Goddess of Chaos?"

She shifted, avoiding his eyes. "Just what the Seers teach. That she was defeated by the God of Strength and that spelled the downfall of the old gods."

"The fact that she could hold her own against the God of Strength says something right there."

Damian hunched her shoulders at that.

"That was only the end of her tale, though. She built up quite a reputation for herself in the Time of Gods and Magic, as much as any of the principal gods."

Damian shivered. She opened her mouth to say something but hesitated. Without facing him she finally said, "I will go get some water from that creek we passed."

Garrick leaned his head back against the folded blanket as she removed the iron pot from his bag and walked out of the shack, leaving him alone.

A figure appeared in the doorway. He glanced over, concerned that Damian had returned and he had lost a moment in time, but instead he found the Crow entering the shack, a pile of branches in his arms. Garrick raised himself on an elbow to watch the mercenary cross to the fire and add more wood. Garrick's eyes narrowed. The mercenary's appearance was highly suspicious. It seemed unlikely that any trial would have exonerated him quickly enough to allow him to follow them here. How could the Crow have gotten out of prison already? Why devote so much energy to finding them? What did he want from Damian?

A glint on the Crow's chest caught Garrick's eye. Garrick had been conscious enough to see the mercenary materialize out of a blur of motion after attacking the fox woman. It took a powerful spell to be able to move that fast. It was another thing Garrick didn't trust about the mercenary.

As Garrick focused on the pulse of the enchanted amulet, he realized its energy was weak, barely clinging to the pendant. He stared at the mercenary.

"That thing is nearly spent, isn't it?"

The Crow glanced over his shoulder at Garrick.

"How many uses do you have left on it?"

Without a word or betraying any emotion, the mercenary faced the fire and held up one finger.

Garrick studied him. The potential for a spell like that was enormous. Yet the Crow used up the second to last charge on the amulet to rescue Damian? She had told Garrick that the mercenary asked nothing in payment for his protection on the journey to Trent and she had little else to offer him now. The Crow had wandered Faneria alone for years and it didn't seem that he and Damian formed any great bond during that journey. Why go to so much trouble for her now? Someone could have hired the mercenary in Trent but who there knew about Damian, and if that was the case why help Garrick out of the forest as well? The man's intentions made no sense.

Garrick decided to try a different tactic. "You know, I heard an interesting story about you from the earldom of Canson. The people there didn't seem to believe all the other rumours about you. That what you did to the Red Hawks wasn't murder, but justice."

The Crow continued gazing at the fire. "They are wrong."

Garrick's eyes narrowed. There had been no emotion in the words. Not apology nor regret nor self-righteousness, merely a statement of fact. Before Garrick could say anything in response the Crow abruptly stood and walked out of the shack. Garrick blinked, so surprised by the sudden departure that he could only watch the mercenary leave.

Outside the doorway Garrick heard Damian's voice. "Domino? Is something wrong?" There was a pause, then she hurried inside, clutching the pot in her hands. "What's going on?"

Garrick stared at the open doorway, suspicion crossing his face. "Something is very strange about him."

Her expression matched Garrick's as she kneeled before the fire with the pot of water, her voice terse. "What?"

Garrick shook his head. "He doesn't deny any charges of murder. If anything, he just denied that he didn't commit murder."

Damian's eyes narrowed as she focused on the pot, harshly throwing in herbs and snatching a vial out of the knight's bag.

Garrick's tone softened. "Doesn't it bother you that he killed his own partners?"

She didn't face him. "No. He has been nothing but kind to me."

"Why? You haven't even been able to pay him."

She glared at him. "Is it so wrong for someone to be nice to me just for my sake?"

Garrick blinked, taken aback. "I didn't mean—"

"I am going to check on the horses," she cut in, standing and walking out of the shack before he could react. He glanced at the pot of herbed water abandoned by the fireside.

Frowning, he rubbed his fingers over his eyes. "Good one, Garrick." With a sigh, he flopped back onto the blankets, cringing as the impact made his head ache again.

Things just keep getting more complicated with this girl.

*   *   *

"Domino!"

Damian hurried around the shack, open plains shrouded in pre-dawn darkness visible between the trees clustering around the small, dilapidated building. Covered in his black cloak, she could just make out the mercenary's form beside his gelding, throwing his saddle over its back. Her throat grew thick.

"Domino, wait!"

"You no longer need my assistance." He didn't face her as she jogged up beside him. "The knight can take care of you now."

Her voice fell as low as his. "He couldn't help me when that malakh attacked."

He paused in his work. The silence stretched for a long moment, Domino staring into the woods beyond his horse. His hesitation to leave should have eased her worries yet her confusion mounted.

Why did Garrick get under his skin when he didn't care what the people of Trent said about him?

As the silence lengthened and Domino still did not look at her, she wondered if Garrick was the reason for his discomfort at all.

"He is right, you know," Domino said abruptly. "I did murder my companions in cold blood. Unprovoked, while they slept."

She stared at him. It was exactly what Filias and the other people of Trent told her when she asked about Domino. Unlike the gossipers, Domino spoke of it as if discussing the weather.

"Why are you telling me this?"

"You deserve to know the truth."

"Is that the entire truth?"

"It is the important part."

"Not to me." She gazed at him firmly as he turned to her. "What matters to me is that you saved my life and guided me to Trent and shared your own food and cloak with me when I could give you nothing in return."

He faced away. "You needed assistance."

Her brow furrowed. That seemed an odd answer. "So why did you come back?"

He hesitated. "I am not entirely certain."

For a brief moment the facade broke. She held her breath at the glimpse of thoughtfulness and confusion that soon clouded over with his usual detachment. She watched him for a moment, struggling to understand where he came from and what he believed. As he shifted, a glint of moonlight against his bag caught her eye.

She peered curiously at it. When she could make out the shape of it, her eyes widened with a gasp.

Her brooch, the tiger iron owl she had given to him outside Trent, was pinned to the flap of his satchel.

"You still have it!"

He nodded once.

Seeing the old ornament again, the pin she had worn nearly every day for most of the past ten years, made her feel complete again.

"I thought you lost it when you were imprisoned."

He shook his head, saying nothing more. She realized she should not have been surprised, given that his other effects, including his black sword and bloodstone amulet, had been returned to him. Yet his bow and arrows were missing and she had expected he would sell the brooch. Her eyes were drawn to it.

Perhaps he didn't have the time to sell it... but then, why would he wear it on the outside of his bag if he meant to?

His eyes flicked between her and his satchel. Wordlessly, he removed the brooch and held it out.

She reached for the pin, bittersweet memories of her father flashing through her mind. She wanted nothing more than to hold the owl close to her. Before she touched it, she stopped herself. Her hand hovered in the air.

"No." She let out a breath, forcing herself to drop her arm. "It was a gift. It is yours now."

Inside, she tried to associate the tiger iron owl with Domino, to accept it as no longer hers. It was not an easy transition to make and letting go of one of the closest relics she had from her father caused images of the barge burning to claw their way to the front of her mind. Tears welled in her eyes as she struggled to push those thoughts away.

I must not look back.

Opening her eyes, she found Domino watching her, betraying nothing. Trying to think of something to say, she glanced at the horse, slate grey with black mane, tail, face, and legs.

"I prayed for you."

His expression didn't change.

She shrugged. "In a Temple of Time. I prayed for Truth for you, like you asked." She gave him a faint smile as she patted the gelding's hindquarters. "I guess it helped."

His eyes turned to the horse. "I bribed the city guard."

Her smile faded. "Oh." That must be where his bow went.

"But thank you."

She turned to him in surprise. A trace of emotion coloured the words, a hint of real gratitude.

"I should be thanking you. You've saved my life again. I don't know how I'll ever repay you."

He looked away.

She felt exposed standing in the forest knowing the fox woman was out there. Though she had spent so little time with Domino before and knew little about him, merely having him stand beside her made her feel safer.

"You trusted me."

She looked at him curiously but he stared into the distance.

"No one has done that in many years."

She could think of nothing to say. Slowly, he faced her.

"It was not fair that I did not return the favour."

Her eyes enlarged. "Is that why you came back?"

He nodded.

"Even… even after what that fox woman said?"

Another nod.

Her throat grew thick. *So easily given and so freely returned. And he has never once looked at me any different because of my eyes. Not even knowing why.*

Cautiously, she reached a hand toward him. Conflicting impulses tore at her. As she looked up, part of her knew she looked into the eyes of an unforgiving, perhaps unrepentant killer.

But he has never shown me that. Though it came from his own mouth, that was not the Domino she had seen. *I will not let what I haven't seen define him.*

Pulling her arm back, she stepped forward and leaned against him. He laid one hand against her back in a halting motion, fingers still curled around the tiger iron brooch, though it felt nothing but warm and soothing to her. She inhaled the scent of his hard leather breastplate, the trees and plains around them silent but for the breath of the horses.

"Twice now you've given me hope when I had none left." Moving back, she looked up, his face impassive as ever. "Will you stay?"

He stared into her eyes for a long moment. Then, he nodded.

She turned toward the shack. "I'm sorry about Garrick. He shouldn't treat you that way."

Domino glanced into the distance and she saw something cross his eyes, but in the darkness she couldn't tell what.

"He has every right to."

She hesitated, his voice matter-of-fact. Her eyes narrowed. "Not when you just saved his life, too." Turning, she led the way back to the shack.

Garrick heard their footsteps return, but he pretended to be asleep. The weight of their situation made that all but impossible. His mind churned with stories of Nephrita, the most infamous of all the lesser gods even if few knew her name. He had not told Damian half of what she was reputed to have done and thought that for the best.

Rash, arrogant, and devoid of empathy, Nephrita claimed sacrifices on a whim and doled her favour out sparingly to those foolish or desperate enough to worship her. Though few prayed to her and only one temple was known to have been built to her she remained a staple of history, the greatest victory of the new gods over the old. Only Annasus, the God of Strength himself whom in her power and confidence she had challenged during the war between the Gods of Light and Time, had been able to stop her. Her defeat dealt a crushing blow to the old gods, who faded away not long afterward.

Even after looking into Damian's energy, Garrick never would have imagined the spirit inhabiting her was Nephrita. The memory of the power he saw there, so immense he felt like an ant beside it, sent a chill down his spine.

I'm an idiot. He hadn't told Damian the complete truth. In fact, he did know the dangers of the technique he used two days ago and why the Agaesi stopped teaching it. He had read about it in the private library of his order. Not only had it become exceedingly rare for a dragon knight to come close enough to a magical being to attempt it but it involved manipulating his spiritual energy on a finer scale than they ever did. Such a connection if done wrong could have killed him and Damian. He had considered it carefully and chose to attempt it in the hope that they would learn how to control her power better.

Only the opposite had happened. Ever since that moment when he felt that spirit nearly escape through the connection he shared with her, he could sense the change in Damian. She could barely keep her power contained even at rest. Between that and the threat of Niabi looming close by, the danger of their journey had heightened. With them barely a third of the way to Misengrad, Garrick didn't know how they were going to make it.

The Century Storm. Something spectacular and terrible had

happened, though what it was remained a mystery. Whatever caused it, the resulting storm was not magic but the will of the gods. Through it Nephrita, securely imprisoned for hundreds of years, had transferred into Damian. Now the thinnest of bonds kept the Goddess of Chaos from awaking and wreaking havoc once more.

The Gods of Light would be most displeased with that.

The more Garrick considered it the more he appreciated the enormity of the situation. What he had not told Damian and what almost no one outside the Order of the Dragon knew was that he was a mage. Agasis was a great and ancient dragon. When Agaesi warriors reached knighthood they forged a spirit bond with Agasis. In battle they could call upon his power, fighting with strength, speed, and agility far beyond what any normal human could possess. Using their power and ability to detect magic signatures they had defended themselves and protected the land from magical threats since the Time of Gods and Magic, before Faneria existed.

Even with the power of a dragon strengthening his muscles, he could not touch Niabi.

If he and Damian both had been utterly helpless against a malakh, how could they possibly hope to subdue Nephrita? Despite being trained for it, Garrick had never faced magic in his life. As a knight of Agasis, it was his duty to vanquish any magical threat to the kingdom. Nothing he had learned or read growing up could prepare him for this. With the only remaining mages in exile and apparently bitter about it, few remained that could even fathom such a challenge, let alone face it. Who could stop the Goddess of Chaos?

A wry grin crossed Garrick's face as he reflected on the mission that originally sent him to Trent. Yanuk and his rogue mages still posed a huge danger to Faneria. Garrick wished he could be tasked with something only that insurmountable.

"Garrick?"

Opening his eyes, he found Damian standing over him, holding his small iron pot. A trace of annoyance remained on her face.

"Here."

Pushing up on his elbow, he took the pot. "Thanks."

She nodded and returned to the fire, the Crow standing vigil at the open doorway. Garrick looked at the heated broth in his hand. Little more than herbed water, he could smell a hint of ether in the concoction. He studied Damian as he gratefully sipped the broth.

And things had been going so well, too, he thought with another grin. He had finally gotten her to open up on their journey in more ways than one. That opportunity was lost, nor could he focus on what he wanted to do with her with the danger hanging close.

What would happen to her if Nephrita was released? He couldn't guess. Nothing similar to what she was had ever been recorded throughout history. At least, nothing had as far as the Agaesi knew and that was more than many modern scholars. The fox woman said that their spirits had become intertwined. Did that mean that if Nephrita was released she would take over Damian, erasing everything that had been the cloth merchant from Aether? Even if Nephrita took her own form to return to this world, would she take Damian's life force to do so? What would it take to prevent Nephrita's return? Would anything short of Damian's death keep the goddess contained?

The thought made him greatly uneasy. Garrick didn't believe in martyrdom at the best of times and certainly not with someone he had grown to know and like. It seemed fundamentally wrong for someone who never asked for any of this to sacrifice herself. He was certain that the malakh's solution was borne out of a lower regard for humanity but he didn't doubt the possibility that it might be the only way to keep Nephrita from returning. He wasn't certain that if the time came he would be able to carry out such a task.

The Way of the Dragon raised him to give everything he had to protect this land and to respect those that lived there. Garrick always strongly believed in those values yet never before had they flown so in the face of each other. He felt utterly at a loss.

I can't do this on my own.

Slowly, his thoughts eased. The rest of the Agaesi would be able to figure out what to do. No message he could send would arrive faster than he could ride. He had to keep pushing them toward Hesperia. If he could help keep Nephrita contained until they reached Misengrad and avoid any further encounters with Niabi then they would get the help they needed. There their hope lay.

Resolved, Garrick set down the empty pot and leaned back against the blankets, surrendering to the dreamy abyss washing over him from the broth.

Sleep did not come easily for Damian. She listened longingly as Garrick's breathing slowed and steadied. She imagined the ether had something to do with that. Now that the dispute between him and Domino had been set aside, her thoughts turned to darker subjects.

For a long moment she crouched before the fire, staring into the red-hot embers that threw flickering light and long shadows across the single room of the shack, before she realized she felt no warmth from the flames. Squeezing her eyes shut, she struggled to still the power surging through her, gradually regaining control of the rush of energy until she could feel the heat of the flames.

After Garrick read her energy outside Rahgden, Damian tried to probe those dark recesses inside her, to find some awareness of the spirit she supposedly kept trapped inside. Little wonder she never suspected the truth throughout her life and part of her still didn't fully believe it. She could feel nothing and had never received any indication that some other being inhabited her body. The only hint of the existence of Nephrita was that memory of the battlefield in the valley, the memory that felt familiar but was not her own.

Damian shook her head. The Seers glossed over what made the Goddess of Chaos so reviled though she knew those teachings were well founded. Cruel and powerful as the chief gods, Nephrita's defeat at the hands of the God of Strength was one of the greatest moments of victory in the history of Light. Strength and the noble virtues of Light at last won out over the vengeful Gods of Time and all followers of the true gods revelled in the relief of knowing that the Goddess of Chaos had been imprisoned.

It seemed too distant, too difficult to fathom for Damian to feel truly horrified by the thought. She felt far more chilled by the thought of Niabi. Up until tonight, like any believer Damian would have given anything for the opportunity to meet a malakh. People spoke of the idea of meeting one as proof of their piety, the ultimate sign that they were favoured by the gods.

A malakh had just tried to kill her as effortlessly as the Goddess of Chaos cut down those warriors in the valley.

Damian shuddered, drawing her knees up to her chest and wrapping her arms around them. Her legs ached where the vines tried to burrow into her body though the bleeding had stopped.

Was it merely luck that caused Nephrita to end up inside Damian or had the goddess chosen her? And if so, why? Was Damian nothing but a vessel for the dark goddess? Or worse, a construct?

Doubts swirled through Damian's mind, reaching all the way back to her birth. Her father told her the truth of her birth only once very reluctantly, nearly ten years ago. He had teared up at the memory of holding his deceased wife in his arms and Damian never pried again. The thought of it made her eyes water and she struggled to lock away the dark thoughts that lingered from the barge sinking.

Those few citizens of Aether who would speak to her knew less and were even more hesitant to discuss it. One of Claude's weavers, from whom Damian learned many of her domestic skills, confirmed his story but they had been close friends for more than twenty years. Could they have misled her? No one else could say otherwise. The midwife who birthed Damian died long before she expressed any interest in the event. Perhaps there was no Damian Sires. Perhaps she was actually Nephrita returned to this world and her father never had the heart to tell her.

The thought that her entire life had been nothing but an incubator for the most dangerous being ever known made Damian's skin crawl. Was there nothing she could do to prevent the goddess from returning? It took all Damian's willpower to keep her power from spiralling out of control and her hold on it grew more tenuous each day. She had no idea what would drive her over the brink and release Nephrita but she knew that it was close.

I don't want to die.

She tried to cling to thoughts of Domino and Garrick, desperately hoping that they could help her, and stopped herself from uttering a quick prayer. If a malakh would not help her without ending her life, what hope did she have for help from any of the gods?

Damian shrank in on herself. *Why did all this have to fall upon me?*

That she could come up with no answer despaired her further.

CHAPTER 13
AN UNLIKELY PARTNERSHIP

THE ATMOSPHERE INSIDE the upscale tavern was jovial. An eclectic crowd filled the common room, many of the patrons local workers with scholars, pilgrims, and government officials sprinkled throughout. The smell of sizzling mutton and bitter ale permeated the air with the smoky fragrance of the large hearth fire set against one wall.

Sitting in a dark and isolated corner of the lively tavern, stripped of his armour and wearing common clothes, Lyle kept his study of the patrons inconspicuous. A mostly full tankard of ale and a well wrinkled note lay before him on the table. The message on the creased page was brief, written in a shaky but practised script.

I have information regarding the theft you suffered recently. Be at the Soaring Falcon tonight at dusk.

The letter was unsigned. One of his soldiers had received it while on duty and paid a young boy to run it to the captain. Lyle had been unable to determine who gave the soldier the letter and could do nothing but leave his office early to follow its instructions. Now the light outside the leaded glass windows faded, the glow of the hearth fire and the chandeliers hanging about the room filling the darkness.

Lyle forced himself not to drum his fingers against the table impatiently. After speaking with almost every soldier under his command and as many people in the neighbourhood of his office as he could find, he had learned nothing to lead him toward the thief who stole the ancient book. Given his interview with the Agaesi commander over a week ago and the fact that no one but a mage would be interested in the book, Lyle determined that the thief gained entry to his office by magic. That meant that there was almost nothing he could do to discover who stole the book.

Then the mysterious note arrived. In all Lyle's questioning he had only told Gravier and the captain of the Agaesi what had been stolen. Lyle had not even told many people that a theft had taken place. The idea that the person who penned the letter would have knowledge of the theft made him suspicious. Much as Lyle hoped that the writer would have information to allow him to search for the missing book, he expected he would be no better off tonight than when he first discovered the theft. So he watched the activity in the tavern, trying to pick out his patron from the varied people inside.

Lyle knew straight away the letter writer arrived when the door swung open. The elderly man's clothes were fine but faded and out of fashion. He hobbled into the tavern on a cane. The look he cast around the common room seemed casual but Lyle could see the searching in his eyes. Lyle didn't move as the older man caught his eyes, then meandered back to his table.

The gentleman smiled as he approached, the creases at the corners of his mouth falling into shadow in the dim corner. "Captain Hitchcliffe. At last we meet."

Lyle neither moved nor offered the old man a seat at the lone chair across the table. Lyle merely watched as the man ordered wine from a passing bar maid and then lowered onto the chair. His face remained impassive but the slowness with which he sat made it clear that the movement pained him.

Lyle said nothing. The more he studied the old man, the more his suspicions rose. The gentleman's accent placed him from Edan and the wine he ordered came from the west as well. Part of Lyle denied the highly implausible conclusion he had immediately jumped to. Yet there were few enough people who knew about the book for all the signs to be coincidence.

The maid soon returned with the drink. Flashing her a smile that looked more like a grimace, the gentleman thanked her as she set a goblet down. Picking it up, he swirled the drink and inhaled its bouquet. "It is interesting that we should meet face to face only now, so many years after you destroyed my position."

All question of who the man was fled Lyle's mind. Here before him sat the catalyst for the adventure Lyle unwittingly undertook almost two decades ago. This was the power-hungry warlord who hunted Lyle's party across southern Edan in search of the ancient sword his companion Kina carried. It seemed absurd that throughout their journey so many years ago Lyle's only interaction with the former Duke of Deverell had been through the legions of soldiers at his disposal, only to have the lord appear now as though no better than a common townsperson.

"You destroyed it yourself, Parn Gawthrain."

Gawthrain grinned, apparently pleased with Lyle's conclusion. "Yes, the loss of confidence by my people might have stripped me of my title, but of course none of that would have happened save for the interference of you and your companions."

Lyle didn't move. "You stole the book."

"I orchestrated its theft." Gawthrain sipped his wine. "Of course, I did not expect the favour to be returned by those with whom I had partnered."

Sarcasm crept into Lyle's voice. "Your partners were not endeared to your personality?"

Gawthrain fixed his eyes on Lyle, the smile fading. "I can tell you exactly where the book will be. All I ask in return is a few days' careful avoidance of a certain location near here."

Lyle's eyes narrowed faintly. "What location would that be?"

The former duke studied the dark wine in his goblet. "A now abandoned rebel base a few days west of here. The inhabitants were unable to take everything of value with them. I merely wish to recoup some of my losses from their treachery with some unimpeded rummaging."

"Fitting. I always thought of you as a jackal."

Gawthrain gritted his teeth but bit back any retort he might have made. "You will not find the book without my assistance. I assure you, their tracks and mine were well covered."

Lyle stared evenly at him.

"You know more than anyone else what a mage with that book is capable of and I can tell you now that you do not have much time before they will cast the spell you fear so much. Grant me what I desire and I will tell you everything you need to know."

Lyle studied Gawthrain for a long moment. The former duke's request seemed innocuous enough and Lyle doubted this so-called rebel base would conceal any considerable wealth. There must be enough to be worth risking a meeting with Lyle, along with vengeance against those who had wronged him. Lyle didn't like the idea of assisting in Gawthrain's plans in any way but he knew it was the only way to track down the book.

Still, something bothered Lyle. "I thought one needed the sword to cast the spell."

Gawthrain was unfazed. "Not the sword specifically. Just some personal connection to the subject of the spell. And I found a new one." He took another sip of his wine. "But I will say no more until I have your assurance—your word—that I will have what I ask."

Lyle frowned, wondering what other personal connection Gawthrain could have discovered. "Fine. You will have peace for your scavenging." His eyes bored into the former duke. "As long as you leave Faneria once you are done."

Gawthrain pursed his lips but eventually nodded. "I would far prefer to return to Edan in any case."

"Where is it?"

"The book travels northeast with a group of mages eighteen strong."

Lyle raised an eyebrow.

Gawthrain flashed him a cutting smile. "It is interesting how hardship brings like-minded people together, is it not? Many of them were cast out I believe shortly after you and your companions thwarted my previous plans with that book. They took up residence in a long-abandoned border fort and began training their own new mages."

The doubtful look remained on Lyle's face. "Eighteen?"

Gawthrain sobered. "Yes. They were already a formidable force, though they dared not act on it."

Lyle's eyes narrowed. "So you offered some encouragement to turn refugees into rebels."

The former duke spread his hands. "Our goals were similar. We both sought power."

"Fortunately for the rest of us, that never seems to go favourably for you." Gawthrain's eyes narrowed, but before he could say anything, Lyle asked, "Where are they?"

Garrick stirred in his sleep, his armour weighing him down. Half waking, he opened his eyes to shift his position. Upon seeing the interior of the shack, he quickly sat up. He felt groggy and a little numb from the ether but forced himself not to lie down. Damian huddled on the floor in her cloak in the opposite corner of the shack, using her bag to pillow her head. The Crow sat up against the wall across from her. In the darkness Garrick couldn't tell whether the mercenary slept. The fire they built had reduced to glowing embers and morning sunlight filtered through the broken shutters.

"Wake up," Garrick said as he rose from his blankets. "We have to get out of here."

Damian started awake, raising her head and blinking blearily at him. "What? What's wrong?"

Garrick marched forward but his legs felt rubbery and his head spun. Before he reached the door of the shack his leg buckled. A strong grip on his upper arm caught him before he fell. He turned. The Crow, now standing, stared at Garrick without emotion while holding him up. Regaining his balance, Garrick wrested his arm free of the mercenary's grip, though the action made him stumble and he grasped the door frame for balance. From the corner of his eye Garrick saw a dark look cross Damian's face. Garrick didn't trust the Crow as far as he could throw him and wanted nothing more than to see the Hawk-killer back in prison. But he said nothing.

"It won't take long for that malakh to break her bonds, and if she has the senses of a fox then it won't take much for her to find us again either. We need to put as much distance between us and her as possible."

"Are you sure you can ride?" Damian asked.

"I'll be fine." Pain rippled over Garrick's back as the ether wore off. He looked out between the thinning trees to the open plains beyond, his voice commanding. "We need to get back to civilization. That malakh must have avoided people for a very long time if there aren't any stories circulating about her. The more towns we pass through, the safer we are."

This part is easy.

Damian looked uncomfortable. "Are… are you certain of that?"

He smiled at her. Reaching out, he pulled the hood of her cloak up and over her head, leaving his hand resting on her forehead. "You'll be fine. Trust me, the judgement of some ignorant villagers worries me a lot less than Niabi does."

A malakh.

Hiding his trepidations, Garrick smiled at her until she nodded, slightly reassured.

"Let's go." Taking up his voulge, resting against the door frame, he limped out of the shack and around where their horses waited. If he expanded his senses he could likely detect if Niabi approached, but even diluted by the medicine Damian's aura had grown so strong he could scarcely detect his own power. He felt the energy churning within her, tearing outward and barely repressed by her efforts.

Garrick led Brenadier in a brisk trot, Damian and the Crow's horses cantering to keep up. Between the lingering dullness of the ether, the overpowering presence of Damian's aura, the aches in his back, chest, and head from the malakh's attack, and his own worries, it was all he could do to focus on the path they took.

My first mission, Garrick thought dryly. When he thought back to their encounter with the malakh the previous night a hollow feeling spread through him. Niabi had taken him down effortlessly and yet her aura was barely a flickering candle against Damian's raging bonfire.

What would he do if the fox woman came back? What could he do?

Maybe I should send word to the captain. But would the captain know any better? Garrick had studied the histories in the hidden library of the Agaesi and never ran across anything remotely like this. A god trapped in a common woman and a callous malakh Garrick had no hope of defeating. He could run but he knew he couldn't run forever. He had to be ready.

This is my chance.

He flicked the reins, pushing Brenadier harder, and heard Hope and the gelding break into a canter to follow.

The travel became much harder and more urgent over the following days. Garrick pushed them as fast as he dared, though Brenadier could not maintain even a trot for any considerable length of time. He traded horses with Damian occasionally to give the stallion a lighter burden to bear. It helped them cover ground quicker but Misengrad seemed entirely too far away, especially after diverting due north for a few days to return to the more developed part of Faneria. Most nights they found refuge in a barn or stable if not an inn or some generous villager's loft. However, each night Damian's magic grew more out of control. Garrick took to giving her small doses of ether to help her sleep better. A trail of scorched, flooded, frozen, petrified, or broken patches of earth and farmland stretched behind them. He could only imagine the rumours that would spread once that evidence was discovered.

Garrick trained when he could, trying to prepare himself for the malakh's reappearance or Nephrita's. Between the long days of riding, the short nights of sleep, and the growing pain in his legs and rear from sitting in the saddle for so many hours, he barely recovered from his initial injuries and felt less able than before.

And if Damian's increasingly uncontrollable magic and the threat of Niabi didn't weigh on his mind too much, then the Crow did. Often Garrick would forget the reticent mercenary was there but as soon as he caught a glimpse of their large shadow, the knight would frequently look over his shoulder at their unexpected companion.

This is the last thing I need to be worrying about right now.

No one knew how many of his companions the Crow killed. The Red Hawks had been a large band, fifty strong as some stories boasted. A few had been caught and sentenced for their crimes, no more than a dozen in total. Garrick doubted the man could have killed the rest single-handed but if there were any other survivors of the massacre they did not make it known. Based on the persistence and consistency of the stories that circled about him, the mercenary had a lot of blood on his hands. He did not deny that he murdered many of his own associates either.

Worse to Garrick was the fact that he didn't know the man's intentions. Garrick might have been willing to accept that perhaps some madness overcame the Crow then or he did what he had out of a misguided sense of justice, if he knew what the Crow's purpose was now. But the mercenary remained a mystery. Garrick couldn't help but wonder if the Crow planned to betray them or was working for someone who did. Nothing the Crow did or said suggested otherwise.

Tense breaks marked their passage and Damian and Garrick spoke almost as little as the mercenary did. Garrick tried to focus on the much more pressing concern of Nephrita but every time they stopped, the knight's eyes were drawn to the mercenary and the sword the Crow kept hidden under his cloak. Throughout the days that followed, Garrick wracked his mind for a way to be rid of the mercenary.

Several times Garrick tried to convince Damian of the danger of keeping the Crow with them, yet it seemed each conversation ended more angrily than the last.

"You can't trust that man."

"Who are you to tell me that? I know him better than you do."

"He barely even talks to you. What *do* you know about him?"

"I know he helped me at a time I needed it most without asking anything in return."

"People like him don't do things like that out of the kindness of their hearts."

"He saved my life, and yours."

"You think that excuses him?"

"I think it entitles him to some respect."

"Look at him. He doesn't care about anything."

"You are judging him based solely on stories. At least he has not lied to me or manipulated me like you have. Between the two of you, I would rather have him as company."

That last barb cut deep, far more than the flare of magic that accompanied her anger, and Garrick's blood boiled merely to reflect on the conversation. A day later he still mulled over the retort he wanted to yell at her. *I gave you a horse, stood up against that malakh for you, and gave you a real chance to control your power, and I'm the one in your bad books?* He could hardly believe she was the same girl he had shared such intimate moments with on their journey.

Normally, such comments even from someone as close to him as Damian would not have bothered him so much. The shame that clung to him after their conversation about manipulation almost two weeks ago made her words fester. Garrick had consciously avoided trying to bend or influence her thoughts since. He wanted to find a way to deal with the mercenary without resorting to that.

A day and a half after dwelling on that last conversation, a new idea occurred to him. Setting aside his emotional exhaustion, Garrick approached the mercenary when they stopped to rest the horses for lunch. From the corner of his eye, Garrick saw Damian's expression darken but he faced the Crow with a steady look.

"Hey. You're a mercenary, right?"

The Crow's impassive look did not change. He nodded once. Nearby, Damian glared a warning to Garrick but the knight remained unfazed.

"And you're here to protect Damian?"

Silence followed Garrick's words. The Crow nodded again.

Reaching into a pouch on his belt, Garrick pulled out a smaller burlap sack inside it. The coins inside jingled as he held it out. "Then you should be compensated for your services."

Damian's anger melted into uncertainty as she watched them. Garrick knew his offer came across as a test, but the Crow remained so much a mystery that Garrick knew he would learn nothing, no matter the outcome.

As Garrick expected, the mercenary betrayed nothing. The Crow merely reached out and took the pouch, dropping it in his satchel without a glance inside. Then, silently, he took up his horse's reins and led it toward a creek to drink.

Garrick exchanged a look with Damian. She straightened, looking relieved, and she nodded at him before following the mercenary with Hope's reins in her hands.

The gesture didn't change anything, but at least Garrick could feel like the mercenary had a reason to stay with them, and the payment appealed to Damian's pride. The thought of continuing to travel with the Crow left a sour taste in Garrick's mouth but he could devote his energy to the true problem. He would have much more to worry about than the mercenary if he failed to help Damian keep her magic in check.

I sure hope we can make it to Misengrad before she loses hold of her power entirely.

CHAPTER 14
RESURRECTION

DAMIAN SIGHED AS a village appeared in the distance.

The late afternoon sun hung ahead as she rode through rolling farm land, Garrick and Domino to either side of her. The warm days from the coming summer had kept her cloak stored in one of Hope's saddle bags but she drew it out now.

The town was a far cry from Dresdin and Trent nor was it as large as Aether but a central market clustered along the road and she could see craftsmen's shops and more than one temple. Unlike the tiny hamlets scattered among the fields where goods and marriages were traded, this was a place where people both lived and worked. It seemed likelier that this town would have an inn where they could stay the night unlike the villages where they had stopped the past nights.

Hope snorted and shuffled uneasily beneath her. Damian patted the pinto's neck though the gesture failed to ease the mare's distress. It took all Damian's focus to keep her power contained, to keep it from leaching out through her skin and disrupting the world around her, and her horse sensed the energy roiling and churning within her. They were a week or more away from Misengrad. Fear that she couldn't keep her power contained that long rose but Damian pushed it aside, trying to focus solely on stilling the energy bubbling within her.

As they reached the outskirts of the village, she pulled the hood of her cloak over her head. Much as she didn't want to hide anymore, she had avoided showing her eyes as her power grew more unstable, not wanting to draw attention to herself.

Riding within the borders of the village, Damian saw that the little town looked busy. Too busy. Far more people scrambled through the main avenue than she would expect in a town this size and at this hour, most appearing to transport food or clothing with others carrying armfuls of metal and leather, along with tools and supplies to work them. A number of the people hurrying through the streets turned curiously to Damian, Domino, and Garrick. Damian caught a glimpse of a woman telling a young boy something and gesturing down another street. The child darted off in the direction she indicated. Damian shot a concerned glance to Garrick. The knight merely smiled with a shrug.

After they travelled a few blocks into the town, a wide square with a fountain in its centre ahead, an older man wearing finer clothes than the other villagers hurried in front of them. The fabric of his clothes, Damian reflected, could have come from Aether last year.

"Good afternoon and welcome to Padura, Sir," the man said breathlessly. "Please forgive us for being unprepared for you, we weren't expecting any more."

Garrick cocked his head. "More?"

The man looked between them. "You're not..." He gestured vaguely over his shoulder. When Garrick only gave a bemused look in return, the man cleared his throat and straightened his doublet. "Forgive me, Sir, I thought you were with the soldiers."

Damian tensed, holding her breath.

Garrick asked, "Soldiers?"

"A patrol from the duke's forces." The man gestured over his shoulder again. "They arrived about an hour ago. You are not with them?"

Garrick smiled at the man. "Mere coincidence." He nodded at Damian. "I am helping this woman recover her son, who was taken by raiders, and have enlisted the help of this tracker." The man nodded, seemingly reassured by this explanation, though Damian couldn't help being surprised by how easily the lie came out. "We merely seek lodging for the night."

The man looked uncomfortable. "I'm afraid the soldiers have already filled up our only inn. It would be my honour to take you in at my home, Sir. I'm Orneth, the magistrate of this area."

Garrick nodded and dismounted, the magistrate bowing before him. "Sir Garrick Magni of Hesperia. We would be glad to take your offer."

Orneth's eyes widened at Garrick's title. The magistrate shook his head and wrung his hands. "I-I fear our houses are not so lavish as you are used to, Sir. We do not have space for your companions as well."

Garrick looked back at Damian and Domino. "Do you have stables for our horses?"

"Oh yes, Sir. Plenty of space to spare."

The knight nodded. "They can sleep in the stables."

Damian frowned, disappointed that she and Domino would get no better lodging this night than the previous ones.

"Please give me a moment to speak with them."

"Of course, Sir."

Damian and Domino dismounted as Garrick strode over. The knight lowered his voice. "Sorry to do this to you but it'll look suspicious if I don't accept. You'll be fine for tonight." He smiled wryly. "Though it would figure we'd stop in right at the same time as a patrol of Aldenese soldiers. You should stay clear of them. We'll leave first thing in the morning."

Damian nodded, not needing Garrick's suggestion to avoid the soldiers.

He gave Domino a quick warning look, then turned back to the magistrate, grabbing Brenadier's reins. "Lead the way, master Orneth."

Damian took Hope's reins and followed, her hips and thighs aching after another long day spent mostly in the saddle.

Orneth called for servants as they approached the stable and a few scrambled out to take the horses. Damian shied away as a young man reached for the reins, though he didn't look at her face as he led Hope inside.

"Resha," the magistrate barked. A round-faced girl scrambled over. Orneth passed a coin to the servant. "Take these two to the inn and be sure old Jared has supper for them."

Damian shot a startled look to Domino, the mercenary returning an expressionless glance. Before Damian could say anything, the servant girl bowed to the magistrate and replied, "Yes, master. Please follow me, miss, mister."

The thought of walking into the inn where the band of provincial soldiers was staying terrified Damian. Objecting now would draw too much attention to her. She turned desperately to Garrick as Resha began walking away. The knight's smile faded just slightly and he nodded toward the servant girl. Reluctantly, Damian turned and followed Resha, Domino walking silently after.

The servant strode briskly through the town and Damian hurried to keep up. The village had grown quieter since they arrived, though people passed through the streets painted orange by the setting sun.

Some came close to Damian while scrambling to their errands. Damian flinched at their nearness but the most reaction she received was a hasty, distracted nod from one older man.

Three soldiers stood beside the entrance to the inn, flickering light glimmering in the yellow windows. Damian slowed ten feet from them but Resha continued to the doors. The soldiers looked at Damian with her hesitation. It would be worse if she turned back now. Pulling her cloak tighter about her, Damian crossed the rest of the distance to the door as the servant held it open.

Damian stopped in her tracks inside the doors, catching her breath. The common room was packed. The soldiers, identifiable by their silver-green surcoats, sat at almost every table, chatting and drinking and eating. They crowded around the large hearth against one wall, two played a board game, and a few more circled a man in a corner who strummed a lyre and sang. There had to be twenty of the soldiers inside. Nearly as many townspeople crowded the room, listening raptly or discussing recent events with the soldiers. Harried bar maids and tenders wove through the crowd, delivering armfuls of drinks or platters of food to tables throughout.

Numerous heads turned in Damian and Domino's direction as they stepped inside and few of those looked away after seeing her. Damian felt her cheeks heat up and she dipped her chin, keeping her eyes shaded beneath her hood. She tried to take comfort in Domino's presence, large and silent beside her, but her hands trembled and she wanted nothing more than to escape.

"You can sit down, miss, mister," Resha said, her voice raised to be heard over the din. "I'll get your food."

Briefly, Damian considered telling the servant not to bother. The aroma of cooked meat that saturated the air caused her stomach to twist hungrily. Before Damian could say anything, Resha departed and squeezed between people as she approached the bar.

Movement to Damian's side caught her eye. One soldier sitting alone at a table near the hearth stood, gesturing at his chair with a smile. Swallowing uncomfortably, Damian made her way to the table. A few stares followed and other patrons spoke to companions in interest. Damian hoped the attention was only the novelty of someone new.

At the table, the soldier stepped aside, still holding the back of the chair.

Damian nodded, her eyes low and hood hanging over them. "Thank you." She sat down, leaning away from his hand until he took it away.

"My pleasure, miss." He stepped over to the group at the hearth as Domino sat in the other chair at the table.

Damian watched the tallow candle flicker on the table, wringing her hands while she waited for the food to arrive. The fires, the candles, and the crush of bodies made heat press down on Damian, sweat dampening the roots of her hair. She opened the sides of her cloak though she dared not move her hood.

She raised her head to send a furtive glance to Domino. He stared back. She couldn't help smiling faintly at the sight. Sitting at an inn with him, neither of them being judged by the townspeople, it felt bizarrely like a casual outing with an old friend. It reminded her of the evenings she spent travelling across the kingdom with her father.

Except her father was gone.

Damian's heart wrenched as the thought struck her suddenly. A flash of the barge wrapped in flames appeared in her mind before she could push it back.

A full-figured bar maid with a mass of strawberry blonde curls, who looked Damian's age, stopped beside their table and set mugs down before them. "Personal guests of the magistrate's! Your food will be right out. I'm afraid our ale's running low. Will cider do for you?"

"That's fine, thank you," Damian replied from beneath her hood, uncertain her voice rose above the clamour in the room. Domino merely nodded as Damian sipped her drink.

The maid put her hands on her hips, beaming at them. "Quite a night this is. I haven't seen this much action around here in years. What brings you out to Padura, then?"

Damian swallowed around a lump in her throat. She remembered the story Garrick told the magistrate but couldn't bring herself to pretend she had a son. "We are only passing through."

The maid tilted her head aside. "Oh, what an interesting accent you have! Where are you from?"

Damian shifted, realizing a few soldiers and villagers nearby had turned to her with the maid's questions. "Aether." Speaking the name caused dark thoughts to creep up from deep inside, intangible but constricting.

"Where's that?"

A bartender called out, "Shureen!"

The maid turned. "Oh, I think that's your food. I'll be right back. I want to hear more!"

Damian squirmed as Shureen strode off, forcefully repelling thoughts of the barge. The heat in the room weighed on Damian and she pushed the sides of her cloak back further.

Shureen soon returned, a platter in each hand. As she came close and glanced at Damian, she drew in a breath, eyes widening.

"Your gown is beautiful!"

Damian smiled a little as the maid set the dishes on the table. "Thank you."

Shureen examined the dress as Damian began to eat. "Did you make it?"

Damian's smile widened. "Yes."

"You are so talented. I wish I could make something that pretty."

Damian chewed a bite of mutton quickly, about to suggest a simpler way of designing her gown, but before she finished the maid went on, "So where did you say you were from?"

Damian swallowed. "Aether. It is in the foothills of the Orthys Mountains."

Shureen perked up. "Wow. Do you ever see any of the barbarians out there?" Damian paused with a bite halfway to her mouth, but before she could answer the maid waved a hand. "I'm sorry, I should let you eat. It's just that we don't often get visitors here, especially from out east."

Damian smiled. Such reactions had been common in the smaller towns along the trade journey and she always enjoyed speaking with the locals about their lives. "It's alright. I have not seen any Zahni at home. They usually trade along the border rather than come over the mountains. We have received some of their pottery, though." Memories of Aether and of the annual journey flashed in Damian's mind and her chest tightened.

The maid pulled a chair over and sat down at the table. "How neat! What is your home like, then? Are you sure this is alright? I'm not bothering you, am I?"

Damian ate another mouthful before assuring the maid, "I don't mind." Damian found it nice to speak of mundane things. It was particularly refreshing to talk to another young woman after spending so much time in the company of such serious or calculating men. Damian stopped herself from saying as much with Domino quietly eating across from her.

Damian told Shureen about Aether, its focus on shepherding and growing flax and how the village had grown over the years, though aside from that it seemed little different from Padura. A lump formed in Damian's throat as she ate and thought back to the home she had not seen in weeks. Aether would never be the same and her house would feel empty without her father. Even as she spoke with

Shureen, Damian's skin crawled to wonder how she could get by on her own.

"Are you married, then?" The maid glanced at Domino as she spoke.

Damian blinked at the mercenary. As ever, he made no reaction. Had she been in a lighter mood, Damian might have laughed at the insinuation. The question only made loneliness and fear grip her tighter. "No."

Shureen turned back to Damian. "So what does your family do?"

Damian swallowed hard, the meat in her mouth dropping like a lead weight in her stomach. She fought to keep a tremor from her voice. "My father ran a cloth trade. He would sell Aether's stock across the kingdom each year." She tried to deflect her thoughts as well as the bar maid's questions. "I think your magistrate might be wearing some of our cloth."

Shureen's smile brightened. "Oh! Is that what your papa's doing now?"

Images of the barge burning flared across Damian's mind in quick succession. She squeezed her eyes shut against the memory, tears gathering. She dropped her hands to the table, giving up any attempt at choking down more of her supper.

"He… he passed away a few weeks ago."

A mortified look crossed the maid's face. "Oh, I'm so sorry. What happened?"

The tears streamed down Damian's cheeks as she relived her last moments aboard the barge for the first time since it happened.

"Miss? Are you alright?"

The disturbing dreams, the cabin wreathed in flames, plummeting through the weakened floor, the barge falling apart around her.

"He… I…"

Damian trembled, the living nightmare she had woken to aboard the barge consuming her thoughts.

He's gone. I'll never see him again. I'm all alone.

"A fire on our ship. I couldn't… I couldn't stop it." Her voice broke as the memory barraged her, consuming her like the flames that destroyed the barge.

"Shining Light! Your hands!"

Startled cries followed Shureen's exclamation. Damian opened her eyes to find Domino sweeping to his feet. The villagers and soldiers nearby scrambled, some racing for flagons of water, others reaching for weapons.

Looking down, Damian found the table top blackened where her hands touched it, embers glowing around the edges of her fingers.

Yelping, Damian leaped to her feet, yanking her hands back. The energy roiled within her, pushing out from her skin with almost tangible force. The candles and hearth fire flared. Shouts and screams filled the common room and people fought to escape from the growing flames.

Damian shook her head, staring at the scene through tear-blurred vision. "Not again. Not again!" She slid around Domino and ran for the door, pushing between people and escaping into the rosy dusk.

Wind howled as she entered the plaza and the air grew frosty and sweltering in waves. Shrieks rang out as people hurried away. Damian stumbled as her foot struck an obstacle on the smooth road. A moment passed as she regained her balance and looked down. A spider web of cracks fanned out in all directions, the dirt road pushed up by the now broken bedrock beneath.

"No, no, no!"

The words came out in a puff of cloud and the road around her glistened in the waning dusk as it coated over with a layer of ice. Damian clasped her hands over her head as she moved back to the fountain. On the edges of the square the soldiers clamoured and shouted and their blades pointed toward her. Other townspeople gathered around the plaza, adding their cries to the soldiers' accusations.

"What's going on?"

"She's a witch!"

"Stop her!"

Damian crouched at the edge of the fountain, crying as guilt and horror swallowed her up. The water churned in the fountain, splashing up in needle-sharp icicles while heat-hazy wind swirled around her, reaching up to the clouds that roiled overhead. The power surged through her body, heedless of her attempts to control it, and the shouting voices tore at her concentration like a raptor at its prey.

Then, another voice called out from nearer by, "Damian!"

Raising her head, she found Domino a few paces away, ice pooling beneath his boots. Aside from a small worry line creasing his brow, he looked as stoic as ever. Unfazed by anything, calm and cool and showing no fear or any other emotion.

"Do not give in."

She wanted to find strength in his calmness, but she couldn't stop crying.

"It's my fault! My father is dead! I've already lost the most important person in my life and nothing will ever change the fact that I killed him."

Domino took a step into the whirlwind blowing around her, flinching when a shard of ice slashed his cheek.

"You will only have more to regret if you let your emotions rule you."

Sniffling, she stared at him standing a few paces away and at the steady, meaningful look he gave. There was something else in his eyes she couldn't quite identify, something that hinted at emotions that ran deep. She swallowed as she considered his words.

I can't let Nephrita be freed. I must not give in to despair.

Closing her eyes, Damian tried to ground herself the way he did. She detached herself from everything except Domino, brushing away the danger, the anxiety, and the helplessness. For a moment, she simply let herself be. Gradually the surge of power diminished. The voices, seeming far away, rose as her body returned to normal though she let them roll past her like a breeze.

Gentle hands took her by the arms. Opening her eyes, she looked up at Domino. His brow was smooth but even in the darkening dusk she saw a questioning look in his eyes. The wind died down, the clouds overhead faded, the ice covering the road was gone, and she heard the fountain fall still behind her. Exhausted beyond belief and barely keeping the guilt and horror from the barge held at bay, she simply nodded.

The townspeople's shouts grew louder. They called her all sorts of names, chief among them 'witch.' Domino turned to face them as the soldiers from the inn, at least a dozen spread along the edges of the plaza, took a few steps forward. Swords were brandished in Damian's direction. Behind them, other villagers stared with angry or terrified looks. Shureen stood outside the inn's doors, face pale and eyes enormous as she watched. The sight made Damian uneasy. Feeling the power within her cling to that worry, feeding off it, she tried to cast it aside.

A middle-aged soldier with sandy hair straightened. "Witchcraft is forbidden. In the name of the Duke of Alden, you're under arrest."

"Don't try anything!" added another.

The villagers around them cheered at the order.

Damian opened her mouth to speak. Before she could say a word Domino stepped forward, standing between her and the approaching soldiers. He said nothing.

Another soldier sneered at the mercenary. "If you've been

sheltering this girl, then you're guilty as well."

"Stand down," added the sandy-haired soldier. "You don't want this getting any uglier."

Domino drew his sword. All the soldiers raised theirs defensively though the mercenary stood ten paces away. Damian's throat grew thick. Although Domino didn't hold the weapon menacingly, the soldiers shuffled their feet and clearly prepared for a fight.

"Wait!" Damian cried, stepping beside Domino to face the soldiers. "We are with Sir Magni. I am under his…" She nearly said 'protection,' but seeing the looks in the soldiers' faces, she finished instead, "guard."

The soldiers looked skeptical, a few scoffing or laughing at her assertion.

"What are you talking about?"

"Who?"

"There's no knight here."

"She's trying to trick us."

"Where's this knight now if he's supposed to be guarding you?"

"He is at the magistrate's house," she tried to explain. Only Domino heard her over the rising clamour of voices.

"That's enough. You're coming with us, witch." With that, the soldiers moved forward.

Domino raised his sword defensively and reached his free arm over to gently move Damian behind him.

"Please," Damian cried, leaning against Domino's arm. "Just go to the magistrate's house and speak with him." The air crackled around her and Domino's arm twitched reflexively. She jumped back with a gasp. A stream of black flames flared out of her and struck the mercenary in the back. He stumbled forward, groaning.

"Domino!" Her power flared and she leaped back to the edge of the fountain. The villagers and some of the soldiers cried out. The clouds billowed yet the lightning was on the ground, small bolts crackling through Damian's body and sparking to the road. Strong winds circled her, dark shadows like wisps of cloth dancing in the gales.

"No…" She pulled her hands close, trying to keep the energy from spreading. Spinning to face her, Domino lunged back and held his arm over his face. Damian tried to calm herself as she had done before but the fear would not be quenched and the energy would not abate. Her body burned from the power of it, the magic so intense it felt like it would take over her flesh entirely. She struggled to breathe as she looked around.

The edges of the square descended into chaos, villagers shoving and attacking each other in a mad dash to get away. The soldiers tried to organize and advance on her but streams of fire and gale force winds threw them back. Screams filled the night sky and dogs barked and cats yowled in the distance. Birds fled their roosts though the storm winds tossed them about like leaves. Tears ran down Damian's face and she dropped to her knees, staring at the horror she wrought.

It doesn't matter what I do. I can't control this.

Around her, the world faded to grey and the sounds of the panicking townspeople droned to an incomprehensible hum. Shadows shifted in the town square as the flares of magic lit up the dusk-darkened roads brilliantly. Everything moved yet nothing seemed to be alive. Inside her, she felt something else moving, trying to tear its way free.

I can't keep from hurting the people I care about.

She faintly discerned a familiar voice calling her name. Garrick, out of his armour and armed only with a dagger, stood a few paces beyond where Domino struggled to remain on his feet. The knight said something but between the roar of the wind and the thickness in her head Damian couldn't make out the words.

Thoughts of her father and the captain and crew of the barge circled around and around in her mind while the townspeople screamed and fled.

And people will always hate and fear me, for good reason.

Spears of ice taller than Damian surrounded her. Only with fierce concentration could she discover the lightning shooting over them and the earth breaking apart beneath them. She couldn't breathe, she lost feeling in her arms and legs, and a fire burned inside her, the heat excruciating. Reality and perception slipped away and her tenuous grasp on consciousness faded. The other presence was escaping her body, leaving her cold and empty.

I killed them. I killed them all.

The last thought that ran through her mind was fear and disappointment that just as her father warned long ago, magic had taken her life. For a moment, she thought she saw him standing beside Domino. More tears streamed down her face.

I'm sorry.

Then, everything faded to darkness.

*   *   *

Wind howled through the plaza, tearing pennants and wooden signs free of their posts and flinging dirt and debris through the air. Tendrils of power ripped free of Damian, sparking in the air with a brilliant crimson glow. The sensation crashed against Garrick, nearly overwhelming him. Her control over her power was gone.

"Damian!"

Garrick could barely hear his own shout over the torrential wind roaring through the square. Beside him, the Crow struggled to stay on his feet, black cloak and brown hair billowing in the gale. Debris slapped Garrick hard all over his body, unprotected by the armour he had left back in the magistrate's house. Plate and mail alike sat uselessly in the magistrate's loft, along with Garrick's voulge and the ether he had bought for this very purpose. The peace of the quiet dinner he had enjoyed with Orneth's family minutes earlier mocked him and he cursed his unpreparedness.

Damian's body emitted a shimmering mist and a glow that illuminated the plaza clearly. Garrick could only make out a vague shape through the towers of icicles surrounding her. She turned to him, her face coming into view through a narrow gap in the ice, and his throat tightened. There was no recognition in her eyes as she looked at him.

He shut his eyes, his body feeling heavy with his failure to prevent this. Damian Sires might already be gone. He had to stop her before the Goddess of Chaos was reborn.

Opening his eyes, he drew his dagger.

Movement from the corner of his eye drew his attention. The Crow stepped in front of him, baring a single-edged black sword.

Garrick spared a brief glance at the Crow. Swinging his foot up, he kicked the mercenary hard in the upper leg. The Crow grunted as he stumbled off-balance. Darting around him, Garrick plunged into the crystalline maze surrounding Damian.

Before Garrick's foot landed, a flare of energy blasted out, smashing against him and flinging him several feet back. He twisted around as he fell, coming to a stop in a crouch and facing her. In that moment, he knew he was too late.

The ice and wind were gone, only Damian and the broken fountain behind her filled the otherwise empty plaza. Her body glowed with a light that hurt to look upon, shining brilliantly against the buildings surrounding the square. The power flooded Garrick from ten paces away.

The light diminished and Damian's form came into view, streams of golden fire swirling around her like leaves in an autumn breeze.

Her eyes were shut, her body limp as she stood there. Slowly, she straightened and then bent over backwards. Her heels lifted off the ground and her body hung limply, suspended as if by a cord attached to her heart. Tongues of fire and bright red smoke swirled around her and floated into the sky. A stream of flames flowed out of her chest, rising as though on a gentle breeze.

After a long moment, the flames fled Damian's body and she collapsed. The mercenary rushed forward but Garrick stared above her, transfixed. The flames that had escaped Damian's body illuminated the square as brightly as she had. They gathered above, swirling into a human form that hovered in the air. Fire melted into ivory flesh so clearly visible in the dark night that it almost seemed the form glowed from within.

The figure above became a nude woman, hanging in midair in the same position as Damian had a moment earlier. As the woman's shape solidified, Garrick felt a chill run through him. The same pearly skin and short, raven hair he had seen depicted in Temples of Light formed in the air. He drew power to him, resigning himself to what would likely be his death.

As the light of her summoning faded, she plummeted to the earth. Without thinking, Garrick raced forward, catching her just before she hit the ground. His vision faded as he touched her. The woman's aura, though far more contained than Damian's, burned so brilliantly that when his skin touched hers the power of her magic overcame all his other senses. Swaying in place, he struggled to support himself on one knee before he dropped her. She moaned as he lowered her to the broken, boggy road, his eyes adjusting to the sudden darkness. He slid his hand, still holding his dagger, out from under her knees.

He hesitated.

This may be my only chance.

The woman seemed surprisingly frail. Though her naked body was shaped in sensuous curves, she hardly weighed more than a child in his arms and her head must barely reach up to his shoulders.

This is the Goddess of Chaos. I have to stop her before she regains her strength.

His arm didn't move as he stared at her small body, lying prone in his arms.

Stirring, she opened her eyes and blinked at him. He tightened his grip on his dagger, his blood rushing through him, but there was no malice in her hazel irises. There was only confusion.

"Garrick? What happened?"

He blinked. "How do you know my name?"

Her expression became more curious. "What do you mean? What's wrong?"

Completely baffled, he could think of nothing to say in response.

She sat up, releasing her faint weight from his arm as she gave him a worried look. "Don't you recognize me?"

He could only stare at her.

"It's Damian."

His power washed away and his grip on his dagger slackened. Slowly, he raised his eyes across the square.

"No…" He stared at the mercenary, who held Damian's unmoving body in his arms inside the dry fountain. "That's Damian."

The dark-haired woman followed his gaze. As her eyes fell on Damian, crimson dress and auburn plait draped over the Crow's arms, she gasped.

"What? But…" Turning her eyes back to herself, she gasped again, trying to cover herself with her arms. A swish from nearby drew Garrick's attention. He and the woman both turned as the Crow tossed his cloak through the air toward them. Garrick caught it and the woman nodded in thanks, her cheeks reddening as she took the cloak and wrapped it around her. She huddled beneath the cloak, trembling as she gazed absently at the ground. Garrick's mind whirled.

"What in *shadows* just happened?"

Footsteps sounded behind him. Garrick turned his head. Silent up until that moment, a crowd of villagers trickled back to the edges of the plaza, most holding torches. The armed men he had seen earlier, likely the duke's patrol filling the inn, fronted the group. Several people in the crowd wore expressions of dumbfounded shock, though many others looked frightened, angry, or both. Their voices rose nearly in unison.

"Who is that?"

"That girl's a witch!"

"Where did that woman come from?"

"She tried to kill us!"

The soldiers pointed their swords toward Garrick though they remained half a dozen paces away. Garrick stood, the woman rising beside him. Indeed, the top of her head barely reached his collar bone. He kept his eyes on the group bordering the square as she pulled the mercenary's cloak close about her.

Oh boy. Time to put my people skills to the test.

"Magic is forbidden," said a sandy-haired man at the front of the group, swallowing uneasily as he spoke in a commanding voice. "That girl's under arrest."

Garrick stepped forward a pace, standing tall and calling back in a firm, unyielding voice. "She is under my protection."

"You have no authority here," barked another of the soldiers. "She's a witch and she's coming with us."

"Is that any way to speak to your superior?" Garrick snapped back.

Some of the men and villagers jumped at the sharpness in his voice and the woman beside him flinched.

He squared his shoulders and raised his voice. "I am Sir Garrick Magni of the dragon knights of Hesperia."

A ripple of murmurs spread through the crowd, villagers and soldiers staring at him with wide eyes.

"And both of these women are my charges." Reaching back, Garrick placed a hand on the woman's shoulder. The surge of power that sparked between them made him shift unsteadily. He was glad at least the cloak hung between his flesh and hers.

The sandy-haired soldier shifted and pointed at Damian. "Sir, that one just attacked us and injured at least three of my men and she admitted to murder."

Oh, Damian. No wonder she lost control.

Keeping his expression calm, Garrick answered, "By starting a fire with a thought. Do you really want to be responsible for someone who can do that?"

The soldiers hesitated and a few glanced at each other.

"Stand down." Garrick stared at them unwaveringly. A tense moment passed.

Finally, the sandy-haired soldier sent uncertain nods to either side. Slowly, the soldiers relaxed though they kept their swords in hand. Garrick glanced over his shoulder at the mercenary.

"Take her back to the stable."

Without waiting to see the Crow's reaction, Garrick touched his fingertips to the cloaked woman's back and walked toward the crowd. Gathering the long, draping folds of the cloak dragging the ground, she followed close behind, her bare feet splashing softly across the drenched dirt road. As they neared the group of soldiers and villagers, those standing directly before Garrick moved aside. A few tightened their grips on their swords. Garrick did not look at any of them or say a word as he led the woman on nor did he look back to check the mercenary's progress. The woman said nothing as they walked.

Beyond the light of the crowd's torches, the streets grew dark as pitch and Garrick could barely make out the outlines of the buildings bordering the roads. Glad for the village's small size, he had small difficulty finding the magistrate's house though he stepped carefully to avoid tripping on any unseen hazard.

All the while, his thoughts remained on the diminutive woman walking beside him. He couldn't attack her now when she showed no signs of aggression toward him or anyone else, but there was no mistaking the fact that he walked beside the Goddess of Chaos. Her aura burned like the sun, eclipsing Damian and Niabi both. Yet here she was, relying on him for protection and blushing at her exposed body like a shy maiden.

It all seemed so absurd Garrick hardly knew what to think.

He hurried his pace when he turned a corner and saw the lanterns lighting the outside of the magistrate's house. Orneth paced in front of his door. Another man dressed in common clothes spoke with the magistrate and his two elder sons waiting in the doorway, illuminated by the fires inside.

The magistrate and his companions spun as Garrick and the woman stepped into the light of the lanterns. Orneth strode forward, glancing uncertainly at the woman as he met them a few paces from his door. "Sir Magni? What happened?"

"Don't worry. Everything is alright." Garrick fixed his eyes on Orneth's teenage daughter peering out from inside. "Do you have clothes you can spare?" Wide-eyed, the girl jerked her head in a nod and darted off.

"What was that disturbance?" Orneth pressed. He gestured at the villager. "He says there were… strange things going on in the square. Storms and ice…"

"It's over now," Garrick spoke as the magistrate trailed off. The knight swallowed, hiding any other reaction from the magistrate. "I saw to that." With that, Garrick led the cloaked woman inside. Orneth and his wife stared at them and exchanged a glance as they passed but Garrick didn't pause as he climbed the stairs to the second floor. Orneth's daughter met him there, holding out a bundle of cloth. Taking the cloth, Garrick nodded in thanks and guided the cloaked woman up the ladder to the loft.

The magistrate of this village didn't take in many personal visitors as was clear from the bolts of cloth, old furniture and clothes, and piles of papers and ledgers that had been shoved quickly to the corners of the loft, and from the sagging straw mattress where Garrick had planned to sleep that night. Before nightfall it had felt an immense comfort after so many nights spent sleeping in barns, mills, or whatever shelter they could find. He took little solace in the accommodations now.

Turning to face the cloaked woman, he held the clothes out to her. She took them silently and retreated behind a screen near the bed.

I should have done it, he thought, brushing the ivory hilt of his dagger with his fingers. He hardly thought it would be so easy to kill a god, but she was clearly weak and once she regained her strength he knew he stood no chance against someone of her power.

And yet she thinks she's Damian. Though she had said nothing since the soldiers and villagers interrupted them in the square, he had seen the uncertainty etched into her eyes. It looked like Damian.

The floor boards creaked. Turning, Garrick saw her as she stepped out from behind the screen. The girl's dress, a simple peasant gown with a green bodice and skirt over a cream-coloured chemise, was too large, the skirts trailing the floor and billowing sleeves falling over her delicate wrists down to her knuckles. She shrugged at him.

The whole image was a bizarre mix of mismatched features like pieces of different paintings cut apart and sewn together. Although the over-large gown complemented her shapely body, the short, raven hair with two locks falling down to her breasts clashed with its simple femininity. The discomfort in her hazel eyes stood out awkwardly against both. He stared at her for a moment, trying to absorb the strange sight.

He shook his head slowly. "Who are you?"

She sighed as she stepped in front of a dusty mirror and glanced at it. A deeply thoughtful look crossed her face as she examined her reflection. "The person I thought I was is someone else." Turning, she fixed her gaze on him. "Me? I am no one."

A lump formed in Garrick's throat and he struggled not to show any reaction. "Who do you want to be?" His voice dropped as he prepared to draw the power of Agasis to him.

She scoffed. "I couldn't imagine being anyone but Damian Sires." Her brow creased. "What am I supposed to think? How would you feel if you suddenly discovered you weren't Garrick Magni, even though you had all his memories and feelings and beliefs?"

If she has Damian's beliefs, he thought inanely, *then does that mean the Goddess of Chaos worships the Gods of Light?* Seeing the look on her face, he suppressed the grin that tried to rise with that thought.

"I don't know."

"I don't either. I thought her life was mine. I've spent my entire life believing that."

Garrick regarded her carefully. He could feel the same thing he sensed in Damian that day outside Rahgden. Not just powerful, not just destructive, but ancient.

"You don't remember anything before then?"

She returned a flat look. "Do you remember anything before your childhood?"

He frowned. Uncomfortable with the look on her face, he glanced out the window over the bed. Aside from the stars glinting above the buildings, outside it was black.

"I have to see her."

Garrick turned to find her expression set.

"Please."

Questions swirled through his mind as he watched her. *Did Damian's mind take over hers? Or did being a part of Damian erase her previous memories? Does she really remember nothing of the infamous figure out of history? What will she think when she sees the person she thinks is herself? What will Damian think when she sees her?*

Then, a more startling thought occurred to him. *Is Damian even alive?* He had been so absorbed in thoughts of Nephrita and the villagers and duke's soldiers that he hadn't asked.

Nodding briskly, he turned and crossed the loft to the ladder, the woman taking up the black cloak and following. Garrick wanted to grab his voulge and don his armour but he didn't doubt she would guess he did so to protect himself from her. He hoped his dagger and his reflexes would be enough if it came to that.

He led the way out of Orneth's home, favouring the magistrate's family and servants with nothing more than a nod along the way. The streets outside had fallen to silence, the darkness beyond the lantern Garrick carried absolute. As he looked down a side street he made out twin glows of torches a block away, illuminating two armed figures facing Orneth's house. Garrick caught a glint of light against mail and leather.

We've overstayed our welcome in this town.

Turning, he walked toward the stable where he had left Brenadier, Damian, and the Crow so recently, looking for signs of other soldiers along the way. Nephrita padded along with him, her bare feet falling silently on the dirt road.

The Goddess of Chaos walks beside me.

His stomach turned at the thought and part of him thought he should bury his dagger in her heart before any memories of her past life returned.

Mercifully, the walk to the magistrate's personal stables was brief. He caught sight of at least three more torches held by soldiers as he stepped inside. Garrick hung the lantern on a peg inside the doors, several burning candles inside providing enough illumination. A pair of torches mounted to either side of a stall drew him down the row to the middle of the building. The door of the stall hung open and another torch or two burned inside. A few snorts or hoof stamps rang through the air but otherwise the stables were silent and empty. Brenadier raised his head and nickered a greeting. Garrick reached out to rub the chestnut stallion's nose absently as he passed.

Shuffling from within the open stall rang out as he came close. The Crow's large form filled the opening, allowing no room to pass. He fixed a steady gaze on Garrick.

The knight returned an annoyed look. Past the mercenary in a nest of straw at the back of the stall, Garrick saw Damian laid out as though sleeping. To his relief, her chest rose and fell faintly.

"How is she?"

The mercenary did not move.

Garrick frowned. "Let me see her." He moved toward the narrow gap between the Crow and the open stall door. The mercenary stepped aside, blocking Garrick's passage.

Garrick glared at him. "I had to do it."

The mercenary didn't budge.

The knight's eyes narrowed. "Look, I didn't want to sacrifice Damian either but Nephrita was going to return. Are you so selfish that you would have let the Goddess of Chaos wreak havoc across all of Faneria just to protect her? Or are you just stupid?"

"And where is Nephrita now?"

Garrick pursed his lips and straightened. He glanced back at the small raven-haired woman in her peasant gown.

Garrick sighed. "I don't know." His eyes travelled past the Crow to the young woman lying in the stall. "She might be in there for all I know." He tried to calm his temper as he faced the mercenary. "Just let me see her."

He stepped a pace forward but the Crow didn't move.

Garrick's expression darkened. "I'm not going to do anything to her. Stand down now." Garrick's hand lowered to the dagger sheathed at his side. The Crow began to slide his sword out of its scabbard. Garrick jumped back, drawing power to him and focusing on the mercenary's hands.

"Enough!"

Garrick straightened as Nephrita grabbed the wrist holding his dagger. With the other, she handed the mercenary back his cloak. "Thank you for letting me use this." The Crow nodded at her with the same impassive look he had worn since he appeared in the red forest. "May I see her?"

The Crow stared at her. For a brief moment, despite the unreadable expression that remained on the mercenary's face, Garrick wondered if the Crow would show some sense of moral judgement. Then the mercenary stepped aside to let Nephrita in. Garrick shot him a dark look as he resumed his position after she stepped into the stall. Garrick folded his arms and stared impatiently at the mercenary wearing his black cloak once more. Garrick noticed that the Crow wore it parted beneath his right shoulder, hiding his black blade from view but keeping the sword arm free.

"Damian?" Nephrita's lilting voice came from within. Around the mercenary's cloak, Garrick saw the raven-haired woman approach Damian's prone form. Leaning over, he tried to watch around the Crow's body. The mercenary moved half a step to the side, blocking his view.

Garrick snapped his attention back to the mercenary, about to spit out an insult. Before he could speak, a spark flashed from within and an echoed cry rang out. One of the voices was Damian's. The Crow spun to look inside and he and Garrick both pushed into the stall and ran over to the women. Damian sat up, leaning back on her hands as she cast a bewildered glance around, her yellow eyes flicking back to Nephrita.

"Damian?" Garrick asked hesitantly.

She turned her questioning look to him.

There was no doubt she responded to the name. Her aura no longer resonated like a beacon. Crouching close to her, he couldn't feel it at all. He opened up his senses, Nephrita's sun-bright glow flowing a few paces away. Focusing on Damian, her aura felt no different from the mercenary's. She was like a perfectly ordinary person.

"What happened?" she asked in a shaky voice, her eyes fixed on Nephrita.

Kneeling at her feet, Garrick reached out and laid a hand on her knee for encouragement. She pulled it away with his touch though the Crow helped support her shoulders. *Definitely Damian,* Garrick thought with a pang of annoyance. "What do you remember?"

Damian paused, then hunched her shoulders and her expression fell. "I... I lost control. I just..." Her eyes shut and her voice was hauntingly hollow. "I couldn't stop thinking about the barge. Beyond that, everything is blurry. I'm not even sure when I fainted."

Garrick looked to Nephrita. She had not ceased to stare at Damian since the spark that flared out a minute earlier, a dazed expression on her face. He narrowed his eyes cautiously, seeing the thoughtful look in her eyes and wondering what was going through her mind. At Garrick's glance, she shook herself, then nodded faintly.

Damian's voice trembled. "Is that..."

The knight frowned as she trailed off. "We're still not entirely sure." He stared at Damian. "She thinks she's you."

Damian's eyes enlarged. "What?"

Nephrita only shrugged.

Damian shook her head. "I... I don't understand."

"Neither do we," Garrick replied. He began to ask her something else but the sound of shuffling and soft voices outside the walls of the stable stopped him. "How do you feel? Are you okay to travel?"

Damian looked surprised. "Now?"

"No, not in the dark. But we should leave at first light if you feel well enough." She nodded uncomfortably and he stood. "Get some sleep. We'll have plenty of time to talk later." With that, he turned and guided Nephrita out of the stall and through the stable, taking up the lantern on his way out.

Left with more questions than answers, Garrick at least felt relieved that Damian was safe. He glanced at Nephrita as they crossed dark streets. A thoughtful look was in her eyes and it deepened as she faced him. He wondered what she was thinking. For all his practice and training to discern precisely that, he had no idea. That made him incredibly uneasy.

Neither of them spoke as they made their way back to Orneth's house. A faint glow of candle light illuminated the yellow windows. Garrick walked inside without knocking, setting the lantern on a table. A servant darted out of view in the next room. Ignoring the reaction, Garrick continued up the stairs, the house now silent.

In the loft, faintly lit by a handful of candles, he rubbed his face roughly. It had been a very long day and he still wasn't sure what to make of Nephrita.

"We should get to sleep. You can take the bed. I'll sleep on the floor."

A brief pause sounded.

"I don't think that's necessary."

His eyes shot open and he turned to face her. The confidence in her eyes, posture, and voice sent a chill through him. He glanced back at the bed beneath the window. The small straw mattress was made for one person and was narrower than most beds he had slept on.

"Uh," he replied heroically.

She stepped toward him. "I have nothing but Damian's memories to define me. I want to experience life for myself."

Garrick stepped back as she approached, his eyes drawn to the sway of her hips and chest. He struggled for words. Lifting an arm, she reached delicate fingers toward his chest, the long sleeve of her borrowed gown sliding down to her elbow.

He cleared his throat. "I don't think…"

His breath fell short as her fingertips gently touched him. Power radiated out of her, stirring and overwhelming his extra sense for magic and heightening the sensation of that soft touch against his skin.

"Just give me this," she whispered, rising on her toes and closing her eyes. He tried to pull away but she grabbed the collar of his shirt and yanked him down into her.

A surge of power roared through him as their lips pressed together, rippling over every inch of his body. Sensation flowed over him in waves. One moment the magic was so strong it overcame all his other senses, the next was filled with the flowery aroma drifting up from her and the sweetness of her lips, the next defined by the feeling of her body against his, the physical sensation stronger than anything he had known. He felt apart from his body, given only a glimpse of control as the feelings swallowed him up.

At once, it felt like an eternity passed and like a single moment lasting for the blink of an eye. When at last he regained enough control to push her away at arm's length, he found himself lying on his back across the small bed, his legs hanging over the edge to the floor and his hair loose. Nephrita straddled him. He breathed hard, staring at her.

She panted, a dazed look on her face. Leaning on one arm, she traced her fingers down his chest, rubbing the fabric of his shirt between them. He moaned softly, his blood rushing with her light touch.

"It's… so real."

Garrick blinked, managing to focus on her face. He couldn't regain enough command to speak.

She shook her head. "I felt things when I was a part of Damian. But it wasn't like this. Everything is so much clearer, so much more real, it's like I never touched," she inhaled deeply, her closed eyelids trembling slightly, "or smelled anything before." She looked into his eyes. "I wasn't alive before. I never even knew what I was missing."

Garrick could only stare at her, Nephrita gazing back. Somewhere deep inside, his mind screamed objections. He couldn't focus on that voice. All he knew was that he couldn't stop.

His arms slackened as she leaned down and kissed him again. Her power flowed over him and his body thrilled at her touch. He lost all awareness of himself and his surroundings, drowning in sensations deeper and more powerful than anything he had ever experienced. All he knew was her.

The candles had burned out by the time Garrick came to his senses enough to realize he stared at the ceiling. The only light in the room came from the moon glowing through the window. He breathed slowly, all thoughts fleeting.

Nephrita's head lay in the crook of his shoulder while the rest of her body pressed against him on the narrow bed. Her warm breath rolled across his bare chest while his arm wrapped around her. No smile marked her face, her expression blank with the serenity of sleep. Her energy resonated through him where her skin touched his, though it had diminished.

One thought lingered in his mind, a characteristic of the Goddess of Chaos that persisted through all the history books he had read.

Impulsive.

He rolled his head over to look out the window. Although he couldn't see the streets, he knew the soldiers lingered outside. Garrick wouldn't be surprised if they heard him and Nephrita a few minutes ago.

If any more of her personality comes out, we are all in big trouble.

CHAPTER 15
THREATS

EVELYN SPOKE SOFTLY, not allowing her voice to carry outside the bedroom as Lyle packed.

"I do not understand. You command the city guard. Your place is here. Why would a mission be given to you that takes you away from Misengrad?"

Lyle focused on folding extra clothes and packing them in his leather bag. He knew his departure would be difficult to explain to his family. Hearing his wife's objections firsthand emphasized the discomfort he felt at leaving them. He didn't mention that this calling had nothing to do with the city guard. He supposed she suspected as much.

"My experience is needed on an urgent matter."

She pursed her lips, clearly seeing his reticence and knowing she would get nothing further out of him. "I suppose nothing I say can persuade you to remain with us."

He sighed as he turned to her, taking in her golden brown hair and firm but not unfeminine chin and cheekbones. Her hair had gone half to grey and lines had formed in her face that were not there when he met her. She remained proud and strong, more so than she had been before they married. Part of him wanted to tell her everything. Instead, he closed the flap of his satchel.

"My knowledge is unique in this situation. There is no one who can take my place."

Sighing, she walked up to him and brushed his hair behind his ears. "Then I will pray for your safe and hasty return."

He leaned down as she reached up to kiss him, then they strode out of the room and downstairs. Marise, Amera, and Daven waited in the common room, looking anxious as they watched Lyle add some food to his pack.

"Where are you going, Father?" Daven asked, leaning over the back of a chair. "Why must you leave us?"

Marise shot him a stern look and Evelyn said, "Daven…"

"It is a dangerous mission that requires my attention," Lyle answered. "I cannot allow this threat to remain unopposed."

Marise stepped forward, squaring her shoulders and drawing up to her full height, much as that was. "Let me come with you, Father."

"No."

The quick rejection seemed to make her hold herself taller. "I can help you. It would be my honour to fight alongside you."

Lyle paused, turning his attention on her fully. Amera and Daven exchanged surprised glances but Lyle's oldest child held his eyes. He remembered what Gravier said about her accomplishments and what Evelyn said of her efforts.

The girl wanted to prove herself. Why did she have to do it like this? Yet he had allowed her to train. It would be unfair to embarrass her.

Straightening, he looked down at Marise with all the command he could display in his bearing. "Kearney has said that you are his brightest student."

She tilted her chin up with the praise, a stubborn look remaining on her face.

"But you are still young and inexperienced. It would do me the greatest honour for you to remain here and continue your training." She opened her mouth to protest but before she could reply, he added, "If you continue to excel at your training, then when I return I will buy you your first real sword."

Marise's eyes widened. She looked like she wanted to argue but after a moment she nodded. "I will train as hard as my body can withstand."

Lyle nodded in return and turned toward the door. From the corner of his eye he saw Evelyn smile in satisfaction.

Amera rose from her chair as he passed by. "Be careful, Father."

Two years Marise's junior, the fair-haired girl looked older for the maturing style of dress she wore. The worry in her eyes shone stronger than most emotion she had expressed to him since she was small. The depth of her concern touched him and he nodded solemnly.

Daven leaped off the chair and darted over. "What about me? Will I get a gift when you return?"

The boy's words twisted like a barb in Lyle's side. Before Lyle let a frown show he turned to Marise, standing stoically behind him. Lyle faced Daven with a calm expression. "You will be rewarded when you prove yourself. Listen to your mother while I am gone." Turning away from Daven's pouting face, Lyle continued across the common room and walked outside without another word. He hoped he had taken the right first steps to handling his children.

Only after the door shut behind him did the thought occur to him. *Father never said goodbye when he left.*

Lyle hissed out a breath. For a moment he hesitated. Giving up, he strode forward.

As he made his way through the streets of Misengrad he tried to shed off concern for his family and focus on his mission. Gawthrain had detailed the rebel mages' destination and the path they took to reach it. Inexperienced travellers weighed down with baggage, they nevertheless had several days' head start on Lyle and his party would have to ride hard to catch up. The thought of facing eighteen mages chilled him. He had found only a few more trained soldiers than that to accompany him. Fortunately, the mages were not experienced in combat and the deposed duke believed several of them had not used magic at all outside their small community. Lyle hoped that surprise and training could overcome the rebel mages. He hoped he could catch up to them before they reached their temple. Lyle never enjoyed placing so much faith in luck.

Finally, he reached the isolated town square where his men gathered with the horses Gravier obtained. They were outfitted for travel, half the horses harnessed with their supplies and the other half saddled for riding.

"It may not be the most comfortable ride," the second explained as he gestured at the stuffed bags hanging from the spare mounts. "I could only acquire two horses per man. I sacrificed some comforts so the horses could still travel quickly. Most of the weight is in arrows and rations."

Lyle nodded, examining his horse. "You have done well." His eyes narrowed as they fell across a dapple grey also bearing a light riding saddle. "I still think that as my second in command you should remain here."

"And I agree." Gravier swung onto the saddle. "But as your friend, there is nowhere else I would feel more comfortable than at your side."

Lyle smiled faintly as he mounted his horse, the rest of the men following suit. He had known Gravier longer than Evelyn. Much as

Lyle knew he should order his second to remain in Misengrad, Gravier's company was welcome. Lyle looked over his shoulder at the men.

"Stay alert and ride hard. Scouts, once we leave the city walls you ride ahead and report any sign of movement back to me. We stop for nothing, men. This is for the protection of all Faneria."

The soldiers let out a shout in response. Digging his heels into his gelding's flanks, Lyle led the charge through and out of the city, townspeople scattering as the horses trotted swiftly past.

Outside the city walls, they urged the horses faster. Lyle didn't bother to consult his map as he turned northeast. They followed the shoreline of Aura Lake, the massive body of water that stretched from Misengrad north to Albrith and beyond. The scouts broke off from the main group and pushed ahead, gradually gaining distance on the rest of the group.

Lyle had begun his preparations for the journey as soon as he finished meeting with Gawthrain the previous night. Procuring the men and supplies delayed their departure until the afternoon, leaving them with only a few hours' daylight to make up time. The group spread out as the horses cantered across the plains, Aura Lake glinting in the sunlight to their left. Minutes drifted past as quickly as the scenery, stretching into hours of hard riding. Focused on the land ahead and pushing his horse as hard as he dared, the pounding of hooves cutting across the silence of the open fields, a meditative calm spread through Lyle.

When the sun hung at eye level above the lake he called a halt and ordered camp set up. Fires were lit, horses tended, and rations divvied out before dusk settled into twilight and Lyle nodded appreciatively as he settled before his fire.

"They are good men," he said to Gravier. "I hope they can continue to push hard."

"As do I. Many of them are inexperienced with long-distance riding though they are eager to impress."

"Not that we have much greater experience with endurance riding than they." Lyle frowned as he rubbed at his thighs, already chafing a little. He wanted to cover as much ground as he could with what hours they had left this first day. He might have pushed a little too hard for city guards who rarely rode horseback.

"This is true," Gravier said, shifting his obviously sore tailbone.

Lyle watched the group for a moment, the men's attitudes boastful and jovial as they settled down for the night. Lyle let out a sigh as he faced the fire. Already he felt very far away from Misengrad.

Gravier leaned back on his elbow, a smile on his face. "It has been many years since I have slept under the stars."

Lyle leaned his head back to the sky, following his second's eyes. The first stars glinted in the sky, a shadow in the violet blanket of what was to come.

"When you told me you wanted men to ride out with you on a journey, I felt invigorated in a way I have not felt in years," Gravier remarked. "I have become quite comfortable in Misengrad but I wonder sometimes if I am still a wanderer at heart. Let us see if my old bones can handle the travel, though."

Lyle grunted at the man all of two years his junior. "You are making me out to be an old man."

Gravier smirked. "You were already a grouchy curmudgeon when we met, what, fifteen years ago?"

Lyle glared at him for the insult but corrected, "Sixteen."

Gravier rubbed his chin. "That long, is it? And yet you're still as stubborn as you were the day you struck me in the face in training." Lyle's expression darkened and his second held up his hands placatingly. "I am not saying I did not deserve it. I'm merely observing that you always seemed more settled in Misengrad."

Lyle turned thoughtfully back to the scattering of stars. "I have worked night shifts and duty has otherwise taken me away occasionally, but the last time I was truly away from Evelyn was before Daven was born."

"Ah, yes. Nice as the open sky is, it is hard to leave our families behind. Celia cried so when I told her I was leaving. I hope she will not trouble Lilana too much while I am gone."

Lyle hoped he could return Gravier to his wife before their second child was born. Lyle hoped he could bring Gravier back alive. Lyle's thoughts turned back to his family as they fell silent.

Gravier's thoughts apparently lay elsewhere. "So are you going to tell what you know of these mages' intentions? I imagine the story of how you came into possession of that book to be an interesting one."

Lyle frowned. It had been a very long time since he thought much on that adventure so many years ago. He knew he owed it to Gravier to tell him the truth. Time had dulled its edges but it remained a bitter memory Lyle preferred to leave buried.

"Of these rebel mages I only know what Gawthrain told me. Him I am more familiar with."

"The lord you met with last night?"

"Once Duke of Deverell, before it fractured and was taken over by neighbouring nobles."

Gravier shook his head. "For all the trouble that man has caused, I am surprised you did not take a knife to his throat."

Lyle shot his second a steely look. "I never take life lightly, nor should you. Not even Gawthrain's. He has no power and no money and was betrayed in his final attempt to regain both. There is no more harm he can cause. Frankly, I would not be surprised if he dies before the week is done."

Gravier mumbled. "If you say so. Go on."

Memories drifted up and Lyle suddenly felt very tired. "He originally had the book, though I did not know of its power then." Lyle hesitated, the weight of the past hanging heavy over his shoulders. He let out a sigh. "I travelled into Edan in search of my half-brother."

Gravier sat up straighter. "You have a brother?"

"His name was Daven."

Gravier's eyebrows rose.

"I found him in the company of a girl on the run from the old duke. She had taken a treasure that Gawthrain sought to use for a magic spell of incredible power and I decided to help them keep it from him."

"This sounds like quite an adventure."

"Yes," Lyle answered dryly. "The long story involves a dragon and a few different gods."

Gravier's eyes widened.

"In the end, we managed to stop the duke. The book was left in my care."

Gravier paused. "And your brother?"

"He perished in the attempt." Lyle stared into the flames. "I returned to Misengrad about a year before you joined the guard. By that time, Daven's death was history and neither I nor the captain spoke of him anymore."

Gravier looked confused for a moment, then said, "Ah, the old captain. Your father."

"Yes." Though Lyle had been captain of the guard as long as he had known Gravier, it felt strange to call his father by any other name.

"I see." Gravier frowned thoughtfully. "So you have a personal investment in this mission."

Lyle shook his head. "Gawthrain was our enemy then, not these mages. But I do know what these mages plan for that book. And that worries me."

*   *   *

Yanuk awoke in a good cheer. They were nearing their destination, they had gathered the ingredients required for the control spell, and from the glow of morning sunlight against the walls of his tent a bright and warm day dawned outside.

It wasn't until he stepped out of the tent that he noticed the uneasy silence settled over the campsite.

Yanuk glanced curiously at his mages milling about but few returned the look. The apprentices seemed uncomfortable and the older mages talked quietly, a few shaking their heads.

Miria's sharp voice rose above the others. "He was a fool. Should never have brought him on."

Heavy footfalls drew Yanuk's attention to the side. The leader of the band of mercenaries protecting them approached, a serious look on his face.

"Vitro, what is going on? Did something happen?"

The scraggly mercenary stopped before Yanuk, sending a glance toward the others in the camp. "One o' your trainees took off in the night. No one noticed but this morning. Didn't take a horse, but he slipped past my men's watch. We haven't been able to pick up his tracks yet."

Yanuk blinked. "One of our apprentices ran away?"

Some of the mages turned at his words. Edrand gave him a firm look. "It seems he no longer had any faith in our motives."

Yanuk's eyes narrowed. "What are you saying?"

Helena stared at him with a pleading look. "Yanuk, we have tried to speak to you a dozen times over the past days and you will not even listen to us. We are worried about you."

He couldn't help laughing. "Worried? Comrades, I have never felt better!"

"You've changed," said an apprentice. "Now that Gawthrain is gone, should we not be looking for a new home?"

"You want to start over?" Yanuk cut in with an incredulous look. "To return to another moldy pen to toil away the rest of our lives in mediocrity and obscurity?"

"We want to know where we are going," Edrand replied. "You march us on every morning without telling us what is our destination just like Gawthrain did."

Yanuk's voice rose along with his frustration. "You all agreed that I would be leader."

"For Gawthrain's sake," Helena said. Even the mercenaries stared as she confronted him. "Listen to yourself, Yanuk! What has happened to you? Do you really want to lay siege to Albrith?"

Yanuk glared at the mages. "Do none of you appreciate what I am trying to do?" Some of the mages straightened at the harshness of his voice while others averted their eyes. Yanuk's voice rose. "We finally have an opportunity to gain power and respect like we never had before. I thought that was all you desired. I thought you all stood behind me!"

A tug on his sleeve interrupted him. He spun, sneering at Vitro, though the mercenary returned a steely look. "A word, m'lord." The mercenary tilted his head toward Yanuk's tent. Yanuk frowned but walked inside the tent with Vitro.

"I know it ain't my place to say, Lord Alganov, but you can't command people just on fear. They have to respect you, too."

Yanuk's eyes narrowed. "Are you challenging my authority as well?"

The mercenary was unfazed. "Not in the slightest. But I can tell you from experience that a rule through fear won't last long. We did that once when we were a much bigger group an' it ended up nearly destroyin' us."

Yanuk stared thoughtfully toward the tent flap. He had noticed the steady leadership Vitro commanded over his mercenaries. Yanuk had even seen one question the decision to turn on Gawthrain and Vitro calmly and satisfactorily explained why the move was best for all of them.

"That surprises me. Your men seem to show a surprising solidarity."

Vitro grinned. "That's 'cause we're the ones who were loyal to each other after the rest of the group broke up. We're like brothers, my men and me."

Brothers. The word rang in Yanuk's mind. That was the least he could call his fellow mages. Shame swept over him as he thought back to what he said outside. Why had he yelled at them? It was the control spell. After ridding their company of Gawthrain, the thought of following the old lord's plans had consumed Yanuk and he could think of little else. He had been unfair to the other mages. Their concerns were well founded and he owed them better than that.

Yanuk straightened. "I should like to know more about your men someday. Thank you, Vitro. I see I have been treating my comrades unfairly."

The mercenary spread his hands. "Throw 'em a bone an' they'll always wag their tails at you. Follow you anywhere, too."

Yanuk sent a wry grin to Vitro at the reference to his brethren as dogs but said nothing in response. Squaring his shoulders, Yanuk stepped outside. A few cautious looks turned his way, including Patrus, who spoke with another some paces away.

Yanuk inhaled deeply. "Friends, please forgive my behaviour a few moments ago. I am only anxious to reach our destination."

Edrand folded his arms, his expression guarded. "Are we really chasing after Gawthrain's plans?"

Yanuk hesitated. He had told Patrus that the decision to cast the control spell was too great to make alone and he believed it. Had believed it. Edrand did not refuse the prospect, he was asking. Leaving the decision in Yanuk's hands. The expressions of the others echoed Edrand's.

"Yes."

Murmurs rippled through the air.

Stepping forward, Yanuk spread his hands. "Think of it. With power like Nephrita's behind us, we could demand recognition from the king. Acceptance. Autonomy! We could build a real home, our own tract of land, fine living quarters. We can truly live in peace and comfort, not slave away and steal what we need to survive in constant fear of being discovered."

Some of the mages seemed skeptical but the murmurs and expressions both softened.

Helena stepped forward. "You could easily have told us this earlier, Yanuk."

Yanuk smiled wearily. "I apologize, my friends. All this excitement and upheaval has wrought havoc on my nerves. I will be more open with you in the future. You know I have only our best interests at heart, yes?"

Several people nodded and many relaxed at his words. A few of the mages remained uncertain or suspicious but others looked calmer. Hopeful. Even Edrand's complaints silenced, though he pursed his lips as he watched Yanuk.

"Come, comrades, let us break camp and continue our journey. If we work together, we could reach our destination this week." Remembering the trust Vitro's mercenaries had in him, Yanuk added, "If you have any concerns, please do not be afraid to voice them to me. I promise to be more receptive from now on."

Turning, Yanuk retreated into the tent he shared with Patrus to pack their belongings. He smiled as shuffling outside announced the mages' work in breaking down the camp site. Everything would work out and before summer began they would have a new home.

And Yanuk would have the power of the Goddess of Chaos at his beck and call.

Silence and a smell of manure hung in the air, only the occasional snort or shifting of a horse ringing through the stable. Candles burned out as Damian sat against the wall in the stall where she awoke, staring unseeing toward the main corridor.

No thoughts crossed her mind. The horror and guilt that consumed her so recently were gone and it seemed like everything else disappeared with them. She had run from those feelings for so long that now that they were past, she had nothing left to fill the void, neither despair nor hope.

Emptiness clung to her. She felt incomplete, as though she had lost one of her senses. Lifting her hands, she tried to summon a spark, a flame, a frosty wind, anything. There was nothing left to draw from. Her magic was gone.

She lowered her hands. Despite wishing for this for a long time, it felt wrong not to have the ability that had been with her as long as she could remember. Now all that power, the magic that surged out of her on the barge, in the forest, in Trent, and in the town square earlier that night was Nephrita's.

Thoughts of what happened in the plaza shamed Damian. Now that she had finally faced the regret she had avoided for weeks, she could hardly believe her emotions consumed her so powerfully.

Cautiously, she glanced to the side. Domino sat two paces away, facing forward.

"You should have killed me." She spoke softly, her quiet voice emphasizing the silence clinging to the stable.

Domino did not face her or show any reaction. "Perhaps."

His straightforwardness didn't bother her. It implied nothing. Yet she knew it was not Garrick's payment to him earlier that week that stayed his blade.

Turning her head, Damian faced the mercenary directly. "Why didn't you?"

He still stared ahead. "I did not want that blood on my hands."

She sent him a curious look. Of all the answers he might have given her, that one she had not expected. The stories she had heard of him, confirmed by Domino himself, rushed through her mind.

Her next words came out cautiously. "Even though you have the blood of the Red Hawks on your hands?"

He showed no reaction to that. "I need no more."

A warm shiver rippled over Damian and her eyes enlarged. He said it with no more emotion than anything else yet it was the nearest thing she had heard to regret for his actions. Was he sorry for killing his former partners?

That burden is far heavier to bear than mine. She let out a slow breath, then yawned. It was the first time she noticed her exhaustion. She hardly knew how late it was.

Domino glanced at her from the corner of his eye.

She pushed to her feet, wincing at the stiffness from the hard stable floor as well as the lingering aches from riding. "I think it is time to sleep."

The mercenary nodded and followed as Damian walked out of the stall and climbed the ladder to the loft. When the shadows of the loft consumed them she said, "Thank you… for sparing me. For being here with me still." He said nothing but knowing he sat close eased her mind and she managed to drift to sleep in a nest of hay.

The stable was dark when a touch on her arm woke her. Damian opened her eyes and sat up. The light of a single torch illuminated the stalls below. Up in the loft, she could barely make out the outline of Domino's form beside her.

"What time is it?" she asked, rubbing sleep from her eyes.

"Almost dawn."

She followed as he descended the ladder. A vague sense of anxiety made Damian's chest tighten. The stable remained silent. The horses shuffled and a few snorted, many of the animals awake. She gathered her things and went to saddle and bridle Hope, Domino tending to his gelding Song of Silence nearby. Pale light seeped under the stable walls as they strapped on Brenadier's tack and led the horses toward the doors.

Damian glanced nervously around as they stepped out of the stable. A few villagers wandered through the streets but as soon as they saw her they scampered out of sight. Swallowing uneasily, she led her mare and Garrick's stallion toward the magistrate's house while Domino guided his gelding behind her. His cloak draped over his left arm, exposing the sword sheathed at his side.

Candle light gleamed in the windows of the magistrate's house. As Damian approached, the front doors opened and Garrick stepped outside. He wore his full suit of plate and mail, voulge strapped over his shoulder and forked cloak hanging over it. The petite black-haired woman followed him out. A lump formed in Damian's throat though Nephrita showed a placid expression and bearing. Garrick nodded to Damian and took Brenadier's reins. Behind him, Damian saw faces peering out through the partially open door, looking as uncomfortable as the other townspeople.

"You ready?" Garrick asked quietly. The stillness of the morning made it seem like all of Padura could hear him.

Damian nodded.

Then, a voice cried out, "Hold it right there!"

Damian turned and her stomach dropped out. She hadn't heard them approach but at least half of the duke's soldiers spread out down the road, swords drawn and pointed toward them.

Garrick straightened, his voice and expression calm. "Let's not start this again."

The same sandy-haired soldier who had addressed her the previous night stood in the middle of the group and stared unwaveringly back. "Those women are under arrest for practising sorcery. Hand them over now."

Her skin crawling, Damian edged closer to Garrick. He didn't react to their order.

"I told you once, as an Agaesi knight they are my responsibility."

The sandy-haired soldier shook his head. "I'm sorry, Sir, but it is our duty to protect Alden against threats to its people. We must take them into custody. We cannot allow you to protect them."

Damian tensed. The soldiers were clearly more organized and more determined this morning. If Garrick's status as a dragon knight didn't deter them, she didn't see how she was going to walk away from this. She felt Domino step closer on her other side.

Garrick seemed unaffected by the soldiers' focus. "I'm not trying to protect them. I'm trying to protect you."

Some of the soldiers shifted and a few raised their sword points higher. Damian's heart raced as the scene unfolded. What did Garrick mean by that? He might be strong, but could he hold his own against this many trained men? Would he want to risk his position by doing so?

The sandy-haired soldier remained firm. "You can accompany us if you wish, Sir, but we cannot allow those witches to go free."

Before anyone could react, Nephrita stepped around Garrick, setting her shoulders back and lifting her chin as she sent the soldiers a hard look. "He said stand down. Do not make us repeat ourselves."

A chill crept up Damian's spine with the threat in her voice.

Instead of answering her, the sandy-haired soldier gestured to the side and shouted, "Loose!"

Damian gasped and lurched back as a handful of archers with

drawn bows appeared around various corners. Domino stepped in front of her and drew his sword.

Widening her stance, Nephrita swung her arm in an arc as the archers released their arrows. A huge flare of crimson light streamed out from her hand with the action. Shouts rose up and Damian leaned back with a gasp as the energy shot forward, scorching the arrows black and casting them away to clatter against the road. Garrick crouched uneasily behind Nephrita and reached for his voulge.

Before the ruined arrows hit the ground, the sandy-haired soldier yelled, "Charge!"

The soldiers rushed forward at once, rapidly closing the distance.

Damian barely had time to gasp and lean closer to Domino before Nephrita threw her arm back around. A wall of blue-white light shot out. Streaking across the road, it slammed into the soldiers with a crackling sound and threw them back with echoed yelps and grunts. Distant shrieks from on-looking villagers rang out as they fled from the blast. The energy faded once it struck the soldiers. All of them collapsed onto the dirt road, several losing their grips on their swords.

Damian's breath fell short and her hands trembled as she looked at the scattered men who groaned in pain and struggled to move. Damian turned a horrified look to Nephrita but the small woman strode forward confidently in her peasant gown. Garrick hurried after with Brenadier's reins clutched tightly in his hand. Domino laid a hand on Damian's shoulder and she trailed after, still shaking.

Nephrita paused beside the sandy-haired soldier, staring down with an imperious look.

"You were warned."

She strode on, Garrick, Damian, and Domino following with the horses. Any townspeople that appeared quickly darted out of sight as they made their way through the streets. The thumps of their footsteps and the horses' hooves rang between the buildings.

A block later, out of earshot of the men who only just stirred, Garrick leaned toward Nephrita and Damian heard him utter, "Don't you think that was a little excessive?"

Nephrita's gaze remained firm. "I will not be bullied by the likes of them." She turned her unyielding look on Garrick. As Nephrita glanced past him to the disturbed expression etched onto Damian's face, her eyes widened and she looked away uncomfortably. Damian frowned.

"Come on," Garrick said, interrupting her thoughts. "We should get out of here as fast as we can." He betrayed nothing as he looked at Nephrita. "You can ride with me." Mounting Brenadier, Garrick pulled his left foot out of the stirrup and held a hand out. Damian climbed onto Hope's saddle as Nephrita took his hand. The goddess could barely reach the stirrup on the huge stallion and the knight hoisted her up almost entirely under his own power. Nephrita settled sideways behind the saddle, Brenadier snorting at the added burden. A strange tightness took Garrick's features as Nephrita wrapped her arms around his waist. Before Damian could say anything the knight tossed the stallion's reins and rode on. Damian hurried to follow, Domino riding beside her.

As they reached the town square where Damian lost control last night, she glanced at the fountain. A large section at the edge was shattered and half the plaza remained damp from the water that drained through the break. Raising her eyes to the statue at the centre of the fountain, she started. The figure carved in the centre was the God of Strength.

I'm sorry, Damian thought hastily as they passed.

Long shadows stretched before them as they passed the buildings at the edge of the village and Garrick urged them into a steady lope. Throughout the morning they alternated pace between a walk and a trot, quickly putting Padura behind them as they returned to the open fields of Alden. Damian didn't ask where they went though she did wonder at the knight's urgency.

They rarely spoke as they travelled, all of them seeming lost in thought, aside possibly from Domino. Damian glanced at the mercenary occasionally, wondering what he thought of Nephrita's return. Did a follower of the Gods of Time look more favourably upon the Goddess of Chaos or was she as maligned among them as she was among the Gods of Light? Or did it even matter to him? Strangely, she doubted the idea of travelling with a goddess affected him much.

Garrick seemed different. Damian couldn't quite identify what had changed about him. If she didn't know him as well as she did, she might not have noticed anything. But after spending more than a week alone with him after they left Trent, he seemed more closed off, more aloof. Even though he flashed them the same smiles, he felt distant. It was not the same reaction as he had after Domino joined them. Garrick clearly hated the mercenary, feelings which had frequently eaten away at him, but he had remained warm to Damian. She wondered what was going on in his mind. With Nephrita clinging to him as they rode, she dared not ask. Damian wondered if she came across the same way with the goddess among them.

As for their new addition, Damian scarcely knew what to think. Nephrita remained as silent as the rest of them, sometimes looking around in wonder, sometimes looking distant, sometimes elated, sometimes confused, and when she met Damian's eyes her expression turned pensive or uncomfortable. The idea that Damian travelled with the Goddess of Chaos terrified her yet she couldn't guess at Nephrita's intentions. Last night, the petite woman seemed uncertain and harmless. The morning's events dashed that image. Her reactions baffled Damian.

Is she just emotional or confused or is she as volatile and unrestrained as a wild animal? Does she want to be the feared figure out of legend or is she content staying with us? She's been imprisoned for hundreds of years, yet she said the only thing she remembers is my life.

Does she feel ashamed of what she did when she looks at me? Is there still innocence inside her or has she already become something dark? Could we keep her from reverting to the person she was in that vision I saw? Or has she already and this attitude is nothing but a show?

That, Damian thought, seemed unlikely, as she watched Nephrita hold out her arms and lean her head back, eyes shut and lips parted while a summer breeze blew over them. The sight sent a shiver unexpectedly through Damian.

When the sun hung directly overhead, Garrick called a halt to rest the horses and eat. Damian hovered close to Domino as she led Hope to a creek. As the mare drank, Damian felt eyes watching her. She sent a furtive glance over her shoulder and found Nephrita staring at her inquisitively. Damian averted her eyes.

"Why do you keep looking at me like that?"

Damian started at the sharpness of Nephrita's voice. Spinning around, she found the petite woman almost within arm's reach. Domino and Garrick turned at Nephrita's words. The knight tensed, a suspicious look on his face, but he hesitated to approach. The mercenary simply watched. Nephrita stared at Damian, a defiant yet desperate look on her face. Her voice had sounded the same. Annoyed and angry, but hurt.

"I'm not the person you think I am. I'm not some bloodthirsty monster. I'm just like you."

"I'm nothing like you! I don't hurt people!" Damian winced and her voice dropped. "At least, not intentionally."

Nephrita shook her head, a baffled expression crossing her eyes. "Neither do I."

"You attacked those men in Padura." Damian realized she put more venom into the words than she intended.

Nephrita leaned back in surprise. "I did that for you."

Damian's breath fell short. "What?"

A serene smile crossed the petite woman's face, utterly unconcerned for the harm she caused. "You shouldn't have to put up with that, but I know you would never stand up for yourself against them. I did it to protect you."

Garrick replied in a warning tone before Damian could find words. "You realize that doesn't help her position."

Nephrita turned a glare to him. "So I was supposed to just let them take us? I'm not going to let her suffer."

Damian trembled as the raven-haired woman looked upon the knight almost as she had the soldiers in the village.

Garrick's eyes narrowed though he didn't step closer. "Don't you understand that she's going to suffer more—"

"Why?" Damian uttered.

Trailing off, Garrick looked at her.

The disturbing smile returned to Nephrita's face as though she forgot Garrick's presence entirely. "Why? Damian, I owe you my life. And I don't mean just my survival. Everything I know, everything I've experienced is from you, and every moment of your life is part of mine."

As Damian considered everything that meant, her cheeks flushed. *She knows all my secrets. All the mistakes I've made, the ridiculous things I've said and done, the embarrassing thoughts I've had, the things I've done while alone...* The thought made her unease with Nephrita grow.

Before Damian could respond, Nephrita's smile darkened and energy rippled through the air around her. "And I will never, *ever* let anyone else hurt you."

All warmth fled Damian's body. Horrified, she stared at Nephrita. The petite woman seemed unaffected by Damian's discomfort. Garrick stepped closer, reaching for the dagger sheathed on his belt.

"No," Damian uttered, barely above a whisper.

Nephrita's smile faded and she looked confused. "What?"

"You can't just go around attacking people! If you really lived my life, you would know that."

The bewildered expression on Nephrita's face intensified. "But those men were attacking us. They deserved to get the same in kind."

"Just because they were attacking us doesn't give you the right to do the same." Damian felt more uncomfortable with each word she spoke. If the goddess didn't believe this already despite living Damian's life, how could Nephrita understand what Damian was trying to tell her? "You have to be better than that."

Nephrita gave her a dubious look. "We are better than them."

The absolute conviction in Nephrita's eyes and voice chilled Damian straight through.

"I'm not going to bow down to people like that and I won't let you do so either."

Struggling to breathe, Damian shook her head and backed away. *She's beyond reasoning.* Nephrita watched as Damian drew near to the creek, the raven-haired woman looking baffled at Damian's reaction.

Movement over Nephrita's shoulder caught Damian's eye. Behind the goddess, Garrick shot Damian a warning look, his hand hovering over the ivory hilt of his dagger. Damian wondered why he didn't reach for his voulge. The meaning was clear. If she couldn't make Nephrita see reason, then the goddess already posed too much of a threat. Damian imagined what would happen if Garrick attacked Nephrita and trembled at the thought. At least one of them would die. As much as the goddess terrified Damian, the mental image of Nephrita dying before her made Damian sick to her stomach. Likely Nephrita would not fall and instead it would be Garrick, Domino, the horses, and maybe Damian. Then no one would be able to stop the Goddess of Chaos.

Damian swallowed around a lump in her throat, her knees trembling and voice tiny. "Just… don't hurt anyone else. Please."

Nephrita stared at Damian, still doubtful but looking concerned. "Very well. But I will protect you."

Damian nodded shakily. As Nephrita turned to face Domino and Garrick, the knight straightened and lowered his hand, his posture at ease.

With a toss of her head that seemed to cast off the entire conversation, the goddess smiled brightly. "Well, shall we eat?"

Garrick nodded and turned toward his bags, lying forgotten in the grass some paces away. Nephrita followed. Damian lingered by the creek, her hands quavering from the confrontation while she watched Nephrita sashay across the grass.

Domino's large form stepped close, his deep voice quiet. "You are not bound to her."

Damian glanced curiously at him.

The mercenary returned an expressionless look. "You could leave."

Damian looked at Nephrita, kneeling beside Garrick as the knight dug in his bag for food. The thought had not occurred to Damian. With no magic left to lose control over, there was no need for her to continue to Misengrad. Part of her desperately wanted to escape, to get away from Nephrita and back to the life she had been taken from. That remained a distant dream.

Damian shook her head. "It's my fault Nephrita is free." She imagined being at home trying to rebuild her father's cloth trade and hearing news that the goddess attacked others. Damian would never be able to forgive herself. "If there is anything I can do to keep her from harming people I have to do it. I can't just walk away from this."

Silence met her words. She turned to look up at Domino. To her surprise, she found a thoughtful, measuring look on his face as he gazed at her. He nodded. Then, he turned to take up Song of Silence's reins. Damian led Hope and Brenadier over to Garrick and Nephrita. The knight leaned over his rations. Nephrita stared intently at Damian as she kneeled in the grass.

Damian shifted uncomfortably. "What is it?"

"I'm just wondering why your eyes are yellow."

Damian blinked. "What?"

"Those aren't my eyes."

Damian paused, not knowing what to say. She had not thought of that either.

Garrick shrugged. "Well, you are the Goddess of Chaos. I suppose what happened was more or less random." He grinned at Damian, but it didn't reach his eyes. "Who knows, you could have come out with a tail."

Damian shivered, repulsed at the thought.

Nephrita shot him a dark glare. "I think Damian has suffered enough because of her eyes without you making light of it."

Garrick held up his hands. "I'm just kidding."

Damian tensed at the exchange but Nephrita seemed mollified by his response. As they resumed eating, Damian considered what they said. She couldn't guess how many ways she could have been affected by Nephrita's influence. For all the fear she had felt through her life at the thought of her eyes being exposed, she supposed she could have dealt with an abnormality far worse. Perhaps she might have suffered some defect so horrible her father would not have kept her.

He loved me. And others have accepted me in spite of my appearance.

Soon, they mounted their horses and resumed their journey across the rolling hills. Their travel continued in silence and at an increased pace. Damian wondered where Garrick led them and why. She never gathered the courage to ask. After their conversation, Damian was afraid to speak to Nephrita at all.

Exhaustion crept over Damian before they sought out a place to make camp for the night. She barely had the strength to tend to Hope and relinquished the pinto to Nephrita's care when the raven-haired woman offered to take over.

"Well, I'm not surprised," Garrick said softly when Damian mentioned her tiredness. He eyed Nephrita, still tending to Damian's horse while the rest of them sat before the fire. "That summoning last night took a lot out of you." A dry smile crossed the knight's face. "Literally."

Too tired and worried to find any humour in his words, Damian said nothing in response.

"So," Nephrita said as she strode toward them, her peasant gown dragging through the grass. "I keep waiting for someone else to bring it up but no one has. Where are we going now?"

Garrick looked into the fire. "Away. Away from Padura, at least." He glanced cautiously at Nephrita from the corner of his eye as she sat beside him. "I don't doubt word will spread fast about what happened there and I want to reach Misengrad before our reputation does."

A heavy weight settled in the pit of Damian's stomach. "What will we do there?"

"Try to keep people from finding out the truth, for one."

Nephrita looked suspiciously at him. "Why?"

He studied her. "If word got out that the Goddess of Chaos was walking among people again, I don't doubt there would be panic. If you really have Damian's memories and beliefs, then you know that."

Eyes narrowing, Nephrita let out a scoffing sound and looked away. Damian swallowed uncomfortably. Garrick seemed compassionate enough but what would the rest of the Agaesi think of Damian? What would they do to Nephrita once they found out who she was? What could they do? That thought sent a chill through Damian.

Sighing, she leaned her head back and looked up at the stars glinting to life. Much as she knew she couldn't just leave, Damian felt uneasy with the thought of entering Misengrad and coming face to face with the Agaesi after what had happened.

Suddenly, Damian noticed some of the stars shifting out of alignment and a few grew larger. She inhaled sharply at the sight, her heart turning cold.

Nephrita sprang to her feet, the others quickly following suit. Domino seemed only to react to their agitation. By the time Garrick stood, his voulge was in his hands and he searched the darkness, his body tensing. Damian tensed as well, wanting to believe the appearance of the sprites was coincidence. She knew that wasn't true.

Nephrita stepped a pace beyond Garrick and Domino at the edge of the fire. A dark smile was clear in her voice. "I've been waiting for this moment." Damian shivered as Domino drew his black blade and peered into the darkness. It wasn't long before the towering shadow appeared.

The fox woman Niabi approached in the night.

CHAPTER 16
THE BINDING

YANUK TENSED AS he saw Vitro galloping back to the front of the column. It wasn't until the mercenary leader slowed his horse near Yanuk that he saw the grin on Vitro's face.

"We've found it, Lord Alganov."

Yanuk's face and heart lit up. "Where?"

Vitro gestured over his shoulder with a jerk of his head. "Jus' over that ridge there. My men're uncovering the entrance now."

A grin spread across Yanuk's face. He turned to face the rest of the horses and wagons. "Brothers and sisters, our hour of triumph is nigh!" Sensing his excitement, his horse pranced and reared and Yanuk struggled to maintain his seat. When he regained control of the horse, he pointed where Vitro indicated. "Beyond that ridge lies our destination, and there ultimate power awaits us!" Various reactions rippled through the group, from murmurs to exclamations. Yanuk glanced up at the retreating spring afternoon. He knew he should wait to penetrate the temple until the following day but his eagerness to finally cast the spell that would make them unstoppable overwhelmed him. "Make haste, for tonight we will stand as gods!" Digging his heels into his horse's flanks, he urged the beast to lope after Vitro, leading him over the ridge.

A forest grew on the far side of the ridge and covered the ravine beyond, tree tops burnished in the sinking sunlight. Vitro's mercenaries cleared a path through the wood, the trees hunching so close together it could barely admit one horse. Yanuk dismounted at the edge of the forest, hips and legs throbbing from sitting astride the saddle, and strode through the shadowy tunnel of trees. The mercenaries held lit torches by the time Yanuk reached them.

The entrance was an unassuming pit in the forest floor, black beyond the edges of the undergrowth. Based on the amount of cut brush piled up, Yanuk imagined it had been well concealed. Yanuk approached the edge of the pit and peered inside. He could just make out tiny lights flickering some three stories down.

"I've got two men down there examinin' the place," Vitro remarked. "Despite it all bein' buried, they say it looks pretty secure."

A few mages crept up as Yanuk straightened. "Good. We will go down tonight."

The mercenary leader grinned. "I thought you'd say that." Vitro turned to his men. "Get the ropes ready." Yanuk picked up a bag that contained the ancient book and the ingredients required to cast the control spell as the mercenaries prepared a harness from their ropes attached to two nearby trees. Soon, they secured the ropes to Yanuk and gently tilted him over the edge.

Beyond the lip of the pit the darkness was absolute. Yanuk clutched his bag closely, unable to see the dirt walls, the ropes supporting him, nor his own hands as he dropped slowly toward the glinting torches. He strained his eyes into the gloom, eager to see what awaited him, but he could not pierce the darkness and swung against his ropes impatiently. The air turned cool and wet as he lowered farther from daylight and a sound of dripping water echoed through a vast chamber.

Finally, Yanuk reached the circle of light where the torches illuminated a mud-speckled stone floor. He regained his footing as the mercenaries freed him from the harness. Taking a torch from one of the mercenaries, Yanuk stepped out of the ropes. His eyes enlarged.

A huge room opened up, towering columns supporting a ceiling that must rest a few feet below the forest floor. In the light of his torch, Yanuk just made out the elaborate carvings covering the walls from floor to ceiling. Heaps of earth piled at various places beneath cracks in the ceiling, along with puddles plinking with dripping water. It wasn't until he turned to the back of the room that he saw the piles of tarnished coins and artifacts and crumbling pottery that drew the mercenaries' hungry looks. The treasures lay about the base of a statue against the far wall of the temple. Yanuk's torch lifted and his head tilted back as he peered to the top of the massive weathered statue, standing just beneath the high ceiling. A grin spread on his face as he took in the countenance of the most infamous of the lesser gods in all the pantheon of Light and Time, brought stunningly to life on a grander scale than he had ever heard of.

He stood in the only known temple to the Goddess of Chaos, Nephrita.

This just keeps getting better and better, Garrick thought.

Niabi appeared unfazed. She strode forward smoothly with her fox head held very high, firelight glinting against her golden fur and silken robe and the grass rising unharmed behind, leaving no trace of her passage. It was exactly the way she approached the first time and it filled Garrick with dread.

He stood beside the fire holding his voulge though the weapon felt little more than a familiar weight in his hands. The malakh had no eyes for him nor for Damian across the fire or the Crow backing closer to her. Nephrita stood a few paces before Garrick and approached the fox woman calmly. Garrick could feel the energy flaring within them both like distant storm clouds flashing with lightning.

And he had no idea what to do.

Nothing, he thought. *I don't have to do anything. This is their battle and I have no obligations to side with Nephrita... right?*

The more he considered it the less certain he felt. Much as he distrusted Nephrita, he had not claimed her as prisoner or enemy and he had tried to defend her against the soldiers in Padura.

He just didn't want to side with her any more than he wanted to side with Niabi.

It felt awkward to do nothing. He wracked his memories of his training in a search for guidance but couldn't shake the desire to simply walk away. Would doing so look bad on him to the Agaesi or to Damian? He had no idea.

I haven't had a right answer in weeks.

The malakh and the goddess stopped simultaneously within ten paces, the petite woman now several steps from the fire.

"You will pay for what you did before," Nephrita said, her voice nearly purring.

Garrick's shoulders stiffened at her casual menacing tone. It reminded him too much of her conversation with Damian that afternoon.

The fox woman didn't react. "You will not remain free, Nephrita. Even if you kill me, the True Gods will come for you."

The sneer was clear in Nephrita's voice. "When I have been alive for one day and have done nothing to earn such malice? And I thought your masters stood for Justice."

Niabi bristled, her black eyes narrowing and the fur on her neck standing on end. "Do not dare to claim knowledge of the gods' intentions. You are their prisoner and so shall you return."

Nephrita's magic rippled through the air and Garrick could hear pleasure in her voice. "I didn't think we would be able to resolve this reasonably."

A thrum of energy threw Garrick back. The blast struck him so suddenly that it wasn't until he regained his footing that he registered the sound and vibration of the ground tearing apart beneath Nephrita. The boom of Nephrita's attack drummed in his ears. The flames of the camp fire leaped and Damian yelped as she and the Crow stumbled from the attack. Energy crackled through the air and the ground trembled beneath Garrick's feet. He backed closer to Damian as Nephrita and Niabi darted across the dark fields, energy surging and plants shooting up. He could barely follow their movements and flinched as flares of magic and furrows of earth and grass shot past almost within arm's reach.

Damian breathed fast. "What should we do?"

Crouching and flinching at each attack that drew close, Garrick's heart raced while he watched. Surges of magic washed over him like gale winds, the power rippling over the plain and filling the air. The sensations reminded him of the last night and his skin crawled. Even if he wanted to choose a side, he knew that there was nothing he could do to influence this battle. He had never felt so overwhelmed, so insignificant, so helpless.

Garrick shook his head, not taking his eyes off the battle. "There's nothing we can do."

An orb of shadowy energy slammed the ground on the other side of the fire. Damian yelped as she and Garrick backed away, the mercenary following to her other side.

Garrick's shoulders eased faintly. This was the excuse he had wanted all day, sitting tense inside his armour while Nephrita clung to him. He no longer cared what anyone else thought. He could leave and Nephrita would no longer be his problem.

Niabi leaped lithely across the grass with all the speed of a fox. As Nephrita slung a stream of violet flames at the malakh, a pillar of earth shot up before Niabi, exploding into dust from the blast with a thrum that resonated in Garrick's heart. He backed away from the fire into the darkness of the land around, eager to leave the confrontation behind.

I hope Niabi wins.

The thought appeared so suddenly that a moment passed before

Garrick realized what occurred to him. His eyes widened, shocked and disgusted that he would think that. Yet he couldn't refute the desire. The thought made him greatly uneasy and not knowing why he wanted Niabi to be victorious only heightened his discomfort.

"I…" Damian attempted as the ground rumbled and sky lit up from Niabi and Nephrita's attacks.

Garrick chanced a glance over his shoulder. Damian watched the battle, mixed emotions written all over her face and eyes.

Good, it's not just me, he thought. Turning to the battle, he slung his voulge in its harness behind his back. Much as he wanted to keep the weapon in hand he knew there was little good it could do.

He reached over to gently push Damian back. "We should get out of here."

Damian stepped swiftly away from the fire as the fox woman veered nearer to its other side, ten paces from where they stood. "You think we should just leave them?" The question was as innocent and uncertain as a child asking why the seasons change. Damian moved unresisting into the darkness of the star-lit night as Garrick urged her on.

"This is far beyond either of us," Garrick answered. He paused, glancing at the Crow. "Any of us," Garrick corrected, tensing and quickening his pace as Nephrita's relentless attacks pushed Niabi to the near side of the fire. "We're better off letting them have it—"

He was cut off as the ground beneath his feet shot upward. His knees buckled from the sudden movement and the column of earth slammed into the small of his back, launching him into the air and scattering the three of them. An enormous blast split the air behind him as he landed and stumbled. He felt the pulse of Niabi's energy nearby as Nephrita's magic flared.

Garrick had just steadied himself on one knee when something shoved him aside hard. The beginning of Nephrita's cry cut off into silence as something smashed into him and everything went dark.

Fatigue crept deep in Lyle's bones as he stole across the grass toward the hill. They had ridden hard for the past days and he knew he would pay for it later but adrenaline and anxiety gave him strength as the sun settled toward the western horizon.

Using hand gestures, he signalled Gravier, the scouts, and the archers to his side. The rest of the men waited with the horses out of sight around another hill. Quietly, Lyle crept up the hill behind whatever brush he could find, well downwind of the wagons parked at the top of the ridge. At the crest of the ridge he paused, peering into the valley as he lay on his stomach. Gravier and the other men crawled up beside him.

In the deepening dusk Lyle saw little beyond a vague glow in the forest. He tilted his head toward the scout beside him. "What can you see?"

The scout focused intensely on the trees. "There's a group of people gathered around what looks like a pit, maybe a score in total. It looks like they're going down into the earth. Some of them are well armed."

"Likely the mercenaries accompanying them." Lyle glanced across the top of the ridge. "And the wagons?"

The scout followed his gaze. "I don't think any mages are left there, only a few hired swords to guard them."

Lyle nodded and fixed his eyes on the forest again.

"What do you think?" Gravier uttered. "Send the archers into the forest, take them down before they realize we're here?"

Lyle frowned. If that pit was the entrance to the temple Gawthrain had spoken of, then undoubtedly a few of the mages already waited inside.

Lyle shook his head. "We would never be able to stop them before they could raise an alarm to those inside."

The scout turned to him. "What are your orders, Captain?"

Lyle's expression darkened as he surveyed the land before him. He might be able to surprise the mages but they were too dangerous to face head-on. How was it he had been able to penetrate the temple eighteen years ago against all the armies at the Duke of Deverell's disposal, as well as a creature far older?

An equally powerful ally, he thought dryly. He sobered. *And a secret entrance.*

He turned to the scouts, his hushed voice hardening with authority. "Search the area. There might be another entrance into the temple."

Nodding, the scout turned to relay his message to the other men.

"Keep out of sight, but stay close together. We cannot afford to miss anything." Rising to a crouch, Lyle descended the hill, Gravier and the scouts following as they entered the forest.

Between the trees, Lyle occasionally caught a glimpse of the group around the pit. Gradually, the crowd grew smaller as more of the mages descended. They did not have long. Lyle bent down close to the forest floor, testing roots and feeling at the earth beneath the leaf litter, searching for any sign of an opening beneath his feet. A few paces away, Gravier's dark shape did the same. The scouts and archers spread out in a wide arc around the pit. Lyle hoped some tunnel could be found that would lead them into the ruins. Soon, he could navigate only by touch as night fully fell over the land and plunged the forest into blackness. More mages dropped into the pit, leaving a handful on the surface, and Lyle's worry escalated. He considered other options and wondered if he had time to set up an ambush on the mercenaries.

Then, movement nearby caught his eye. In the darkness, Lyle just made out the hand signal Gravier made, signifying that one of the men had found another way into the temple. Lyle relayed the signal to the scout behind him, then crept as quickly as he could through the forest after his second, stepping carefully to avoid making noise that might alert the mages.

Following in Gravier's cautious footsteps, Lyle made his way across the bottom of the ravine and around to the steeper hill behind. There he found his men gathered around a ledge made from the earth sinking in below some protruding roots. One of the scouts held a burning stick no larger than a knitting needle over the dark hole.

"Does it go all the way down?"

The scout with the tiny torch nodded. "We've already been all the way inside, Captain. It's a tight fit but it goes straight into a chamber off the main room of the temple."

Without another word, Lyle crouched down to enter the tunnel.

"Captain," the scout interrupted.

Lyle shot him a look.

Swallowing, the scout pointed at his sheathed sword. "You might want to take off your sword belt and tie it around your ankle."

Lyle gave the belt a brief glance before complying. Sword dragging behind him, Lyle wriggled his way underneath the hard roots and into the tunnel.

Complete blackness enshrouded him as he crawled through the narrow passage. The earthen walls were damp and cool and smelled of mildew. Lyle crept along in utter darkness, feeling his way with barely enough room to crawl on hands and knees. An occasional stone or root scraped at his shoulder or knee and his helmet bumped against the dirt as he tried to find his way. A primeval fear settled in his stomach as the encroaching walls and darkness pressed against him. He moved on, confident in his soldiers' guiding and urgency driving him toward the mages. Behind his sheathed sword flopping over his foot he heard others crawling after him.

The tunnel seemed to veer deeper into the earth as it turned. Disoriented and ill from the meandering path, Lyle continued, feeling nothing give in the walls. As he crawled, his thoughts turned to the young woman whose misfortune brought him in to Gawthrain's quest to bind Nephrita to his will so many years ago. Lyle couldn't imagine how Kina had enjoyed traversing such musty, narrow passages. She would have had a far easier time getting through this one than he did. Years had passed since he last corresponded with her and years more since he had seen her. Not so young any longer, he tried to picture how time had changed her. Grey in her hair, lines on her face. It was an odd mental picture compared to his memories of Kina but perhaps his years would surprise her as much.

Lyle was truly feeling his age when his right hand dropped into open air. Flailing his hand around for balance, he struggled to lean back before pitching forward. Reaching out, he found the passage didn't widen as it took a sudden downward turn over a stony ledge. The drop unnerved him but once more he took strength in the scouts' confidence. They had examined this passage without such assurances. Bracing his arms before him, Lyle slipped over the edge and skidded down the dirt walls.

The slide was brief and as Lyle tumbled onto more level ground, light appeared ahead. He eagerly scrambled toward the exit lined in aged blocks of stone. A room opened beyond the blocks. Two of his men grabbed his arms and helped him out of the tunnel onto the floor. Lyle emerged in a small chamber with a high ceiling furnished with the decaying ruins of couches and an empty stone fountain dominating the centre of the room. Likely it had once been a room where temple priests cleansed and purified themselves for whatever rites were performed here. *A little cleansing of my own would be nice,* Lyle thought. Dirt crusted in his hair and beard, mud caked in the joints of his plate armour and between the links of his hauberk, and his entire body was sore from the crawl.

Pushing his discomforts aside, Lyle glanced at one of the men who held a small torch. The torch-bearer gestured toward the only exit in the room, leading to a much larger chamber where light flickered and voices spoke. Lyle replaced his sword belt around his waist and cautiously approached.

Through the doorway he saw the mages gathered in the huge chamber. A number of torches illuminated the soaring room with a massive statue to Nephrita. At the top of a few stairs before the statue stood a man Lyle assumed to be Yanuk, holding his book as he addressed the crowd that watched silently. Lyle didn't listen to Yanuk's speech, instead focusing his attention on examining the room. Lyle didn't like the options. Only a few of his archers could shoot through the small opening at once and magic would likely cut straight through them. An unexpected charge supported by the archers might succeed in incapacitating many of the mages but a single spell against them could turn the tables no matter the numbers. And if the odds did turn against Lyle's men they would be trapped. There was no way any of the soldiers would have time to escape out the tunnel through which they had entered. Even if his men were willing to lay down their lives to stop these rebel mages, Lyle couldn't risk it. If they failed, no one would be left to warn the king of the mages' plans.

Gravier slid up behind him. "This is not a favourable position. It would be far too easy to turn our ambush into theirs."

Lyle nodded faintly. If he could coordinate an attack from the main entrance and their side chamber at the same time they might be able to stop the mages, but they had run out of time to arrange such a manoeuvre. Only something subtle could disrupt this ceremony now and Lyle wracked his mind hopelessly for an idea.

"Our only chance is to distract them long enough for us to rush in," Lyle uttered. "Have you any ideas?"

Gravier paused briefly before answering, "You could walk in there and tell them to stop."

Ignoring the jest, Lyle turned to face their small room. Twice as many men stood inside as when he emerged from the tunnel but it was still too few to face the mages. He could see nothing that would help them confuse their quarry.

"Wait," the second stated suddenly. "Something is happening."

Lyle looked into the chamber. Yanuk held the book open and chanted in a low voice. Light streamed in ethereal clouds around him, the strange powders and objects at his feet emitting a brilliant glow. The other mages stared, awestruck.

I cannot let this ceremony complete.

Lyle wrapped his fingers around the hilt of his sword.

"Garrick!" Damian cried.

Everything happened so fast that she barely registered the movement. Nephrita had attacked. A column of earth launched Damian, Domino, and Garrick into the air. Niabi stumbled as Nephrita attacked again. Niabi threw Garrick into the path of the blast. Nephrita cried out as the energy smashed into him and flung him through the air.

Then, as Damian sat up, she saw a calculating look in the malakh's dark eyes as she looked at Garrick, the knight moaning on the ground several paces away.

Niabi swept to her feet and shouted, "Stop!"

The fields, so recently surging with power and motion, fell silent. Nephrita halted beside the fire and Damian stood frozen.

Garrick hung in the air, suspended by a long rope of grass growing at his feet and wrapped around his neck beneath the armour around his throat. He wheezed and gasped, clawing at his neck and kicking frantically as the grass tightened.

The air in a five-foot radius around Nephrita crackled and shimmered with heat, the grass beneath her feet blackening and smoking as she glared at Niabi with hatred beyond any Damian had ever seen.

"If you harm him, you will know pain beyond the boundaries of flesh and soul." Her voice thundered through the air, dropping so low that Damian felt Nephrita's final words more than she heard them.

Niabi held a furred hand toward Garrick, standing tall though she swayed and blinked blood out of one eye. "There is no pain you can deliver that will stop me."

The impossibly tall cluster of grass rustled and Garrick struggled harder, no air passing through his mouth at all.

"Garrick!" Damian shrieked, shoving to her feet to run toward him. With her first step her foot sank into the earth and stuck fast. The other quickly followed.

"Surrender, Nephrita," Niabi continued, not sparing a look for Damian. "Or this one's life is forfeit."

Damian looked down. Her legs to the knees and part of her dress disappeared into the ground, grass pressed up against her as though it had grown around her. From the corner of her eye, she saw Domino buried in the field as well. Damian tried to pull her legs free. The earth near the surface shifted but the weight pressing around her ankles and feet was so great it might have been stone.

Nephrita stared unmoving at Niabi, the goddess growing more enraged with each passing moment. Garrick's face darkened as he desperately yanked at the grass wrapping around his throat. Releasing one hand, he drew his voulge from its harness, swinging it around blindly as he tried to sever the grass.

"How dare you," Nephrita snarled. "You drag these people into your petty grudge match and now you threaten him because you are afraid of losing to me? Maggots and leeches have better morals than you."

The malakh's eyes narrowed but she did not stir. "The life of one human is a small price to pay."

The polearm dropped from Garrick's hand. Pulling his dagger out of its sheath on his belt, he stabbed at the grass rope. His bonds did not budge and the blade smashed against the plants with a sound like steel on wood. The sight made Damian sick. Niabi's fox face remained implacable.

"Let him go!" Damian screamed. "I thought you served the Gods of Light. How can you do this to an innocent person?" Before she could say another word, something slapped against her mouth and pressed it shut. Damian grabbed at her face to find a net of dandelion leaves tied around her head. She could breathe but no sound greater than a muffled moan escaped from the weedy gag. The leaves were as firm as the earth over her feet.

The plain around Nephrita turned into an inferno. Fire streamed around the goddess like ink in water, the grass glowing red and shrivelling up, and flames rose from her body and eyes. Heat blew over Damian but she felt cold.

Nephrita's voice seemed to rise out of the ground and thunder through the air, the entire world echoing her fury. "Release him now or I will ensure your suffering is remembered throughout history."

For all the destruction circling Nephrita, she did not move closer.

Niabi remained unfazed as she stared back at the goddess. "If you value his life, then surrender."

Damian's eyes darted between them, her breath racing in desperation as she yanked at her legs. Beside Niabi, Garrick's struggles faded and his arms dropped to his sides. Damian let out a muffled shriek.

Then, the fire surrounding Nephrita disappeared. Damian, Niabi, and Nephrita straightened in confusion as a strange shimmering mist danced around the goddess.

"What…" Nephrita attempted.

Niabi's eyes shot open. "No!" She lunged toward Nephrita, arm outstretched. When Niabi's fingers reached the petite woman's peasant dress, light flared and then faded, leaving only darkness behind.

Nephrita was gone.

The fox woman stumbled as her furred fingers grasped at open air, no trace of the goddess remaining. "*No!*" Niabi roared, her voice booming through sky, leaf, and earth. The rope of grass fell limp and Garrick dropped to the ground. The earth gripping Damian's legs grew soft and the web of leaves around her mouth fell away. Stumbling from the sudden freedom of movement, Damian pulled each leg out as though it was buried in sand.

Niabi leaped forward, stretching her arms in front of her. By the time her hands struck the ground, they had become canine paws. Hind legs followed as she raced across the plains as a wolf-sized fox, golden fur glinting silver in the moonlight. Damian could only watch the malakh flee as Domino pulled free and Garrick wheezed and gasped for breath.

Shaking herself, Damian raced across the grass. "Garrick!" She fell to her knees beside the knight as he lay on the ground and scratched at his throat. "Are you alright?" Gently pulling his hand away, she peered close to see if anything still gripped his neck. Aside from a dark line circling his throat, she saw nothing different. The air rattled and whined as it passed through his lungs.

Garrick groaned as he rolled onto his elbow. "What happened?"

"I don't know." Damian took his arm as he struggled to rise. "Nephrita just disappeared. I don't think the malakh had anything to do with it."

Damian turned in the direction Niabi fled. After a moment Damian caught sight of the distant figure bounding across the plain. The danger had passed yet Damian felt no less anxious.

I have a very bad feeling about this.

Lyle leaned forward, preparing to charge into the main chamber as he drew his sword.

Gravier grabbed his arm, pulling him back. "Captain, no!"

Lyle wrested out of the grip. His eyes turned to one of the men standing near the gap in the wall where they entered the temple. Lyle pointed into the dark tunnel. "You, go back and tell the rest of the men to run if we cannot subdue the mages. You must warn the king of Yanuk's intentions."

The soldier snapped into a hasty salute. "Yes, Captain!" With that, he turned and dove into the tunnel. Gravier opened his mouth to say something, but before he could speak, Lyle turned to address the rest of the few men gathered in the chamber.

"Archers, prepare your bows."

Lyle knew that against so many mages as well as the trained mercenaries accompanying them, this attempt might very well kill him. But he had to stop Yanuk before the mage summoned Nephrita.

"The rest of you, get ready to follow me."

The men quietly drew their swords while the archers nocked arrows to their bows.

"On the count of—"

"Lyle."

Gravier's firm grip on his arm stopped him. Lyle shot his second a hard look but hesitated. A chagrined expression marked Gravier's face as he stared through the opening at the main chamber. Brilliant light illuminated him. Turning, Lyle followed the second's eyes.

The entire temple shimmered with light, so bright it hurt to look upon. The mages looked around in awe or uncertainty and many of the mercenaries standing at the edges of the temple stepped away from the glowing walls, hands on their weapons. The brightest lights shone from the statue of Nephrita and from the jars and powders at Yanuk's feet. On the stairs below him a human form crouched, glowing with the same sheen that flared through the temple and surrounded by streams of moving light.

"Darkness and Light," Lyle said under his breath. "We are too late." He slid his sword into its scabbard, dread settling over him.

The soldiers behind Lyle shifted uneasily. Without taking his eyes from the ceremony, Lyle held up a hand, willing his men to stillness.

Then, the light shining through the outer room flared, filling the temple and their side chamber with blinding light. Lyle tensed as he heard his men gasp and yelp. The shouts of surprise in the main chamber drowned them out.

When Lyle looked back, he found a petite woman lying on the stairs below Yanuk, raven-haired and clad in an oversized commoner's gown that was singed in several places. She glanced around the chamber, confused, before her gaze turned wide-eyed to her own hand. Lyle's fingers tightened over the stone doorway. He didn't need Yanuk's next words to know who this was. The resemblance was unmistakable.

"Behold!" the rebel mage leader cried out, drawing the woman's eyes to him. "Nephrita, the Goddess of Chaos!"

Now we can no longer merely stop Yanuk, Lyle thought. *We must kill him.*

Gravier's confusion was clear in his voice. "That's the Goddess of Chaos?"

Despite the discomfort that filled Lyle at the sight, he had to agree that this small woman in her peasant dress hardly looked threatening. In response, Lyle leaned his head back, gazing up the immense statue at the back of the main chamber. Gravier sobered. The face, hair, and figure of the statue precisely matched the woman kneeling before it. Lyle watched the diminutive woman intensely, taking in her expressions and mannerisms. The chamber lay eerily silent as the other mages and mercenaries watched.

Nephrita stared scornfully at Yanuk. "Who are you?"

Yanuk grinned imperiously down at her. "Your new master."

She sneered. "What have you done—"

"Silence," Yanuk cut across her.

Her mouth moved to shape another word, but her voice choked off. She placed a hand over her throat, struggling to speak. Lyle's skin crawled, surprised at the suddenness and effectiveness of the command.

Yanuk smiled in satisfaction. "Now rise."

Her eyes widened as she stood, her head leaning back to look up at him a few stairs above.

"This spell has bound you to me. My word is your law. Whatever I command, you shall obey."

Nephrita turned an icy glare to him.

"Interesting," Gravier remarked softly. "He can control her actions but her mind remains free."

Lyle didn't respond. The revelation didn't surprise him and he was more interested to know the limits of Yanuk's control over her.

"And it seems she objects to his mastery over her," the second added.

"Would you not?" Lyle uttered, watching Yanuk descend the stairs to where Nephrita stood. Only a small, empty bottle and burlap pouch remained on the step where his spell ingredients had been.

Yanuk addressed the mages as he stood beside the goddess. "Together with the power of Nephrita, nothing will stand in our way. We shall have our dignity and our freedom once more!"

One of the mercenaries at the back of the room applauded and tentative cheers rose from the mages in response. Many eyed Nephrita warily.

"Perhaps her reluctance can be used to our advantage," Gravier continued.

Lyle nodded slowly, his eyes fixed on the goddess. Displeasure was written all over her face as she stood beside Yanuk but she looked distracted, lost in thought.

"Let us go." Lyle turned away from the doorway and crossed the chamber to the gap in the wall. "We must be ready to follow them as soon as they leave but we must remain out of their sight." He turned to one of the men waiting beside the tunnel. "Keep an eye on them and report any developments as quickly as you can." Without another word, Lyle climbed into the tunnel and crawled toward the surface. Darkness closed in on him and he feared this wasn't the last of it.

CHAPTER 17
THE GODS' WRATH

DAMIAN AWOKE TO a warm, late spring morning, the scent of flowers and grass rich on the air. She sat up, finding no sign of life anywhere aside from her, Domino, and Garrick. No trace of Nephrita or Niabi could be seen. Under the light of day, evidence of their battle lay all around. Damian had felt the scorched grass crunch beneath her boots when they returned to the fire last night. Now she could see the earth blackened in a fifteen-foot radius, nothing remaining of the grass but ash. Other patches of destroyed earth marred the ground along with sharp ditches and towers of soil and roots. The sight chilled Damian as the memory of the confrontation flashed through her mind.

Garrick stirred and looked at her.

She turned to him. "How are you feeling?"

Wincing, he pushed to a sitting position. "Never better." His voice was hoarse and a whining noise accompanied his breath.

He dug bread out of a saddle bag and offered some to her as Domino woke. Damian looked at the mercenary, suddenly guilty that she had not asked about him in her worry over Garrick. Domino stared back, nodding in response to the unspoken question.

They ate in silence under the newly risen sun, Damian lost in thoughts of what transpired the last night. Her eyes were drawn to Garrick as the memory of him writhing at the end of a noose of grass gripped Damian's mind, along with Niabi's utter disdain for his life.

Damian shook her head, her skin crawling. "I don't understand how a creature that serves the Gods of Light can be so cruel."

Garrick stared at the ashes of the fire, looking weary. "The dealings of the gods are not as simple as the Seers would have us believe."

She looked skeptically at him but he didn't meet her eyes. She bristled at the suggestion that the priests of Light spread the word of their gods wrong.

Instead of arguing, she simply asked, "How do you know that?"

He rubbed at his neck as he spoke, his words coming out raspy. "Learning is an important part of an Agaesi's training. We still study the ancient histories even if most people choose to forget."

Damian remained uncertain, though her ire diminished as she watched him. When he leaned forward, she peered into his throat armour and saw a jagged, inky blue line drawn across his neck.

Catching her eyes, he smiled wryly. "It's bruised, isn't it?"

She looked away uncomfortably and exchanged a glance with Domino. The look the mercenary returned was deeply thoughtful. She couldn't discern what was going on in those clear blue eyes.

Before she could say anything, Garrick let out a resigned sigh. "I think you're right, something bad may have happened to Nephrita. Anything that could steal her out from under Niabi's claws is very dangerous indeed." Something shifted in his eyes but it disappeared before Damian could identify it. "We have to find out what happened."

Flipping his saddle bag closed, he stood and gazed across the plains. Damian thought he faced the direction Niabi fled. With no tracks or disturbed grass to show for it, Damian couldn't be certain.

"That's the way she went?"

Damian frowned at Garrick's tone of voice. The lighthearted demeanour she associated with him was gone, his usual smile replaced by a serious look. She was about to answer when she caught movement to the side. Domino, following Garrick's eyes, nodded once.

"I think so," Damian answered for him.

Garrick nodded. "She may have changed course along the way anyway. It's a start. Come on." With that, he turned to saddle Brenadier and Damian hurried to follow suit. She exchanged a look with Domino as she approached Hope.

They pushed on at a steady trot, their travel as tense and silent as it was the previous day. Damian spent the hours replaying the time they spent with Nephrita in their company and trying to imagine what had happened to the goddess. Damian considered asking Garrick his opinion but she didn't entirely trust his supposed knowledge of the gods.

In the middle of the afternoon, a tingling spread through her. She reined Hope in with a gasp. Garrick and Domino drew their horses up to either side.

"What's wrong?" Garrick asked.

Damian fell still, examining the strange sensation creeping through her. It felt strangely familiar yet distant. It affected her in a way she couldn't define, a thrum of energy swimming through her blood.

"I don't know. I feel something… strange."

Garrick gave her a hesitant look. "Like what?"

Damian's eyes enlarged as she recognized the sensation. "Like magic. But far away."

"Could it be coming from Nephrita?"

She turned to him in surprise. "How would I be able to feel that?"

He shrugged. "You were very close. You might still have a connection to her."

Frowning, Damian focused on the feeling for a moment. "I don't know." She pointed north. "But it's coming from that direction."

Garrick's eyes glazed over as he followed her eyes. "Well, if you can feel it from here…"

He trailed off and they all knew what he didn't say. If it was Nephrita, she was casting a very powerful spell. Damian turned to Domino. He said nothing.

Suddenly, the horses all put their ears back as one. Hope tossed her head as Song of Silence snorted and pawed at the ground.

"What's going on?" Damian asked.

Hope and Song of Silence shuffled and tossed about and Brenadier shook his head. Hope champed at the bit as Song of Silence stamped the ground.

Garrick suddenly straightened and faced north. Damian turned to follow his eyes. A beat later she heard it, a deep rumbling through the ground. Hope whinnied and Song of Silence screamed and reared onto its back legs. Brenadier merely lowered his head and snorted. Damian struggled to remain on the saddle as her mare danced uneasily and breathed hard. The rumbling rose to a thunderous boom. Domino tightened his grip on the saddle and the reins as he fought to get his horse under control.

"What's going on?" Damian cried out, nearly yelling to be heard over the deafening roar.

Garrick leaped off Brenadier, stumbling as he hit the ground. He knelt, laying his palm flat over the earth, and struggled to remain upright on the violently shaking earth. "It's ground thunder!"

Damian's eyes widened as she shifted atop the mare. Domino

dismounted, grabbing the reins of his struggling horse as he fought to keep his balance on the shaking ground.

Finally, the horses calmed and the rumbling gradually subsided. Damian patted her mare's mane as Domino soothed his gelding.

Garrick frowned as he stood. "I've never heard of ground thunder that strong in this part of Faneria." He stared across the fields in the direction Damian had felt the disturbance, his eyes narrowing. "I do *not* like that that came from the same place you sensed magic." He leaped on to Brenadier and spurred into the fields without another word. Damian and Domino galloped after him, plunging into the tall grasses after the huge destrier.

Scarcely an hour passed before a town came into view in the distance from atop a hill. Damian peered at the village, but with the bouncing of Hope's gait she could make out little when she caught a glimpse of it between the hills. The town looked strange, the buildings too uniform and the streets so indistinct she couldn't make them out.

When they reached the base of the last hill before the town, she saw people standing or kneeling in the grass at its peak, looking down at the settlement. Damian, Domino, and Garrick slowed the horses to a walk as they climbed the hill. A few people glanced back at them as they approached. Most of the people at the top of the hill, fewer than twenty, simply stared down or talked quietly to each other. A child huddled nearby sobbed alone, knees drawn up to his chin and arms wrapped around them. A lump formed in Damian's throat at the sight.

As Garrick, riding in the lead, came up beside the group of people atop the hill, he drew up short, his eyes widening as he followed their looks. Damian's discomfort rose as Hope reached the top of the hill.

Damian's breath fell short and her chest tightened as she stared at the town. Swinging her leg off the saddle, she collapsed to her knees in the grass, hands over her mouth.

"What happened here?" Garrick asked quietly.

The people on the hill answered though Damian couldn't take her eyes off the town to face them.

"We were attacked."

"We didn' even see them coming."

"They were just suddenly here."

Domino dismounted beside Damian, stoically staring at the ruins. The edges of fields and pastures and the narrow roads leading in showed where the village had once stood. Nothing remained but rubble. Brick had been scattered, stone pillars shattered, wood beams torn apart and turned to ash, and burn marks marred much of the debris lying across the desolate field. A jagged seam cut through the entire town, over a foot of earth separating one side from the other as the near side sank toward it. None of the surrounding land had been touched.

Garrick's voice was even. "How many?"

"A dozen?"

"I'd say a score."

"Only one did all this, though. A woman. Short with dark hair. She burned and knocked down everything."

Damian's blood ran cold. She could not tear her eyes away from the destruction. Bodies lay in the remains of the streets.

"That rift doesn't look like it was caused by the same hand," Garrick remarked.

An old man with his head half stained with blood let out a heavy sigh. "No. That was the vengeance of the gods."

That drew Garrick's attention.

Damian turned to the old man in surprise. "The Gods of Time?"

He shook his head. "No. The true gods."

She recoiled.

The man nodded toward the shattered remains of a marble building beside the seam cutting through the town. The pile of rubble remaining suggested a small structure but the thick marble columns and elaborate entablature had clearly come from a massive building. At least half the remains of the building were gone.

"That was one of the oldest Temples of Wisdom in Faneria."

Damian glimpsed a toppled statue in front of the rubble. An upraised arm was shattered from the impact but it clearly depicted the God of Wisdom. The head was missing.

"It was the pride of the town. Pilgrims came from all over to visit it. When that woman destroyed it, the gods were so angry that the ground thunder came and swallowed up the town."

Damian shrank in on herself. She followed the crack in the earth to the eastern border of the village. The outer wall had collapsed, large stones lying askew in all directions. The rift faded into smooth plains shortly beyond the wall, though the wall on the lower side of the break ran into the rubble of buildings half a block in on the upper side. Streets veered toward the furrow only to disappear at its edge. The layout of the higher side looked completely different from the lower. How much of the town had disappeared into the seam, Damian could only guess.

Dark thoughts tumbled through her mind as Garrick spoke with the survivors.

It wasn't the old, vengeful gods that did this.

"How many people lived here?"

It was the Gods of Light.

"About a hun'erd and fifty."

Paragons of virtue. Upholding the highest of ideals.

"Is there anywhere you can go?"

The beings that stand for all that is good and pure in this world...

"With no food, no clothes, and no transportation?"

... wiped an innocent town off the map.

Garrick laid a hand on the old man's shoulder. "I'll send for help."

Damian shook her head mutely, unable to tear her eyes away from the destruction. "Why?" she uttered. "Why would they do this?"

The knight sighed. "The Gods of Light have been away from this world for a long time. It probably wasn't until Nephrita destroyed the temple that they realized she had returned." His voice hardened. "Realizing that would be a sure way to invoke their wrath."

Nephrita's words the last night came back to Damian.

And I thought your masters stood for Justice.

Like nearly everyone she knew, Damian had spent her entire life worshipping the Gods of Light, striving to live to the pure standards they set. Despite that Niabi was a servant of the gods, Damian thought the malakh's words and actions only expressed the fox woman's own disdain for humanity. Damian could not imagine the gods themselves being so callous.

Not only did those holy beings not care about the welfare of those that followed them but they would be so petty as to destroy innocents in their rage against the long rivalry with the Gods of Time.

The dealings of the gods are not as simple as the Seers would have us believe.

Damian's hands curled into fists, squeezing blades of grass hard between her fingers.

Everything I've ever believed in is wrong.

"Where did they go when they left?"

"North."

She heard Garrick shift. "What's north of here?"

"Albrith."

Damian opened her eyes as Garrick cursed.

The gods bicker and we suffer.

Inhaling deeply, she rose, standing straight as she gazed at the town.

I'm tired of watching innocent people die.

Without another word, she turned and mounted Hope.

"Damian?" Garrick asked as Domino smoothly followed suit. Damian said nothing as she pushed Hope into a canter down the hill, ignoring Garrick calling after her while Song of Silence followed.

Veering around the town, she rode with her eyes on the horizon to the north, not looking back or at the wreckage of the village as she pressed on.

Garrick could only watch as Damian rode away. She owed him nothing and he had no reason to keep her under his guard. He had seen the emptiness in her eyes and guessed how she felt. Perhaps she felt the same way he did.

I could have prevented this.

Garrick rubbed his neck as his eyes turned back to the ruined town. Though he had been free of the grass that tried to strangle him for nearly a day, it still felt as though something wrapped tightly around his neck, a constant discomfort.

Movement in the village caught his eye. He turned curiously. He had been so absorbed in examining the damage Nephrita and the Gods of Light wrought that he hadn't noticed a group of people milling in the remains of the town, a large number of horses with them.

"Wait. Who are they?"

One of the villagers followed his eyes. "Soldiers from Hesperia. They showed up shortly after the attackers left."

"Hesperia?"

A couple of the villagers turned to Garrick at the question. Only then did he realize that his natural western accent crept into his voice. He gave the injured townspeople a glance before mounting Brenadier and riding down the hill.

The soldiers straightened and saluted as Garrick rode up, his destrier picking its way carefully over the rubble littering the remains of the streets. The largest man among them, middle-aged but built much like the Crow, saluted as Garrick came to a stop before them.

"Sir."

Garrick nodded as he dismounted, slightly uneasy with the deference given him by the large man old enough to be his father. "Sir Garrick Magni of the Agaesi knights."

"Captain Lyle Hitchcliffe of the Misengrad city guard." He gestured to the man standing beside him, also his age. "My second in command, Tauros Gravier."

Garrick straightened as he looked at them. "The city guard of Misengrad? What are you doing here?"

The captain frowned. "I sent word to the Agaesi when I left."

Garrick shifted. "I've been away from Misengrad for a while."

The captain seemed hesitant but continued, "I received privileged information regarding the people who attacked this town and I felt it my duty to pursue them."

The captain hid his emotions well but Garrick could see in Hitchcliffe's eyes that there was more to the story than that. Before he could say anything, the second piped in, "And they stole a book from him."

Garrick examined them both in interest. "What kind of book?"

"An ancient magic book," Hitchcliffe answered with a dirty look to his second.

Ignoring the look, Gravier added, "With a spell that allowed them to bind a god to their will."

Garrick's eyes widened as he studied the destruction. "Nephrita."

This caught the soldiers' attention. Gravier blurted out, "How do you know that, Sir?"

Garrick gave him a wry smile. "It's a long story." He shook his head. "Please, continue."

"We have been tracking these mages since Misengrad," the captain explained, "but we were unable to stop the spell when they bound Nephrita."

Garrick fixed his eyes on the captain. "Mages? Led by Yanuk Alganov?"

The second looked surprised though the captain only eyed him as he responded, "Yes."

The knight shook his head as his eyes travelled over the ruins. "This is not good."

"No, it is not."

Gravier took a half step forward. "But perhaps we stand a greater chance of stopping them with a dragon knight at our head."

Garrick frowned as he took in the destruction surrounding him. The town looked worse up close than it had from the top of the hill. No structures remained untouched nor could he see more than a handful of walls still standing. Deformed cookware, shattered pieces of furniture and clay goods, smashed vegetables, and rotting meat littered the streets with the broken stone, timbers, and charred remains of thatch scattered everywhere. Black smoke wafted on the breeze from various points throughout the town. Not many bodies were visible, though Garrick could see a pile that the captain's soldiers gathered beneath a singed length of cloth that had once been drapes. At the jagged scar of earth running through the town, the ruins on each side looked distinctly different. The broken houses of the lower side gave way suddenly to what had once been shops. He had no idea how much of the town had been swallowed up when the Gods of Light let loose their fury on this village.

This is my fault.

A few people hobbling in pain or swaddled in makeshift bandages meandered through the streets, picking through debris as they struggled to recover belongings. Aside from the occasional coins spilled, little was salvageable. Garrick's frown deepened as he watched them. Some looked into the collapsed remains of a well, others desperately picked through the litter of crushed bread scattered around a destroyed bakery, others flung shards of glass and pottery aside as they dug through the rubble of an apothecary's stand.

This will happen again, and again, if Yanuk isn't stopped. And now that the Gods of Light know Nephrita has returned, it will be much worse.

Garrick looked away, imagining how much destruction would tear across the land if the rebel mages continued unchecked.

"They plan to storm Albrith," the second added as Garrick remained silent with his thoughts.

The knight didn't react. He had assumed as much when the villagers told him which way the mages left. Even with a large standing army and the most fortified castle in the kingdom, that huge city with its massive population didn't stand a chance against the power of the rebel mages with Nephrita at their head.

Garrick couldn't tear his eyes away from the people struggling to pick up enough pieces of their life to start over somewhere else, or to find out for certain how much they lost. He glanced up to the hill where the few survivors he had met when he arrived lingered.

I could have saved these people.

Garrick shut his eyes, unable to face the soldiers standing so close. "I can't leave these people like this."

The captain's voice was hesitant. "We cannot linger here."

"I know." Garrick opened his eyes, watching two people overturning the bricks of what used to be a house. "But these people will die as well if I do not help them. I'll catch up to you as soon as I've seen to their care."

Hitchcliffe glanced at his men. "Then with your permission, Sir, I will leave the rest of this town's needs to you."

Garrick followed the captain's eyes to the stack of bodies. Garrick's throat tightened at the sight but he nodded.

The captain turned to his soldiers. "Move out, men."

Without question, all of them efficiently returned to their horses. As Garrick surveyed the destruction, they rode out and soon passed the jagged seam running through the town.

The townspeople remaining watched the men from Misengrad go, haunted looks in their eyes, then turned to Garrick. They looked at him for guidance.

If only they knew the truth.

The desperate, imploring expressions on the villagers' faces felt like accusations to Garrick. He kept his expression neutral but couldn't look any of them in the eye.

All I had to do was stick my blade in her. The memory of holding Nephrita in his arms in the city square resurfaced. *One simple action, nothing I haven't tried in practice hundreds of times. I knew it was her. I knew that was my best chance to stop her. But I couldn't. How many people are dead because I didn't kill her when I had the chance?*

The thought of facing the captain of the Agaesi rather than these townspeople rose unbidden to Garrick's mind. What would the captain say to him right now? Garrick knew what he would say if he was in the captain's place.

You are weak, Garrick Magni of the Dragon Knights. You are unfitting of our ranks and of the title Sir if you cannot perform the acts necessary to support our goals. Your goals. To protect your brothers and sisters. The oaths you swore to uphold when you became empowered with the strength of Agasis are bound by blood and your very soul. I want you to remember this disgrace, Garrick. I want you to live with it. To know you could have saved these people and all the others who will now die. You could have avoided this disaster by simply holding true to the ways of the Agaesi. But you didn't. Because you are weak.

Garrick's already constricted throat tightened and his breath fell short as the words rang in his mind. It took every ounce of self-control he had to maintain his composure before the townspeople.

"Sir?" asked a quiet voice. "What should we do?"

Garrick's attention returned to his surroundings.

Yanuk is still out there. He got away with this in one town and he will think he can do the same everywhere he goes. Nothing will make him turn back.

Garrick's gauntleted fingers curled into tight fists, the leather creaking and metal rustling.

I can't change the past. But I can fight for a better future. I might have failed but I will not give up.

Squaring his shoulders, Garrick turned to the woman who had spoken, a handful of other people milling nearby.

"Gather everyone together in that square and await my instructions."

The authority in his voice snapped them to attention and they hastened to comply. Garrick pointed at one able-bodied young man. "You, go tell those survivors at the top of the hill to come join us." The boy scampered away with a nod.

Garrick glanced at Brenadier, knowing the chestnut stallion wouldn't be able to move quickly for long. The knight laid a hand on the horse's neck. "I'm sorry, Bren." He looked at the group gathered in the town square nearby.

"Tell me you have a horse that survived the attack."

The tall grass whipped past all four of Niabi's legs as she ran. She saw none of the scenery around, her attention focused entirely on finding the surge of energy she could feel, now far distant. Anger heated her blood as much as exertion as the events of the past season rushed through her mind. Her defeat ate away at her like a parasite and she could not help reliving it again and again.

Shame and fury had swept through Niabi when she lost the girl bound to Nephrita, surprised so despicably by the human with the spell that allowed him to move so quickly. Then, when Niabi seemed so close to capturing Nephrita, to redeeming herself and proving her worthiness to her masters, her prize had been stolen from her again. Niabi didn't recognize the spell that had taken Nephrita but its energy was old. Very old.

Centuries drifted into the distance like the earth beneath her feet. Things had happened so quickly that Niabi's timeless existence descended into a sigh. Every movement, every decision, had to be carefully considered though she had but a blink of an eye to act. Passion kept her from giving up all hope. She did not like the ground thunder she had felt at all. Events threatened to spiral out of control and only she stood in the path of the Goddess of Chaos, the bane of Light.

Niabi's muscles burned from fatigue, her chest aflame and her eyes parched, but she dared not relent in her chase. Blind to the world around her, unable to gather the strength to consider her strategy when she would face Nephrita, she could only run.

"Niabi."

The voice rippled through every leaf and blade of grass, every grain of dirt, and bored through the entirety of Niabi's being. Niabi lunged to a stop with a gasp, a rumble of energy filling the air. She felt the world open up behind her, energy streaming out of it so pure that it was like a ray of light washing over her. As soon as her feet came to a stop, she spun, rising to two legs, to behold a visage she had not seen in hundreds of years.

Niabi immediately fell to one knee, bowing her head. Her voice came out faint and breathless. "Master!"

The figure that approached Niabi looked human though she fairly glowed with energy. With each step that she took, grass and flowers sprang up beneath her feet, buds opening and leaves spreading as she passed. Songbirds whirled around her rippling hair and the wreath of living laurel perched there.

Ganodu, the Goddess of Life.

"Well met, my child."

Niabi could barely breathe as the master she had fought and worked for over centuries of silence stood before her. Niabi didn't look up from the ground, seeing only Ganodu's feet. "You greatly honour this worthless soul with your presence, my master," Niabi said, struggling to keep a tremor from her voice. "I have failed in my duties to maintain your peace. I do not deserve to beg your forgiveness."

"None is necessary." Ganodu's silky voice echoed through every living thing, the air trembling with the power of it. "You have done everything within your power to prevent this abomination and you have acted with integrity. My kin and I have watched your actions from our sanctuary and they all send their appreciation and regard."

Niabi's breath raced and she stammered. She could not imagine that she would be so favoured by the gods that had been gone for so long. Niabi had survived only to serve them. All her efforts of late had met with such failure that she could not fathom they would approve of her.

"Thank you, my master. My life is yours to give to any task you desire."

"I would not wish to take it." The patch of grass and wildflowers around Ganodu's feet continued to bloom, the leaves and stalks reaching past her ankles. "Life, after all, is precious."

"It would be my honour to give my entire being to you if I could serve you better, master."

Though Niabi's eyes remained focused on the sprouting plants beneath the goddess, she could hear the smile in Ganodu's voice. "Yes, I know that I can count on your devotion, my faithful servant. There is a task I would ask of you."

"I will do anything you require, my master."

The goddess's words grew more serious. "Nephrita must be recaptured. We cannot allow her to remain free. However, we have interfered too much already." Ganodu raised a hand as a blackbird wheeled around her open fingers. "My brother Wyshied deeply regrets the suffering he caused to that village of humans. His rage got the better of him, as it had with us all when he discovered that his most beloved temple had been destroyed by none other than the patron of Chaos, who should have remained imprisoned."

Niabi raised her head slightly as Ganodu reached inside her gown.

"Our foes started this battle already. This is proof of their treachery, their malicious intent."

As her slender fingers emerged, Ganodu held out a dagger, plain in design but old and sturdy. Reaching out, Niabi carefully took the dagger. Only when she touched it could she feel the dark energy clinging to it. It belonged to the Gods of Time. Niabi's lip curled in a snarl over her sharp teeth as she clutched the dagger in her hand.

Ganodu dropped her arm. "We must not interfere with this world further. Therefore, it is with the blessing of my brothers and sister that we assign this task to you. You, Niabi, most loyal of our servants, must see to Nephrita's recapture. If you succeed, we would be glad to see you return to our home."

Niabi felt like her heart stopped. After six centuries of exile, she had given up hope that this day would ever come. Trapped in the human world, unable to return to the realm of the gods, her masters and her only reason for existence, what could she do but live alone with only wilderness for company? After all these years, Ganodu was ready to welcome Niabi into their home.

Niabi's heart raced as she thought of her past failures. Confidence and dedication made her body tremble with anticipation. "It will be done, my master."

Ganodu nodded. "Yes, it will. But you shall not face this task unassisted."

Niabi raised her head as her master held a hand out.

"The power of the Gods of Light will go with you."

Niabi inhaled sharply as Ganodu lightly touched her fingers to the bridge of the fox woman's muzzle. Power surged through Niabi, roaring through her body with incredible force. She drew in a breath, her eyes twitching behind their closed lids as she struggled to absorb the energy Ganodu endowed her.

"You shall be our manifestation in this land. Our actions and our motivation are yours. All of the gods give you this power so that you may fulfil your sacred duty."

Niabi could barely focus on the words as the energy flooded through her, bathing her in a white light. Her body shivered and screamed from the force of it, power she could never imagine would be hers.

"Go now, our servant, our avatar. The security of this land and the domain of the gods is in your hands. Go with our blessing and our strength and rid the world of this evil once and for all."

As Ganodu pulled her hand back, the flow of energy faded. Niabi's body surged with power, crackling over her fur as she struggled to contain and control it. She fell to her hands and knees, panting, though the exertion had left her more energized than she had felt in her long life.

"It is up to you now, Niabi. Show us your faith and we will await the news of your success."

Unable to summon her voice, Niabi stared at the knee-high plants around her master's feet. The goddess stepped back, away from Niabi, and suddenly Ganodu was gone.

Slowly, Niabi caught her breath, gradually gaining mastery of the energy roaring through her. Fingers twined through the long grass, ears and tail twitching. She lay still for a long moment. The idea tumbled through her mind that with a single thought she could cause ground thunder like she had felt earlier. Or with a single breath she could turn a desert into a blooming garden.

Finally, she pushed to her feet, managing to control the meagre, fragile body that housed such enormous power. The trust the gods had given her filled her even more. She alone had been bestowed with this all-important task and they had given their own power to her so that she may succeed. She could not fail now. She would not.

Niabi looked down at the dagger in her hand. Eyes narrowing, she clenched her fingers tightly over the hilt.

CHAPTER 18
NOTHING LEFT TO LOSE

DAMIAN FOCUSED SO intently on the land before her and the thoughts swimming through her mind that she didn't hear the thunder of hoof beats until they were almost upon her.

"Damian."

She looked aside with a start. Domino rode alongside her. In her agitation she had forgotten about him. She found his presence welcome. As she met his eyes, he gestured behind them.

Twisting around on the saddle, she glanced back. Her eyes widened. A group of men at least twenty strong, heavily armed and with twice as many horses, approached a hundred feet away. If the men meant trouble, it was already too late for her to flee. She had slowed to a modest trot since they passed the destroyed village though the men behind came up fast at a light canter. Damian didn't want to risk exhausting Hope by pushing the mare into a gallop. With spare mounts there was little she could do to escape the men if she had to. Damian exchanged a glance with Domino. Without showing any other reaction, he slid his cloak farther up his left arm, exposing his sword for easier access.

As they drew closer, the large man riding at the front of the group veered aside and the rest of the men turned to move past Damian and Domino without slowing their pace. Damian watched curiously as the leader, dark-haired and as old as her father, passed fifteen paces away. Her attention was caught by the style of his horse's bridle, subtly different from the bridles she saw back home. With a brief glance at her, he rode on before Damian could examine his horse's tack further.

The rest of the riders sent her looks as they followed their leader. Spread out, a few of the men passed her and Domino almost within arm's reach. She studied the bridles and saddles closer.

Then she recognized the style and inhaled sharply. The same griffin and swords marked the riders' tack as Brenadier's. These men were from Hesperia.

They're riding toward Albrith, Damian thought as the extra horses passed, the pounding of hooves fading as the men continued on their course without a word to her.

She glanced at Domino. The mercenary lowered his black cloak, hiding his sword now that the men had moved on. Domino returned a steady, thoughtful look.

Damian turned her eyes to Hope. The mare plodded faithfully along, though its coat glistened with sweat. Damian patted the horse's neck, Hope nickering in response. Then, Damian put her heels to the mare's flanks and pressed on at a canter after the men.

If they ride for Albrith, then their goal is the same as mine.

Damian followed the riders as best she could through the rest of the waning afternoon. The men stopped twice to rest the horses and switch mounts. With only Hope to carry her, Damian couldn't ride as fast as them.

It wasn't until after the sun sank below the horizon that the men stopped. Damian saw fires spark to life in the distance. She slowed Hope to a walk, hoping that the horses wouldn't stumble as she continued toward the encampment with Domino riding at her side. Gradually, Damian and Domino drew closer as darkness fell over the land.

A stone's throw from the edge of the camp, they came upon a lone man standing watch on the plains with a torch in hand. He held a strung bow in his other hand as he watched them approach. Damian stopped ten feet from the scout.

"Follow me. The captain wishes to speak with you. We'll take care of your horses."

Damian exchanged a glance with Domino, then nodded at the scout. Dismounting, she led Hope after the scout, reluctantly relinquishing the mare to another soldier before following the scout through the camp.

The eyes of all the men turned to watch them pass. Damian inhaled deeply, forcing herself to stand straight and not look down. The night had grown dark enough that it was unlikely the soldiers could see her eyes but she felt exposed under the scrutiny of all the men staring at her. The party was small, scarcely a score of them, and all hardened warriors bearing swords and leather armour or mail. There were no camp followers and no dedicated healers, cooks, or grooms, and there was not a single woman among them. Damian's cheeks heated up at that thought as she strode between the men. Domino loomed close, a comforting presence, but she began to regret her decision to approach these men.

Her guide brought her and Domino to the second fire from the northern edge of the camp and saluted. "Captain." Damian recognized the man who had ridden at the front of the group sitting before the fire with crossed legs beside another man his age.

The leader nodded. "Thank you, Tenner. Return to your duties."

"Yes, Captain." With a bow, the scout scampered away, leaving Damian and Domino with the captain and his companion.

The leader gestured to the ground before them. Damian noticed that his eyes were on Domino and not her as he spoke. "I am Captain Lyle Hitchcliffe of the Misengrad city guard. My second, Tauros Gravier."

Damian nodded and sat beside the fire. "I am Damian Sires of Aether." She held a hand out to Domino as the mercenary lowered to the ground. "This is Domino." The captain's second raised an eyebrow at the mercenary's introduction. Only then did Damian realize how odd it sounded that she had no surname or home to offer for Domino.

Before she could say anything more, the captain straightened and stared evenly at them. "You have been following us for some time." His eyes drifted to Domino more than to Damian.

Damian pursed her lips, annoyed by the dismissal. "I thought you were riding for Albrith. I thought..." She trailed off, realizing how foolish it seemed that she had wanted to meet with the men without knowing who they were or what they were doing.

"And you wish to go to Albrith as well?" the second asked nonchalantly. "Despite knowing what awaits you there?"

Damian examined him cautiously. *How much do they know?*

"Our men saw you arrive at Raven Point with Sir Magni," Lyle explained.

Gravier's eyes passed between Damian and Domino. "Though you left his company in rather a hurry."

Damian didn't know what to say.

The second smirked. "Perhaps you don't know as much about the people who attacked that town as I suspected."

The captain grunted. "There is much the Agaesi do not speak of, and I suspect that one keeps more secrets than others."

Thoughts whirled through Damian's head as she struggled to absorb what the men said. She had been so stricken by thoughts of what Nephrita did to that village that she had forgotten what the survivors said of the people who accompanied the goddess. It seemed irrelevant to Damian at the time but now she felt like she was missing a large part of the conversation. She reeled at the idea that Garrick was keeping important information from her. Somehow she found she couldn't deny the captain's claim. That made her more uncomfortable.

In the silence, Gravier asked, "So why do you ride for Albrith?"

Hesitating, Damian looked between the captain and his second for a moment. What did it mean that they didn't trust Garrick or his order? She wasn't certain if she should be more wary of them for it or less. What would they think if she told them the truth? What would they think if she didn't?

What would the merchant Damian do?

She would be honest. There is no sense in speaking otherwise.

Squaring her shoulders, Damian inhaled deeply and answered, "I ride for Nephrita."

Gravier raised an eyebrow as he turned to face her directly for the first time. "Now why would you—"

He cut himself off with a gasp and start as he looked in her eyes. She didn't look away. Captain Hitchcliffe only narrowed his eyes faintly. Turning her attention back to him, Damian found his gaze on her suddenly more intense.

Gravier looked ready to flee or attack. His hand moved toward his sword. "Shadows be damned, who are you?"

Beside her, Damian heard Domino shifting his hand toward his blade.

Staring at Damian with an unreadable look on his face, Captain Hitchcliffe casually reached over and laid a hand on Gravier's arm, stopping him from drawing the sword. Gravier reluctantly relented though a suspicious look remained on his face.

Damian inhaled slowly, facing the men without fear. "My father was Claude Sires. He ran a cloth trade out of Aether until…" Her chest tightened but she forced the words out. "Until I destroyed our barge. Up until very recently, Nephrita was a part of me, trapped in my body, which gave me a gift, or rather a curse for magic that I could no longer control."

The second blinked, wide-eyed. "What?"

Lyle studied her. "How long was she a part of you?"

"Since I was born."

"The Century Storm."

Damian watched the captain carefully, wondering how many

secrets he held. "Yes."

Gravier turned to Lyle. "I think I shall have to hear the full tale of this adventure you went on."

"Tonight is not the night," Lyle answered without shifting his attention from Damian. "So she was released from your body last night."

Damian straightened. "No, two nights ago. You know what happened to her last night?"

"You do not?" the second asked curiously.

"Yanuk," Lyle said, "the leader of a band of rebel mages, used an ancient magic spell to bind her to his will. He controls her."

Damian's eyes widened and she swayed back as if from a blow. "You mean… what she did to that town might not have been her choice?"

The captain nodded.

Gravier scoffed. "She is the Goddess of Chaos. I doubt she objected to the idea of causing such destruction."

Damian reflected on the conversation she had with Nephrita yesterday. Had the goddess lied or had she only attacked Raven Point on the orders of her new master?

What is the truth?

Damian looked at Domino, but the mercenary gazed silently at her.

"What can you tell us about Nephrita?" the captain asked.

Shifting, Damian thought back to her few interactions with Nephrita. "She is very dangerous. She seems like a child—reckless, impulsive, she does not consider the consequences of her actions and she sees the world as black and white. With her or against her.

"But… she said she does not remember anything of her past life. Until she was released, she thought she was me. I don't think she even realized she was a separate person." Damian paused, taking in the intense looks on the men's faces. "And she has not harmed or even threatened anyone who was not already attacking us." She squirmed. "Of course, she did not have much opportunity until she was taken away last night, but… I don't know…"

The conversation fell silent as Damian trailed off. The captain and his second both looked thoughtful as they considered her words. Gravier looked at Lyle.

Finally, the captain said, "You should not go to Albrith. It is far too dangerous for a young girl."

Damian gawked at Lyle a moment before anger set in. "I am not a 'young girl,' I am a grown woman. And I am not going to sit idly by while others rush to give their lives for my mistake. If there is anything I can do to stop the bloodshed, then I will do it."

Gravier gave her a flat look. "What would you do? Even if you somehow managed to convince the Goddess of Chaos to stand down, Yanuk controls her, and he will not be talked down from his goals."

"I will not allow a defenceless young woman to accompany us to war," Lyle added.

Damian opened her mouth to respond but another voice cut her off.

"What about another sword hand?"

All eyes turned to Domino.

Gravier remarked to Lyle, "Well, it is a good thing I didn't get the chance to bet you he was mute."

Lyle studied Domino carefully. "Only if I am certain I can trust that hand."

Domino remained placid. "Then allow her to accompany you, as my payment and collateral."

Damian stared wide-eyed at the mercenary, her heart racing. At first she was shocked that he would use her as a bargaining piece. As she stared into his blue eyes, she realized the bargain was not for him. He was giving up his freedom and risking his life to join these men so that she could do the same. He was sacrificing himself for her. A shiver spread through her.

She turned to Lyle. The captain did not take his eyes off the mercenary and hardly showed any more emotion than Domino. The silence stretched out for a long moment.

"Miss Sires, you will assist my men in caring for our horses."

Damian straightened, momentarily startled. "Yes, Captain. Thank you."

Lyle stood and the rest of them scrambled to their feet as he walked away. "Save your thanks until you are assured you made the right decision. We leave before dawn and ride hard." Gravier hurried after the captain with a distrustful look to Damian and Domino.

I do know this is the right decision, she thought as she watched the captain and his second walk away.

A pleased smile crossed Yanuk's face as he waved the goblet beneath his nose and inhaled. Many years had passed since he last enjoyed a treasure such as this.

"Temple ceremonies always use the finest wines."

The woman sitting across from him uttered darkly, "I find it hard to believe you were ever pious enough to taste any without stealing it."

Yanuk glared back at Nephrita. "You are the last person to speak to me of piousness, goddess. Or to judge me."

Nephrita did not turn to face him, her small frame perched on the floor of their tent with arms folded.

"The deaths in that pathetic little village pale in comparison to the blood reputed to be on your hands." His expression darkened. "Besides, do not forget that we suffered from that attack as well." The memory left a bitter taste in his mouth and he lowered his goblet to the small table beside his chair, suddenly uninterested in the drink.

Truthfully, the wine—and the taking of it—had been intoxicating. There had been a thrill when Yanuk first devised the spell that made him and his mages pass unseen, allowing them to take what they needed from right in front of people without being caught. Over the years, the novelty faded as the spell became a necessity to obtain supplies they needed merely to survive in their isolated community.

Taking such treasures as the wine from Raven Point made him feel more powerful than he had since his exile. He threw a few simple spells in the attack. To conserve his energy he allowed Nephrita to handle much of the destruction. She was far better suited to it though he had to admit he was hardly impressed with the meagre show of force she displayed in comparison to all the stories about her. The townspeople stood no chance against them and Yanuk revelled in his supremacy.

The ground thunder took them all by surprise. He remembered a brilliant light flaring out from the broken Temple of Wisdom where they acquired the wine before the earth trembled so violently he fell to the ground. His knee still ached from the impact. Barely had he pushed to his hands and knees than he looked out and saw the entire town split in two. The two halves on either side of the chasm poured into it as fast as a waterfall. Entire buildings disappeared, bodies speckled in the broken streets like leaves caught up in its flow. The screams around him drowned out his cry to retreat, though his mages and Vitro's mercenaries already fled.

To Nephrita's credit and Yanuk's surprise, five of their number had been swept into the pit and she hurried to retrieve them without being ordered to. Only three returned with her before the fissure slammed shut, burying over half the town within and the rest shaken to rubble by the movement.

Yanuk had crouched frozen for a long moment, staring in wonder and horror at the uneven seam running through what was left of the town. The suddenness and intensity of the assault rocked him. It took Vitro, who had lost three of his own men to the fissure, tugging on Yanuk's arm to come to his senses and gather his comrades to escape. That had resulted in an unpleasant confrontation from the mercenary leader. Vitro's complaints silenced when Yanuk promised him half the treasures from the vaults beneath the king's castle when they reached Albrith.

Only later did Yanuk learn that two of the mages had been lost to the fissure. Miria, dear old Miria, bristly as a thorn bush, blunt as a hammer, restrained as a wolverine, with her never-ending streams of criticism and a life rich with experience and knowledge, now lay buried in the earth. She never had a nice thing to say nor ever showed affection to anyone yet she had seemed amiable to Yanuk in her harsh ways and he had liked her honesty. Her loss left a hole in his heart that none other in their community could fill.

White had been Miria's recruit from three years hence, a sturdy and somewhat slow-witted boy who nonetheless pulled more than his own weight in his chores, as well as showing some promise for magic when he could recite the incantations properly.

The thought of both their bodies crushed when that fissure slammed shut sent a chill through Yanuk's body. With the others who had deserted along the way it brought their number down to twelve. Even young Rhyslen, Yanuk's most loyal pupil, seemed to have deserted them. The apprentice had failed to catch up to them as Yanuk ordered over two weeks ago and no longer responded to Yanuk's attempts at contact.

"Oh yes," Nephrita remarked dryly, dragging Yanuk's thoughts back to the present. "Of course the loss of your old grouch and your dullard hurts you just as much as the losses suffered by the handful of survivors in the innocent town you razed to dust."

Yanuk bristled.

Patrus, sitting in the other chair in the tent, lunged to his feet in anger, goblet clinking in his hook. "Those very 'innocents' are the same type of people who ostracized and mutilated us and scorned us for years when we had done nothing wrong. Miria and White were worth a thousand of their number each."

Yanuk gestured to Patrus to calm, pushing away his own irritation at the goddess's spite. The amputee reluctantly backed off as Yanuk stood and stared at the woman kneeling a few paces away.

"Darkness knows why you should care, but I know that it disturbs you to have those deaths on your head." He smiled in satisfaction as she seethed. "But rest assured, word shall spread like wildfire before us of the destruction caused by the Goddess of Chaos. All across Faneria and to every corner of Elderra, people shall know and fear the name of Nephrita once more."

His smile faded as he stepped closer to her. "And I will not have the most infamous god ever to walk this land strutting around looking like some common wench."

As he spoke, he plucked at the sleeve of her chemise with a sneer, the cloth marred with burn marks. She tugged her arm out of his grasp, glaring at him.

A dark grin crossed his face. "You will don yourself in a gown that invokes the name and power of Nephrita."

Slowly, she rose, her eyes smouldering. Light shone from her body and Yanuk squinted as the peasant dress melted and re-formed. The fabric darkened as the gown changed shape. He covered his eyes as the glow shimmering from her grew too intense to look upon.

After a moment, it faded and he turned to her. His smile widened. The robe now covering her looked precisely like the one on the statue in her temple. The wide sleeves and low collar hung off her shoulders and chest and the raised hem exposed her bare calves and feet. The fabric shimmered like black silk with large red and purple flowers patterned across it. She looked mysterious, proud, and exotic.

Acid laced her voice. "Will this suffice?"

His eyes roved over her. "It suits you well."

She looked away.

"Yes, this is a visage worth showing off. With me." Turning, Yanuk strode out of the tent, not looking back to see if Nephrita followed.

He drew back the tent flap and stepped into the dark night, the circle of tents illuminated by the large fire burning in its centre. His mages sat or stood around it conversing quietly or reading books. It took Yanuk a moment to locate Vitro's mercenaries, a handful hovering around the edges of the circle or standing in the darkness between tents. The rest presumably rested for a later shift or kept patrol around their camp.

"Comrades," Yanuk said with a smile, drawing the attention of all gathered around the fire. "Behold, the Goddess of Chaos reborn." He pulled the tent flap aside and Nephrita stepped out, firelight gleaming off her robe. "Our vanguard and ally, Nephrita."

Looks of modest or stunned surprise fell upon her along with a few uneasy or suspicious frowns. A torrent of emotion roiled in the goddess's eyes. She kept her expression otherwise neutral. As Yanuk gauged his mages' reactions, his smile faded. A few showed discomfort with Nephrita's presence. All looked weary and not from physical exertion. Their hearts were heavy and their minds ill at ease.

Yanuk sighed, stepping closer to the fire. "Comrades, I know you feel guilt over the events that transpired in that town yesterday. And I know you do not merely grieve for the loss of our dear, beloved Miria and White but for the many innocent victims of the attack. In truth, the young, naive Yanuk that still hides deep within this old, bitter man feels shame for my actions in that assault." A few of the mages looked surprised, if not pleased with this confession. Several gave each other bewildered glances.

Yanuk stared at each of his remaining companions in turn. "But I ask you, if the people in that town did not hate us, would they love us?" In the eyes of the mages, he could see that they knew the answer before he had to say it. "No." Pacing slowly around the fire, Yanuk addressed the mages personally. "Crain, do you think if you walked into that village with no ill intent, would those villagers beat you to the edge of death as was done to you years ago? Of course they would.

"Helena, do you think the people who expelled you from the only home you had ever known with nothing other than the clothes on your back and a threat of death should you ever return, do you think they regret doing that to you? Of course not.

"Edrand, if those people seventeen years ago were given the choice today to attempt to burn you at the stake, would they take it? They would not even hesitate.

"And to all our apprentices, even if you kept your gifts secret, would the people you fled welcome you home with open arms? No."

Yanuk saw the looks in their faces shift. Jaws clenched, bitter tears gathered, and sneers formed at the memories Yanuk resurfaced.

"We have been kicked down, trod underfoot, and spat on all our lives. We took such abuse gracefully and quietly, hoping we would one day earn their respect.

"And it has never come. We have done everything in our power to endear ourselves to others and yet people continue to berate and chastise us merely because they can. And I am tired of it. I am sick of being the whipping boy for ignorant and spiteful peasants.

"You know I never wished for it to come to this. But if no amount of diplomacy will get others to treat us with fairness, then we shall earn our respect with blood. I have had enough, and if it means being hated, so be it. The rest of the world has shown us enough spite for so long that I see no point in continuing to be civil."

Circling to the front of his tent, Yanuk spread his arms at the entire group. "Brothers and sisters, we will not cow to anyone ever again. The time has come to be treated with dignity. The time has come to stand up against those who thought of us as carpets."

Though the only immediate response was murmuring, Yanuk could see in their eyes that he had invoked painful memories in each of them. The apprentices, outcasts in their own right who had gladly walked out of their mundane past lives where they were taken advantage of and toiled in mediocrity, looked determined and hardened.

Yanuk smiled. "Let us rest. A great battle awaits us and we shall need all the energy we can spare." He turned to the goddess, still standing outside his tent, Patrus looming in the opening. "Nephrita shall continue to bear us toward Albrith with great haste and make light work of setting up and tearing down our camp each day. Rest, my friends. Use this time to regain your strength and refresh your memory of your incantations."

Yanuk inhaled slowly. His relief at completely abandoning the complaisance he had clung to for so long, which gave him such grief, lifted a weight off his heart so great it felt like an ache.

The other mages nodded and bid him good night as they retreated into their tents. Some brought books inside and left lanterns lit within. Yanuk smiled up at the stars.

Soon. Soon all will be right.

Turning around, he said to Nephrita, "You are not to leave the camp." With that, he disappeared inside his tent.

CHAPTER 19
TIDES OF FATE

DAMIAN SHIFTED AS she stood in the middle of the line of men waiting to receive their share of supper from the stores Captain Hitchcliffe brought with them. The travel that day had been harder than anything she experienced in her life but more than physical discomfort made her fidget.

She peered into the darkness. The half-moon overhead illuminated empty fields beyond the camp. No fires burned and no trace of daylight remained in the cobalt sky. The men who had received their share of rations choked them down hastily or sprawled on the ground, many without removing their sword belts. The sight hardly surprised Damian. Throughout the long day of travel they hadn't even stopped for meals, being forced to eat on horseback, and had pushed on without pause until they finally collapsed here. The only break in the constant riding came when they had to switch mounts or allow the horses to rest, graze, and drink.

Damian's tailbone ached from the hard riding, her thighs and knees sore from standing in the stirrups to ease the discomfort. Hunger twisted her stomach from having to wait for her share until after helping tend to the horses, a long process with so many mounts.

The looks cast her way made her squirm even more. Under the light of day it hadn't taken long for one of the men to see her eyes and word spread quickly throughout the camp. The hard riding felt a reprieve as she couldn't hear the murmurs that circled now that they stopped for the night.

More still, the men had identified Domino and whispers of *the Crow* rippled among the crowd. As Damian stood there, the mercenary's large form looming protectively close, the soldiers gave Domino a wide berth and many scowled or kept their hands on their weapons. Damian hadn't spoken to the captain or his second since the previous night but she dreaded knowing what they thought of being accompanied by Domino. She hoped the captain would not rescind their bargain knowing who Domino was.

Rubbing her eyes, she stepped forward as the line moved on, eager to get her share and slip away from the camp to sleep. She wished she had considered the fact that she had no food of her own and that Garrick had provided her everything she ate along their journey before she rode away from him the previous day.

Damian clung to the hope that she could make a difference, knowing she couldn't walk away without doing everything she could to prevent the same tragedy in Albrith as befell Raven Point. The pain of seeing that village destroyed by the hand of the gods she had followed all her life never faded through that long day. Despite the discomfort of the ride, distrust of the soldiers, and demands of the horses, Damian was glad for the opportunity to travel with Lyle and his men.

'Damian, are you out there?'

She started and gasped at the voice that rang out to her. "Nephrita?" Damian searched for the source of the voice, but she saw only Lyle's soldiers in the line for rations or lying on the ground nearby.

'Damian! You can hear me?' Nephrita's tone lifted eagerly.

"Where are you?" Damian looked around, vaguely noticing the startled reactions of the soldiers nearby. Some reached for swords, others peered into the darkness, and some stared straight at Damian. Even Domino watched her intently.

Nephrita's voice seethed. *'A spell was placed upon me. A man named Yanuk Alganov—'*

"I know that Yanuk controls you," Damian cut across Nephrita's voice. The goddess's words seemed to come from everywhere at once. Despite the rising clamour around Damian, the sound of Nephrita's voice rang out as clearly as if she stood right beside Damian. The soldiers closed in to form a ring around Damian while Domino turned to face them and reached for his sword.

'Yes,' Nephrita snarled. *'That pompous, conniving, two-faced, black-hearted, darkness-spawned...'*

The soldiers around Damian shouted, breaking into her concentration and overwhelming Nephrita's words. Damian edged closer to Domino. Shouts of 'witch' and 'spy' rang out.

Closing her eyes, Damian tried to project a thought back to Nephrita the same way she heard the goddess's voice. *'Nephrita… can you tell us how to stop Yanuk?'*

Lyle and Gravier pushed their way through the circle around Damian. The second shot a hard look at the soldiers. "What is going on here?"

One of the soldiers spat out a response, but Damian didn't hear him as Nephrita's maliciously ecstatic voice came to her.

'Nothing would please me more.'

Damian shuddered at the sound of those words, much like the way Nephrita spoke two days ago. Damian wondered if her initial impressions of the goddess had been right.

'Tell me the truth. Did you mean to attack those people at Raven Point?'

In the ensuing silence from Nephrita, Damian heard the angered accusations the soldiers spat out.

"She's spying on us for Yanuk!"

"I heard her! She's talking to the Goddess of Chaos!"

Before Damian could say anything, Nephrita's quiet voice came back.

'Did you mean to burn down your father's barge?'

Damian's eyes widened in fury. The goddess continued before she could respond.

'I could not stop myself from killing those people any more than you could control your magic—well, my magic—on the ship. No, I did not know those people, but I feel the same way.'

"Miss Sires!" Gravier snapped impatiently.

Damian recoiled at the sharpness in his voice, but before she could answer, her attention was captured by Nephrita's next words.

'I understand now what you were trying to tell me the other day. I almost wish I didn't. These memories will never go away.'

A chill spread through Damian. Weeks of guilt and remorse rushed through her. What would it feel like to know she had attacked and murdered dozens of innocent people, fully aware of what she was doing yet unable to do a thing to stop it? Part of Damian still questioned the goddess's sincerity but one thing she knew she could count on was Nephrita's hatred for her new master.

Squaring her shoulders, Damian looked up at Gravier. "Yes, I am speaking with Nephrita, but I am not spying on you. She is spying on Yanuk."

A chorus of murmurs rose in response.

Damian fixed her eyes on the captain, watching the scene silently.

"She despises Yanuk. She will give us information to stop him."

Surprised and dubious exclamations rose from the soldiers, the entire camp listening in.

Lyle regarded her quietly for a moment. Then, he asked, "How are they moving so quickly now?"

The group fell silent as Damian relayed the question to Nephrita.

'I have been displacing the earth underneath the group. They do not move, the ground moves beneath them. One of the other mages made the suggestion when Yanuk demanded I make them travel faster.'

Lyle and Gravier looked at each other as Damian repeated what the goddess told her.

"Those curious patterns we have seen in the ground," remarked one of the scouts who rode ahead of the rest. Damian, who spent the day riding near the spare horses at the back, had not noticed anything.

Gravier's brow knit suspiciously. "How are we certain we can trust Nephrita's word? Or hers?"

Damian gazed firmly at them. "I can only give you my word. But if you want information to help you stop Yanuk from the person closest to him, then you will have to trust me."

Many of the men looked apprehensive, including Gravier. Damian stared her challenge to the captain. He didn't speak as he watched her. She could see thoughts whirling in his eyes.

One of the soldiers was the first to break the silence. "With all due respect, Captain, I think it's a bad idea to keep someone who can talk to the Goddess of Chaos with us."

At his words, other soldiers chimed in with their arguments. Damian frowned at the soldiers' responses, frustration growing.

"Men," Lyle spoke over them. His voice was even but the soldiers fell silent at his interruption. "We know that Nephrita objects to her binding. Gravier and I saw it with our own eyes. If Yanuk's first line of defence and attack wishes to tell us how to stop him, then it is foolish to ignore it."

The men fell quiet in the wake of Lyle's words.

The captain turned to Damian. "Tell us about the people in his party."

Damian nodded, some of the stiffness in her shoulders easing. Closing her eyes, she sent Lyle's request to Nephrita.

"There are twelve mages, including Yanuk. Sixteen mercenaries accompany them, led by a man called Vitro Norgssen."

Domino straightened, looking distant. Damian glanced at him

curiously but Gravier's voice cut into her thoughts.

"Twelve?" Gravier's eyebrows rose as he turned to Lyle. "I thought you said there were eighteen."

'*We thought there were eighteen mages,*' Damian projected back to the goddess while Lyle responded to his second.

"Gawthrain told me eighteen, though I trust his word little."

"Four deserted since they set out," Damian told them, "and two were killed during the attack on that town."

"Desertions?" Gravier remarked. "It would seem their group is not very close-knit after all."

Lyle nodded, his eyes fixed on Damian. "Tell us about the mages. Their names, appearances, strengths and weaknesses, temperaments, whatever she knows."

The soldiers around shifted, some leaning closer and others trying to push their way through the outer ring to listen to Damian. Lyle gave them a dirty look but said nothing as Damian silently contacted the goddess.

Damian closed her eyes and relayed messages to and from Nephrita, her own contribution diminishing until she acted as a translator, repeating the goddess's thoughts verbatim and returning the questions asked by Lyle, Gravier, and the men similarly.

Murmurs rose as the men discussed strategies while Damian gave them information. Lyle remained focused on her, giving demand after demand without pause. Nephrita answered obediently, clearly eager to put an end to Yanuk's rule over her, and answered honestly when she did not know certain information and vowed to try to learn it. Damian and the men eventually sat down as the conversation continued, although she wasn't the only one to shift uncomfortably on the ground while they spoke.

Damian didn't know how much time passed before Nephrita exhausted all the information she had on Yanuk's group and Lyle's requests finally fell silent.

"I promise I will try to discover as much as I can about them while we travel," Damian spoke for Nephrita. "I would like nothing better than to wring the life from Yanuk's neck with my own hands but I cannot harm him. I must ask you to do it for me."

Lyle's eyes widened before he covered them with his hand. "Oh no…"

"Then our goal is simple," Gravier said. "Before we attack the rest of the mages, we must destroy Yanuk so that he can no longer use Nephrita against us."

"No," Lyle replied wearily. "You cannot kill him. None of you can. The limitations of the spell forbid it."

A flurry of murmurs rang up among the men.

Gravier shot Lyle an annoyed look. "You could not have told us of these limitations before now?"

"I was not planning to have contact with Nephrita," Lyle grumbled.

The second let out an exasperated noise. "Do you have any other information that might result in a little less certain death? Because I think now would be a good time to share it."

Damian shook her head. "I don't understand. What limitations are you talking about?"

A distant look crossed Lyle's face. "The spell that binds Nephrita forbids her from telling others to kill Yanuk for her. Anyone who sets out to kill him from her request will perish in the attempt. None of you can kill Yanuk now."

Eyes widened and more murmurs rippled through the group.

A calculating look crossed Gravier's face. "How is it you so know so much about this spell?"

Lyle simply answered, "Coincidence."

One soldier spoke up, "So there is nothing we can do? We can only hope some unrelated party will do the job for us?"

Damian thought of Garrick, who had not caught up to them. Lyle's answer interrupted her contemplation.

"No. I will do it."

"Captain!"

"Are you daft?" Gravier asked. "You just told us that we cannot kill him."

"I was prepared to kill Yanuk before tonight," Lyle responded. "I am the only one among us who can stop him."

"Are you willing to risk your life on that assumption?"

"I must."

The men fell silent with his conviction. Damian's eyes widened as she watched him. She didn't know the captain but she felt uncomfortable at the thought of killing even Yanuk. Her stomach turned over to think Lyle might be going to his death.

Lyle straightened. "Go to sleep, men. We will need our strength to continue the chase tomorrow. When we make camp tomorrow evening we will plan our strategy of attack, since it seems unlikely we will catch up before they reach Albrith."

With nods and murmurs, the men rose and spread out, re-forming the line for rations or returning to belongings they laid out earlier. Damian stood, hesitating as they dispersed. Her eyes fixed on Lyle as he stood with a grimace. Gravier looked at the captain from the corner of his eye but said nothing.

Damian frowned. "I am sorry, Captain. I did not mean to make things so difficult."

Lyle rubbed his face. "No, Gravier is right. I should have said something sooner." He turned toward where he had left his things, not looking at her. "Go to sleep. The travel will only get harder from here."

Damian glanced at Domino. She was surprised to find a thoughtful look on the mercenary's face. She shook her head, trying to clear her thoughts as she faced the captain.

"Well, thank you for trusting me."

With that, she made for the soldier doling out rations, Domino at her side. Lyle said nothing more as he walked away, Gravier quietly following.

Damian considered the discussion she and the men had while she waited in line to receive her share of cold supper. As she stepped away from the rest of the camp her thoughts shifted. She reflected on the brief period she had spent with Nephrita, less than a day. Had she judged the goddess too harshly? Damian had been too disturbed by the thought of releasing the Goddess of Chaos into the world to try to see it from her eyes. She tried to imagine what it must have been like for Nephrita, to awaken suddenly with apparently no memory of her past life and no idea that she was not Damian. Then she was spurned by the person whose life she had shared.

These memories will never go away.

Damian let out a sigh as she sat down to eat. Nephrita might have shown a disturbing propensity for attacking people who meant her harm but she seemed more remorseful for attacking innocent people than the Gods of Light had in Raven Point. Nephrita had halted her attacks on Niabi to spare Garrick's life when the malakh who served the Goddess of Life used him against Nephrita like a coin.

My whole world has been turned upside down. The gods I have worshipped since birth are just as malicious as the ones I have been taught to spurn, and the one more despised than any other might not mean others any harm. I cannot trust the word of a knight, yet I trust a traitor implicitly.

She shut her eyes, the world feeling heavy.

How do I know what to believe anymore?

Damian's eyes were drawn to her mercenary companion.

"You follow the old gods," she said softly, her voice fluctuating between question and statement. "Why?"

Something shifted in his eyes but the change was so minute she couldn't place it. "Anyone can claim to work for the Light. Use it as a screen to excuse any behaviour. But no one can claim to control Time."

Damian couldn't help staring at him as he spoke, distant and emotionless as ever.

"They are what truly run the world."

She paused, considering his words and remembering the statues in the Temple of Time in Trent. Fortune, Fate, Mystery, Truth, and Change. Their personalities more flawed, but their essences untouchable. Damian could see the reality in Domino's words.

"But, doesn't it frighten you that you can't control those things?" she asked.

"It comforts me. They are constant and unchanging and humanity cannot taint them."

Damian's eyes dropped to the dark earth in front of her feet, unable to shake the feeling of betrayal by the gods she had followed her entire life. She found Domino's focus on man's use of the gods peculiar. "How long have you followed them?"

Whether his expression shifted, she couldn't tell in the darkness. "Since I left the Red Hawks."

Her eyes enlarged as it struck her. The Red Hawks had also been known as the Champions of Light. They had claimed to fight for the virtues of the true gods only to be uncovered as corrupt sellouts. She studied Domino, the expressionless ease with which he took in the world, and wondered what happened with the Red Hawks and how it changed him. Clearly, it had been powerful enough to rattle his core beliefs and resulted in his self-imposed isolation.

As she thought back to Raven Point, destroyed by the wrath of the Gods of Light, Damian wondered if she would have preferred to have her beliefs shaken by the actions of man rather than the gods themselves.

The silence stretched out for a long moment as Lyle returned to his blanket laid on the ground. He heard Gravier follow but the second said nothing until he sat down nearby.

"So you do not know what that book says but you know the limitations of the spell Yanuk cast from it. Why is that?"

"That is another long story, one that no one else knows of yet."

A wry grin crossed Gravier's face. "All these years I assumed you were merely terse. I had no idea you had such secrets about you."

Lyle didn't respond as he watched the men settle down. He admitted there was much of his life that he kept hidden, even from those as close to him as Gravier or his own wife. It had not seemed important to speak of those days and Lyle liked to focus on the simple things in life. He never expected to be taken away from them into another grand adventure.

As the rest of the camp fell silent, Lyle let out a breath. "Is this where you pictured your life would take you?"

Gravier chuckled. "If you meant that I would be riding to Albrith to battle a god, no, I can truthfully say I never expected that."

"I meant back home."

That gave the second pause. "Honestly, no. I requested a position on the guard mainly for money and esteem. I had planned to leave and start mercenary work after completing my service obligation. Perhaps in Edan. There was plenty enough work to go around for a sword-for-hire in those days."

Lyle stared into the distance. "So why have you remained in Misengrad all these years?"

Gravier shifted. "Actually, when I saw what you had with Evelyn when you married her, I was envious. I had never met a woman I cared to settle down with before, but despite all the wanderlust of my youth it looked very appealing."

Lyle nodded slowly.

"You fear for them, in case you should fall in this attack."

"I do not fear death," Lyle answered. "Evelyn and the children would be cared for. But I have found what I desired from life."

"You do not have to risk yourself to put an end to Yanuk. Albrith is well defended, we need only tell another that he leads the charge and he would be made a quick target anyway."

"It would still be passing on Nephrita's request. We cannot stake our hopes on chance, nor will I jeopardize others. I must stop him."

"Captain." Reaching out, Gravier laid a hand on his shoulder. "Lyle. I have known you many years now and you are not one to risk yourself needlessly. Do not throw your life away now, after all we have been through."

Lyle glanced askance at his second. "I have no intention of throwing it away. Besides, if my theory is wrong I will be struck down before ever drawing near Yanuk. So if I suffer heart failure or get struck by lightning before we reach Albrith, I recommend avoiding him."

Gravier grinned. "Well, at least your mulishness and optimism have not been affected by all this. Just remember, courage and stupidity come from the same place. Neither increases your chances of survival."

Lyle ignored the barb. "I merely want to see an end to this, though with Nephrita involved I doubt it shall be as simple as killing Yanuk."

Lyle had heard too many stories to believe freeing Nephrita would be the end of their battle and he knew with certainty that he would not be able to defeat the Goddess of Chaos. He suspected that one way or another he would not survive the coming encounter. An old conversation he had not thought about in years came to the front of his mind and he wondered if she had foreseen this. *Yes,* he thought dryly, *tell him a god once said you were destined for greatness, that will go over well.*

Instead, he added, "I have faced greater foes than an old mage with a vindictive streak."

"Even one who commands a goddess?"

"Well," Lyle remarked, "if I survive her I shall have one more story to tell over a mug of ale."

Gravier laughed. "As though you are one to tell stories."

Lyle smiled wryly. "Enough chatter. It is late and we will need our strength."

The thunder of hooves drummed a steady rhythm throughout the long day that followed. It was easier for Lyle to focus his attention on the sounds and the land they passed to try to take his mind off the many aches all over his body that grew worse through each hour of travel. His thighs were rubbed raw, his tailbone was jounced into putty, and a knot formed in the small of his back from riding.

Stopping to rest at night did little to relieve Lyle's pain. Sleeping on the ground night after night had left his joints sore and gave him a headache and stiff neck that persisted longer each passing day. He was very much feeling his age but pushed on without complaint. The travel took a heavy toll on the men and he worried that some of the horses would not survive the journey.

Yanuk's group continued at great speed and the only sign of their passing was the strange column of displaced land behind them. Lyle's scouts kept the mages and mercenaries in sight though they rarely returned to the main group. There was little need for such stealth, nor for Lyle to see them at all. He pushed his men toward Albrith though it became increasingly clear that they would not reach Yanuk and his rebel mages until they were already attacking the capitol.

Lyle's mind drifted to unexpected places during the long hours of travel. Although he tried to keep focused on exploring strategies for attacking Yanuk and preparing alternate plans in case something failed, he often found himself reflecting on old memories. The adventures he had unwittingly undertaken before he met Evelyn, the births of his children, the moments of tension that occasionally broke up the routine duties of guarding a well fortified city. He wondered what his younger brother would have been doing at this stage in his life had he survived. What would he have thought of the life Lyle now led? Almost nineteen years later Daven's legacy continued to pull him into grand, heroic adventures he never planned to be part of.

Lyle called a halt for the day well after the sun set and the last rays of daylight had almost completely washed out of the sky. The thought of sleep did not encourage him though he was glad to dismount at long last. He oversaw the men divvy out rations gathered earlier in their journey and see to the care of the horses. They had fallen into such a routine since they left Misengrad that little input was needed on his behalf. Instead, he lowered to the ground to stuff down stale bread and cheese and dried meat before he gathered the more senior guards together to discuss strategy. The men fell silent as they hurriedly ate, as famished from the hard ride as Lyle was.

Out of the corner of his eye, he watched Damian and her mercenary shadow help care for the horses. They were an odd addition to the group. Lyle knew Gravier wasn't the only one uncomfortable with the thought of riding with a yellow-eyed witch who could speak with the Goddess of Chaos and the man known for murdering over half the Red Hawks. Lyle didn't trust the Crow either and had ordered the night watch to be extra cautious of the mercenary. If Domino was still around, Lyle planned to take the man in for questioning at least after this was all over. Damian Sires was a different matter and Lyle had not yet decided what he thought of her.

He watched her as she got in line for rations alone, the mercenary waiting away from the rest of the men with their belongings.

Gravier nodded at her as she passed by. "Miss Sires."

She stopped and bowed. "Captain. Master Gravier."

Gravier scoffed. "Second is an honorary title, Miss Sires. Mister will do."

"Of course. My apologies, Mister Gravier."

Gravier gestured at him and Lyle. "Would you care to sit with us?

There is no need to distance yourself from the rest of us every night."

Lyle shot Gravier a look, recognizing the shift in his tone when he went prying for information.

Gravier smiled innocently back. "If you do not mind, Captain?"

Narrowing his eyes suspiciously, Lyle grunted through a mouthful of bread.

Hesitantly, Damian glanced between them. She held up the food in her hands. "I have to get this to Domino."

The second let out a snort of laughter. "It will get no colder than it is now. Waiting a few more minutes might actually improve its flavour."

She didn't respond to the jest. "I appreciate your offer. I would be happy to return after we've eaten." She turned toward where the mercenary waited but Gravier's serious voice stopped her.

"Actually, I would prefer to speak with you alone."

Even in the darkness Lyle could see her shoulders tense and eyes narrow.

"I need to go."

"Miss Sires," Gravier answered before she left, his words gentler, "you know how dangerous he is, right?"

Her voice was hard. "Yes." She took a few steps more though the second didn't allow her to get far.

"Then why do you defend him?"

"I have to," she snapped back, still trying to leave.

"What makes you believe that?" Lyle asked, suddenly more interested in the conversation.

Her hands trembled. "Because if I can't forgive him for what he did, then I can't forgive myself."

That gave them both pause.

"What are you saying?" Gravier asked quietly.

She let out a shaky sigh. "I told you that I burned down my father's barge. What I did not tell you was that Domino and I were the only survivors. Everyone on the ship, the captain, the crew, my own father... they're all dead because of me."

Lyle's attention diverted as he saw the mercenary approach.

Gravier clearly missed the black-cloaked man. "That is not the same as what he did."

"Yes, it is!" Damian spun to face Gravier, anger and misery etched into her young eyes. "Just because I didn't intend to do it doesn't make them any less dead or the fire any less my fault." She nodded toward Domino, standing a few paces from her. "He may admit to what he's done but how do you know he doesn't regret it? How do you know guilt doesn't harry every step he takes? How do you know those faces don't haunt his dreams asleep and awake? How do you know he wouldn't give everything he had to take it back?"

Her voice broke and as her head bowed, tears streamed down her face. Silence fell over the area and Lyle noticed a handful of soldiers nearby had fallen quiet as they listened.

"I did something horrible," she uttered, "and nothing will ever change that."

Lyle watched the Crow carefully, but the mercenary did not move nor betrayed any emotion as he stood within a few paces of Damian.

Lyle was the first to break the silence. "Including shouldering more guilt than you earned."

Everyone in the vicinity turned to Lyle. Raising her head, Damian gave him a questioning look, but before she could speak he turned to one of the men hovering nearby. "Tenner, gather the senior guards together. It is past time we discussed our strategy for when we reach Albrith."

The lanky soldier snapped into a salute. "Yes, Captain."

Lyle faced Tenner as the soldier jogged away. Lyle watched Damian and the mercenary slink away from the corner of his eye. The rest of the men surreptitiously strode or scooted farther away.

"Had I but half your way with words when you choose to use them," Gravier remarked as he watched the crowd disperse. "Have you ever considered becoming a diplomat?"

Lyle only grumbled at Gravier.

Garrick leaned over the horse as it cantered swiftly across the plains. The bay mare felt strange and unfamiliar though its gait was notably smoother than Brenadier's. Garrick regretted leaving the destrier with the survivors from Raven Point but he knew Brenadier would never have been able to handle the hard pace across Alden. The stallion was not built for endurance riding nor was it a particularly forgiving beast. Brenadier was bred for the chaos of war and the Agaesi did not ride horses into battle.

It was only the first in a series of decisions Garrick knew he would have to face, and soon. Had he the gift of foresight or the opportunity to relive the past season he might make different decisions but it didn't matter now. He couldn't regret his choices even as he ran a strange horse to exhaustion, hoping that he could find another town where he could switch mounts before the beast collapsed under him. He hoped he could continue the pattern and arrive in Albrith before Yanuk reached it.

Garrick had made so many mistakes along the way. He hoped that staying behind to help the survivors of Raven Point was not one of them. He could have left them and perhaps he should have. They might have made it to safety on their own. With scarcely a third of the population of the village remaining and their spirits too broken to accept that they had any hope left, he doubted they could have organized themselves.

They lay far behind, as did the mule he had taken from them in exchange for the use of Brenadier and promise of a hefty payment should Garrick get the stallion back. Hopefully, by now they had encountered the same band of provincial soldiers who had threatened Garrick and Damian in Padura. They had been none too happy to see him, nor had Magistrate Orneth when Garrick made it back to the village. They all felt the same ground thunder that swallowed up Raven Point. Warnings of what would happen if Yanuk succeeded in his endeavour frightened them into submission.

Garrick did not doubt that a few of the soldiers now struck for Windermere to pass on the news of what happened with the Duke of Alden. Nor did he doubt that the magistrate only allowed the knight to switch mounts in his village due to the substantial coin Garrick offered in exchange. If the rest of the soldiers sought to help the survivors from Raven Point and the magistrate took them in at his village, then at least Garrick would have done something right. The consequences of choosing them over riding out with Lyle Hitchcliffe could be dire, Garrick knew, but looking in the eyes of the villagers who had lost everything made it impossible for him to abandon them. Just as it had been impossible for him to sacrifice Damian when that could have prevented it all.

How many people were dead or their lives ruined because of the decisions Garrick made? How many decisions he thought were right at the time were failures? Abandoning the quest that originally sent him to Trent, attempting to use an ancient technique to read Damian's magic, sheltering her from a creature that might have been able to keep Nephrita from returning, and all the little choices in Padura had left him unable to prevent her resurrection and subsequent binding to Yanuk's will.

He could have chosen otherwise. He could have taken one life and it might have saved many. But if he were to do it over again, would he make different decisions? Would killing Damian, or attempting to kill Nephrita, have saved the people from Raven Point?

The thoughts swirled through Garrick's mind, uncertainty piling upon uncertainty. As he reflected on the events that brought him here, he knew one thing was sure. He had believed every decision he made was right at the time. Whether that turned out to be the case he didn't know, nor did he care to dwell on what might have been. The only thing that mattered now was to lend his aid to Albrith.

So two days had passed, riding hard from town to town as Garrick tried to make up the ground he had lost. The wind rushed through his hair as he wove between the rolling hills in central Faneria, focused on his destination and determined to do whatever he could to serve his liege and make things right.

One way or another, he thought as a village came into view and he pushed the exhausted mare into a gallop for the remaining stretch, *this ends soon.*

CHAPTER 20
THE BATTLE OF ALBRITH

DAMIAN INHALED SLOWLY as she stared up at the entrance to Albrith. The massive city wound up a ravine between two hills, crested by the king's castle at the top of the rise on the far side of the town. Nothing lay beyond, as the back of the city came up against a cliff face overlooking Aura Lake. The water stretched farther than anyone could see, more like an inland sea than a lake. The hill to the left was smaller and sank toward the shore of the lake though the sun had fallen behind it and darkened the city. Standing a stone's throw from the towering outer wall that surrounded the city and crowned the hills to either side, Damian could only see the upper reaches of the town and castle, along with a curious series of narrow towers and raised paths weaving above the buildings. The immensity of Albrith was mind-boggling, bigger than Trent and seemingly twice as dense.

Though the higher part of the city seemed intact, wisps of black smoke rose over the wall from within, along with the light of flames too large and bright for watch fires. A lump formed in Damian's throat at the sight.

'Nephrita,' she sent into the city. 'We're here.'

'Good,' the goddess replied into her mind, pain and fury etched into her voiceless words. 'I cannot wait to see Yanuk's life ripped from him.'

The wall loomed above as Damian sat atop Hope on a wide stone bridge over a creek running before the city. Domino waited beside her. Shattered wagons and smashed vegetables and dry goods littered the ground along the well paved road, along with a few lumps Damian hoped were not bodies. No people could be seen though at this hour the entrance should be crowded with people trying to file into the city for the night.

Inhaling deeply, Damian turned to face Domino. The mercenary's eyes did not stray from the wall before them.

A faint smile crossed Damian's face. "Thank you for staying by my side this whole time. I don't think I could have handled everything that's happened without you." She faced the wall, barely making out the flicker of firelight in the gateway into the city. "And I certainly couldn't face this without knowing you were here with me." She clenched her fingers over the reins while the clatter of metal and creaking of straps rang behind them.

"Your faith is misplaced."

Damian turned to Domino with a start but he didn't look away from the wall. As ever, his voice and expression were impassive. However, there was a seriousness to his words she had rarely heard from him.

"I am not someone worth fighting for."

She stared at him, bewildered.

Before she could respond, Domino continued, "Nor are the people from Raven Point." He faced her. "Or the memory of your father."

She recoiled, staring wide-eyed at him.

He made no reaction. "You will not find peace if you fight for justice or penance."

For a moment, Damian could do nothing but stare at him, her blood chilling. With each passing second she hoped he would apologize or tell her that he misspoke. He only gazed steadily at her, his expression unchanging.

"Leave the spare horses and supplies here," Lyle's voice rang out.

Swallowing hard, Damian glanced back at the men from Misengrad. In a few minutes, they had clad themselves in leather and mail and armed with swords, spears, and bows. At the front of the group, Lyle wore an old but sturdy suit of plate, a pentagonal wooden shield banded with iron strapped to his arm. He slid a helmet that matched the rest of the armour over his head. Damian couldn't make out the captain's face in the T-shaped opening in the helmet, despite that the gap was a finger's length wide. As she glanced at Domino, garbed the same as he was that day she met him aboard her father's barge, she suddenly felt more comfortable with the captain of the guard from Misengrad than with the man who had accompanied her and kept her hope alive throughout her journey. She tried to think of something to say to the mercenary but Lyle continued before she spoke.

"Time is of the essence." Mounting his horse, Lyle turned to face the rest of the men. "If we do not find Yanuk before the light fades it will be impossible to stop this attack."

Damian shut her eyes. *This changes nothing. I know why I am here.*

She straightened and drew in a breath. "I can find him. Nephrita will guide us right to him."

Lyle said nothing but the clop of his horse's hooves approached. With that, Damian rode toward the gate. Domino didn't say another word but rode by her side. Lyle and Gravier rode to her other side with the rest of the men from Misengrad spread behind them, the extra horses and gear left at the bridge.

The first thing Damian saw as they approached the gateway through the thick wall was the portcullis. The one on the outside of the wall had apparently been in the process of lowering when Yanuk and Nephrita reached the city, as it was half raised. The exposed part of the gate had crumpled like paper, the two-inch-thick iron bars twisted inward and some of the stone above it marred with large cracks. Through the corridor in the walls thick enough to hide a house inside, arrows littered the ground along with pools of oil that still burned. Torches mounted on the walls illuminated armoured bodies scattered throughout. Hope snorted and shied away from the burning pitch and bloodied city guards, nostrils flaring and the whites of her eyes showing. Whinnies and shuffling from the other horses covered up the sounds of their hooves on the stone, the animals' agitation echoing through the passage. There was no sign of movement in the guard towers lining the entrance. A few horses slipped as they marched over the puddles though they didn't stumble and continued through the wall into the city.

Damian soon found the inner portcullis lying on its side against a building a stone's throw from the wall, dented severely in the middle with broken links of chains scattered in the street around it. Lyle's men drew their swords as distant scuffling and screams floated across the air. Damian glanced at the buildings immediately inside the wall, similar to those in Trent but styled differently. A few of the buildings had sections of roof or walls gouged out and a fire consuming one down the block lit up the street. Otherwise the dwellings had suffered little damage. Much debris littered the streets. At first glance Damian saw three more bodies. Some of the horses stamped their hooves and snorted at the scene that greeted them. Damian felt the small amount of food she choked down for dinner hours ago rising in her stomach. She resisted the urge to turn and flee outside the city walls.

I can do this, she thought to herself, inhaling slowly to settle her stomach. *For Nephrita and for the innocent victims here and at Raven Point.* Damian couldn't help feeling uncomfortable as she reflected on what Domino said to her outside the wall but she pushed those feelings back.

Lyle turned to her, his shadowed eyes barely visible through his helmet. "Lead us."

She nodded. *'Nephrita, show us where Yanuk is.'*

'I will guide you,' the goddess's thoughts came back. *'I can feel your presence. Go straight for now.'* Damian pointed down the road they faced and they continued in the same order as they had approached the city.

They had only moved a few paces forward when commotion at the back of the group gave them pause. Damian turned along with the others to watch the men to one side of the group shift aside, someone else pushing through. Damian straightened when the new figure appeared around the side of the men.

"Garrick!"

"Sir Magni," Lyle greeted with a nod.

"You made it." Damian stared in surprise at the lathered black gelding he rode, wondering what became of Brenadier.

"Wouldn't miss it for the world," the knight answered simply as he rode to the front of the group. "And I see we've no time to waste." He nodded ahead and Damian led them on. "What's the plan?"

"Surprise," Lyle answered simply. "We intend to set up an ambush for the mages and try to take down as many of them as possible before they can retaliate."

Damian shifted, thoughts of what was to come making her skin crawl.

Gravier leaned over to look at Garrick. "Unless you have any more appropriate recommendations, Sir?"

The knight smiled wryly. "Not unless you happen to know another god who can help us out."

Gravier frowned at that but Lyle didn't react.

"A surprise attack is probably our best shot," Garrick continued. "We need to break up the formation of mages." He let out a sigh. "And somehow handle Nephrita. I'm open to suggestions on taking care of the Goddess of Chaos."

Gravier grinned dryly. "We would likely have a better plan if we knew how to do that. These mages seem to be all over the city."

Lyle turned to face Damian, his helmet shadowing the narrow opening at its front. "Then I think now is the time to learn Yanuk's strategy."

She nodded, though she heard the bewilderment in Garrick's voice as he asked, "You can find that out?"

Gravier and Garrick continued speaking but Damian closed her eyes and sent to Nephrita, *'What are the mages doing?'*

Damian could hear the enraged tone in the words returned to her. *'Not much of anything besides walking. Yanuk ordered me to attack the city.'*

"Of course," Garrick muttered after Damian repeated Nephrita's words. "He gets to destroy the city without any of the stigma of being seen doing it."

"And while conserving his own energy to defend himself," Lyle added. "What else can she tell us?"

Damian sent the question to Nephrita and responded, "The mercenaries aren't with them. She doesn't know why but Yanuk has them spread out several blocks around them. She thinks they're keeping watch for anyone who comes too close to them."

From the corner of her eye, Damian noticed movement. She sent Domino a curious look as he raised his head and stared down the street, showing no emotion.

"How prudent of Yanuk," Gravier remarked flatly.

"Scouts!" Lyle called over his shoulder.

Several men trotted up through the ranks. "Captain!"

"Ride ahead and find those mercenaries. We cannot allow them to alert Yanuk of our approach."

"Yes, Captain."

Damian watched for a moment as the scouts threaded between them and hurried on.

"We must hurry."

Nodding at Lyle, Damian continued, leading the way. It wasn't long before the road they followed curved. She lost her bearings not three turns later as she followed Nephrita's instructions down the streets winding through the city and up the higher hill. Although the streets they passed through remained fairly wide, the frequent turns and rubble littering the road caused the men to spread out in a narrower line. Even Garrick and Gravier fell back a few paces as Damian led at the front with Lyle.

As they rode, Damian's eyes were drawn up to the platforms that spread out like a web from the slender towers rising at even intervals throughout the city. "What are those?"

"The catwalks," Gravier answered. "Albrith may be a trading hub but the city is designed for defence. The layout is confusing so as to slow invaders and the catwalks allow city guards to always have a vantage point." They watched a pair of guards race along a catwalk a few blocks away, scrambling at their bows and arrows. In another direction, a raised bridge was shattered.

Garrick's expression darkened. "Unfortunately, the same measures that hinder standard invaders don't defend so well against a group of mages with a goddess at their head."

Damian frowned.

As Damian's head turned around to follow the path of the suspended bridges, she caught a glimpse of the rest of their party. Starting, she looked between the men, eyes frantically searching.

"What is it?" Garrick asked.

Her breath came up short as she looked ahead. "Wh… where's Domino?"

The knight's eyes enlarged. "*What?*"

"The Crow?" Gravier said.

Lyle looked over his men and the roads they had passed before he focused on the soldiers in the middle of the group. "Did you see him leave?"

One of the men shook his head. "I didn't notice, Captain."

Another added, "I saw him fall back, but I didn't see him leave."

Damian stared through the late afternoon streets, a sinking feeling in the pit of her stomach.

Garrick cursed. "I knew he couldn't be trusted. He was probably one of Yanuk's mercenaries this whole time."

Gravier regarded him cautiously. "That is a rather swift conclusion to jump to, Sir." The second sent a brief look to Damian. "I think it likelier he is merely concerned only with his own welfare."

Garrick's eyes narrowed. "And you find that thought reassuring? What if he gets caught by Yanuk's mercenaries and tells them everything or they make him a better offer?"

Gravier raised an eyebrow. "That man talk? I doubt he would ask for a bandage if his arm was cut off."

The jest did nothing to ease Damian's fear. She hunched her shoulders, her hands trembling.

Was he spying on us for Yanuk this whole time? Or did he just not care about us… about me at all? She thought of the owl brooch Domino wore on his bag and her throat grew thick.

"Miss Sires," Lyle said, a prompt in his voice.

She shrank in on herself, trying to hold back the tears that threatened to spill from her eyes. "I… I don't—"

"Did Nephrita have any indication that any of Yanuk's mercenaries was missing?"

Damian blinked as she turned to him. "No."

Lyle was unfazed. "Even if he intends to betray us he does not know where we plan to set up our ambush. We will keep to our plan."

Garrick held an arm out. "Captain, if he tells Yanuk everything he knows, then it's hopeless."

Damian swallowed hard.

Lyle regarded the knight calmly. "If you have any better suggestions, Sir, then I welcome them. We can either reduce our numbers to send men in a desperate search for the Crow or we can focus on the true enemy here."

Garrick's expression darkened but he said nothing as he faced forward.

"We never had much hope to begin with." Lyle glanced at Damian through the opening in his helmet. "Keep leading us."

Damian felt small and her heart twisted inside but she tossed Hope's reins and rode on. Damian glanced through the streets around them though she saw no sign of Domino.

Was I wrong about him this whole time?

The group fell silent as they advanced through the city though it was clear the mercenary's sudden departure weighed on everyone's minds. An annoyed look remained etched onto Garrick's face as he followed Damian and Captain Hitchcliffe.

How many times did I tell her that man wasn't to be trusted?

As he looked at her, his expression softened. The hurt was clear in her eyes and she hardly seemed to notice their surroundings as she remained lost in thought. With a sigh, Garrick urged his exhausted gelding forward until he rode beside Damian, so close their knees almost bumped each other. Reaching out, he laid a hand on her shoulder.

"I'm sorry, Damian. I'm sure he didn't mean to hurt you."

Her eyes narrowed and she wrenched her shoulder out of his grip. "You don't believe that."

He huffed out a breath. "Well, I figured you'd appreciate that more than me saying 'I told you so.'"

Glaring at him, she nudged Hope a pace closer to Captain

Hitchcliffe. "So you think after Domino abandons us with no explanation that I'd prefer you lied to me?"

Garrick threw up his hands in exasperation. "Excuse me for trying to comfort you."

She faced forward, her face set in a scowl.

That's better, Garrick thought. *Anger is easier to focus.* Guilt swept over him and he couldn't help remembering her disgust at his manipulations. *I'm sorry, Damian, but we have more important things to worry about right now.*

The shame didn't dissipate. The captain sent him a brief cautious look but they all lapsed into silence. Garrick glanced at Damian as she guided them down another turn in the road, wondering what she and Nephrita discussed silently.

Following Damian, they rode deeper into the city, the golden light of the sunset gradually waning. The signs of struggle became more apparent as they continued. Burns scored walls, houses were shattered and collapsed, and an increasing amount of debris and bodies were scattered in the road. The men spread out as they manoeuvred around the litter of broken boards, refuse, food, and clay and metal fragments. The horses grew agitated as they continued into the chaos, many showing the whites of their eyes and a few whinnies ringing up despite their riders' attempts to keep them quiet.

"The horses are not meant for battle," Gravier said.

The captain nodded. "We shall need to dismount. How far are we from Yanuk?"

Damian paused for a moment, her gaze distant, then answered, "Another eight blocks."

"We'd better leave the horses here, then," Garrick said. "We don't want them giving us away."

Nodding, the captain called a halt and they dismounted. Garrick rubbed the black gelding's nose as it heaved its breath, its coat lathered from the hard ride. He smiled at the exhausted horse. "Thanks. You've earned a rest."

As he glanced to the side, he caught a glimpse of Damian patting Hope's neck and looking miserable. Her expression reminded Garrick of the way he felt when he left Brenadier with the survivors from Raven Point. Stepping closer, he laid a gauntleted hand on her shoulder. She turned warily toward him but softened when she saw the smile on his face. He nodded down the road. With a nod in return, she stepped away from the mare and darted ahead, Garrick and the captain behind her and the rest of the men following.

They rarely spoke as they made their way higher up the hill toward the castle, the rattle of armour and thumping footfalls not spreading far in the close walls and with the sounds of panic all around. Garrick wondered about the scouts Lyle sent out earlier to search for Yanuk's mercenaries. His thoughts returned to Yanuk as they made another turn in the streets.

Finally, Damian slowed a handful of buildings from an intersection. Garrick stepped behind her as she crept toward the corner. With a hand signal over his shoulder, the captain and his second followed, the rest of the men waiting down the block. Garrick moved carefully, keeping his armour from rattling and his voulge from bumping against the ground as he followed Damian.

At the corner of the intersection, she leaned against the wall and peered around the building, then caught her breath. Garrick waited behind her for a moment. The captain and his second moved around her to look into the next street. Slipping between them, Garrick glanced down the next street. He raised an eyebrow. No one was there.

"Are they down that street?" Lyle asked.

Turning, Damian gave him a puzzled look. "That's them right there."

Garrick glanced back and forth, looking for some obstacle that the mages might be hiding behind, but saw nothing. "Where?"

Her stunned look turned to him. "Right there, in the middle of the street."

Garrick blinked at her before turning into the road. He still saw no sign of anyone. Shutting his eyes, he expanded his senses, feeling into the connecting street for any sign of magic while the others spoke.

"Miss Sires, no one is there."

"They're right there, barely a block away."

Garrick's head twitched as he thought he detected something, but it flitted out of his awareness as soon as he noticed it. He tried to search for it again but couldn't sense anything unusual nearby.

Was that magic? I don't know how I could miss something like that.

"Miss Sires—"

"They're using a spell," Garrick uttered, cutting off the captain. All eyes turned to Garrick. He thought back to what the captain of the Agaesi told him before Garrick set off on his mission over a season ago. "They must be using magic to keep themselves hidden from sight. That's how they must have escaped our spies this whole time."

Lyle and Gravier straightened and the second turned to his captain. "And that must be how they broke into your office to steal that book."

Lyle nodded soberly.

Garrick faced Damian. "But you can see them?"

She glanced around the corner as if making certain of it and nodded. "Yes."

Garrick followed her eyes, wondering where the mages were as they stood in plain sight yet unable to be seen. "Then I guess it's up to you to coordinate the attack."

She recoiled, staring wide-eyed at him. "What?"

"Sir Magni," Lyle began, a warning in his voice.

Garrick turned to him. "Captain, I think it's time you got your archers into the catwalks."

"How will we know where to set up the ambush?"

"There is a city square not far from here," Gravier said. "If the mages keep to the main roads like they have been, they will pass through it. We can get into position there and Miss Sires can tell us when to strike."

Garrick looked at Damian as Lyle nodded.

"I…"

Lyle strode swiftly down the street and gave orders to his men who quickly scrambled to their tasks. Turning, Garrick took Damian's shoulders.

"Don't worry. They'll pick out a good target to aim for. You just need to tell them when Yanuk and his mages walk into it. Once it starts, you should get back and hide. Alright?"

She nodded shakily.

"Stay safe. We need you, especially if the first attack doesn't work." With that, Garrick turned and jogged down the street after the city guards from Misengrad.

"Wait!" Damian called softly after him. "Where are you going?"

He glanced over his shoulder at her. "The Agaesi aren't archers, Damian. I have to be close when the attack begins. Closer than I want you to be."

Colour drained from her face. Without another word, Garrick hurried down the street, following the group of archers who struck for one of the towers connected to the catwalks.

Closing his eyes, Garrick focused his senses on his aura, on the presence he always felt but never noticed. He reached out along the thread that connected him to Agasis, the great and ancient dragon that gave him power, and drew energy. Garrick's muscles tensed and strained against the strength that filled them, causing his movements to become effortless and the weight of his armour and voulge to lift away. The world came into sharper focus, sounds ringing out clearer, details easier to see, and shadows lighter. His body reacted quicker than he noticed it move.

Garrick moved at a light jog down the road though he swiftly passed most of the archers that had a head start on him. Entering a tower, he climbed the dark, narrow, winding staircase inside after two more men.

At the top of the tower, Garrick stepped onto the catwalk. The city climbed up the hill toward the castle perched at the edge of the cliff. As he faced the setting sun, Albrith spread out below, row after row of buildings marching down the ravine and up the other side. Garrick's eyes narrowed faintly. Buildings burned throughout and destruction littered the streets over at least half the city.

The archers conferred before pointing down the platform stretching west from the tower. Garrick crouched low along with them as they ran down the catwalk. The crenellated walls of the catwalks were low, not even waist high, but five stories off the ground no one below could see them as they moved. They darted above the city in silence for a few minutes, turning twice after peering at the streets winding below.

Finally, the archers came to a stop at the entrance to another tower and pointed as they looked over the short walls.

"There's the square."

Garrick followed the man's pointing finger as the rest of the archers caught up. The plaza was easy to pick out, a starkly open space among the tightly woven streets and buildings crowding the city. The square was designed like a wheel with six spokes, each path beginning where a road entered the plaza and ending at a fountain in the centre. Patches of grass and flowers and statues sat between the paths. The catwalks stopped at the edge of the square, the space below entirely open. One building lining the plaza burned brightly, scarcely anything left of it but the framework.

"Where are they coming from?" Garrick asked quietly. With the twists and turns of the streets in Albrith he could hardly be certain which direction they had travelled or from which road the mages would emerge.

An archer pointed down a road entering the square. "That way, Sir."

Garrick nodded, looking down the road. He still saw no sign of the mages. The only people he could see were city guards scrambling through the plaza, some directing groups of townspeople who cried out as they raced across the square seeking cover. To one side of the entrance where the mages would emerge stood a statue of a woman with flowing hair and gown atop a stallion as magnificent as Brenadier. A stone flower box lined the other side.

"Better get yourselves into position, then."

With that, Garrick crouched low and hurried along the catwalk past the intersection of the road the mages travelled. He darted to the next connecting road before he slowed and glanced over the wall at the buildings below. Stepping onto the parapet, he leaped off the catwalk.

Garrick landed near the peak of a roof, bending his knees as he slid down the slope of the wooden shingles. He skidded straight over the edge of the roof, falling a story down to the roof of a porch over the front door. From there, he leaped to the ground, the plaza opening up before him. He rushed across to the statue of the mounted woman, keeping its thick stone form between him and the road the mages travelled.

Garrick's heart raced as he came to a stop by the statue, turning around to press his back up against it. He swung his voulge out of its harness over his back and breathed slowly, steadying his nerves.

This is the hour of destiny, he thought as he slid his gauntleted hand over the ironwood haft of his voulge, the blade gleaming in the late afternoon light. *This is what I've trained for my entire life.*

Carefully, he crept to the edge of the statue and peered around the stone horse's tail. Focusing carefully, he noticed movement in the catwalks but it soon fell still and he saw no sign of anyone around. Garrick examined the area around the intersection of the street with the plaza. He could make it there within a few seconds, just after the arrows fell if the archers fired precisely when the order was called out.

Glancing around, he looked for signs of the rest of Captain Hitchcliffe's men. His vantage point gave him little view of the other alleys and roads that connected to the plaza. It wasn't an ideal location for an ambush. There was plenty of room to manoeuvre but too much space for the mages to do the same. It would be too easy for the mages to disappear if Lyle's soldiers weren't able to break the invisibility spell. There weren't many easily accessible places for the men to hide and attack at once. Garrick could be alone among Yanuk's group once the arrows fell.

Twelve mages, he thought, his mouth going dry at the thought.

Even if I could see them there's no way I could disarm or incapacitate them all on my own. Unless they are too foolish to coordinate their attacks they will be unstoppable, even without Nephrita's aid. Captain Hitchcliffe was right. We never did have any hope.

Garrick tightened his fingers around his voulge. *All of my training, all of my choices, all of my mistakes, my entire life, have led to this. I will not be afraid of death.* Breathing slowly, he waited and watched.

Yanuk smiled as he imagined the coming weeks. With Nephrita ably handling the task of terrorizing Albrith and enacting vengeance for his and his comrades' exile years ago, he had time to discuss with the others exactly what he would demand of the king. The image of their future that crystallized from their conversation filled his heart with joy.

A new home, modern and spacious and well-kept, with all the essentials they needed and servants to retrieve, tend, and maintain them. Access to any scholarly text on magic they desired to further their study. Autonomy and freedom from the restrictions of taxes or the whims of demanding lords. Recognition from the kingdom of their prowess and new status within the kingdom.

It was, in fact, much like the sanctuary Yanuk had built in their old border fort, which they had all been content enough with. But never again would he have to cower in fear that the common man should know he could use magic, nor would they have to scavenge or steal for the bare essentials they needed to live. Theirs would be a true community at last, not the gathering of exiles they had been until so recently.

"It will be glorious," he said to himself as he walked, hands clasped behind his back. "We shall have a library to rival that in the castle of Misengrad, studies and parlours where we devise new spells and mix ingredients and experiment with new ones, with new brass scales and glass jars and crow quills and everything we could want, and never have to worry about toiling in gardens or mucking out stables or cleaning or preparing food."

Patrus, walking beside him, smiled as Yanuk mused. Edrand stepped forward as they strode calmly through the streets of Albrith. The few people visible hurried for shelter or ran toward the crashes and roars of Nephrita's destruction. No one looked at the group of mages making their way leisurely through the city.

"They will come for us one day," Edrand said evenly.

Yanuk let out an annoyed sigh. "If you fear that so much you are free to strike out on your own, and good luck to you."

Edrand rolled his eyes. "You know I desire the same as you, Yanuk. I think your methods foolish but I would not have followed you this far were our goals different. But we must be prepared. No matter how you attempt to convince these people that you are holding back Nephrita they will not abide our peaceful settlement for long, not after this." He nodded to indicate the city, debris strewn over the roads and smoke from numerous fires rising over the buildings.

Yanuk scoffed. "We are mages, we can defend ourselves."

"I would not place utter faith in our small community," Crain remarked behind him.

"I would prefer some additional measure of security as well," Helena added.

Patrus straightened. "Then we shall demand a force of our own for defence."

Yanuk waved a hand. "Besides, we have Nephrita to protect us."

"I do not have much faith in her, either," Crain muttered.

"She is volatile," one of the apprentices remarked. "She is the Goddess of Chaos, for Light's sake!"

Helena nodded in agreement. "She will turn on us the first opportunity she gets."

Edrand leaned closer to Yanuk, his voice dropping. "And it seems you do not place any faith in her either. I notice you have not entrusted her with the secret of our unseeing spell."

"She is dangerous," another apprentice said. "I think it would be unwise to rely on her any longer than we must to achieve our goals."

Yanuk frowned, glancing south. He heard and felt rumbling in the earth where Nephrita assaulted another sector of the city. It was true, part of the reason he sent her away to wreak havoc on Albrith was to prevent her knowing about their unseeing spell. He didn't trust her.

"I will handle Nephrita. I still control her, remember? For now, she is serving her purpose." His grin darkened as they passed a side street dropping down the hill, affording him a view of the destruction spreading over the city. "And she is doing it very well."

Turning, he spread his arms as he faced each of his mages. "Take heart, comrades. All our years of struggles are coming to an end, and after our long journey, we shall soon have all we desire." He pointed toward the palace at the top of the hill. Nothing but orange sky and violet clouds stood behind it.

"Once we reach that castle, victory will be ours, and our new home will make all of it worthwhile."

Smiles spread on several faces while others looked more determined. Facing forward, Yanuk continued. He considered using the enchanted crystal around his neck to contact Vitro, wondering how their mercenary companions fared, but decided against it. Vitro would have contacted him had he any idea that they would encounter any trouble. Yanuk thought reticence was better so as not to risk the mercenaries finding out about their unseeing spell. That was a secret he wanted to keep among his mages and no one else.

"After all," he said under his breath with a smile, "if no one can see us and not even our allies know why, what have we to fear?"

Followed by a handful of his men and Damian, Lyle stole through the back streets as quietly as his armour would allow. His legs from waist to heel ached powerfully from the hard ride and his back, shoulders, and neck remained sore from sleeping on the ground.

I am getting too old for this, he thought, shifting against the weight of the plate that seemed heavier now than it had when they set out from Misengrad. He was nearly as old as his father had been when he passed away and the senior Hitchcliffe had already taken strictly commanding duties for some time prior to that. Although Lyle had kept his body in shape and his training fresh, he had noticed his reflexes slow, his strength begin to deteriorate, and his endurance shorten. Over the past days, he realized he was no longer fit to take an active role in these adventures, not only for his own sake but for the safety of the men he led. As he panted while he jogged through the dusky streets, sweat dripping down his forehead and hair beneath his helmet, he wondered if he should have sent men on this mission without accompanying it himself.

That, of course, was no longer an option. He slowed momentarily to catch his breath and stretch his limbs, the city guards with him stopping as they waited. Lyle lowered the bow and quiver of arrows he held to the ground, relieved for the lessened burden he had traded to one of the men for use of his shield. He wasn't an expert archer but better to shoot at a blind target than try to fight an invisible opponent with a sword, especially one that commanded magic. The idea of facing enemies he couldn't see greatly unnerved him. He didn't show that to his men. His exhaustion was harder to hide.

Gravier leaned over to look at Lyle. "Are you alright, Captain?"

Lyle noticed his second breathed hard and locks of dark hair plastered to Gravier's forehead beneath his mail hood. Without answering, Lyle nodded, then picked up the bow and quiver and continued.

The men peeled off to take up different positions as they neared the circular plaza. Eventually, Gravier left his side to hide in an alley across the road, leaving Lyle alone with Damian as they reached an alley near the square. Lyle located the nearest catwalk and just made out the silhouette of one of his men leaning over the parapets high above.

Lyle leaned on his knees, pressed up against the wall as he caught his breath. "Any sign of them?"

Damian crept to the end of the alley and peered around the corner. "They're a little ways down the road, coming this way."

"How far down are they exactly?"

Her eyes passed slowly down the street as she mouthed a few words. "Eleven buildings away from here."

Nodding, Lyle straightened, his breath gradually slowing. "Are they showing any signs that they are aware of the ambush? Do they look wary or cautious?"

She watched them a moment, then shook her head. "No." A trace of disgust crept into her voice. "They look as if they haven't a care in the world."

Lyle said nothing in response. He supposed he would have little to worry about if he expected no one could see him. Turning, Lyle faced the man in the catwalks above and signalled the mages' location using hand gestures. The man nodded, then slipped back from the wall, disappearing from sight. Sliding the helmet off his head, Lyle wiped the sweat off his face, relishing the coolness of the late afternoon air against his skin. He paused a moment to inhale deeply before replacing the helmet.

Damian glanced over her shoulder from the corner, anxiety clear on her face. Lyle couldn't help feeling uncomfortable as well. No misfortune had befallen him so far, but he had no idea when his conviction to kill Yanuk would strike him down if the limitations of the control spell applied to him. Entirely too many concerns stacked up against Lyle.

He examined the alley, looking for ways to make himself hidden when the mages would pass by. A few casks and a broken barrel lay scattered about the alley, hardly enough to conceal him from view without his armour. On one side of the alley a door hung open, the top hinge broken. Picking up the bow and quiver, he stepped to the entrance and pushed the door open, the wood creaking as it strained against the lone hinge supporting it. Seeing him, Damian hurried over and slipped into the building.

A strong smell of leather struck him as soon as he stepped in. He stopped two paces inside and squinted into the gloom but the modest glow of the shadowy alley outside failed to illuminate more than a small square of the floor immediately inside. Giving up, he turned around.

Damian leaned around the mostly closed door, only her face lit by the dusky light as she peered down the alley. Lyle idly ran a gauntleted finger down the string of the bow, trying not to think of the limitations of his age, his lack of proficiency with the only weapon he dared to use, the danger of the foe they faced, or the fact that they relied entirely on a single young girl to know where their enemies stood. He might feel better about their odds if at least one of those factors didn't apply. Then again, a force of a dozen mages had not threatened Faneria in centuries, if ever in its history.

Such strange times we live in.

Suddenly, Damian tensed. Lyle fixed his eyes on her.

"They're passing by," she uttered, so softly he barely heard her. Leaning back from the door, he swung the quiver over his shoulder, leaving the arrows hanging at his hip against his sheathed sword. A long, quiet moment passed. Lyle cursed the spell that left him unable to see or hear the mages.

Finally, Damian's shoulders relaxed. "They've passed the alley."

Reaching over her, Lyle pulled the door open as gently as possible, then he hurried down the alley after Damian to the corner. He slowed to gesture to the men in the catwalks that the ambush was about to begin. At the edge of the alley, he looked over Damian's head toward the street. It remained as empty as ever, only a few survivors or city guards struggling to get to safety across the plaza.

"Tell me what they are doing," Lyle said under his breath.

Damian's breathing hurried, though she kept her voice quiet. "They are one building away from the plaza. They still don't seem to suspect anything."

Silently, Lyle slid an arrow out of the quiver and nocked it to the bowstring. "Keep telling me where they are."

"They aren't moving very fast."

All the thoughts that filled Lyle's mind moments earlier faded. He focused on the paving stones just inside the plaza where the street entered it, mentally placing the mages there and deducing the best place to aim. A feeling of serenity washed over him, the calmness of giving his thoughts and reactions over to his body without anything coming between his movements and the training ingrained into him for decades.

"Yanuk is entering the plaza. The others are not far behind."

Lyle drew the arrow back along the string, raising the arrowhead to aim it toward the centre of the open space.

"Almost there."

Lyle stretched his arm out on his eye level, sighting along the shaft of the arrow to his target. Whatever was about to occur, he was as ready as he would ever be.

"Now."

CHAPTER 21
AMBUSH

"*ATTACK!*"

Screams accompanied the call and noise and motion roared around Yanuk before he could turn to face the voice that shouted it. Arrows rained down from all directions and armed men charged across the plaza with swords in hand. Yanuk yelped and shielded his head with his arms as his mages screamed and shouted warnings and attempts at incantations.

"We have been seen!"

"Watch out!"

"Laryn!"

"Loose!"

Yanuk's breathing sped and his entire body trembled. Strange figures crashed into them and threw his mages in all directions as blades slashed and arrows fell and his comrades collapsed, howling from pain. The chaos overwhelmed him, too much motion and noise to absorb at once. Yanuk struggled to raise his head and look at one form that darted and spun right in their midst, striking the mages with a polearm with enough force to fling them through the air. Yanuk could barely make out the figure for how fast it moved but the strange style of armour and bare head made it clear who attacked them.

"Dragon knight," Yanuk uttered, unable to hear his own voice over the din of battle. "W-what's going on?"

Flashes of light flared as the mages struggled to organize themselves and fight back, slinging spells at their enemies in the catwalks and all around. Quivering from fright, Yanuk backed away from the action as the attacks descended upon them.

As he glanced toward the open space of the plaza, he glimpsed the glow of a fire illuminating a dark plume of smoke rising in the distance. In all the terror, he had forgotten about the destruction spreading throughout the rest of the city.

Yanuk struggled to steady his voice as he called out, "Nephrita, protect us!"

A blue gleam shone above Yanuk's head. He glanced toward it as it faded. An arrow spiralled away from him and clattered uselessly to the ground. Lowering his arms, he looked around at the mages. Bubbles of invisible energy shimmered around them with an azure glow whenever some weapon or danger drew close to them. Even the dragon knight's blade was stopped by the barriers around each of his comrades. As Yanuk watched, he found the Agaesi's attacks wild and unfocused. The knight swung through empty air or glanced awkwardly off one of the mage's barriers, eyes not fixing on any of them.

"We are safe," Yanuk uttered, though his heart pounded and his hands trembled from fright. "They cannot see us and we are protected."

An arrow zipped through the air toward him. Yanuk yelped and leaped backward, though the arrowhead struck the side of the invisible barrier around him, flaring blue as the arrow flew away. More men rushed in from various directions as other arrows streaked through the air.

"Yanuk, do something!" Helena snapped.

"We must retreat!" shouted an apprentice.

Yanuk swept his eyes around, struggling to think in the commotion. Nephrita now stood in the plaza, glancing curiously back and forth without focusing on any of them. Yanuk's eyes fixed on her as he swept an arm around to encompass all the soldiers. "Attack them!"

A surprised look crossed her face and she leaned her head back. Without a word, she lifted into the air, floating a handspan above the ground, and flung her arms wide. A wave of shining energy shot through the air in all directions. Yanuk lifted his arms to cover his face, but as the blast streaked toward him, the barrier around him shimmered and he felt nothing.

The blast smashed into the dragon knight and the other soldiers and threw them to the ground. The Agaesi, standing so close to the spell, flew through the air like a rag doll and crashed through the wall of a building on the edge of the plaza. The blast spread, smashing into the buildings with a boom like thunder that reverberated through the ground. Several buildings collapsed as voices shouted in all directions, Nephrita's spell flinging people into the air or against the sides of buildings. The blast faded less than a block down the street from whence they came, but the rumbling and crashing seemed to echo eternally.

Pulling his arms away, Yanuk looked around. One of the catwalks on the edge of the plaza crumbled and fell from the sky, a handful of soldiers screaming as they plummeted to the ground. Yanuk swiftly turned away but the sounds of their fall reached his ears. Clouds of dust rose from buildings that cracked and collapsed. The building where the dragon knight had been thrown caved in on itself, the roof crashing through the second story as bits of the wall exploded outward. Bodies lay everywhere, many groaning.

"Yanuk!"

Starting, he turned his attention to the mages scrambling nearby. A sickly feeling rose in his stomach as he noticed two apprentices and old Crain lying unmoving in the road, brightly fletched arrows protruding from their bodies. While one of the younger mages still breathed, the puncture in his chest made it clear he would not last long. Other mages sported large gashes or bruises or clutched smaller, but badly bleeding wounds that had clearly come from other loosed arrows. Two limped and it seemed only four others beside Yanuk had escaped the attack unharmed.

"My friends," he uttered with a hollow voice. He hurried to Crain and felt for a pulse but there was none. Yanuk's hands trembled and curled into fists as his eyes narrowed.

"They saw us," whimpered an apprentice. "We are not safe. We cannot win. We are undone!"

"Gather your wits, you cretin," Edrand snapped, holding a rag against a wound on his arm. "We could not expect that we would cross the entire city and breach the king's castle unmolested."

"They cannot see us," Patrus added, favouring a leg as he looked around.

Yanuk followed the amputee's eyes. The soldiers that lingered nearby struggled to find shelter. One man crawled toward Yanuk without looking at him. Yanuk glared as the soldier shuffled past, never turning to face him. Yanuk resisted the temptation to crush the man's head beneath his boot.

"This cowardly attack and murder of our friends will not stand." Yanuk straightened, setting his shoulders back as he faced the surviving mages. "Do not lose hope now, my brothers and sisters. We are not undone, and our beloved comrades' death shall not be in vain. These ignorant fools thought they could destroy us once, but we persevered. We survived for nearly two decades outside of their notice! We will not turn back now. We have fought too hard and sacrificed too much to give up so close to victory. Anyone who is too injured to proceed, take shelter here and we shall return. Everyone else, with me."

With that, Yanuk helped an apprentice who nursed what appeared to be a twisted ankle to her feet and strode on. Nearly all the surviving mages gathered themselves and followed.

Damian coughed as dust filled the air, her eyes stinging and heart racing. Silence replaced the screams and clashes of battle as the crashes and crumbling in the alley behind her fell still. She crouched behind the row of buildings that faced the road. Closer to the plaza she saw the debris of houses and shops that collapsed from the blast. This far from the square and behind the buildings along the open road, she had remained safe.

Damian rose to her knees, listening carefully. The sounds of other buildings crumbling faded away and she heard people talking and moaning. The sky was starkly open above, many of the catwalks that stretched overhead now gone.

Some of the voices grew clearer and she recognized Yanuk's, though she could not make out the words he spoke. Her throat grew thick. He still lived, and that meant he still controlled Nephrita.

I have to find the captain.

The sounds of the battle when the ambush began caused Damian to flee but now she turned and ran back to the alley where she had hidden with Lyle moments ago. At the end of the passage, she stopped in her tracks. The support beams for the overhanging second story of a building lining the alley had snapped and half the upper story had collapsed. Damian could see right inside the building, the wall torn away and part of the roof missing. The debris from the fallen walls choked the passage so thoroughly Damian couldn't see Lyle. Her heart tightened at the sight, unable to tell how much of the alley was buried. Unease heightened as she reflected on the control spell limitation Lyle had mentioned. She hurried behind the buildings toward the next alley leading to the street, hoping Lyle wasn't buried beneath the rubble.

As she reached the next corner, a figure appeared from the passage coming the other way. She half crouched with a gasp, preparing to flee, but straightened as she recognized the tall form.

"Domino."

A torrent of emotion roiled through her as he fixed his blue eyes on hers. She stared at him, unsure what to think or say. She thought of his disappearing without a word while they made their way through Albrith as well as the callous words he said to her outside the city walls. Yet the sight of him was so familiar as to be comforting. Her heart whirled between trust and unease.

A shadow of movement appeared down the alley. Light glinted off the blade of a sword.

"Behind you!"

Domino spun, cloak swirling about him as he faced the intruder before she finished calling out her warning. He swiftly moved back as the new figure, a rough-looking man nearly as tall as Domino, raised his sword but stopped before he swung. As she examined the man's mussed blonde hair and leather clothes with bare arms, she realized this was the leader of Yanuk's mercenaries that Nephrita had told her about. The name Domino had reacted to so strangely. Vitro Norgssen.

A wry grin crossed Vitro's face and he snorted out a dry laugh. "To think, I almost sunk to your level." The smile disappeared. "I jus' thought you should know what it feels like to be stabbed in the back by someone you once trusted."

Damian's eyes enlarged and her breath fell short. This man was once part of the Red Hawks.

There was no emotion in Domino's voice. "I have no quarrel with you." He had drawn his sword but held it calmly beside him with the tip barely off the ground.

A sneer crossed Vitro's face. "What about my sister? Did y' have any 'quarrel' with her?"

Damian saw and heard no reaction from Domino. "There were no women among us."

Damian blinked, knowing she needed to find Captain Hitchcliffe but unable to drag herself away from this glimpse of the history Domino had kept so well shrouded. She stood in the middle of the alley but Vitro and Domino only had eyes for each other.

Vitro's glare darkened. "Maybe you'd remember her better as Preston. She was all I had left, y' two-faced son of a whore. We dressed her up like a boy so we could stay together. She was sixteen years old and you slit her throat while she slept."

Damian's blood ran cold and her eyes grew huge as she watched them. Still Domino showed no reaction.

"And for what?" Vitro went on with a snarl. "Some stupid, snot-nosed, silk-pant whelp who'd as soon spit on you? Tell me how she deserved that. Tell me how any o' them deserved it!"

Damian's hands trembled and her heart clenched as though in a vise. *It's not true,* she pleaded silently to Domino. *It can't be. He only killed heartless cutthroats, not an innocent girl.*

Domino looked away from Vitro. It put his face in Damian's view. His eyes shut. Damian held her breath as she watched him, begging for him to deny the charge.

"Well, whaddya have to say for yourself?!"

Domino opened his eyes but did not face the mercenary. "There is no excuse for what I did."

It felt like Damian's stomach dropped out of her body.

Vitro snarled. "That's it? Y' ain't even sorry for murderin' dozens of your own comrades? People who watched your back when you stabbed theirs? Well, I should've expected no less from you. It don't matter, anyway. It's not me you have to worry about. You'd better get ready to beg Peony's forgiveness in person!"

Raising his sword over his head, Vitro charged Domino with a yell. Damian gasped as Domino smoothly lifted his black blade and blocked the blow. Sparks glinted as the blades clashed. Barely had the flash of orange faded before the two separated only to lunge toward each other again.

Damian's breath raced as she watched their blades clash. Her heart felt empty as she stared at Domino. She wondered once what he had used his black sword on. Unbidden, the image of him slicing it across the neck of a girl younger than Damian sprang to her mind. The thought made her ill.

The mercenaries' battle brought them a step closer to Damian, though neither looked at her. She backed down the alley toward the road, sliding her hands along the wall of the building behind her. Some paces away, while the clashes of swords rang out, she fell still, squeezing her eyes shut.

I was wrong. I was wrong about him this whole time.

Shuffling and footsteps in the street drew her attention. She turned toward the noises, trying to will the battle behind her out of her mind.

Then, a voice thundered through the air.

"NEPHRITA!"

The force of the shout rocked the air and the earth itself and Damian fell to her hands and knees. Her ears rang from the blaring call and the power of it trembled through her arms and legs. The voice ripped through the air and seemed to ring over the entire city, echoing off buildings and booming through the countryside.

Damian's eyes enlarged. "Oh no…"

Pushing to her feet, she hurried to the street and glanced toward the plaza where the voice had emanated. Damian gasped at the figure down the road.

"Divine Light."

CHAPTER 22
CHOSEN ONE

PROFOUND SILENCE HUNG over the street for a long moment as all eyes turned toward the figure that strode forward a block away. It nearly hurt to look upon as it emitted a brilliant white glow that shone onto the streets and buildings all around. It moved with a liquid grace, the air and the earth thrumming with energy around it.

"What is that?" Helena uttered.

None of the other mages moved as they watched the strange being approach. Yanuk stared along with them, unable to think of anything to say. The figure stood taller than anyone he had met though was slender as a reed. Squinting, Yanuk could just make out the shape of the strange robe covering its body and the canine head bathed in the shimmering light that emanated from it.

Only through a strong effort of will could Yanuk tear his eyes away from the creature and turn to the diminutive form of Nephrita. A few paces in front of him, the goddess stepped forward and faced the glowing figure that towered over her.

The shining form stopped and the muzzle lifted as it stared at Nephrita. Yanuk swallowed hard, feeling the power that radiated out from the creature.

"Nephrita, your time in this world has come."

Each syllable thrummed with energy, the air rippling as it spoke. A flurry of murmurs rang through the mages and droned from the edges of the plaza and nearby streets.

"It's a malakh," one of the apprentices uttered beside Yanuk, her voice full of reverence.

Nephrita placed a hand on her hip as she faced the creature, her voice light as though discussing the weather. "You get to decide that, do you? Funny, I haven't even been here a week."

A tug on Yanuk's sleeve drew his attention away from the incredible confrontation. "Master Yanuk!"

Turning, Yanuk found another apprentice shifting his weight anxiously from foot to foot, though he clutched a bleeding wound on his shoulder. As Yanuk's eyes drifted past the youth he saw the rest of his mages, most of them still wounded from the attack.

The malakh's voice rang out from the plaza as it faced Nephrita. "In the name of the Gods of Light and all that is good and pure that they represent, surrender now or face the wrath of all the gods."

Yanuk gestured toward the next side road leading out of the plaza. "Hurry, comrades. We must seek cover and quickly." With that, he shuffled swiftly around the edges of the plaza, the rest of the mages hobbling behind.

Yanuk looked at the raven-haired woman standing nearly in the centre of the plaza. Small she may be but her clothes, hair, and the way she stood straight and unyielding before the malakh reminded him of the immense statue of her in the temple where he bound her to his will.

Although he could not make out her face from this distance, Yanuk heard the dark smile in Nephrita's voice as she lifted a hand toward the malakh. "Your gods, you mean. My wrath is yours to taste."

Light flared over the street and an enormous thunderclap split the air. Yanuk felt the earth tremble beneath his feet as he winced and covered his ears from the boom of the thunder. More tremors followed along with crackles and crashes. He shouted at the mages to hurry, barely able to hear his own voice and struggling to pick out details in the dusk-darkened street, while crashes and booms rocked the earth from the plaza. Screams and shouts rang out in all directions as the thunder of the battle filled the air.

Yanuk stumbled from the ground quavering beneath his feet and leaned against a building for support. He turned to face the plaza and his eyes grew huge.

The square had become a maze. Towers and pillars of earth and stone shot into the air, the ground a field of debris. Gouges and scorch marks larger than a man cut straight through them and some had cracked into sharp spires, leaving huge chunks of rock littering the jagged ground.

Were it not for the brilliant light shining from the malakh, Yanuk could not tell which was which. They both moved in a blur, Nephrita streaking through the air in sharp arcs like a swallow and the malakh darting and leaping over the upturned earth like a panther. Huge flares of energy shot through the air as Nephrita moved, blocked by walls of stone and earth that sprang out of the ground in the blink of an eye. Vines as thick as Yanuk's leg and twisted roots tore up and snapped toward Nephrita like a whip, smashing through anything in their way as they tried to snare the goddess. The swiftness and ease with which they both flung their spells at each other seemed like a dance but for the destruction around them. An area the size of a city block had been levelled along the edge of the plaza. As they attacked each other the radius grew larger with each passing moment.

"What have we unleashed on the world?" Edrand said.

Patrus gestured toward the battle raging. "That malakh was not of our doing."

"We must retreat and take shelter," Helena urged.

"No," Yanuk shot back, though he flinched as a crash rang out from the plaza entrance they had just left and another building crumbled. "We will not turn back now, so close to victory."

An apprentice waved a hand toward the city square. "Master, they will destroy everything in their path, including us. They are gods."

Yanuk straightened. "And we are mages. We can use this to our advantage."

Exclamations and protests rang up and a few exchanged concerned looks.

Yanuk grinned. "Do you not see what an opportunity this presents? With such danger occupying their minds, those men who attacked us will be too concerned to turn their attention back to us."

"As will the king," Edrand retorted. "He will never treat with us if he has this to worry about."

Yanuk was not fazed. "Remember, I still command Nephrita. She must surrender to that creature if I order her to do so." His smile darkened as he turned toward the castle rising at the top of the city. "And we shall let the king know it."

Garrick groaned in the darkness, the floor trembling and his extra senses surging from the magic he could feel beyond the rubble that buried him. He had dived for shelter beneath a table when the ceiling caved in, leaving a pocket free beneath the debris. The legs on one side of the table snapped beneath the pressure and now that side leaned on his shoulder. His armour pressed against his calves from the debris that lay across his lower legs which stretched beyond the shelter of the table. His entire body ached and his head swam from the blow that threw him into the building and he could see nothing in the complete blackness of the rubble.

His thoughts, however, lay outside.

The silence underneath the rubble had been nearly as absolute as the darkness until the shout filled the air. Garrick had felt the voice almost as much as heard it. Worse, he recognized it.

What he didn't recognize was the power behind the voice. Now that power surged outside, so strong he couldn't tell where or how it was being used, but he heard the muffled crashes and felt the earth trembling.

"Oh, this is bad," he said into the darkness.

Placing his free hand against the floor beside his chest, Garrick pried his upper body out from the broken side of the table. The rubble shifted and settled as the edge of the table dropped to the floor. Then he slid his voulge backward and levered the debris up enough to pull his legs out from beneath it. He let out a breath as he crouched beneath the broken table, his feet stinging as his blood flowed freely once more.

Something had happened to Niabi. That much he could tell just from the sensation of her shout rippling over him, far more powerful than the overwhelming energy he had detected in her before. It sent a chill up his spine. He very much wanted to be out from this pile of rubble.

Crawling forward, he felt around the wall of broken building pieces on the other side of the table. He hoped he could tunnel his way out without the rest of the debris falling on top of him and before whatever happened outside reached a peak.

Suddenly, something smashed through the rubble in a long streak just beyond the broken side of the table. Garrick leaned away from it as more and larger crashes followed. Thin beams of light shone through the debris around the table. He hesitated as another huge boom drummed out a few paces from where he crouched. The destroyed building rocked as something else careened through the rubble.

Then, everything fell quiet, only the distant trembling breaking the silence.

Scrambling around the table, he pushed his way out of the debris and climbed onto the remains of the thatched roof. He sucked in a deep breath of fresh air and squinted against the hazy light of the evening sky. His eyes widened as he glanced at the source of the activity.

"Mother of darkness."

For a moment, Garrick forgot where he had been a minute earlier. The plain of twisted roots and pinnacles of rock stretching before him looked so unfamiliar he felt disoriented and wondered if he had been thrown farther than he thought. Only the absence of the catwalks overhead made him realize this jagged field was the remains of the plaza where they had ambushed Yanuk's mages, unrecognizable in its upturned disorder. The statue he had hidden behind, the stone flower boxes, the benches, and the paths were gone.

He could barely follow the figures darting over the broken earth and plants with his eyes though he could not shield himself from their auras with all his concentration. Niabi's power gleamed even brighter than her body, the waves of energy radiating out of her so powerful they overwhelmed his senses. Nephrita's power seemed much more concentrated though no less intense. It was an awesome sight.

I will never witness anything like this again.

Flares of energy and walls of stone, earth, and vine shot through the square too fast to evade. He saw glimpses of unmoving bodies scattered throughout. Screams rose in the waning dusk as people struggled to flee.

Garrick's thoughts dredged back to his surroundings. He swallowed hard as he watched Nephrita and Niabi battle. *I couldn't do a thing against Niabi before. Nobody can stop them. They'll tear the entire city apart.*

Turning his attention away from the divine figures, he glanced through the streets nearby. Buildings all around had collapsed to timbers and dust and more bodies were visible. Some had been dragged together or covered with cloth. A few people fled through the streets, mostly townspeople from the look of them. Garrick caught glimpses of some mail-clad men among them.

A glint of armour caught his eye. Turning his head, Garrick stared toward it. The person soon disappeared behind a building down another street, though not before Garrick recognized the armaments of one of Lyle's men.

Garrick glanced over his shoulder. Niabi and Nephrita sparred at least a block deeper into the city on the southern side of the ruined plaza, all the buildings around them levelled.

Facing forward, Garrick hurried over the rubble and onto the next street, running after the figure he had seen.

*   *   *

Screams rang out from the square as the people who had watched Nephrita and Niabi face each other struggled to escape. The ground tore apart, blasts of energy cut through statues, and buildings crumbled to dust with a single blow from the combatants. Damian heard someone cry out in pain as a vine ripped through the earth and toppled towers of stone. Another person howled as a stream of white-hot flames roared through the air and struck a house on the edge of the plaza.

'*Stop this, Nephrita, please!*' Damian desperately sent to the goddess. As with her last three attempts at contact, Nephrita didn't respond.

The destruction in the plaza thrummed through the ground, making buildings quake around Damian. She winced, tears welling in her eyes as she leaned against the corner of a building.

You said you didn't want to hurt anyone else.

The sounds of the sword fight in the alley broke through the clamour of the battle in the square, raging despite the incredible confrontation a few blocks away.

I was wrong. Wrong about everything.

Another crash resounded as Nephrita and Niabi's battle drew them out of the plaza, destroying several buildings at once.

About Domino, about Nephrita, about even the gods themselves.

Frantic voices spoke down the road, desperate for help or instruction. Townspeople and city guards fled, not knowing where to go.

Nothing I believed in is worth fighting for.

Niabi roared, her canine growl thundering through the air. Nephrita let out a vicious laugh in response as a crackle of stone and snap of a vine sounded out the malakh's retaliation. A row of buildings down the street from Damian collapsed from one of their attacks.

Damian leaned into the building and hunched her shoulders. All she wanted to do was run, to leave everything behind. But she couldn't gather the strength to rise and there was nowhere to go. Nowhere she could escape.

Shuffling from the next street over drifted down the alley, less urgent than the movement of the other people scattered through the streets. Damian turned her head morosely. The alley did not lead straight through to the next street but a large gouge cutting through the wall of a building at its end let her see the next road over. She focused for a moment on the figures she saw on the other side. As she caught a glimpse of the people making the noise, she raised her head. It was Yanuk's mages. Watching them, Damian could hear some of what they said.

"Remember, I still command Nephrita," Yanuk said. "She must surrender to that creature if I order her to do so." Damian heard the smile in his next words, much like Nephrita's a moment ago. "And we shall let the king know it."

Damian drew in a breath. Turning, she glanced down the road. Three city blocks or more had been levelled as Niabi and Nephrita fought. Neither seemed to be taking the upper hand on the other nor did anything deter them from their battle or the destruction they caused.

Clenching her fingers around the building, Damian glanced through the gap at the end of the alley to the other road. The last of the mages slipped past, leaving open street beyond.

Damian's eyes hardened as she ran down the street toward another alley. All her anxiety and feelings of betrayal from a moment before disappeared, along with the fear from the collapsing buildings and the other concerns that rocked her mind since she entered Albrith. She focused on the path ahead and she ran.

Finding her way through proved difficult but when she reached a dead end she merely turned around and searched for another way to the next street. She ignored the crashes blaring from the plaza and beyond, the screams that rose now and then, and the ground rumbling beneath her feet.

Finally, she found a passage leading to the next road. Rushing through, she turned away from the ruined square and ran after the mages, now several blocks ahead. At their unhurried, deliberate pace, she soon caught up to them.

"Hey!"

The mages did not so much as look at her. She yelled louder.

"Wait!"

One or two of the younger mages turned their heads but didn't quite look back at her.

As Damian came up to one building behind them, she hardened her voice.

"Yanuk Alganov!"

The entire group stopped and turned at that. Damian came to a stop several paces away from them and panted as the crashes and bangs of the battle down the road raged.

"Yanuk, please," she attempted, though the mages' voices

drowned her out.

"She can see us?"

"Who is that?"

"Check the spell!"

"How does she know us?"

One of the older mages, leaning heavily on a younger and with a bloody rag tied about his shoulder, narrowed his eyes at her. "She must have arranged the attack at the plaza!"

Damian stood firm as the mages shuffled and stared at her. One figure strode between the others to send her a bewildered but calculating look. In the waning dusk, she could just see the scar on his forehead.

"Yanuk, you must order Nephrita to stop."

Yanuk glared at her. "What makes you believe you are in any position to tell me what to do?"

Damian shook her head. "These people do not deserve this."

A flurry of murmurs rang among the group and the older one who addressed her before, Edrand by Nephrita's description, barked out a sour laugh. "These people hated and scorned us for years."

Damian's expression darkened. "No, these people never even knew you until you marched into their home and attacked them. They still do not know you because you cower behind your spell rather than face them."

The murmurs escalated to shouts and many of the mages glared at her.

"How dare you insult us!" snapped the amputee.

Yanuk remained calm as he laid a hand on Patrus's shoulder. "So how can you see us? Who are you?"

Letting out a breath, she straightened and faced them head on. "My name is Damian Sires and I know the persecution you have suffered."

A number of the mages scoffed at that. Several muttered to each other wondering how she could see through their spell.

Yanuk merely sniffed in disdain. "You know nothing of what we have endured."

"You of all people should not be so quick to judge." Damian strode forward a few paces. "I know what it is like to be incriminated for something over which you have no control. To be blamed and shunned, even attacked over a part of you that you never chose. To be hated for using magic, even when you never meant anyone any harm."

As she drew near to them, several of the mages started or leaned their heads back in surprise.

"Her eyes…"

Yanuk's expression darkened as he shook his head. "So you do understand how it feels to suffer merely for being. And yet you defend these same people?" He waved a hand, the gesture encompassing the entire city. "These people hate and fear magic and they hate us for practising it."

Damian glanced around, catching glimpses of movement but unable to see anyone aside from her and Yanuk's mages. She stood alone. Memories of how she had been treated since she left her home, particularly those who had reacted to her magic, bubbled up to her mind.

"You know it is true," Yanuk went on. "They care nothing for you and they never will, even if you never do anything to earn their spite. Why do you fight for them?"

Damian shut her eyes, her heart feeling heavy. She knew Yanuk was right. Some people, perhaps many, would never look upon her favourably for what she could once do no matter what good she tried to do. Likely not even the survivors from Raven Point would appreciate her trying to stop Yanuk if they knew she was a mage. Trying to defend them would bring her no satisfaction.

You will not find peace if you fight for justice or penance.

Slowly, Damian set her shoulders back. She inhaled deeply and felt strength course through her, clarity she had not known since before she set out from Aether so many weeks ago.

"I am not fighting for them." Raising her head, she opened her eyes. "Or anyone else. Not any longer." Standing tall, she faced Yanuk, unyielding. "I fight for myself. And I will not let you harm any more innocent people."

Silence fell over the street as she and Yanuk stared at each other, his expression unreadable. Most of the mages looked skeptical. A few glanced between her and Yanuk.

Yanuk responded with a small scoffing sound. "No one is innocent."

Before Damian could react, he threw his hand forward and barked out a strange word. A handful of pebbles flew from his hand, bursting into flares of light and heat as they streaked toward her. Yelping, she threw her hands in front of her and twisted her head away.

A tremble of energy swam through her body and a light gleamed in front of her. The pebbles cracked as they came near her only to fly back and fall to the ground with a series of taps before crumbling to dust. Damian stared at the remains of the stones for a moment, then at her hands. She reached for the energy she had felt coursing through her. It was unlike the magic she wielded before.

"Attack her!" Yanuk screamed as he dug in the satchel hanging over his shoulder.

Half a dozen mages converged on Damian, shouting foreign words and flinging strange powders or other objects. Damian gasped and backed away, holding her hands forward and struggling to repel the attacks descending on her. The earth trembled under her, stronger than the tremors from Nephrita and Niabi's battle. Tendrils of energy lanced out at Damian and other flares glowed against the invisible barrier in front of her outstretched hands.

"We have no time for this," Yanuk snapped after throwing some other object that burst into a shower of flame and smoke before her. "You two, finish her off. We must continue to the castle."

"Wait!" Damian cried as Yanuk and most of the others turned and walked away. The spells flared against Damian's barrier like jolts of lightning in her hands, making her stumble in place. She tried to run around the mages standing a few paces before her but they quickly moved in her path and spouted off another spell that rocked her back several steps.

Then, the older mage threw some strange objects on the ground at Damian's feet. As the older woman shouted her words, the paved road parted beneath Damian. Slabs of stone shot up, smashing into Damian's legs. Damian cried out, trying to move away, but the stone held fast, digging into her ankles and holding her against the ground.

"Keep her right there," the younger mage said as he reached for a dagger on his belt. "I will take care of her."

Wincing from the pain, Damian struggled to raise her head and look toward Yanuk. He and the others walked calmly away, several limping from the effort. Damian breathed hard, the pain overwhelming her. Desperately she glanced around but she saw nothing aside from destruction, bodies, and the young man with a blade in his hand as he closed the distance to her. Closing her eyes, Damian reached for the energy she had felt swimming through her moments before, gathering as much as she could feel.

Suddenly, a crack rang out below her and some of the pressure eased off one of her legs. She stumbled as she pulled her leg free, focusing on the power she summoned. A metallic clash rang out below her other leg and the two mages shouted exclamations. Damian pushed them from her mind.

She drew all her energy into her hands, her legs and body going numb. The unworldly feeling of magic coursed through her like the warmth of a hearth fire. More shouts rang out that droned incomprehensibly in ears that seemed waterlogged.

When she leaned over and nearly toppled from lack of strength, Damian flung her hands forward with a shout and forced the energy out. She felt it ripple over the street and distantly heard the cries and thumps of the mages.

Unable to feel anything else, she tipped over and fell, the world blurring. A pair of strong arms caught her. Draped over them, she could barely turn her head and look at the one holding her. In the twilight and with her vision fading, she struggled to make out the face staring back. A pang of anxiety rippled through her as she recognized Domino. Then, everything faded to darkness.

Lyle crouched in an alley, sword bared as he peered into the empty street.

If the gods intend to strike me down, this is the moment that they should do it.

For a heartbeat he thought his end had come when the building bordering the alley where he attacked the mages collapsed. The supports for the second story above him held. Only the pain of the blast smashing into him and flinging him against the far wall of the alley remained, along with dread at the thought that Damian was gone.

Flares of light and tongues of energy streaked through the air to Damian down the road, seemingly bursting to life from nothingness. The mages stood closer than she did and Lyle could not see them. Her voice had drawn him here and it was still the only one he heard. Lyle tightened his fingers about his sword but held a hand out to keep Gravier back as the second moved forward.

"Captain," Gravier said.

Lyle's skin crawled to watch the attacks bearing down on her yet he remained still. "If we try to approach them blindly, we will fare worse than her."

Gravier said nothing as he crouched beside Lyle.

"Wait!" Damian cried as she struggled to hold back the spells beating against her. Her gaze shifted farther away.

"They are coming this way," Lyle uttered. He stepped back a few paces, leaning close against the wall. He heard Gravier suck in a breath as he followed suit. From where he crouched, Lyle could no longer see Damian, though he heard her cry out in pain.

"This does not bode well," Gravier uttered.

"We can still warn the guards at the castle gates if Damian cannot assist us," Lyle whispered back, hoping that the mages would not see him as they walked past.

"And we shall leave her?"

Lyle didn't respond.

A crack sounded down the street, followed by the yelps of two unfamiliar voices. One of Lyle's men barked an order that was drowned out by Damian yelling.

Lyle winced and turned away as a flash of blue flared down the road, much like the blast that had struck him during the ambush. A chorus of voices young and old cried out as the spell faded beyond the alley where they hid.

And as Lyle turned back to face the street, he found several people sprawled on the ground where no one had been before, most of them injured.

Lunging to his feet, Lyle hurried into the road, Gravier close behind. Sir Magni rushed down the street from a block away, brandishing his voulge, while several of Lyle's men and some city guards of Albrith appeared out of alleys. Lyle swiftly spotted Yanuk among the groaning bodies and strode directly over to him.

The mage blinked blearily up as Lyle approached. "What…"

Without a word, Lyle ran his sword through Yanuk.

Shouts of protest rang out as the mages watched. The amputee, on his elbows and knees beside Yanuk, reared to his feet with an enraged look and shouted, "No!" His hooks reached for a pouch on his belt.

Lyle swiftly pulled his sword free to defend himself, but found Gravier standing a pace away, holding his own blade to the amputee's throat.

"Make one move and you shall meet the same fate," Gravier said evenly.

The amputee lowered his hooks with a scathing glare. A third mage, a young woman, made to rise, but Lyle swung his sword around and pointed it at her with a steady look. Stepping in, Sir Magni held the blade of his voulge close to one of the less injured mages as the rest stirred.

"Not a word, any of you," the knight said.

Lyle held his sword to the young woman's throat as his eyes swept across the mages, challenging. Some of them sent him smouldering looks while others looked horrified. Inside, Lyle's shoulders eased as he finally accepted that it was over. The spell had not taken his life for trying to take Yanuk's. The old mage no longer moved.

City guards and Lyle's men rushed up to point more blades at the mages. The survivors held up their hands as armed soldiers surrounded them.

"Take all their effects," Sir Magni ordered. "They cannot have anything, no jewelry, no baubles, no medicine, nothing but their clothes. Does anyone have cuffs or rope to bind their hands?"

Lyle sent the young woman at the end of his sword a warning look before pulling the blade back and kneeling beside Yanuk. Lyle opened the flap of the satchel hanging around the mage's neck. There on top lied the book, along with a sheaf of papers tied to it with twine. Letting out a breath, Lyle pulled the book out.

He turned to glance down the road as the men rushed in and swiftly relieved the mages of their bags and personal effects. The sudden silence weighed on Lyle now that the battle was finally over. It wasn't until others followed his eyes that he realized why the stillness felt so stark, so blatant.

No movement came from the destroyed plaza.

Lyle blinked, staring where Nephrita and the malakh had fought moments ago. The ground remained torn apart, spires and chasms larger than houses marring the square, but Lyle saw no sign of either of the combatants. He glanced across the rubble of buildings to either side of the ruins. He had heard nothing while he focused on slaying Yanuk nor did he have any indication now of what happened to either of them. They were simply gone.

As Lyle's attention swept across the road, his eyes dropped and settled on Damian. She draped limply across the Crow's arms. Upturned slabs of stones laid at his feet, one split in half with the shaft of an arrow sticking out of the break. While Lyle watched, one of his men strode up within a few paces of the mercenary and said something while gesturing to Damian. The Crow merely nodded in response.

"Stand up," the knight's voice barked out. "Hands behind your backs."

Lyle let out a sigh and faced the mages as more city guards ran in, swords bared. At last, weariness crept into his muscles, his aches too powerful to set aside any longer. Sliding his sword into its scabbard, Lyle gratefully stepped away as the guards came in with cuffs and rope and bound the mages' hands behind them. Outside the circle, Lyle found Gravier, holding a torch against the deepening darkness of the approaching night. His second smiled knowingly as Lyle strode over.

"You alright, Captain?"

Lyle nodded heavily and pulled his helmet off. "Yes. It is over." He glanced down at the book in his hand, the one he had not looked upon in years.

He could hear the grin in Gravier's voice. "Does that mean you will finally tell me that grand tale of dragons and gods and how you came into possession of a book that can bind a god to one's will?"

Lyle shot his second a flat look.

Gravier's eyebrows rose inquiringly.

Then, Lyle gave him a wry smile. "Only if you are buying the ale."

Gravier laughed and clapped him on the back. "Come, Captain. Let us round up the men."

CHAPTER 23
DECISIONS

AFTER SLEEPING COMATOSE throughout the night and eating a breakfast fit for an entire family, Damian finally felt well enough to take in her surroundings. She stared out the window as aches throbbed all over her body. Her stomach twisted and turned as the food worked its way through her, her back and legs remained sore from the hard ride to Albrith, and her ankles pounded from the stone that crushed them last night.

Here in the inn where she awoke, halfway up the hill again from the plaza where everything came to an end the last night, there was less damage than deeper in the city. Much of the rubble had been cleaned from these streets by the time she rose, though great burned gouges remained in several buildings. She had seen a wagon pass by draped in a sheet that could not completely conceal the bodies piled up within.

What happened to the men who brought her to Albrith or to Garrick, she had yet to learn. She had no idea how many of the city's inhabitants had fallen in the attack. She had only seen two people since she awoke. The cook who brought her breakfast, and subsequent helpings of the same, seemed eager to leave her company and had said nothing. The other had not left her sight but said no more than the cook.

Damian turned toward the other window along the wall in the room. Her chest tightened. Domino stood impassively staring outside. Without moving any of his body, his blue eyes turned to her. She swallowed, trying to think of something to say, but she didn't know where to begin. To her surprise, he spoke before she did.

"Captain Hitchcliffe was correct. My crimes far exceed your

misfortune."

Damian shifted, trying not to think of Domino murdering a young girl while she slept. "What really happened with them?"

He glanced at her.

She squirmed under the scrutiny. "I'm just trying to understand who you are. Everything I have seen about you tells me you would never kill innocent people for no reason. You say it doesn't matter why you did it but I feel more uncomfortable not knowing."

He looked at her without facing her for a long moment, his expression as unreadable as ever. Damian tried to keep her face neutral as she watched him though her heart wrenched. As much as she needed to know the truth about what he had done, the thought of it terrified her.

The silence stretched out for ten seconds or more. Then, he shut his eyes, still unmoving. "I joined the Red Hawks when I was younger than you."

Damian drew in a breath.

"It took me a while to realize what they were. Not all they did was evil but they had no morals for the commissions they took. I joined them on many missions before I came to hate them. There was little I could do. I was not the first Red Hawk to hate them for what they did but I was the first to survive."

His eyes opened and a distant look crossed them as he stared outside, morning sunlight shining against his face. Damian didn't move as she sat at the small table at the other window and listened raptly.

"We were hired to recover an earl's son who was presumed kidnapped by a rival. It turned out the boy ran away. On the way back to his father, the same rival who was accused of kidnapping offered us a greater payment to kill him ourselves."

Damian's eyes widened.

"I stood back and watched as ten of the Red Hawks laughed and ran their swords through the child. That night, I got up and told the night watchman that I needed to stretch my legs and instead I turned around and slit his throat."

She flinched.

Domino's expression didn't change. "I remember little of that night. I was consumed by rage. I never knew how many of them I killed before I fled into the night. The Red Hawks' immoral deeds were soon brought to light but my crimes stayed with me. As they should. I may have despised their goals but I lived with the men I murdered."

Damian hesitated as he fell silent. "So, what you did, you did out of a desire for justice."

He showed no reaction. "No. What I did was kill people I knew in anger. It does not matter that they did evil or that I regret my actions. I still did something inexcusable and you should not make light of it."

Damian's throat tightened. She said nothing for a long span of time. Domino admitted he was a traitor and a murderer since he was arrested in Trent weeks ago. Despite his admission and the persistence of the stories that circulated about him, she had refused to believe he had done something so horrible. She thought she was seeing past the embellishments of stories, even his own, to see the true person he was. She had deluded herself.

Yet looking at him, she couldn't help reflecting on the things he had done for her. His rescuing her from the barge and river, protecting her from Niabi, staying by her side when he seemed to have no reason to do so.

"Why did you come back?"

He looked at her.

"You told me outside the red forest that you came back because you felt it unfair that you didn't trust me the way I trusted you. But it took until now for you to tell me the truth about the Red Hawks. So what really brought you back?"

He looked away. To Damian's surprise, a weary look touched his eyes. "I saw you succumbing to your emotions and harming others."

Her eyes enlarged. His mouth opened as if to say something else but he hesitated.

Pushing her chair back, she rose. "Domino…"

Several knocks pounded against the door. She started and the mercenary spun to face it.

"Damian Sires," came a voice from outside. "You have been summoned to a meeting with the king. Come with us at once."

Damian froze. In the silence, Domino strode toward the door. He picked up his satchel and sheathed sword, lying on a table near the door, and left, walking between the armoured soldiers and down the upstairs hall of the inn.

A cold feeling spread through Damian. She raced after, just stopped by the guards grabbing her arms. "Hey!"

"Wait!" Damian exclaimed.

Domino stopped in his tracks. His eyes narrowed faintly as he glanced over his shoulder. "Do not pretend you wish to keep company with a traitor and murderer."

Damian shivered at the hardness in his voice. She swallowed roughly with a glance at the guards. "I just don't want to be alone, especially not now."

Domino's eyes and voice softened to their usual unconcern. "My company will not help your position."

"It will help my discomfort."

The mercenary stood still for a moment, showing no change in his bearing or expression. She waited tensely. Finally, he straightened and turned to face her expectantly. The men eased their grips as one led the way down the hall. The other followed as Domino fell into step beside Damian.

In the street, people swept and picked up the debris from the attack and many had opened shops. The smells of smoke and baking bread and the banging of hammers filled the air. A few people looked at them as they passed but the stares showed curiosity, not disgust or suspicion. The farther they went through the city, the less damage Damian could see. Sky and open catwalks appeared overhead instead of buildings.

Finally, they came upon the castle entrance. The towering outer wall and gate, nearly as tall as the wall surrounding the city, were surrounded by open sky as though standing at the edge of the world. Through the gate and a bustling courtyard framed by barracks and towers, the guards led Damian and Domino beneath a smaller gate to a suspended stone bridge.

A cool breeze with a smell of water brushed over Damian as they headed toward the immense bulk of the castle proper, perched atop a spire of rock rising from the lake. She took in a breath as she looked out from the bridge. The city dropped away behind them and nothing else lay around as they crossed the stone bridge wide enough to let three wagons pass abreast.

From where she stood high above the lake, she could see farther across the land than she ever had in her life. The lake stretched to the horizon, the rippling waves seemingly as endless as the sea along Faneria's southern border.

Soon, they drew close to the castle entrance. Damian's head leaned back as she looked at the towers rising above, shining in the morning sunlight. The doors alone, hanging open as servants passed inside and out, were taller than most buildings she saw on a regular basis.

The soldiers led them inside. Damian's footfalls echoed in the immense entrance hall. The steps of the guards drowned them out along with the murmuring and movement of the others scattered through the huge corridor, but she heard her presence announced throughout an open space that could have fit her entire house inside four times over and twice again as high. Soaring fluted pillars supported the arched ceiling high above, pale marble and gilded accents gleaming in the sunlight streaming through the arched windows in the roof. Enormous tapestries and portraits three times life size hung in a careful formation on the walls. Polished brass candelabras on tall poles perched between them along with regular rows of silent armoured guards. Elaborate statues, inlaid mosaics, and engravings in the walls marked every available surface.

Damian swallowed uncomfortably at the opulence of it all. Though the guards flanking her looked as common and dirty as her, she felt wholly out of place in the elegant palace.

She glanced at Domino. He met her eyes impassively, looking just the same as he had since she met him aboard the barge. She drew in a breath, trying to take comfort in his presence even as she remained uneasy with what she had learned about him.

Their taciturn escorts led them through a courtyard, up a half-flight of stairs, and down another passage before taking them into a grand hall more exquisite than the entrance. A crowd of people milled inside, murmurs echoing off the walls and high ceiling. Knights in full suits of armour ringed the room, keeping a careful watch on the people within. Damian looked across the crowd, finding mostly city guards and other knights filling the room with only a handful of townspeople.

At the far end of the room, a half-flight of stairs led up to a dais where two elaborate gilded chairs perched. On either side stood cloth-draped tables. Huge pennants hung against the back wall. Several men dressed in silk doublets and finely embroidered coats sat at the tables, chatting quietly and sipping from goblets as they watched the crowd. Damian swallowed around the increasing lump in her throat. She stayed near the doors and tried to remain out of sight but enough people waited that she had little room to hide. A few people on the edges of the crowd stared at her when they caught a glimpse of her. She realized she was one of very few women in the room.

Then, glancing between the others in the hall, she caught a glimpse of Garrick standing near the base of the stairs. Damian raised her head in interest but the crowd shifted and she lost sight of him. The knight was busy speaking with someone and had not noticed her.

A horn blared from the top of the stairs at the back of the room and the crowd fell silent. The trumpeter lowered his horn and called out in a strong voice, "All rise for His Majesty, King Riselius II of Faneria, lord of the twelve kingdoms, the Great Plains, and the western march, chosen by the true gods and voice of Justice and Wisdom in Elderra, and Her Majesty, blessed mother of the heir to the throne, Queen Imala."

The men seated at the table stood and a round of applause rang out as two figures appeared from behind one of the pennants at the back of the room. The king and queen waved to the crowd as they strode to the thrones. A chill spread over Damian at the sight. Never in her life had she thought she would stand this close to the regents of Faneria. The crowd silenced as the king and queen stopped in front of their thrones and looked at the people gathered in the hall.

The king held up a hand for silence. "I thank you all for coming this morning. The assault our great city suffered last night took us by surprise in more ways than one, and I know that many of you are very busy dealing with the aftermath. I know also that a number of you have already filed reports with your superior officers. However, this attack was anything but simple and the best way we will understand what happened is for all of us to hear your reports in person." The king nodded to the men standing behind the tables to either side of the thrones. "Gentlemen, I thank you for coming on such short notice. I shall not delay you any longer than is necessary. Let us bear in mind that we are not assembled to pass judgement nor make any decisions. We are here simply to hear official reports from those who had significant roles to play in the battle the last night." Gathering his cloak about him, the king lowered onto his throne. The queen followed suit and the men behind the tables returned to their chairs.

The captain of the guard for the city of Albrith was the first to speak and the room silenced as he relayed his report. Minutes later, another name was called. Damian wondered how long this meeting would last as the second man began his story. She gained a better view of what happened in the city but her feet grew sore as she waited.

Damian wasn't certain how many men had spoken when she heard a familiar name called out.

"Sir Garrick Magni of the Agaesi knights of Hesperia."

Perking up, she dared to step forward a pace. The crowd shied away from her so that she caught a glimpse of Garrick standing before the stairs leading up to the king and queen. Many people straightened and murmured to each other at the mention of a dragon knight in their midst.

The king nodded. "I know you have already given a full report but I ask you to please repeat it for my advisers' sake."

"Of course, Your Majesty."

Damian smiled to hear a familiar voice. Though he stood so far away, the comfort of another friend in the room eased her mind.

"The men your guard mentioned apprehending last night were in fact mages."

Gasps and exclamations rang up as Garrick stated this casually. The king banged a sceptre against the floor to will the crowd back to silence.

"They were led by Yanuk Alganov, once personal assistant to the Duke of Hesperia. The Agaesi had been aware for some time that Yanuk was gathering outcast mages around him but had been unable to locate them. I was in Trent on a mission to track down one of his underlings when I met a young woman named Damian Sires."

Damian's smile faded. To her horror, Garrick told the king and the entire room everything about her. Surprised whispers rose to a murmur that spread through the crowd and multiple times during Garrick's tale the king had to silence the attendees. Many of the men waiting to speak turned around to stare at her and a few edged away with disturbed looks on their faces. Some of the knights lining the room stepped closer, helmets pointed straight toward her.

The men's voices raised to a shout when Garrick spoke of Niabi appearing in the red forest and telling them that the spirit trapped within Damian's body was the Goddess of Chaos, and again when the knight related Nephrita's resurrection in Padura. Even the lords seated at the tables added exclamations as Garrick's story drew close to the attack the previous day. Garrick's tone was matter-of-fact and he reminded his audience of her attempts to prevent what happened but it clearly did not mollify the others in the room. Damian's shoulders tightened. Several men stared at her, their bodies tensed and prepared to move. As Damian looked at the raised seats on the far side of the room, she noticed that the queen's eyes were fixed on her.

One of the advisers at the table beside the queen's throne raised his head as the king banged his sceptre against the arm of his throne. "This Damian Sires sounds far more dangerous than Yanuk Alganov was."

Damian let out a sigh, suddenly feeling tired.

"What power she still commands I cannot say," Garrick answered. "But I do not believe she would use it to harm anyone."

"How certain are you of that, Sir Magni?" asked another of the lords.

"I would stake my reputation on it."

Another ripple of murmurs spread through the crowd.

The king nodded. "Please continue, Sir Magni."

The crowd listened as Garrick's tale resumed, only a few uttered conversations breaking the silence. Even those faded as he told, simply and briefly, about the ambush and his being buried under a building. The murmurs resumed when he spoke of emerging to find Nephrita and Niabi engaged in battle. He finished his story by telling how he followed Damian and stepped in to apprehend the remaining mages after her final attack broke the spell that kept them hidden.

The king raised his chin as he regarded the knight. "So what became of the malakh and the Goddess of Chaos?"

"I don't know, Your Highness. A moment after Yanuk died, I heard what might have been the malakh growling, but after that they both disappeared."

One of the advisers banged his fist on the table. "You cannot believe all this, Your Majesty! Gods walking among us, the Goddess of Chaos returning to Faneria, and a malakh attacking innocents? It is preposterous."

Another of the advisers shot the first a wary look. "Do you doubt the word of an Agaesi, Lord Haestus?"

"The Agaesi keep many secrets."

A chill spread over Damian as she remembered what Lyle said of Garrick. *So I was wrong about Garrick, too.* The thought made her feel wearier.

"Enough," the king cut across the advisers. "Sir Magni has given his report as requested and it falls in line with what others have spoken already."

Lord Haestus reluctantly sat back in his chair as the advisers grew quiet.

"We are not here to interpret any information, only to hear what was witnessed last night and before. Sir Magni, we owe you a great debt for protecting our city, especially being so far from your own."

"I was only doing my duty, Your Majesty."

"Still, bravery such as yours does not go unrewarded," spoke the queen. She glanced sidelong at the king. "And I believe that a Sword of Annas is in order for your deeds."

The king nodded once. "I agree." He faced a messenger standing to the side. "Have the goldsmith make up a Sword of Annas."

Damian glanced at the king, unable to feel joy for Garrick receiving the highest medal for bravery in the kingdom.

"You honour me, Your Majesties," Garrick answered.

A few people clapped and the applause spread through much of the crowd.

The king nodded. "Thank you for your report, Sir Magni."

Garrick's armour rattled softly as he stepped aside.

"I think now we should hear the testimony from Captain Lyle Hitchcliffe of Misengrad. Captain?"

Another set of armour jingled to the open space in front of the stairs. Damian's head bowed, prepared to face another round of suspicion.

"I received privileged information regarding Yanuk's group and his intentions and gathered men to join me in an attempt to stop him."

Damian listened with mild curiosity as he told of meeting the former Duke of Deverell and Lyle's ride to the temple to Nephrita, though his information was sparse. She couldn't help tensing when he came to his arrival at Raven Point. The murmurs resumed when he told of Damian and Domino joining his men on the ride. However, he said nothing incriminating about her, omitted her admission to causing the fire on her father's barge, and did not explain how she obtained information on Yanuk's mages and how she knew where they were in the city. He did not even mention Domino by name. She let out a breath though a few people on the edge of the crowd stared at her anew. Of course, Garrick had already revealed all those secrets.

The murmurs rose when Lyle told of Damian attacking the mages. Several of the guards in the hall inched closer to her, eyes fixed on her and hands hovering over the hilts of their swords.

"So you saw this Damian Sires use magic inside the city, after lying that she could not?" sneered one of the advisers.

Lyle did not seem to react. "What happened with Miss Sires before she came to join us, I cannot say. But were it not for her assistance, then none of us would stand here before you now, My Lords. Perhaps not you, either. She was the only one who could see the mages."

Damian's shoulders remained stiff but Lyle's words comforted her faintly. The king nodded and gestured for Lyle to continue. He had little left to say and silence fell as he briefly spoke of his defeat over the rebel mage.

One of the lords at the table regarded him. "So as Sir Magni tells it and you concur, you slayed Yanuk Alganov without giving him a chance to surrender."

Damian heard no reaction from Lyle nor did his voice seem any less composed. "I thought it the only way to break the spell that bound Nephrita to his will."

Damian watched the advisers carefully, knowing that Lyle knew more than he let on. Some looked doubtful but none rebuffed him.

"So," the king said, "two men from Misengrad protected my city better than we ourselves could."

A few of the knights and city guards in the room shifted.

"How long have you held the command of the guard in Misengrad, Captain?"

"Sixteen years, Your Majesty."

"This position has been held by your family for some time?"

"Generations, Majesty."

"Well, I think it is time that another line take command of the city guard in Misengrad, if you will take your vows and swear your sword to my service." The king stood and drew a sword sheathed by his throne.

Damian's head rose. Through the people gathered in the throne room she could just see Captain Hitchcliffe kneel.

"My sword and my strength are yours, my liege."

The king lifted the sword at the base of the stairs leading to the dais.

"Then I dub thee Sir Lyle Hitchcliffe."

A round of applause spread through the room, the people crowding too close for Damian to watch. She clapped along with them, some of her unease fading.

"Thank you, Your Majesty," Lyle said as the applause died away.

"As appreciative as we all are to our heroes of the hour," Lord Haestus spoke, "let us not forget that both Sir Magni and Sir Hitchcliffe have shared greatly concerning testimony regarding this Miss Sires."

Damian shut her eyes as the king replied.

"I agree. Damian Sires, step forth."

This was the impression she would leave upon the King of Faneria. She might as well be addressing the entire country. Here her fate would be decided and nearly everyone in the room already distrusted or hated her.

I know who I am.

The room fell silent and half the people in the crowd turned to look at her. Setting her shoulders back, she raised her head and strode forward. The crowd parted before her and many gasped as she passed and they saw her eyes up close. Some of the men muttered under their breath and a few spoke curses. Her footsteps rang louder than the voices speaking. Damian did not face any of those who stared at her.

Passing beyond the ring of men standing some paces away from the base of the stairs, she stepped forward and looked up unflinchingly. The knights at the front of the room crowded closer around the king and queen and advisers, many putting their hands on their swords.

"Miss Sires," the queen said, "have these men spoken any untruths about you?"

"No, Your Majesty."

The murmuring rose and the king held up a hand for silence.

"Are you prepared to give your own account of the battle last night, as well as of your own… abilities?"

"Yes, Your Majesty."

The king waved a hand. "You may begin."

Closing her eyes for a moment, she inhaled deeply.

"I have lived with this ability my entire life. It is clear to me now that it was given to me at birth, and I never chose nor desired it, though I will admit I once found wonder in it."

She spoke as though the room was empty, holding herself straight and at ease. Ignoring the conversations that began as she told of her journey, she continued without pause, not looking at anyone other than the king himself. His gaze remained fixed on her as she spoke, his face betraying nothing.

Some of the advisers seemed more agitated as she concluded her tale than they had been before and they quickly argued among themselves. Their voices rose as they all tried to speak over each other, more discussions from the men milling below ringing through the hall.

"Enough!" the king roared, banging his sceptre so hard against his throne Damian jumped. The roar of voices died abruptly away, the echoes bouncing off the cavernous walls and ceiling as the throne room fell still.

The queen glanced between the tables of previously bickering advisers. "Need we remind you gentlemen that this is not a trial?"

"We are here merely to understand what happened last night," the king added. "We shall discuss Miss Sires's fate once we have a complete report from all present." Damian didn't react as he turned to regard her again. "Miss Sires, you will remain in the castle until such time as we reach a decision. Sir Ramsay, please assign a guard to her in the meantime. She is not to go anywhere without an escort. Thank you for your report."

With a stiff bow, Damian turned to walk through the crowd. Domino waited near the front of the group. To Damian's surprise she found a deeply thoughtful look on his face. Tearing her eyes away, she continued past him and moved between the men toward the back of the room.

"Wait a moment," called out one of the advisers. "You, in the black cloak! Stop! Were you summoned to this meeting?"

Damian froze in her steps as Domino stopped walking.

"No."

"Why have you come? Who gave you permission to attend?"

Damian heard the guards who had brought her and Domino to the castle shifting uncomfortably.

Domino didn't turn, still facing her. "I came only to accompany Damian."

A shiver spread through Damian's body.

"What is your name?" the king demanded.

Domino hesitated, the thoughtful look returning to his eyes as he stared at her. Then, he answered, "Henricksson, Your Majesty. Liam Henricksson."

Damian's eyes widened.

A man seated at the table leaped to his feet, his chair scraping behind him. "Wait, that is the mercenary that Sir Magni mentioned. That is the Crow!"

As the voices in the room rose, the king held up a hand. "Do you have anything to add to our report, Mister Henricksson?"

The hall fell quiet as everyone awaited the mercenary's answer. Many of the men around looked tense, hands halfway to their weapons.

Domino still did not react. "Only that Miss Sires is being treated worse than I am when she has only ever acted with respect and fairness to all around her."

The room roared with voices, the advisers shouting over each other. Damian barely heard the shouts as she stared at Domino, her breath falling short.

The king silenced the crowd. His voice grew hard. "Mister Henricksson, you are not to leave the castle either, and you will have an escort at all times until such time as we have made a decision regarding your fate. Do you understand?"

Domino nodded.

"Let us continue. We all have duties we must attend to and none of us wishes to stay here longer than is necessary. Who is next?"

Without another word, Domino walked toward Damian. She stared up at him as the herald announced the next man to come forward and make his report, at a loss for what to think. Domino merely looked impassively back.

The rest of the meeting passed in a haze and Damian barely heard the remaining reports. When the meeting was dismissed and she and Domino filed out of the throne room after half the morning passed, the same guards that had summoned her to the meeting shadowed them as they left. Damian hurried ahead of the rest of the people called to the meeting. When they reached the courtyard they passed along the way, she veered away from the main path and watched the others leave, many sending uncertain looks in her direction.

After most of the men passed, she turned to Domino. "Liam Henricksson? That's your real name?"

He nodded. "All of the Red Hawks used an alias. I thought it best to continue using it." He hesitated, then looked away. "I did not want my reputation connected to my family name."

She blinked. After all she had seen of him and what he told her, she found it hard to imagine his family. "So what made you tell everyone your real name now?"

He turned to her, his eyes focusing intensely on hers. She caught her breath at the depth of that look.

"It seems true strength is in accepting oneself despite one's mistakes, regardless of what others believe."

Damian stared at him. She had not looked at anyone else when she spoke to the king. The only reactions she was aware of were the ones she heard. Had what she said affected Domino and she didn't realize it?

"Miss Sires."

She turned, finding Lyle and Garrick standing nearby. A pang of unease spread through Damian at the sight of Garrick though it soon faded. Scuffs and scratches marked their armour and bare heads. Beneath Garrick's throat armour she saw a blue-green bruise circling his throat. Lyle looked unharmed but dark circles marked his eyes and the lines in his face seemed deeper than she recalled.

She smiled. "Captain… forgive me, Sir Hitchcliffe."

He nodded. "I apologize for my part in your confinement."

She shook her head. "No, I appreciate your speaking so well of me. I owe you a great debt of gratitude." She looked away. "I know I was probably a burden on you and your men on the journey here, and I deeply appreciate your defending me in there."

"It was the least I could do. Your information on Yanuk's group was invaluable and we could not have stopped him without your assistance. I only regret that we cannot do more to help your case before we leave."

She raised her head in surprise. "You're leaving?"

Garrick nodded. "Sir Hitchcliffe and his men have found passage on a ship sailing back to Misengrad in the morning. I'm going with them."

A lump formed in Damian's throat. She felt uneasy with the thought that she would be trapped in the castle with the only familiar company having as low a standing among the nobility as her. "So soon?"

Garrick shrugged with a wry smile. "I've been gone a long time and this was what I set out to do. I need to return."

"But… I don't know when we'll get to see each other again."

Garrick stared into the distance, his expression falling. "There's a lot you don't know about me."

She stared speechless at him. Lyle gave Garrick a sidelong glance through narrowed eyes.

After a moment, Garrick returned his attention to Damian, grinning as though nothing had happened. He winked, taking her hand and raising it to his lips. "Don't worry, I'm sure we'll meet again one day." He kissed her hand before releasing it. "Take care of yourself, Damian."

A suspicious look remained on Lyle's face as he watched Garrick turn to leave. Facing Damian, Lyle sobered and bowed his head to her. "Good luck, Miss Sires."

Still taken aback by Garrick's abrupt change of attitude, Damian barely managed to utter, "Goodbye." Soon, they disappeared into the entrance hall of the castle and she and Domino were left alone in the courtyard with the guards hovering nearby. She sighed.

At least we were able to keep Yanuk and Nephrita from destroying the city. She leaned her head back, gazing up at the sky framed by the towers of the castle.

I helped stop them. I know I did the right thing at last.

Damian smiled faintly at Domino. "Well, I have never been to the king's castle before. Would you like to look around?" He nodded in response and together they walked out of the courtyard.

EPILOGUE

DAMIAN IGNORED THE stares she received as she and her small retinue walked through the streets. Her feet ached fiercely from the travel but she pressed on, relieved to have finally arrived. She glanced around at the buildings as she walked, each familiar sight invoking a memory, but she said nothing while she made her way through the town.

Finally, she came to a stop. Standing in the middle of the street, she looked up at the house she faced. Paint peeling in places and weathered around the edges, it looked much like every other house in the town, yet a lump formed in her throat as she gazed at it.

Her black-cloaked shadow moved closer as she hesitated. She gave him a faint smile and wiped her eyes with the back of her hand.

"I'm home."

The silence hung over the street for another moment. Then, inhaling deeply, she strode forward and laid her hand on the doorknob.

The door creaked as she opened it, the sound echoing in the common room. She stepped inside with a sigh, her companions trailing in after her, then faltered.

The hearth was lit.

"Damian?" came a voice from across the room. "Is it really you?"

Her eyes enlarged.

"Papa?"

ABOUT THE AUTHOR

A perpetual temp who has worked for a number of evil empires, Catherine decided to forgo things like a salary and regular human interaction to start a business. She lives near Toronto, Ontario with her husband, daughter, and a large, Himalayan-shaped hole in her life. Visit her website at thejinx.wordpress.com.

www.ingramcontent.com/pod-product-compliance
Lightning Source LLC
Chambersburg PA
CBHW021456110726
47899CB00001BA/180